RAVES FOR JAMES PATTERSON

THE PARIS DETECTIVE

THREE DETECTIVE LUC MONCRIEF THRILLERS

JAMES PATTERSON

AND RICHARD DiLALLO

GRAND CENTRAL
PUBLISHING

NEW YORK   BOSTON

Copyright © 2021 by James Patterson

Grand Central Publishing
Hachette Book Group
1290 Avenue of the Americas, New York, NY 10104
grandcentralpublishing.com
twitter.com/grandcentralpub

First Edition: December 2021

French Kiss was first published by Little, Brown in October 2016.
The Christmas Mystery was first published by Little, Brown in December 2016.
French Twist was first published by Little, Brown in February 2017.

Grand Central Publishing is a division of Hachette Book Group, Inc. The Grand Central Publishing name and logo are trademarks of Hachette Book Group, Inc.

The publisher is not responsible for websites (or their content) that are not owned by the publisher.

The Hachette Speakers Bureau provides a wide range of authors for speaking events. To find out more, go to hachettespeakersbureau.com or call (866) 376-6591.

ISBN 978-1-5387-4996-8 (trade paperback) / 978-1-5387-1904-6 (large-print paperback) / 978-1-5387-1886-5 (ebook)

Cataloging-in-publication data is available at the Library of Congress.

Printed in the United States of America

LSC-C

Printing 1, 2021

CONTENTS

FRENCH KISS

JAMES PATTERSON
AND RICHARD DiLALLO

CHAPTER 1

THE WEATHERMAN NAILED IT. "Sticky, hot, and miserable. Highs in the nineties. Stay inside if you can."

I can't. I have to get someplace. Fast.

Jesus Christ, it's hot. Especially if you're running as fast as you can through Central Park *and* you're wearing a dark-gray Armani silk suit, a light-gray Canali silk shirt, and black Ferragamo shoes.

As you might have guessed, I am late—very, very late. *Très en retard*, as we say in France.

I pick up speed until my legs hurt. I can feel little blisters forming on my toes and heels.

Why did I ever come to New York?

Why, oh why, did I leave Paris?

If I were running like this in Paris, I would be stopping all traffic. I would be the center of attention. Men and women would be shouting for the police.

"A young businessman has gone berserk! He is shoving baby carriages out of his path. He is frightening the old ladies walking their dogs."

But this is not Paris. This is New York.

So forget it. Even the craziest event in New York goes unnoticed. The dog walkers keep on walking their dogs. The teenage lovers kiss. A toddler points to me. His mother glances up. Then she shrugs.

Will even one New Yorker dial 911? Or 311?

Forget about that also. You see, I am part of the police. A French detective now working with the Seventeenth Precinct on my specialty—drug smuggling, drug sales, and drug-related homicides.

My talent for being late has, in a mere two months, become almost legendary with my colleagues in the precinct house. But...oh, *merde*...showing up late for today's meticulously planned stakeout on Madison Avenue and 71st Street will do nothing to help my reputation, a reputation as an uncooperative rich French kid, a rebel with too many causes.

Merde...today of all days I should have known better than to wake my gorgeous girlfriend to say good-bye.

"I cannot be late for this one, Dalia."

"Just one more good-bye squeeze. What if you're shot and I never see you again?"

The good-bye "squeeze" turned out to be significantly longer than I had planned.

Eh. It doesn't matter. I'm where I'm supposed to be now. A mere forty-five minutes late.

CHAPTER 2

MY PARTNER, DETECTIVE Maria Martinez, is seated on the driver's side of an unmarked police car at 71st Street and Madison Avenue.

While keeping her eyes on the surrounding area, Maria unlocks the passenger door. I slide in, drowning in perspiration. She glances at me for a second, then speaks.

"Man. What's the deal? Did you put your suit on first and *then* take your shower?"

"Funny," I say. "Sorry I'm late."

"You should have little business cards with that phrase on it—'Sorry I'm late.'"

I'm certain that Maria Martinez doesn't care whether I'm late. Unlike a lot of my detective colleagues, she doesn't mind that I'm not big on "protocol." I'm late a lot. I do a lot of careless things. I bring ammo for a Glock 22 when I'm packing a Glock 27. I like a glass or two of white wine with lunch...it's a long list. But Maria overlooks most of it.

My other idiosyncrasies she has come to accept, more or less. I must have a proper *déjeuner.* That's lunch. No mere sandwich will do. What's more, a glass or two of good wine never did anything but enhance the flavor of a lunch.

You see, Maria "gets" me. Even better, she knows what I know: together we're a cool combination of her procedure-driven methods and my purely instinct-driven methods.

"So where are we with this bust?" I say.

"We're still sitting on our butts. That's where we are," she says. Then she gives details.

"They got two pairs of cops on the other side of the street, and two other detectives—Imani Williams and Henry Whatever-the-Hell-His-Long-Polish-Name-Is—at the end of the block. That team'll go into the garage.

"Then there's another team behind the garage. They'll hold back and *then* go into the garage.

"Then they got three guys on the roof of the target building."

The target building is a large former town house that's now home to a store called Taylor Antiquities. It's a place filled with the fancy antique pieces lusted after by trust-fund babies and hedge-fund hotshots. Maria and I have already cased Taylor Antiquities a few times. It's a store where you can lay down your Amex Centurion card and walk away with a white jade vase from the Yuan dynasty or purchase the four-poster bed where John and Abigail Adams reportedly conceived little John Quincy.

"And what about us?"

"Our assignment spot is inside the store," she says.

"No. I want to be where the action is," I say.

"Be careful what you wish for," Maria says. "Do what they tell you. We're inside the store. Over and out. Meanwhile, how about watching the street with me?"

Maria Martinez is total cop. At the moment she is heart-and-soul into the surveillance. Her eyes dart from the east side of the street to the west. Every few seconds, she glances into the rearview mirror. Follows it with a quick look into the side-view mirror. Searches straight ahead. Then she does it all over again.

Me? Well, I'm looking around, but I'm also wondering if I can take a minute off to grab a cardboard cup of lousy American coffee.

Don't get me wrong. And don't be put off by what I said about my impatience with "procedure." No. I am very cool with being a detective. In fact, I've wanted to be a detective since I was four years old. I'm also very good at my job. And I've got the résumé to prove it.

Last year in Pigalle, one of the roughest parts of Paris, I solved a drug-related gang homicide and made three on-the-scene arrests. Just me and a twenty-five-year-old traffic cop.

I was happy. I was successful. For a few days I was even famous.

The next morning the name Luc Moncrief was all over the newspapers and the internet. A rough translation of the headline on the front page of *Le Monde*:

OLDEST PIGALLE DRUG GANG SMASHED BY YOUNGEST PARIS DETECTIVE – LUC MONCRIEF

Underneath was this subhead:

Parisian Heartthrob Hauls in Pigalle Drug Lords

The paparazzi had always been somewhat interested in whom I was dating; after that, they were obsessed. Club owners comped my table with bottles of Perrier-Jouët champagne. Even my father, the chairman of a giant pharmaceuticals company, gave me one of his rare compliments.

"Very nice job...for a playboy. Now I hope you've got this 'detective thing' out of your system."

I told him thank you, but I did not tell him that "this detective thing" was not out of my system. Or that I enjoyed the very generous monthly allowance that he gave me too much.

So when my *capitaine supérieur* announced that the NYPD wanted to trade one of their art-forgery detectives for one of our Paris drug enforcement detectives for a few months, I jumped at the offer. From my point of view, it was a chance to reconnect with my former lover, Dalia Boaz. From my Parisian *lieutenant* point of view, it was an opportunity to add some needed discipline and learning to my instinctive approach to detective work.

So here I am. On Madison Avenue, my eyes are burning with sweat. I can actually feel the perspiration squishing around in my shoes.

Detective Martinez remains focused completely on the street scene. But God, I need some coffee, some air. I begin speaking.

"Listen. If I could just jump out for a minute and—"

As I'm about to finish the sentence, two vans—one black, one red—turn into the garage next door to Taylor Antiquities.

Our cell phones automatically buzz with a loud sirenlike sound. The doors of the unmarked police cars begin to open.

As Maria and I hit the street, she speaks.

"It looks like our evidence has finally arrived."

CHAPTER 3

MARTINEZ AND I RUSH into Taylor Antiquities. There are no customers. A skinny middle-aged guy sits at a desk in the rear of the store, and a typical debutante—a young blond woman in a white linen skirt and a black shirt—is dusting some small, silver-topped jars.

It is immediately clear to both of them that we're not here to buy an ancient Thai penholder. We are easily identified as two very unpleasant-looking cops, the male foolishly dressed in an expensive waterlogged suit, the woman in too-tight khaki pants. Maria and I are each holding our NYPD IDs in our left hands and our pistols in our right hands.

"You. Freeze!" Maria shouts at the blond woman.

I yell the same thing at the guy at the desk.

"You freeze, too, sir," I say.

From our two pre-bust surveillance visits I recognize the man as Blaise Ansel, the owner of Taylor Antiquities.

Ansel begins walking toward us.

I yell again. "I said freeze, Mr. Ansel. This...is...a... drug...raid."

"This is police-department madness," Ansel says, and now he is almost next to us. The debutante hasn't moved a muscle.

"Cuff him, Luc. He's resisting." Maria is pissed.

Ansel throws his hands into the air. "No. No. I am not resisting anything but the intrusion. I *am* freezing. Look."

Although I have seen him before, I have never heard him speak. His accent is foreign, thick. It's an accent that's easy for anyone to identify. Ansel is a Frenchman. Son of a bitch. One of ours.

As Ansel freezes, three patrol cars, lights flashing, pull up in front of the store. Then I tell the young woman to join us. She doesn't move. She doesn't speak.

"Please join us," Maria says. Now the woman moves to us. Slowly. Cautiously.

"Your name, ma'am?" I ask.

"Monica Ansel," she replies.

Blaise Ansel looks at Martinez and me.

"She's my wife."

There's got to be a twenty-year age difference between the two of them, but Maria and I remain stone-faced. Maria taps on her cell phone and begins reading aloud from the screen.

"To make this clear: we are conducting a drug search based on probable cause. Premises and connected premises are 861 Madison Avenue, New York, New York, in the borough of Manhattan, June 21, 2016. Premises title: Taylor Antiquities, Inc. Chairman and owner: Blaise Martin Ansel. Company president: Blaise Martin Ansel."

Maria taps the screen and pushes another button.

"This is being recorded," she says.

I would never have read the order to search, but Maria is strictly by the book.

"This is preposterous," says Blaise Ansel.

Maria does not address Ansel's comment. She simply says, "I want you to know that detectives and officers are currently positioned in your delivery dock, your garage, and your rooftop. They will be interviewing all parties of interest. It is our assignment to interview both you and the woman you've identified as your wife."

"Drugs? Are you mad?" yells Ansel. "This shop is a museum-quality repository of rare antiques. Look. Look."

Ansel quickly moves to one of the display tables. He holds up a carved mahogany box. "A fifteenth-century tea chest," he says. He lifts the lid of the box. "What do you see inside? Cocaine? Heroin? Marijuana?"

It is obvious that Maria has decided to allow Ansel to continue his slightly crazed demonstration.

"This—this, too," Ansel says as he moves to a pine trunk set on four spindly legs. "An American colonial sugar safe. Nothing inside. No crystal meth, no sugar."

Ansel is about to present two painted Chinese-looking bowls when the rear entrance to the shop opens and Imani Williams enters. Detective Williams is agitated. She is also *très belle.*

"Not a damn thing in those two vans," she says. "Police mechanics are searching the undersides, but there's nothing but a bunch of empty gold cigarette boxes and twelve Iranian silk rugs in the cargo. We tested for drug traces. They all came up negative."

I think I catch an exchange of glances between Monsieur

and Madame Ansel. I *think*. I'm not sure. But the more I think, well, the more sure I become.

"Detective Williams," I say. "Do you think you could fill in for me for a few minutes to assist Detective Martinez with the Ansel interview?"

"Yeah, sure," says Williams. "Where you going?"

"I just need to . . . I'm not sure . . . look around."

"Tell the truth, Moncrief. You've been craving a cup of joe since you got here," says Maria Martinez.

"Can't fool you, partner," I say.

I open the shop door. I'm out.

CHAPTER 4

THE SUFFOCATING AIR ON Madison Avenue almost shimmers with heat.

Where have all the beautiful people gone? East Hampton? Bar Harbor? The South of France?

I walk the block. I watch a man polish the handrail alongside the steps of Saint James' Church. I see the tourists line up outside Ladurée, the French *macaron* store.

A young African American man, maybe eighteen years old, walks near me. He is bare-chested. He seems even sweatier than I am. The young man's T-shirt is tied around his neck, and he is guzzling from a quart-size bottle of water.

"Where'd you get that?" I ask.

"A dude like you can go to that fancy-ass cookie store. You got five bills, that'll get you a soda there," he says.

"But where'd you get *that* bottle, the water you're drinking?" I ask again.

"Us poor bros go to Kenny's. You're practically in it right now."

He gestures toward 71st Street between Madison and Park

Avenues. As the kid moves away, I figure that the "fancy-ass cookie store" is Ladurée. I am equidistant between a five-dollar soda and a cheaper but larger bottle of water. Why waste Papa's generous allowance on fancy-ass soda?

Kenny's is a tiny storefront, a place you should find closer to Ninth Avenue than Madison Avenue. Behind the counter is a Middle Eastern–type guy. Kenny? He peddles only newspapers, cigarettes, lottery tickets, and, for some reason, Dial soap.

I examine the contents of Kenny's small refrigerated case. It holds many bottles, all of them the same—the no-name water that the shirtless young man was drinking. At the moment that water looks to me like heaven in a bottle.

"I'm going to take two of these bottles," I say.

"One second, please, sir," says the man behind the counter, then he addresses another man who is wheeling four brown cartons of candy into the store. The cartons are printed with the name and logo for Snickers. The man steering the dolly looks very much like the counterman. Is he Kenny? Is anybody Kenny? I consider buying a Snickers bar. No. The wet Armani suit is already growing tighter.

"How many more boxes are there, Hector?" the counterman asks.

"At least fifteen more," comes the response. Then "Kenny" turns to me.

"And you, sir?" the counterman asks.

"No. Nothing," I say. "Sorry."

I leave the tiny store and break into a run. I am around the corner on Madison Avenue. I punch the button on my phone marked 4. Direct connection to Martinez. All I can think is: *What the hell? Twenty cartons of candy stored in a shop the size of a closet? Twenty cartons of Snickers in a store that doesn't even sell candy?*

She answers and starts talking immediately. "Williams and I are getting nowhere with these two assholes. This whole thing sucks. Our intelligence is all screwed up. There's nothing here."

I am only slightly breathless, only slightly nervous.

"Listen to me. It's all here, where I am. I know it."

"What the hell are you talking about?" she says.

"A newsstand between Madison and Park. Kenny's. I'm less than two hundred feet away from you guys. Leave one person at Taylor Antiquities and get everyone over here. Now."

"How—?"

"The two vans, the garage...that's all a decoy," I say. "The real shit is being unloaded here...in cartons of candy bars."

"How do you know?"

"Like the case in Pigalle. *I know because I know.*"

CHAPTER 5

ONE MONTH LATER. IT'S another sweltering summer day in Manhattan.

A year ago I was working in the detective room at the precinct on rue Achille-Martinet in Paris. Today I'm working in the detective room at the precinct on East 51st Street in Manhattan.

But the crime is absolutely the same. In both cities, men, women, and children sell drugs, kill for drugs, and all too often die for drugs.

My desk faces Maria Martinez's scruffy desk. She's not in yet. Uh-oh. She may be picking up my bad habits. *Pas possible.* Not Maria.

I drink my coffee and begin reading the blotter reports of last night's arrests. No murders, no drug busts. So much for interesting blotter reports.

I call my coolest, hippest, chicest New York contact—Patrick, one of the doormen at 15 Central Park West, where I live with Dalia. Patrick is trying to score me a dinner reservation at Rao's, the impossible-to-get-into restaurant in East Harlem.

Merde. I am on my cell phone when my boss, Inspector Nick Elliott, the chief inspector for my division, stops by. I hold up my "just a minute" index finger. Since the Taylor Antiquities drug bust I have a little money in the bank with my boss, but it won't last forever, and this hand gesture certainly won't help.

At last I sigh. No tables. Maybe next month. When I hang up the phone I say, "I'm sorry, Inspector. I was just negotiating a favor with a friend who might be able to score me a table at Rao's next week."

Elliott scowls and says, "Far be it from me to interrupt your off-duty life, Moncrief, but you may have noticed that your partner isn't at her desk."

"I noticed. Don't forget, I'm a detective."

He ignores my little joke.

"In case you're wondering, Detective Martinez is on loan to Vice for two days."

"Why didn't you or Detective Martinez tell me this earlier? You must have known before today."

"Yeah, I knew about it yesterday, but I told Martinez to hold off telling you. That it would just piss you off to be left out, and I was in no rush to listen to you get pissed off," Elliott says.

"So why *wasn't* I included?" I ask.

"You weren't necessary. They just needed a woman. Though I don't owe you any explanations about assignments."

The detective room has grown quieter. I'm sure that a few of my colleagues—especially the men—are enjoying seeing Elliott put me in my place.

Fact is, I like Elliott; he's a pretty straight-arrow guy, but

I have been developing a small case of paranoia about being excluded from hot assignments.

"What can Maria do that I can't do?" I ask.

"If you can't answer that, then that pretty-boy face of yours isn't doing you much good," Elliott says with a laugh. Then his tone of voice turns serious.

"Anyway, we got something going on up the road a piece. They got a situation at Brioni. That's a fancy men's store just off Fifth Avenue. Get a squad car driver to take you there. Right now."

"Which Brioni?" I ask.

"I just told you—Brioni on Fifth Avenue."

"There are *two* Brionis: 57 East 57th Street and 55 East 52nd Street," I say.

Elliott begins to walk away. He stops. He turns to me. He speaks.

"You *would* know something like that."

CHAPTER 6

WHAT'S THE ONE QUESTION that's guaranteed to piss off any New York City detective or cop?

"Don't you guys have anything better to do with your time?"

If you're a cop who's ever ticketed someone for running a red light, if you're a detective who's ever asked a mother why her child wasn't in school that day, then you've heard it.

I enter the Brioni store at 57 East 57th Street. My ego is bruised, and my mood is lousy. Frankly, I am usually in Brioni as a customer, not a policeman. Plus, is there nothing more humiliating than an eager detective sent to investigate a shoplifting crime?

I'm in an even lousier mood when the first thing I'm asked is, "Don't you guys have anything better to do with your time?" The suspect doesn't ask this question. No. It comes from one of the arresting officers, a skinny young African American guy who is at the moment cuffing a young African American kid. The minor has been nabbed by store security. He was trying to lift three cashmere sweaters, and now the kid is scared as shit.

"You should know better than to ask that question," I say to the cop. "Meanwhile, take the cuffs off the kid."

The cop does as he's told, but he clearly does not know when to shut up. So he speaks.

"Sorry, Detective. I just meant that it's pretty unusual to send a detective out on an arrest that's so...so..."

He is searching for a word, and I supply it. "Unimportant."

"Yeah, that's it," the young officer says. "Unimportant."

The officer now realizes that the subject is closed. He gives me some details. The kid, age twelve, was brought in for petty robbery this past February. But I'm only half listening. I'm pissed off, and I'm pissed off because the cop is right—it's unimportant. This case is incredibly unimportant, laughably unimportant. It's ridiculous to be sent on such a stupid little errand. Other NYPD detectives are unraveling terrorist plots, going undercover to frame mob bosses. Me, I'm overseeing the arrest of a little kid who stole three cashmere sweaters.

As Maria Martinez has often said to me, "Someone with your handsome face and your expensive suit shouldn't be sent on anything but the most important assignments." Then she'd laugh, and I would stare at her in stony silence...until I also laughed.

"We have the merch all bagged," says the other officer. The name Callahan is on his nameplate. Callahan is a guy with very pink cheeks and an even pinker nose. He looks maybe thirty-five or forty...or whatever age a cop is when he's smart enough not to ask "Don't you have anything better to do with your time?"

"Thanks," I say.

But what I'm really thinking about is: *Who the hell gave me this nauseatingly* petite *assignment?*

I'm sure it's not Elliott. Ah, *oui,* the inspector and I aren't exactly what they call best buds, but he's grown used to me. He thinks he's being funny when he calls me Pretty Boy, but he also trusts me, and, like almost everyone else, he's very pleased with the bust I (almost single-handedly) helped pull off at Taylor Antiquities.

I know that my partner, Maria Martinez, puts out good press on me. As I've said, she and I are simpatico, to say the least. I like her. She likes me. Case closed.

Beyond that, anyone higher than Elliott doesn't know I exist. So I can't assume that one of the assistant commissioners or one of the ADAs is out to get me.

"There's a squad car outside to bring him in," Callahan says.

"Hold on a minute. I want to talk to the kid," I say.

I walk over to the boy. He wears jeans cut off at midcalf, very clean white high-top sneakers, and an equally clean white T-shirt. It's a look I could live without.

"Why'd you try to steal three sweaters? It's the goddamn middle of summer, and you're stealing sweaters. Are you stupid?"

I can tell that if he starts talking he's going to cry.

No answer. He looks away. At the ceiling. At the floor. At the young cop and Callahan.

"How old are you?" I ask.

"Sixteen," he says. My instinct was right. He does start to cry. He squints hard, trying to stem the flow of tears.

"You're a lousy liar *and* a lousy thief. You're twelve. You're in the system. Don't you think the officers checked? You were picked up five months ago. You and a friend tried to hold up a liquor store on East Tremont. They got you then, too. You *are* stupid."

The kid shouts at me. No tears now.

"I ain't stupid. I kinda thought they'd have a buzzer or some shit in the liquor store. And I kinda felt that fat-ass guy here with the ugly-mother brown shoes was a security guy. But I don't know. Both times I decided to try it. I decided...I'm not sure why."

"Listen. Good advice number one. Kids who are assholes turn into grown-ups who are assholes.

"Good advice number two. If you've got smart instincts, *follow them*. You know what? Forget good advice. You've got a feeling? Go with it."

He sort of nods in agreement. So I keep talking.

"Look, asshole. This advice is life advice. I'm not trying to teach you how to be a better thief. I'm just trying to...oh, shit...I don't know what I'm trying to teach you."

A pause. The kid looks down at the floor so intensely that I have to look down there myself. Nothing's there but gray carpet squares.

Then the kid looks at me. He speaks.

"I get you, man," he says.

"Good." A pause. "Now go home. You've got a home?"

"I got a home. I got a grandma."

"Then go."

"What the fu—?"

"Just go."

He runs to the door.

The young officer looks at me. Then he says, "That's just

great. They send a detective to the scene. And he lets the suspect go."

I don't smile. I don't answer. I walk to a nearby table where beautiful silk ties and pocket squares are laid out in groups according to color. I focus on the yellow section—yellow with blue stripes, yellow with tiny red dots, yellow paisley, yellow...

My cell phone pings. The message on the screen is big and bold and simple. CD. Cop Down.

No details. Just an address: 655 Park Avenue. Right now.

CHAPTER 7

COPS AND LIGHTS AND miles of yellow tape: POLICE LINE DO NOT CROSS.

Sirens and detectives crowd the blocks between 65th and 67th Streets. Even the mayor's car (license NYC 1) is here.

People from the neighborhood, doormen on break, and students from Hunter College try to catch a glimpse of the scene. Hundreds of people stand on the blocked-off avenue. It's a tragedy and a block party at the same time.

Detective Gabriel Ruggie approaches me. There will be no French-guy jokes, no late-guy jokes, no Pretty Boy jokes. This is serious shit. Ruggie talks.

"Elliott is up there now. The scene is at the seventh floor front. He said to send you up right away."

I walk through the fancy lobby. It's loaded with cops and reporters and detectives. I hear a brief litany of somber "hellos" and "hiyas," most of them followed by various mispronunciations of my name.

Luke. Look. Luck.

Who the hell cares now? This is Cop Down.

Detective Christine Liang is running the elevator along with a plainclothes officer.

"Hey, Moncrief. Let me take you up," Liang says. "The inspector's been asking where you are."

What the hell is the deal? Ten minutes ago I'm supervising New York's dumbest little crime of the day. Now, all of a sudden, the most serious type of crime—officer homicide—requires my attention.

"Good—you're here," Elliott says as I step from the elevator. I feel as if he's been waiting for me. It's the typical chaos of a homicide, with fingerprinting people, computer people, the coroner's people—all the people who are really smart, really thorough; but honestly, none of them ever seem to come up with information that helps solve the case.

I'm scared. I don't mind saying it. Elliott hits his phone and says, "Moncrief is here now."

"Who's that?" I ask.

"Just headquarters. I let them know you were here. They were trying to track you down."

"But you knew where I was. You sent me there," I say, confused.

"Yeah, I know. I know." Elliott seems confused, too.

"What's the deal?" I ask.

"Come with me," Elliott says. The crowd of NYPD people parts for us as if we're celebrities. We walk down a wide hall with black and white marble squares on the floor, two real Warhols on the walls. Suddenly I have a flash of an apartment in Paris—the high ceilings, the carved cornices. But in a moment I've traveled back from boulevard Haussmann to Park Avenue.

At the end of the hallway, an officer stands in front of an

open door. Bright lights—floodlights, examination lights—pour from the room into the hallway. The officer moves aside immediately as Elliott and I approach.

Three people are huddled in a group near a window. I catch sight of a body, a woman. Elliott and I walk toward the group. We are still a few feet away when I see her. When my heart leaps up.

Maria Martinez.

A black plastic sheet covers her torso. Her head, blood speckling and staining her hair, is exposed.

Elliott puts a hand on my shoulder. I don't yell or cry or shake. A numbness shoots through me, and then the words tumble out.

"How? How?"

"I told you this morning, she was on loan to Vice. They had her playing the part of a high-class call girl. It seems that . . . well, whoever she was supposed to meet decided to . . . well, take a knife to her stomach."

I say nothing. I keep staring at my dead partner. Elliott decides to fill the air with words. I know he means well.

"The owners of this place are at their house in Nantucket. No servants were home . . . no . . ."

I've stopped listening. Elliott stops talking. The police photographers keep clicking away. Phil Namanworth, the coroner, is typing furiously on his laptop. Cops and detectives come and go.

Maria is dead. She looks so peaceful. Isn't that what people always say? But it's true. At least in this case it's true. In death there is peace, but there's no peace for those of us left behind.

Elliott looks me straight in the eye.

"Ya know, Moncrief, I'd like to say that in time you'll get over this." He pauses. "But I'd be a liar."

"And a good cop never lies," I say softly.

"Come back to the precinct in my car," Elliott says.

"No, thank you," I answer. "There's someplace I've got to be."

CHAPTER 8

IT'S THE SOUTHWEST CORNER of 177th Street and Fort Washington Avenue. Maria and Joey Martinez's building. I had never been there before, although Maria kept insisting that Dalia and I had to come by some night for "crazy chicken and rice," her mother's recipe.

"You'll taste it, you'll love it, and you won't be able to guess the secret ingredient," she would say.

But we never set a date, and now I am about to visit her apartment while two cops are standing guard outside the building and two detectives are inside questioning neighbors. I was her partner. I've got to see Maria's family.

A short pudgy man opens the apartment door. The living room is noisy, packed. People are crying, yelling, speaking Spanish and English. The big window air conditioner is noisy.

"I'm Maria's brother-in-law," says the man at the door.

"I'm Maria's partner from work," I say.

His face shows no expression. He nods, then says, "Joey and me are about to go downtown. They wouldn't let him—

the husband, the actual husband—go to the crime scene. Now they'll let us go see her. In the morgue."

A handsome young Latino man walks quickly toward me. It has to be Joey Martinez. He is nervous, animated, red-eyed. He grabs me firmly by the shoulders. The room turns silent, like somebody turned an Off switch.

"You're Moncrief. I know you from your pictures. Maria has a million pictures of you on her phone," he says.

"Yeah," I say. "She loves clicking away on that cell phone."

I can't help but notice that he calls me by my last name. I don't know why. Maybe that's how Maria referred to me at home.

I try to move closer to give Joey a hug. But he moves back, blocking any sort of embrace. So I speak.

"I don't know what to say, Joey. This is an incredible tragedy. Your heart must be breaking. I'm so sorry."

"Your heart must be breaking also," Joey says.

"It is," I say. "Maria was the best partner a detective could hope for. Smart. Patient. Tough . . ." Joey may not be weeping, but I feel myself choking up.

Joey gestures to his brother. It's a "Let's go" toss of his head.

"Look, my brother and I are going down to see Maria. But Moncrief . . ."

There's that last-name-only thing again. "I need to ask you something."

Now I'm nervous, but I'm not at all sure why. Something is off. The room remains silent. Brother is now standing next to brother.

"Sure," I say. "Ask me. Ask me anything."

Joey Martinez's sad and empty eyes widen. He looks directly

at me and speaks slowly. "How do you have the nerve to come to my house?"

I feel confusion, and I'm sure that my face is communicating it. "Because I feel so terrible, so awful, so sad. Maria was my partner. We spent hours and hours together."

Joey continues speaking at the same slow pace. "Yes. I know. Maria loved you."

"And I loved her," I say.

"You don't understand. Or you're a liar. Maria *loved* you. She really loved you."

His words are so crazy and so untrue that I have no idea how to respond. "Joey. Please. You're experiencing a tragedy. You're totally...well...you're totally wrong about Maria, about me."

"She told me," he says. "It's not a misunderstanding. She didn't mean you were just good friends. We talked about it a thousand times. She *loved* you."

Now he pushes his face close to mine. "You think because you're rich and good-looking you can get whatever you want. You think—"

"Joey. Wait. This is insane!" I shout.

He shouts even louder. "Stop it! Just shut up. Just leave!" He shakes his head. The tears are coming fast. "My brother and I gotta go."

CHAPTER 9

WHEN I GET HOME, Dalia is waiting for me in the apartment foyer. Her hug is strong. Her kiss is soft—not sexual per se—just the perfect gentle touch of warmth. The tenderness of Dalia's kiss immediately signals to me that she's already heard about Maria Martinez's death. I'm not surprised. The DA's office has access to all NYPD information, and Dalia knows her way around her job.

Dalia is an ADA for Manhattan district attorney Fletcher Sinclair. She heads up the investigation division. The two qualities that the job requires—brains and persistence—are the two qualities Dalia seems to have in endless supply. Nothing and no one stands in her way when she's hot on an investigation.

Every day at work she tones down her tall and skinny fashion-model look with a ponytail, sensible skirts, and almost no makeup. When Dalia's at her job, she's all about the job. Laser-focused. Don't mess with the ADA.

Some evenings, when Dalia's dressed for some ultrachic charity dinner, even I have a hard time believing that this breathtakingly *belle* woman in her Georgina Chapman gown is one of the toughest lawyers in New York City.

"We got word about Maria at the DA's office late this morning," she says. "I was going to call or text or something, but I didn't want to butt in. I didn't want to nudge you if you didn't need me...."

"You can always nudge me, because I always need you," I say.

"I opened a nice Chilean Chardonnay. You want a glass and we can talk?" she asks.

"Yes," I say. "Mix a glass of wine with a quart of tequila and we'll have a drink that *might* make me forget what a miserable day this has been."

"Maria, Maria, Maria," Dalia says. She shakes her head as she pours the wine into two wineglasses. Then she says, "I hate to ask, but... any ideas yet?"

"I sure don't have any guesses. I don't even have all the details yet. Plus Maria's husband is a crazy mess right now." I decide to skip the details.

"Understandably," Dalia says.

I cannot shake the mental picture of Joey Martinez's hurt and anger as he spat out the words "She *loved* you."

Then Dalia says, "But what about you? How are you feeling?"

"How *can* I feel? Maria was my partner, and she was as good a partner as anyone ever had. She was damn near perfect. As my rugby coach used to say, 'The best combination for any job is the brains of an owl and the skin of an elephant.'"

"What was the name of the genius who came up with that little saying?" Dalia asks.

"Monsieur Pierre LeBec. You must remember him—the fat little man who was always smoking a pipe. He coached boys' rugby and taught geometry," I say. A reminiscence is about to open up.

Dalia and I speak often about the school in Paris we both attended. We became girlfriend and boyfriend during our second year at Lycée Henri-IV. And we fell in love exactly the way teenagers do—with unstoppable passion. There wasn't enough time in the day for all the laughter and talking and sex that we needed to have. Even when we broke up, just before we both left for university, we did it with excessive passion. Lots of door slamming and yelling and crying and kissing.

Ten years later, when Act II of *The Story of Dalia and Luc* began, it was as if we were teenagers all over again. First of all, we "met cute." Dalia and I reconnected completely accidentally three months ago at one of the rare NYPD social functions—a spring boat ride on the Hudson River. I was standing alone at the starboard railing and must have been turning green. About to heave, I was one seasick sailor.

"You look like a man who needs some Dramamine," came Dalia's voice from behind me. I'd know it anywhere. I turned around.

"Holy shit! It's you," I said. We hugged and immediately agreed that only God himself could have planned this meeting. It may not have been an actual miracle, but it was certainly *une coïncidence grande.* Two former Parisian lovers who end up on a boat and then...

Dalia reminded me that she was not Parisian. She was Israeli, a sabra.

"Okay, then it's a fairy tale," I said. "And in fairy tales you don't pay attention to details."

By the time the boat docked at Chelsea Piers, we were in

love again. And—holy shit indeed—had she ever turned from a spectacular-looking teenager into an incredibly spectacular-looking young woman.

She invited me back to her ridiculously large penthouse at 15 Central Park West, the apartment that her father, the film director and producer Menashe Boaz, had paid for. That night was beyond unforgettable. I couldn't imagine my life if that night had never happened.

After the first week, I had most of my clothes sent over.

After the second week, I had my exercise bike and weights sent over.

After a month I hired a company to deliver the three most valuable pieces from my contemporary Chinese art collection: the Zao Wou-Ki, the Zhang Xiaogang, and the Zeng Fanzhi. Dalia refers to them as the Z-name contemporary art collection. She said that when those paintings were hung in her living room, she knew I planned to stay.

But now we have *this* night. The night of Maria's death. A night that's the emotional opposite of that joyful night months ago.

"Will you be hungry later on?" Dalia asks.

"I doubt it," I say. I pour us each another glass of wine. "Anyway, if we get hungry later on, I'll make us some scrambled eggs."

She smiles and says, "An eight-burner Garland range and we're making scrambled eggs."

That statement should be cute and funny. But we both know that nothing can be cute and funny this evening.

"I want to ask you something," I say.

"Yeah, of course," she says. She wrinkles her forehead a tiny bit. As if she's expecting some scary question. I proceed.

"Are you angry that I'm so sad about Maria's murder?"

Dalia pauses. Then she tilts her head to the side. Her face is now soft, tender, caring.

"Oh, Luc," she says. "I would only be angry if you were *not* sad."

I feel that we should kiss. I think Dalia feels the same way. But I also think something inside each of us is telling us that if we did kiss, no matter how chaste the kiss might be, it would be almost disrespectful to Maria.

We sit silently for a long time. We finish the bottle of Chardonnay.

It turns out that we never were hungry enough to scramble some eggs. All we did was wait for the day to end.

CHAPTER 10

THE PERSON RESPONSIBLE FOR whatever skill I have in speaking decent English—very little French accent, pretty good English vocabulary—is Inspector Nick Elliott. No one has mastered the art of plain speaking better than he has.

"Morning, Pretty Boy. Looks like it's going to be a shitty day" is a typical example.

This morning Elliott and a woman I've never seen before appear at my desk. Looks like I'm about to receive an extra lesson in basic communication skills.

"Moncrief, meet Katherine Burke. You two are going to be partners in the Martinez investigation. I don't care to discuss it."

I barely have time to register the woman's face when he adds, "Good luck. Now get the hell to work."

"But sir..." I begin.

"Is there a problem?" Elliott asks, clearly anxious to hit the road.

"Well, no, but..."

"Good. Here's the deal. Katherine Burke is a detective, a *New York* detective, and has been for almost two years. She knows police procedure better than most people know their own names. She can teach you a lot."

I go for the end-run charm play.

"And I've got a lot to learn," I say, a big smile on my face.

He doesn't smile back.

"Don't get me wrong," Elliott says as he turns and speaks to Burke. "Moncrief has the instincts of a good detective. He just needs a little spit and polish."

As he walks away, I look at Katherine Burke. She is not Maria Martinez. So, of course, I immediately hate her.

"Good to meet you," she says.

"Same here." We shake, more like a quick touch of the hands.

My new partner and I study each other quietly, closely. We are like a bride and groom in an arranged marriage meeting for the first time. This "marriage" means a great deal to me—joy, sorrow, and whether or not I can smoke in the squad car.

So what do I see before me? Burke is thirty-two, I'd guess. Face: pretty. No, actually *très jolie*. Irish; pale; big red lips. A good-looking woman in too-tight khakis. She seems pleasant enough. But I'm not sensing "warm and friendly."

And what does she see? A guy with an expensive haircut, an expensive suit, and—I think she's figured out already—a pretty bad attitude.

This does not bode well.

"Listen," she says. "I know this is tough for you. The inspector told me how much you admired Maria. We can talk about that."

"No," I say. "We can forget about that."

Silence again. Then I speak.

"Look. I apologize. You were trying to be nice, and I was just being...well..."

She fills it in for me: "A rude asshole. It happens to the best of us."

I smile, and I move a step closer. I read the official ID card that hangs from the cord around her neck. It shows her NYPD number and, in the same size type, her title. These are followed by her name in big bold uppercase lettering:

K. BURKE

"So you want to be called K. Burke?" I ask her as we walk back to the detective room.

"No. Katherine, Katie, or Kathy. Any of those are fine," she says.

"Then why do you have 'K. Burke' printed on your ID?"

"That's what they put there when they gave me the ID," she says. "The ID badge wasn't high on my priority list."

"K. Burke. I like it. From now on, that's what I'm going to call you. K. Burke."

She nods. For a few moments we don't speak. Then I say, "But I must be honest with you, K. Burke. I don't think this is going to work out."

She speaks, still seriously.

"You want to know something, Detective Moncrief?"

"What?"

"I think you're right."

And then, for the first time, she smiles.

CHAPTER 11

THE LOBBY OF THE Auberge du Parc Hotel is somebody's idea of elegance. But it sure as hell is not mine.

"Pink marble on the walls *and* the floor *and* the ceiling. If Barbie owned a brothel it would look like this." I share this observation with my new partner as I look out the floor-to-ceiling windows that face Park Avenue.

K. Burke either doesn't get the joke or doesn't like the joke. No laughter.

"We're not here to evaluate the decor," she says. "You know better than I do that Auberge du Parc is right up there with the Plaza and the Carlyle when it comes to expensive hotels for rich people."

"And it affords a magnificent view of the building where Maria Martinez was killed," I say as I gesture to the tall windows.

Burke looks out to the corner of 68th Street and Park Avenue. She nods solemnly. "That's why we're starting the job here."

"The job, you will agree, is fairly stupid?" I ask.

"The job is what Inspector Elliott has assigned us, and I'm not about to second-guess the command," she says.

Elliott wants us to interview prostitutes, streetwalkers, anyone he defines as "high-class lowlife." Enormously upscale hotels like the Auberge often have a lot of illegal sex stuff going on behind their pink marble walls. But asking the devils to tell us their sins? I don't think so.

This approach is ridiculous, to my way of thinking. Solutions come mostly by listening for small surprises—and yes, sometimes by looking for a few intelligent pieces of hard evidence. Looking in the *unlikely* places. Talking to the *least* likely observers.

Burke's theory, which is total NYPD style, is way more traditional: "You accumulate the information," she had said. "You assemble the puzzle piece by piece."

"Absolutely not," I replied. "You sink into the case as if it were a warm bath. You *sense* the situation. You look for the fingerprint of the crime itself." Then I added, "Here's what we'll do: you'll do it your way. I'll do it mine."

"No, not *your* way or *my* way," she had said. "We'll do it the NYPD way."

That discussion was a half hour ago. Now I'm really too disgusted and frustrated to say anything else.

So I stand with my new partner in a pink marble lobby a few hundred yards from where my old partner was murdered.

Okay. I'll be the adult here. I will try to appear cooperative.

We review our plan. I am to go to the lobby bar and talk to the one or two high-priced hookers who are almost always on the prowl there. You've seen them—the girls with the perfect hair falling gently over their shoulders. The delicate pointy noses all supplied by the same plastic surgeon. The women who are drinking in the afternoon while they're dressed for the evening.

Burke will go up to the more elegant, more secluded rooftop bar, Auberge in the Clouds. But of course she'll first stop by the hotel manager's office and tell him what he already knows: the NYPD is here. Procedure, procedure, procedure.

If Maria Martinez is watching all this from some heavenly locale, she is falling on the floor laughing.

After agreeing to meet Burke back in the lobby in forty-five minutes, I walk into the bar. (I once visited Versailles on a high school class trip, and this place would have pleased Marie Antoinette.) The bar itself is a square-shaped ebony box with gold curlicues all over it. It looks like a huge birthday present for a god with no taste.

At the bar sit two pretty ladies, one in a red silk dress, the other in a kind of clingy Diane von Furstenberg green-and-white thing, which is very loose around the top. I don't think von Furstenberg designed it to be so erotic. It takes me about two seconds to realize what these women do for a living.

These girls are precisely the type that Nick Elliott wants us to speak to. Yes, a ridiculous waste of time. And I know just what to do about it.

I walk toward the exit and push through the revolving door. I'm out. I'm on my own. This is more like it.

CHAPTER 12

K. BURKE THINKS A good New York cop solves a case by putting the pieces together. K. Burke is wrong.

You can't put the pieces together in New York because there are just too goddamn many of them.

One step out the revolving door onto East 68th Street proves my point. It's only midday, but everywhere I look there's chaos and color and confusion.

Bike messengers and homeless people and dowagers and grammar-school students. Two women wheeling a full-size gold harp and two guys pushing a wheelbarrow full of bricks. The Greenpeace recruiter with her clipboard and smile, the crazy half-naked lady waving a broken umbrella, and the teenager selling iPad cases. All this on one block.

The store next to the Auberge bar entrance is called Spa-Roe. According to the sign, it's a place you can visit for facials and massages (the "spa" part) while you sample various caviars (the "roe" part). Just what the world has been waiting for.

Right next to it is a bistro...*pardon*...a bar. It's called Fitzgerald's, as in "F. Scott." I stand in front of it for a few moments and look through the window. It's a re-creation of a 1920s speakeasy. I can see a huge poster that says GOD BLESS JIMMY WALKER. Only one person is seated at the bar, a pretty young blond girl. She's chatting with the much older bartender.

I walk about twenty feet and pass a pet-grooming store. A very unhappy cat is being shampooed. Next door is a "French" dry cleaner, a term I'd never heard before moving to New York. There's an optician who sells *discounted* Tom Ford eyeglass frames for four hundred dollars. There's a place to have your computer fixed and a place that sells nothing but brass buttons. I pause. I smoke a cigarette. The block is busy as hell, but nothing is happening for me.

Until I toss my cigarette on the sidewalk.

CHAPTER 13

A MAN'S VOICE ISN'T ANGRY, just loud. "What's with the littering, mister?"

Littering? That's a new word in my English vocabulary.

The speaker is a white-bearded old man wearing brown work pants and a brown T-shirt. It's the kind of outfit assembled to look like a uniform, but it isn't actually a uniform. The man is barely five feet tall. He holds an industrial-size water hose with a dripping nozzle.

"Littering?" I ask.

The old guy points to the dead cigarette at my feet.

"Your cigarette! They pay me to keep these sidewalks clean."

"I apologize."

"I was making a joke. It's only a joke. Get it? A joke, just a joke."

This man was not completely, uh...mentally competent, but I had to follow one of my major rules: talk to anyone, anywhere, anytime.

"Yes, a joke. Good. Do you live here?" I ask.

"The Bronx," he answers. "Mott Haven. They always call

it the south Bronx, but it's not. I don't know why they can't get it right."

"So you just work down here?"

"Yeah. I watch the three buildings. The button place, the animal place, and the eyeglasses place. They call me Danny with the Hose."

"Understandably," I say.

"Good, you understand. Now stand back."

I do as I'm told until my back is up against the optician's doorway. Danny sprays the sidewalk with a fast hard surge of water. Scraps of paper, chunks of dog shit, empty beer cans—they all go flying into the gutter.

"Danny," I say. "A lot of pretty girls around here, huh? What with the fancy hotel right here and the fancy neighborhood."

He shuts off his hose. "Some are pretty. I mind my business."

A young man, no more than twenty-five, comes out of the pet-grooming shop. He has a big dog—a boxer, I think—on a leash. Danny with the Hose and the man with the dog greet each other with a high five. The young man is tall, blond, good-looking. He wears long blue shorts and a pathetic red sleeveless shirt.

"Hey," I say to him. "Danny and I have just been talking about the neighborhood. I'm moving to East 68th Street in a few weeks. With a roommate. A German shepherd."

"Cool," he says, suddenly a lot more interested in talking to me. "If you need a groomer, this place is the best. Take a look at Titan." He pets his dog's shiny coat. "He's handsome enough to be in a *GQ* spread. I've been bringing him here ever since we moved into 655 Park five years ago."

My ears prick up. I go into full acting-class mode now.

"Isn't 655 the place where that lady cop got killed?"

"They say she was a cop pretending to be a hooker. I don't know."

"Luc...Luc Moncrief," I say. We shake.

"Eric," he says. No last name offered. "Well, welcome. I said 'pretending,' but I don't know. Women are not my area of expertise, if you know what I mean. All my info on the local girls comes from one of the doormen in my building. He says all the hookers hang out at the Auberge."

"That's where I'm staying now," I say.

"Well, anyway, Carl—the doorman—says most of the girls who work out of the Auberge bar are clean. Bang, bang, pay your money, over and out. He says the ones to watch out for are the girls who work for the Russians. Younger and prettier, but they'll skin you alive. I dunno. I play on a whole other team."

"Yet you seem to know a great deal about *mine*," I say. "Nice meeting you."

The guy and the dog take off. Danny with the Hose has disappeared, too.

I look at my watch. I should be meeting up with K. Burke.

But first I'll just go on a quick errand.

CHAPTER 14

IF YOU EVER NEED to get some information from a New York doorman, learn from my experience with Carl.

A ten-dollar bill will get you this: "Yeah, I think there's some foreign kind of operation going on at the Auberge. But I'm busy getting taxis for people and helping with packages. So I can't be sure."

I give Carl another ten dollars.

"They got Russians in and outta there. At least I think they're Russian. I'm not that good with accents."

I give him ten more. That's thirty so far, if you're keeping track.

"I heard all this from a friend who works catering at the Auberge. The Russians keep a permanent three-room suite there... where they pimp out the hookers."

Carl gives me a sly smile. It would seem my reaction has given away my motives.

"Oh, I see where you're headed. You wanna know if the Russians had anything to do with the murder on seven. The cops talked to me, like, twenty times. But I wasn't on the door that day. And how the girl got in? No clue."

Perhaps that's true. But I have a feeling Carl might be leading me to some other clues. I give him ten bucks more.

"Strange, though. Those Russians specialize in young, pretty, all-American blondes. You know. Fresh, clean, sort of look like innocent little virgins. Nothing like the woman who got iced. But...there is something else."

I wait for Carl to keep talking, but he doesn't. Instead, he hustles outside the building just as a yellow cab pulls up. He opens the door, and a weary-looking gray-haired man in a gray pin-striped suit emerges. Carl takes the man's briefcase and follows him down a long hallway that leads to an elevator. The old man might as well be *crawling*, he's going so slowly. Finally Carl returns.

"Sorry. Now, what was I saying?"

Damn this sneaky doorman. I know he's playing me, but I'm hoping it's worth it. Because all I've got left is a fifty. I give it to Carl with a soft warning: "This better be worth fifty bucks."

"Well, it's a little thing, and it's from my buddy at the Auberge, and you never know when he's telling the truth, and...."

"Come on. What is it?"

"He says that the girls never wait in the lobby or the suite or the back hallways. The Russian guys keep 'em in the neighborhood somewhere. I don't know where. Like a coffee shop or a private house. Then the girl gets a phone call and a few minutes later one of the blondies is taking the elevator up to the special private suite."

Bingo. I'm ready to roll. And—if you're keeping track—it cost me ninety bucks.

But it was *definitely* worth it.

CHAPTER 15

I WALK INTO THE lobby of the Auberge. Standing there is K. Burke. She's easily identifiable by the smoke coming out of her ears.

"Where have you been?" she demands. "I checked the bar, then the restaurants, then...anyway. What did you find out?"

"Nothing," I say. "And you?"

"Wait a minute. Nothing? How many people did you talk to?"

"Beaucoup."

"And nothing?"

"Oui. Rien."

She shakes her head, but I'm not sure she believes me.

"Well," she says as she gestures me out the front door, "while I was standing around, waiting for a certain someone I won't name, I texted a contact in Vice, who gave me access to some of their files. And I have a theory." Detective Burke begins to speak more quickly now, but she still sounds like a first-grade teacher explaining simple arithmetic to the class.

"There have been three call-girl murders in the past three

months, including Maria Martinez. All Vice cops posing as
call girls. The first was..."

I cannot keep quiet. We've already looked into this.

"I know," I say. "Valerie Delvecchio. Murdered at a con-
struction site. A *rénovation* of a hotel. The Hotel Chelsea, on
23rd Street and Seventh Avenue. The second cop was Dana
Morgan-Schwarz. She was offed in a hotel on 155th and
Riverside. A drug-den SRO so bad I wouldn't go there to
take a piss."

This does nothing to dampen Burke's enthusiasm for her
theory.

"Don't you see, Moncrief? You're not putting the pieces
together. This is a pattern. Three Vice cops posing as call girls.
All of them murdered. This is—"

"This is ridiculous," I say. "This is *not* a *pattern.* It is at best
a *coincidence.* The Chelsea murder is unsolved, yes. But the
detective's body was dumped there *after* she was murdered.
And Morgan-Schwarz was probably involved in an inside
drug deal. No high-class hooker would go to that hotel."

But Burke is simply not listening.

"I set up a meeting for us with Vice this afternoon at four.
We're going to get the names, numbers, and websites of *every*
expensive call-girl service in New York."

"Good luck with that," I say. "That should only take a few
weeks."

"Then we're going to meet all the people who run them.
I don't care if it's the Mafia, Brazilian drug lords, Colombian
cartels, or other cops. We're going to see every last one."

"Great. That should only take a few *months.*"

"You've got a bad goddamn attitude, Moncrief."

I'm not going to explode. I'm not going to explode. I'm not going to explode.

"I will see you at four o'clock for our meeting with Vice," I say calmly.

"Where are you going till then? We've got work to do."

"I'm going to work right now. Want to come along?"

Burke folds her arms and frowns. "You lied to me, didn't you? You did find out something."

"Come with me and see for yourself."

CHAPTER 16

"WELCOME TO THE ROARING Twenties," I say to K. Burke as we enter Fitzgerald's Bar and Grill, on East 68th Street.

"Not much roaring going on," Burke says. The room is empty except for the bartender and one female customer.

The same girl I watched through the window earlier.

The lone woman at the bar is young. She's blond. She's pretty. And after we flash IDs and introduce ourselves as detectives with the NYPD, she's also very frightened.

"Try to relax, miss," says Burke. "There's a problem, but it's nothing for you to worry about. We're just hoping you can help us out."

I'm astonished at the genuine sweetness in Detective Burke's voice. The same voice that was just loud and stern with me is now soothing and gentle with the pretty blonde.

"Could you tell us your name, please?" I ask, trying to imitate Burke's soft style.

"Laura," she says. Her voice has a quiver of fear.

"What about a last name?" Burke asks.

"Jenkins," says the girl. "Laura Jenkins."

"Let's see some ID," I say.

The girl rustles around in her pocketbook and produces a laminated card. Burke doesn't even look at it.

"You're aware, Ms. Jenkins, that in the state of New York, showing a police officer false identification is a class D felony punishable by up to seven years in prison."

Holy shit. I'm in awe of Burke. Sort of.

The girl slips the first card she removed from her purse back into it and hands over a second. It reads: LAURA DELARICO, 21 ARDSLEY ROAD, SCARSDALE, NEW YORK.

"What do you do for a living, Miss Delarico?" I ask.

"I'm a law student. That's the truth. I go to Fordham. Here's my student ID." She holds up a third plastic identity card.

"Do you work?" I ask. "Perhaps part-time?"

"Sometimes I babysit. I do computer filing for one of the professors."

"Look, Miss Delarico," I say, raising my voice now. "This is serious business. Very serious. Detective Burke was being genuine when she said you have nothing to worry about. But that only happens if you help us out. So far, not good. Not good at all."

Laura looks away, then back at me.

"We know that you work for a prostitution ring," I continue. "A group that trades in high-priced call girls. We know it's controlled by a Russian gang."

Laura begins to cry. "But I'm a law student. Really."

"A few days ago a female detective posing as a call girl was murdered. Somebody who meant a lot to me. We need your help."

I pause. Not for dramatic effect but because I feel myself choking up, too.

Laura stops crying long enough to say, "It's just something I'm doing for a little while. For the money. I live with my grandfather, and law school costs so much. If he ever found out…"

A few seconds pass.

Then K. Burke says, "Off the record."

K. Burke is staring deep into Laura's eyes. But Laura is frozen. No response.

"Let me show you something," I say.

Laura looks suspicious. K. Burke looks confused. I reach into my side pocket. Next to my ID, next to the place where I kept the cash for Carl the doorman, are two small photographs. I take them out. One shows Maria Martinez on the police department's Hudson River boat ride. I took that picture. The other shows Maria Martinez dead. It was taken by the coroner.

I show Laura the photos. Then she looks away.

Finally, she says, "Okay."

CHAPTER 17

PROSTITUTES DON'T KEEP traditional hours.

Laura Delarico tells us that she's "on call" at Fitzgerald's for another thirty minutes. She's certain she'll be free by late afternoon. "Even if I do get a client," she says, "I'll be in and out quickly." (No, I don't think she was trying to be funny.)

I suggest that Laura, K. Burke, and I meet at Balthazar, where a person can get a decent *steak frites* and a pleasant glass of house Burgundy. "This will put everyone at ease," I say.

K. Burke suggests that we schedule an interview at the precinct this evening. "This is an investigation, Moncrief, not happy hour. Plus, *I'm* going to that meeting with Vice."

Because proper police procedure always trumps a good idea, at six o'clock the three of us are sitting in an interrogation room at the precinct.

Laura is surprisingly interested in the surroundings. The bile-colored green walls, the battered folding chairs, the crushed empty cans of Diet Coke on the table. I don't think I'm wrong in thinking that Laura is also interested in me.

"So this is, like, where you bring murderers, drug dealers, and...okay, prostitutes?"

"Sometimes," I say. "But today is strictly informal, off the record. No recordings, no cameras, but as much of the cold tan sludge my colleagues call coffee as you can drink."

Laura is wearing a black T-shirt, jeans, and a gold necklace with the name *Laura* on it. She could be a barista at Starbucks or a salesgirl at the Gap or, yes, a law student.

"We're very glad that you agreed to try to help us," K. Burke begins.

Laura interrupts: "Listen. I don't think I want to do this anymore. I think I've changed my mind."

"That would not be a good idea," I say. My goal is not to sound threatening, merely disappointed.

"We're counting on you," K. Burke says. Where does she hide that beautiful soothing voice?

"I don't think there's much I *can* tell you," Laura says. "I get a call. I turn a trick. That's how it goes."

"Tell us anything," I say.

"Anything?" Laura says. Her voice is suddenly loud, suddenly scared. "Like what? What does 'anything' mean? What I ate for lunch? What classes I went to? Anything?"

The conversation needs K. Burke's smooth-as-silk voice. Here it comes.

"Maria Martinez was found murdered on Tuesday," K. Burke says. "Were you working Tuesday morning or Monday night?"

Laura closes her eyes. Her lips curl with disgust. She spits out three little words: "Paulo the Pig."

Burke and I are, of course, confused. I picture a cartoon character in a Spanish children's television program.

But Laura repeats it, this time with even more venom. "Paulo the Pig."

"That's a person, I assume," Burke says.

"A person who deserves his nickname. If you're a girl on call and you get assigned to Paulo the Pig, you never forget it."

Her hands shake a bit. Her eyes begin to water.

"That's where I was the night your friend was murdered. I was with Paulo. Paulo Montes."

"Tell us, Laura," I say. "We need to know what happened that night with you and Paulo. Everything you remember. You're safe with us."

Her story is disgusting.

CHAPTER 18

Auberge du Parc Hotel
Monday evening

PAULO MONTES, A BRAZILIAN drug dealer, is usually followed everywhere by two bodyguards. Tonight, however, he sends them away and waits alone for the arrival of his hired girl.

The fat middle-aged man has dressed appropriately for the occasion—a sweat-soaked sleeveless undershirt. Thick curly black hair grows like an unmown lawn over both Paulo's chest and back. The hairs crawl up and down his shoulders and neck. He wears long white silk shorts—longer than boxers, almost long enough to touch his fleshy pink knees. Montes has greased himself up with a nauseating combination of almond oil and lavender cologne. He has used this same overwhelming oil-and-cologne concoction to slick back the greasy hair above his fat round face.

Paulo answers the door himself. "You're much prettier than that dark-haired bitch they sent up an hour ago," he says.

He is speaking to Laura Delarico—tall, slim, blond. With her fine youthful features, Laura is easily Paulo's fantasy come to life—a combination of Texas cheerleader and Italian fashion model. Fresh and clean, lithe and athletic. Just what Paulo is longing for.

He begins quickly, clumsily unbuttoning Laura's white oxford-cloth shirt. "The first one they sent was the kind I could find for ten dollars in an alley in São Paulo. Dark hair, dark skin. Screwing her would be like screwing myself."

Paulo Montes laughs uproariously at his little joke. Laura smiles. She's been taught to smile at a client's jokes.

Paulo pulls her onto the bed. His fingers are fat, and he has become bored with trying to unbutton Laura's shirt. So he pulls it up and over her head. He tugs at Laura's panties, ripping them.

Soon she is naked. Soon Paulo the Pig is naked. Every inch of Laura's flesh is disgusted by him. She feels he might crush her with his weight, but she's skilled at positioning her shoulders and hips in such a way as to minimize all discomfort. She tries to ignore the garlicky alcohol smell as he roughly kisses her face and lips, as he squirms slowly downward to kiss her breasts. He suddenly slaps her face. For some sick reason this makes him laugh. Paulo Montes then pulls hard at her hair.

"Stop it," Laura says. "You're hurting me."

"Like I give a shit," Paulo says. Now he grabs her genitals. His filthy fingernails travel harshly around her vagina. She feels scratching, bleeding. With his other hand he pulls hard at another handful of hair. "I'm paying good money for this!" he yells. "I'm in charge."

He pushes himself back up, again closer to her face. His saliva is dripping onto Laura's cheeks and lips. The kisses begin to feel more like bites. She is certain the skin on her right cheek has been punctured by his teeth. Then more hair pulling. Her vagina is full of pain.

This time Laura screams. "Stop. Slow down!" She pushes at his fat neck.

Then suddenly Paulo makes a huge noise—a kind of explosive grunt. His breathing immediately slows down.

Laura realizes that she doesn't need to protest any longer. It's over. He's finished. He never even entered her. Paulo the Pig begins panting like a tired old horse. He is resting, she thinks. He remains on top of her for a few minutes.

Finally Paulo rolls off and rests at her side.

For a moment, Laura becomes a kind of waitress in a sexual diner. "Can I get you anything else, sir?"

But Paulo Montes merely keeps his heavy breathing pumping. "That was good, very good. Go into the next room. Take what you want. Within reason, of course." He laughs again. What a comedian!

Like all the girls who work for the Russian gang, Laura knows Paulo Montes is one of the most significant importers of what are called travel packages: drugs that are smuggled along strange geographic routes—say, from Ankara to Kiev to Seoul to New York to São Paulo—in order to confuse and evade the narcs.

"No, thank you," Laura says, slipping into her torn underwear, her jeans, and her shirt. She plucks a few of his many sweaty curly hairs from her stomach.

"Don't be ungrateful, bitch," Paulo says. This time he's not sounding funny. He doesn't laugh. "Scag, maybe. I got it in the plastic containers. Or some good China white."

"I just need to use the bathroom," Laura says.

Paulo snaps at her quickly. "Use the maid's bathroom at the end of the hall. You can't use this one. I have personal items in there."

Laura simply says, "Okay." She's tired and frightened and disgusted.

"Now go in the next room and treat yourself. Even something simple. Take a little C. Have a party later with your friends."

To appease him she says, "Do you have some weed? I'll take some weed."

He laughs again, the loudest of all his laughing jags.

"Weed? You're joking. Like Paulo would ever deal low-class shit like that."

She watches Paulo on the bed, naked, laughing.

As Laura leaves the room all she can think of is that line from the Christmas poem: "...a little round belly / That shook when he laughed, like a bowl full of jelly."

CHAPTER 19

LAURA DELARICO HAS FINISHED her story.

"So that's it. The clients don't pay us girls directly. It's all online, I guess. I don't really know. When it was over, I just left."

Burke speaks. "Detective Moncrief and I want to thank you. We know this has been tough."

"I wish I could have helped more," Laura says. "I'm not afraid. I just ... well, that's what happened."

"You've helped us more than you can imagine," I say. Sincerely, softly. "What you gave us was big. I'm fairly certain Maria Martinez visited Paulo's room as well."

Burke agrees. "There's a very real possibility she was the dark-haired girl he rejected before you."

"You don't know that for sure," Laura says.

"You're right," I say. "Not yet. But it is a logical deduction. He may have killed her and disposed of her. *Or* he may have put her body in the bathroom."

"The one he wouldn't let me use," she says quietly. "I guess that makes sense."

K. Burke holds up her hand. "Or we may be completely off base. Maybe it was not Maria Martinez. Maybe we've got it all wrong."

I cannot resist. I say, "Ah, K. Burke, ever the jolly optimist."

I reach over and gently touch Laura Delarico's hand. She does not pull away. She is so much less frightened than she was a few hours ago.

"And that is why..." Suddenly, I must stop speaking. Oh, shit. Oh, no.

I feel my throat begin to burn. I'm having trouble breathing. Maria is on my mind, in my heart. Because of Laura's information, we may actually have a shot at solving Maria's murder.

K. Burke senses the emotional hole I've fallen into. She finishes my remarks.

"And that's why...we need you to help us just a little bit more."

CHAPTER 20

LAURA SAYS NOTHING FOR a few long moments.

"Well?" I say.

Laura is suddenly businesslike. Sharp. Composed.

"I know what you'll do if I don't keep helping you," she says.

"You *know* what we'll do?" I ask. "I don't even know what we'll do except ask you to help us."

"No," Laura says. "You'll play the Grandpa card."

"The what?" I ask.

K. Burke is far quicker than I am in this matter.

"Laura thinks we'll tell her grandfather how she's been making money," says Burke.

For the first time I see a toughness in Laura. I am beginning to think that Laura Delarico is not so naive and innocent as I first thought. She'll make a good lawyer someday.

"Believe whatever you want, Laura," I say, "but I promise you with my heart that we will never do such a thing."

"I guess I'll believe you because...well, because I *want* to believe you," Laura says. "I want to help...at least, I think I want to help. Oh, this sucks. This whole thing sucks."

Time for a bottom line. Laura agrees to continue to help. "But just one more time."

Later, after Laura leaves, K. Burke and I walk the dirty gray hallway back to the detective room.

"Nice job," Burke says. "Your performance won her over."

"Did you think that was a performance, K. Burke?" I ask.

"To be honest, I don't know."

Back at our desks, we learn that Paulo Montes will not be in New York for three days. He is on a quick drug trip through San Juan, Havana, and Kingston.

I tell Burke that I'm going to take one of those three days off.

"Impossible!" she exclaims. "Your presence is critical. We have Vice files to examine. We have a reinspection of the murder scene as well as forensics at Montes's suite. I need you to—"

I cut her off immediately. "Hold it," I say sharply. "Here's what I need from *you*. I need you to stop thinking that you're my boss. You're my partner. And I don't mean to throw this in your face, K. Burke, but we would not be progressing if I had not pursued my very *un*professional way of doing things."

K. Burke gives me her version of a sincere smile. Then she says, "Whatever you say, partner."

CHAPTER 21

A MAN KNOWS HE'S in love when he's totally happy just watching his girlfriend do even the simplest things—peeling an apple, combing her hair, fluffing up a bed pillow, laughing.

That is precisely how I'm feeling when I walk into the ridiculously tricked-out media room of Dalia's apartment: the Apologue speakers, the Supernova One screen, the leather Eames chairs. A room that is insanely lavish and almost never used.

As I walk in I see Dalia standing on a stepladder. Her back is to me. She is frantically sorting through the small closet high above the wet bar. She neither sees nor hears me enter. I stand and watch her for a moment. I smile. Dalia is wearing jeans and a turquoise T-shirt. As she stretches, one or two inches of her lower back are exposed.

I walk toward her and kiss her gently on that enticing lower back.

She gives a quick little yell.

"Don't be scared," I say. "It's only me."

She steps off the ladder and we embrace fully. I know a great kiss cannot wash away a bad day, but it surely can make the night seem a little bit brighter.

"When did *this* closet become the junk closet?" she asks as she climbs back up the ladder and begins tossing things down to me.

A plastic bag of poker chips. These are followed by three Scrabble tiles (*W, E,* and the always important *X*). A plastic box containing ivory chess pieces, but no chessboard in sight. And a true relic from the Victorian era: a Game Boy.

"This is for you," she says as she pretends to hit me on the head with a wooden croquet mallet. I add the mallet to the ever-expanding pile of items next to me.

"And you'll like *this,*" she says with a smile. Dalia leans down and hands me a small gold box. I open it. It contains two little bronze balls the size of small marbles. Never saw them before. I shrug.

"Give up?" she asks. "They're those Chinese things they use for sex, for the vagina."

"The vagina?" I say. "Yes. I think I've heard of it." She laughs and punches me lightly on the arm. I decide not to ask where she got them—or how often she used them or with whom.

"Well," she says. "At least we've solved *one* mystery. This closet is not a junk closet. It is obviously a game closet."

"What exactly are you looking for, anyway?" I ask.

"This," she says as she steps down off the ladder. She is holding a slim burgundy leather book. I recognize it immediately. It's the yearbook for our class at Lycée Henri-IV.

She opens it and turns to the page that has her graduation picture. "I was thinking of getting bangs. The last time I had them was when I was a kid. I wanted to see if I was as goofy-looking as I remember." She frowns. "Guess I was."

I say exactly what is expected of a man in this situation. The only difference is that this man means it with all his heart.

"You were beautiful," I say.

"You're mad. Braids on the side and bangs in the front. I look like a goatherd."

I reach toward her and touch her face.

"If so, then you are *la plus belle* goatherd since the beginning of time." I lean in and kiss her. Then I speak. "How about we have something nice to drink?"

"How about a nice warm bath, with lavender perfume?" she says.

"A bath?" I say. "I don't know. I don't think I'm *that* thirsty."

Dalia taps me playfully on my nose. Then she heads toward the bathroom.

CHAPTER 22

Auberge du Parc Hotel
Three days later
1:20 a.m.

LAURA KNOCKS ON THE hotel-room door. Everything feels just as it did the last time she visited Paulo.

She wears a white oxford-cloth shirt. Just as she did the last time. The tiny entrance hall where she waits stinks of liquor and bad cologne. Just as it did the last time. One other thing that's the same, one other thing she cannot deny: she's horribly frightened. Her arm shakes as she knocks on the door again.

Yes, Moncrief and Burke have assured her that everything is set up to keep her perfectly safe. This time, hidden in Paulo's bedroom are two minuscule video surveillance cameras: one is attached to a large bronze lamp on the writing desk, the other to the fake-gold-leaf-and-crystal chandelier hanging directly over the king-size bed. The videos play on monitors that are being watched two doors away by five people: Luc Moncrief, K. Burke, Inspector Nick Elliott, and two officers from Vice.

Paulo opens the door and steps back. He smiles at her.

This time Paulo manages to look even more disgusting than before. Laura Delarico quietly gasps as she takes in the repellent sight: Paulo the Pig is completely naked except for a pair of short brown socks.

"So," he says. "They sent you back like I asked. I'm glad. You're the best."

Laura and the five people watching in the other room realize immediately that Paulo Montes is drunk or drugged or both. He stumbles. He slurs his words. His feeble erection collapses as he lunges toward her, and he begins half spitting and half kissing, half hugging and half groping her.

"Hold on. Come on. Just hold on," Laura says. Then she uses one of the first conversation starters that a woman learns in "prostitute school."

"Let's get to know each other."

Laura wonders how she will ever get Paulo to talk about the dark-haired woman, the woman who may have been Maria Martinez. Laura wafts in and out of that nightmare. She must keep reminding herself she is there to help uncover the truth of the death of a woman she never even knew.

Paulo is even more impatient this time at bat. He tugs hard at Laura's shirt. Two buttons snap off and onto the floor. He pushes his greasy face into her breasts as if he is trying to suck in oxygen from the space between them.

Within a few seconds, he has her on the bed. They are, for the moment, side by side, facing each other. The slobbering. The saliva. The boozy breath.

"So," Laura ventures, trying to cajole him into a calmer, gentler mood. "Just tell me how much more you like me than that dark-haired girl who was here."

Paulo is in no mood for conversation. He is somewhere between crazy drunk and crazy turned on.

"Dark?" he shouts. "Was her hair dark? I don't remember. Does any bitch have the color she's born with? In Brazil they all lie. Lie and dye. That's the joke in Rio and São Paulo. Let's check you. Let's see if you're telling the truth."

Laura fears a harsh inspection of her pubic hair. Instead Montes rolls over and on top of her. He grabs a great chunk of her hair and pulls it hard with his fat heavy hands. She yells for him to stop.

"I have to find the roots!" he screams and laughs simultaneously.

In the surveillance room, Inspector Elliott speaks loudly: "We've got to stop this immediately, Moncrief. We can haul him in right now for aggravated assault."

"I don't want him arrested. I want him to talk," says Moncrief. "I want to get the story on Maria."

"I swear, Moncrief. This whole thing is a half-assed setup. I should never have let it get this far."

"Inspector! Look!" K. Burke says. All five in the surveillance group peer intently at the screen. Paulo Montes is grunting and making animal-like noises as he pinches one of Laura's nipples hard and fiercely bites the other.

"That's it!" yells Elliott.

"Give it five seconds," says Moncrief as he grabs Elliott by the arm to urge him to remain. "The guy might calm down."

Almost as if Montes actually heard Moncrief speak, Paulo begins gently massaging Laura's breasts.

"There, there," Paulo says softly. "You are beautiful. I could love a woman like you."

Paulo gently brushes his lips against Laura's beautiful soft cheeks. He touches her chin and runs his hand down her neck.

"Kiss me," Paulo says. "Kiss me like you love me."

Laura knows her job. She kisses him softly on his lips.

Then suddenly, horribly, Montes slaps Laura against her right cheek, so violently that her head snaps to the side. She lets out a scream.

"You are just another dumb bitch!" Montes shouts, saliva dripping from his mouth onto Laura's face.

"Get away!" Laura screams. "Get the hell off of me!"

Paulo slaps her again, then holds her down by her wrists. She is fighting as hard as she can. But it's useless.

Again she screams, "Get off! Stop it!"

As Paulo is about to sink his teeth into her, the door to the room swings open.

"NYPD! Freeze!" The voice belongs to Moncrief.

Moncrief, Burke, and both Vice officers are holding guns. They all rush toward the bed.

With the help of one of the Vice cops, Moncrief pulls Montes away from Laura.

Laura quickly rolls away from her attacker. Then she grabs a pillow and holds it up to cover her nakedness. Montes thrashes about in a futile attempt to free himself from Moncrief and the cop. He keeps struggling and manages to push his one free hand under another pillow. He pulls out a pistol. He shoots it once. The bullet hits the TV screen. It shatters into a small mountain of glass pieces. Moncrief pushes his own index and middle fingers into Montes's face. The drunken Montes manages to get off one more shot. The bullet hits a

Vice officer's forearm. As Moncrief and the two officers struggle to pull the naked fat man to his feet, Montes struggles to bring his arm around. Montes aims the gun at Laura.

A final shot. It comes from Moncrief's gun.

The bullet goes right into Montes's neck via his Adam's apple.

Laura Delarico is sobbing. K. Burke is on her cell, calling for reinforcements, forensics, the coroner, police attorneys, the DA's office. Nick Elliott closes his eyes and shakes his head back and forth.

When she finishes her phone calls, K. Burke takes a gray jumpsuit from one of the police kits. She walks to Laura and helps her slip into it. For just a moment Burke's eyes meet Moncrief's.

The two of them are thinking the same thing. They are no closer to solving the case of Maria Martinez. And the one person who might have helped them is now dead.

CHAPTER 23

PHOTOGRAPHERS AND MORE photographers. Detectives and more detectives. Statements are made and then repeated. Hotel guests wander into the hallway.

We go to the precinct. More detectives. Two police attorneys. Everyone agrees: my bullet was justified. The surveillance video verifies what happened. My colleagues can easily rationalize that the world is a better place without Paulo Montes. I want to rationalize it also, but I cannot ignore the fact that I'm the cop who made it happen.

I go home.

"I'm awake," I hear Dalia shout. "Be right out."

I move toward the bedroom.

We meet in the hallway, and we stand directly in front of a black-and-white Léger poster, a drawing of four people artfully intertwined. Dalia and I do not kiss, but we hug each other with all our strength, as if we are afraid that the other person might slip away.

A few minutes later we are seated on a sofa. We watch the city sky slowly brighten. We both sip a snifter of Rémy. I devour a bowl of cashews. I tell her about my evening. Her face fills with horror, her eyes widen when I tell her about the horrific ending.

"Oh, my God, Luc. You must feel...I don't know...I don't know how you must feel."

"I don't think I know, either," I say. "I've never killed anyone."

I find myself remembering the shooting range near Porte de la Chapelle, where I spent so many hours learning how to load and shoot, load and shoot. The paper dummies, the foolishly big ear protectors. One-handed aim, two-handed aim, shoot from a prone position, shoot from a standing position. But shoot, always shoot. You got him. You got him. You missed him. You got him.

My plan for Montes would have worked. I am sure it would have worked.

I take the last gulp of my Cognac. I swipe the inside of the cashew bowl with my index finger. I touch my salty finger to the tip of Dalia's tongue. She smiles. I hold her tightly.

I tell Dalia that all I want to do now is sleep. She understands. We begin walking toward the bedroom. I stop for a moment. So Dalia stops also.

I have an idea. A very good idea. So good I want to share it with someone. But I'd be a fool to share it with Burke and Elliott. What about Dalia? I usually tell her everything, but not this time, not this idea. She'd kill me if she knew.

Dalia looks up at me.

"You're smiling," she says. "What are you thinking about?"

"Just you," I say. And as we fall on the bed, I consider crossing my fingers behind my back.

CHAPTER 24

I CALL GARY KUEHN at Vice. He's one of the few guys in that department who's smart enough to appreciate what he calls my shenanigans.

Shenanigans. English is a wonderful language.

Gary emails me a list of names of "superior sex workers" (translation: high-class hookers) and their managers (translation: drug-dealing abusive johns). I specifically request names of girls who regularly service the toniest areas of the Upper East Side.

I tell my new plan to no one—not K. Burke, not Nick Elliott, not even Gary. At midafternoon, I take an Uber car across town and check into a room at the Pierre, on Fifth Avenue at 61st Street. A mere seventeen hundred dollars a night. I silently thank my father for the large allowance that makes this expensive escapade possible.

I arrange for a series of these high-priced call girls to visit my room—one girl every thirty minutes. I do all the scheduling—the phoning and texting and emailing—myself.

At three o'clock a girl with incandescent mahogany skin appears. Her skin is so shiny it looks polished. Her hair is short and dark. She smiles. I am sitting in a comfortable blue club chair. She approaches me and touches my face.

"Please have a seat over there," I say, pointing to the identical blue club chair opposite my own. No doubt she thinks we're about to begin a freaky fantasy.

"Here is the first piece of news: I'm not going to touch you, but I will, of course, pay you for this visit." I hand her three hundred-dollar bills. (The agreed-upon price was two fifty.)

"Here is the second piece of news, and perhaps it is not quite so welcome. I am going to ask you some questions."

She smiles. I quickly add, "Nothing uncomfortable—just some simple talking and chatting. I am a detective with the NYPD."

Her face becomes a mask of fear.

"But I promise. You have nothing to worry about."

The questions begin:

Have you ever serviced a client at 655 Park Avenue?

Have you ever serviced a client at the Auberge du Parc Hotel?

Have you ever serviced a client who acted with extreme violence?

A client who hurt you, threatened you, brandished a weapon, a gun, a cane, a stick, a whip? A client who tried to slip a tablet or a powder or a suspicious liquid into a beverage?

Have you ever met with a client who was famous in his field—an actor, a diplomat, a senator, a governor, a foreign leader, a clergyman?

The answers are all no. And the pattern remains the same for every woman who follows.

A few of them tell me about men with some odd habits, but as the woman in the tight yellow jeans says, "A lot of guys have odd habits. That's why they go to prostitutes. Maybe their fancy wives don't want to suck toes or fuck in a tennis skirt or take it up the ass."

Other statements are made.

A tall woman, the only woman I've ever seen who looked beautiful in a Mohawk haircut, says, "Okay, there is this congressman from New Jersey that I see once or twice a month."

A very tan woman in a saronglike outfit says, "Yeah, one guy was *sort of* into whips, but all he wanted was for me to unpin my hair and swing it against his dick."

A woman who shows up in blue shorts cut off at mid-thigh, her shirt tied just above the navel, gives me some hope, but she, too, is a waste of time. "I think I was at 655 Park once. But it was for a woman. I hate working chicks. The few I've done were all, like, just into kissing and touching and petting. They're more work than the guys."

No information of any value. Yes, two of the girls have been slapped—both of them by men who were drunk. Yes, the girl-on-girl prostitute at 655 Park works for the Russian gang, but she knows nothing about the death of Maria Martinez, and she has never even heard of Paulo Montes.

What I am learning from these few hours of wasted interviews is the knowledge that the world is filled with men who are happy to pay to get laid. That's it. That's the deal. Over and out. It is a gross and humiliating way for a girl to make money, but, in most cases, each has made her separate peace with it.

The interviews end. Thousands of dollars later I have nothing to show for my work.

It is definitely time for me to leave the Pierre.

It is definitely time for me to return home to Dalia.

CHAPTER 25

EVERY MORNING AT THE precinct, K. Burke and I have the following dialogue.

Instead of saying the words "Good morning," she looks at me and says sternly, "You're late."

I always respond with a cheery "And good morning to you, *ma belle*."

It has become a funny little routine between the two of us, the sort of thing two friends might do. Who knows? Maybe K. Burke and I are becoming friends. Sometimes a mutually miserable situation can bring people together.

But this morning it's different. She greets me by saying, "Don't bother sitting down, Moncrief. We have an assignment from Inspector Elliott."

All I know is that unless Elliott has had an unexpected stroke of genius (highly unlikely) I am not interested in the assignment. I must also face the fact that my mood is terrible: interviewing the call girls has led to absolutely nothing, and I can share my frustration with no one. If I were to tell Burke or Elliott about my unapproved tactic they would both be furious.

"Whatever it is the inspector wants, we'll do it later."

"It's already later," Burke says. "It's one o'clock in the afternoon. Let's go."

"Go where? It's lunchtime. I'm thinking that fish restaurant on 49th Street. A bit of sole meunière and a crisp bottle of Chablis…"

"Stop being a Frenchman for just one minute, Moncrief," she says.

I can tell that K. Burke is uncomfortable with what she's about to say, but out it comes: "He wants us to visit some high-class strip clubs. He's even done some of the grunt work for us. He's compiled a list of clubs. Take a look at your phone."

I swipe the screen and click on my assignments folder. I see a page entitled "NYC Club Visits. From: N. Elliott."

Sapphire, 333 East 60th Street

Rick's Cabaret, 50 West 33rd Street

Hustler Club, 641 West 51st Street

Three more places are listed after these.

As a young man in Paris, full of booze and often with a touch of cocaine in my nose, I would occasionally visit the Théâtre Chochotte, in Saint-Germain-des-Prés, with some pals. It was not without its pleasures, but on one such visit I had a very bad experience: I ran into my father and my uncle in the VIP lounge. That was the night I crossed Chochotte and all Parisian strip clubs off my list. Even a son who has a much better relationship than I have with my father does not ever want to end up in a strip joint with the old man.

As for clubs in New York...I am no longer a schoolboy. I am no longer touching my nose with cocaine. And I now have Dalia waiting at home for me.

The fact is that my assignment would be the envy of most of my colleagues. But I am weary and frustrated and pissed off and...it seems impossible for me to believe, but I am growing tired of so much female flesh in my face.

"I won't do it," I say to Burke. "You do it alone. I'll stay here and do some detail analysis."

"No way am I going alone, Moncrief. C'mon."

"I cannot. I will not," I say.

"Then I suggest you tell that to Inspector Elliott."

I feel my whole heart spiraling downward. The entrapment with Laura. The death of Paulo. The futile interviews with the call girls. Now I am expected to go to these sad places, where a glass of cheap vodka costs thirty dollars, and try to talk to women with breast implants who are sliding up and down poles.

"I am sick. I am tired," I tell Burke.

"I know you are," Burke says. And I can tell she means it. "But you need to do it for Maria. This is—"

I snap at her. "I do not need a pep talk. I know you're trying to be helpful, but that kind of thing doesn't work with me."

Burke just stares at me.

"Tell Inspector Elliott we will make these 'visits' tomorrow. Maria will still be dead tomorrow. Right now, I'm going home."

CHAPTER 26

BURKE WILL TELL ELLIOTT that I went home because of illness. And, of course, Elliott won't believe it.

But I think that K. Burke and I are now simpatico enough for her to cover for me.

"Suddenly he's sick?" Elliott will say. "That's pure bullshit."

The answer Burke might produce could go something like, "Well, he was out sick all day yesterday."

It makes no difference. For the moment I am engaged in a very important project: I am in a store on Ninth Avenue selecting two perfect fillets of Dover sole. The cost at Seabreeze Fish Market for a pound of this beautiful fish is one hundred and twenty dollars. I have no trouble spending that much (or more) on a bottle of wine. But—Jesus!—this is fish. In the taxi uptown to Dalia's apartment I hold the package of fish as if it were a newborn infant being brought home from the hospital.

The moment I walk through the door of the apartment I feel lighter, better, stronger. It's as if the air in Dalia's place is purer than the air in the dangerous, depressing crime scenes I frequent.

I place the precious fish in the refrigerator.

I unpack the few other items I've bought and remove my shirt. I'm feeling better already.

In a moment I'll start chopping the shallots, chopping the parsley, and heating the wine for the mustard sauce. This preparation is what trained chefs call the *mise en place*.

I decide to take off my suit pants. I toss them on the chair where my shirt is resting. I am—in my mind—no longer in a professionally equipped kitchen overlooking Central Park. I am in a wonderfully sunny beach house on the Côte d'Azur. I am no longer a gloomy angry detective; I am a young tennis pro away for a week of rest, awaiting the arrival of his luscious girlfriend.

I press a button on the entertainment console. Suddenly the music blares. It is Dalia's newest favorite: Selena Gomez. "Me and the Rhythm." I sing along, creating my own lyrics to badly match whatever Selena is singing.

Ooh, all the rhythm takes you over.

I chop the shallot to the beat of the music. I scrape the chopped pieces into my hand and toss them into a sauté pan.

I am moving my feet and hips. I drop a half pound of Irish butter into the pan, and now I feel almost compelled to dance.

I sing. I dance. When I don't sing I am talking to an imaginary Dalia.

"Yes," I am saying. *"Your favorite. Dover sole."*

"Yes, there is a bottle of Dom Pérignon already in the fridge."

"Yes, I left early to make this dinner."

"The hell with them. They can fire me, then."

The music beats on. I rhythmically slap away at the parsley leaves with my chef's knife.

In the distance I hear the buzzing of a cell phone. The sound of the phone at first seems to be a part of Selena's song. Then I recognize the tone. It is my police phone. For a moment I consider ignoring it. Then I think that perhaps there is news on Maria Martinez's case. Or it might merely be Nick or K. Burke calling to torment me. But nothing can torment me tonight.

I let the music continue. Whoever my caller is can sing along with me.

I yank my suit jacket from the pile of clothing. I find my phone.

Ooh, all the rhythm takes you over.

"What's up?" I yell loudly above the music.

My prediction is correct. It is Inspector Elliott on the line.

He speaks. I listen. I stop dancing. I drop the phone. I fall to my knees and I scream.

"Noooooooo!"

CHAPTER 27

BUT THE TRUTH IS "yes." There has been another woman stabbed, another woman connected to the New York City police. Only this time the woman is neither an officer nor a detective. This time the woman is also connected to me.

"Who is it, goddamn it?"

Elliott's exact words: "It's Dalia, Moncrief."

A pause and then he adds quietly, *"Dalia is dead."*

I kneel on the gray granite floor and pound it. Tears do not come, but I cannot stop saying "no." If I say the word loudly enough, often enough, it will eradicate the fact of "yes."

For a few moments I actually believe that the call from Nick Elliott never happened. I am on the floor, and I pick up the phone. I observe it as if it were a foreign object—a paperweight, a tiny piece of meteorite, a dead rat. But the caller ID says N/ELLIOTT/NYPD/17PREC.

An overwhelming energy goes through me. Within seconds I am back in my pants and shirt. I slip on my shoes, without socks. I go bounding out the door, and the madness within me makes me certain that running down the back stairs of the apartment building will be faster than calling for the elevator.

Once outside, I see two officers waiting in a patrol car.

"Detective Moncrief. We're here to take you to the crime scene. Take the passenger seat."

I don't even know where the crime scene is. I grab the shoulders of the other cop and shake him violently.

"Where the hell are you taking me? Where is she?" I shout. "Where are we going?"

"To 235 East 20th Street, sir. Please get into the car."

Within moments we are suffocated in midtown rush-hour traffic. How can there be so much traffic when Dalia is dead?

At Seventh Avenue and 45th, the streets are thick with sightseeing buses and cabs. Some people are dressed up as Big Bird and Minnie Mouse. The sidewalks teem with tourists and druggies and strollers and women in saris and schoolchildren on trips and...I tell the driver to unlock the doors. I will walk, run, fly.

"This traffic will break below 34th Street, Detective."

"Unlock the fucking door!" I scream. And so he does, and I am on the sidewalk again. I don't give a shit that I am pushing people aside.

Within minutes I am at Seventh Avenue and 34th Street. The streets remain packed with people and cabs and cars and buses.

I cross against the light at 34th Street, Herald Square, Macy's. Where the hell is Santa Claus when you need him?

Sirens. Cars jostle to clear a route for the vehicle screeching out the sirens.

I am rushing east on 32nd Street. I am midway between

Broadway and Fifth Avenue, a block packed almost entirely, crazily, with Korean restaurants. Suddenly the sirens are fiercely loud.

"Get in the car, Moncrief. Get back in the car." It is the same driver of the same patrol car that picked me up earlier. They were right about the traffic, but I am vaguely glad that I propelled myself this far.

In a few minutes we are at 235 East 20th Street. The police academy of the New York City Police Department. The goddamn police academy. Dalia is dead at the police academy. How the hell did she end up here?

"We're here, Detective," says one of the officers.

I turn my head toward the building. K. Burke is walking quickly toward the car. Behind her is Nick Elliott. My chest hurts. My throat burns.

Dalia is dead.

CHAPTER 28

"THIS WAY, LUC," K. Burke says. Both Burke and Nick Elliott guide me by the elbows down a corridor—painted cement blocks, an occasional bulletin board, a fire-alarm box, a fire-extinguisher case.

The usual cast of characters is standing nearby: police officers, forensics, the coroner's people, two firemen, some young people—probably students—carrying laptops and water bottles. A very large sign is taped to a wall at the end of the corridor. It is a photograph of four people: a white male officer, an Asian female officer, a black male officer, a white female officer. Above the big grainy photo are big grainy blue letters:

SERVE WITH DIGNITY. SERVE WITH COURAGE.
THE NEW YORK CITY POLICE DEPARTMENT

Burke and Elliott steer me into a large old-fashioned lecture hall. The stadium seating ends at the bottom with a large table at which a lecturer usually stands. Behind it are a video screen and a green chalkboard. In this teaching pit also stand two officers and two doctors from the chief medical examiner's office. On the side aisles are other officers, other detectives, and, as we descend closer to the bottom of that aisle, a gurney on which a body rests.

K. Burke speaks to me as we reach the gurney. She is saying something to me, but I can't hear her. I am not hearing anything. I am just staring straight ahead as a doctor pulls back the gauzy sheet from Dalia's head and shoulders.

"The wound was in the stomach, sir," she says.

She knows I need no further details at the moment.

Need I say that Dalia looks exquisite? Perfect hair. Perfect eyelashes. A touch of perfect makeup. Perfect. Just perfect. Just fucking unbelievably perfect.

How can she be so beautiful and yet dead?

In my mind I am still screaming "No!" but I say nothing.

I look away from her, and I see the others in the room backing away, looking away, trying to give me privacy in a very public situation.

I must touch Dalia. I should do it gently, of course. I take Dalia's face in both my hands. Her cheeks feel cold, hard. I lean in and brush my lips against her forehead. I pull back a tiny bit to look at her. Then I lean in again to kiss her on the lips.

The room is silent. Deadly silent. I have heard silence before. But the world has never been this quiet.

I will stand here for the rest of my life just looking at her. Yes, that's what I'll do. I'll never move from this spot. I stroke her hair. I touch her shoulders. I stand erect, then turn around.

Nick Elliott is looking at the ground. K. Burke's chin is quivering. Her eyes are wet. I speak, perhaps to Nick or K. Burke or everyone in the room or perhaps I am simply talking to myself.

"Dalia is dead."

CHAPTER 29

"DO YOU WANT TO ride in the ambulance with her?"
Elliott asks. And before I can answer he adds, "I'll go with
you if you want. We've got to get Dalia to the research
area."

The research area. That is the NYPD euphemism for "the
morgue." It is what they say to parents whose child has been
run over by a drunk driver.

"No," I say. "There's nothing to be done."

K. Burke looks at me and says what everybody says in a
situation like this: "I don't know what to say."

And me? I don't know what to say, either—or what to
think or feel or do. So I say what comes to mind: "Keep
me posted."

I walk quickly through the lineup of colleagues and strangers
lining the cement-block hallway. I jump over the giant stone
barricades that encircle the police academy in case of attack. I
am now running up Third Avenue.

"May I help you, monsieur?" That is the voice I hear. Where
have I run? I don't recall a destination. I barely remember

running. Did I leave Dalia's dead body behind? I look at the woman who just spoke to me. She used the word *monsieur.* Am I in Paris?

She is joined by a well-dressed man, an older man, a gentleman.

"Can I be of some help, Monsieur Moncrief?"

"*Où suis-je?*" I ask. Where am I?

"*Hermès, Monsieur Moncrief. Bonsoir. Je peux vous aider?*"

The Hermès store on Madison Avenue. It is...was...Dalia's favorite place in the entire world to shop.

"*Non. Merci, monsieur. Je regarde.*" Just looking.

On the glass shelves is a collection of handbags, purses, and pocketbooks in red and yellow and green. Like Easter and Christmas. I feel calm amid the beauty. It is a museum, a palace, a château. The silk scarves hanging from golden hooks. The glass cases of watches and cuff links. The shelves of briefcases and leather shopping bags. And then the calm inside me dissipates. I say, "*Bonsoir et merci*" to the sales associate.

I have neither my police phone nor my personal cell. I do not have my watch. I do not know the time. I know I am not crazy. I'm simply crazed.

It's early evening. I walk to Fifth Avenue. The sidewalks are crowded, and the shops are open. I walk down to the Pierre. I was recently inside the Pierre. Was I? I think I was. I continue walking south, toward the Plaza. No water in the fountain? A water shortage, perhaps? I turn east, back toward Madison Avenue, then start north again.

Bottega Veneta. I walk inside. No warm greeting here. A bigger store than Hermès. Instead of a symphony of leather in color, this is a muted place in grays and blacks and many degrees of brown. Calming, calming, calming, until it is calming no longer.

I leave. My next stop is Sherry-Lehmann, the museum of wine. I walk to the rear of the store, where they keep their finest bottles—the Romanée-Conti, Pétrus, Le Pin, Ramonet Montrachet, the thousand-dollar Moët. The bottles should all be displayed under glass, like the diamonds at Tiffany.

I am out on the sidewalk again. I am afraid that if I don't keep moving, I will explode or collapse. It is that extraordinary feeling that nothing good will ever happen again.

A no-brainer: I cannot return to Dalia's apartment at 15 Central Park West. Instead I will go to the loft where I once lived. The place is in the stupidly chic Meatpacking District. I bought the loft before I renewed my life with Dalia. I sometimes lend the place to friends from Europe who are visiting New York. I'm pretty sure it is empty right now.

Will I pick up the pieces? There is no way that will ever happen.

Move on, they will say. Mourn, then move on. I will not do that, because I can't.

Get over it? Never. Someone else? Never.

Nothing will ever be the same.

As I give the address to the cabdriver, I find my chest heaving and hurting. I insist—I don't know why—on holding in the tears. In those few minutes, with my chest shaking and my head aching, I realize what Elliott and Burke and probably others have come to realize: first, my partner, Maria Martinez; then my lover, Dalia Boaz.

Oh, my God. This isn't about prostitutes. This isn't about drugs. This is about me.

Somebody wants to hurt me. And that somebody has succeeded.

CHAPTER 30

A LOFT. A BIG space; bare, barren. Not a handsome space. It is way too basic to be anything but big.

I lived here before Dalia came back into my life. Even when I lived here, I was too compulsive to have allowed it to become a cheesy bachelor pad—no piles of dirty clothing; no accumulation of Chinese-food containers. In fact, no personal touches of any kind. But of course I was spending too many of my waking hours with the NYPD to think about furniture and paint and bathroom fixtures.

I turn the key and walk inside. I am almost startled by the sparseness of it—a gray sofa, a black leather club chair, a glass dining table where no one has ever eaten a meal. Some old files are stacked against a wall. Empty shelves near the sofa. Empty shelves in the kitchen. I have lived most of my New York life with Dalia, at Dalia's home. That was my real home. Where am I now?

I stretch out on the sofa. Fifteen seconds later, I am back on my feet. The room is stuffy, dry, hot. I walk to the thermostat that will turn on the air-conditioning, but I stare at the controls as if I don't quite know how to adjust the temperature. I remember that there is a smooth single-malt Scotch in a cabinet near the entryway, but why bother? I need to use the bathroom, but I just don't have energy enough to walk to the far side of the loft.

Then the buzzer downstairs rings.

At least I think it's the buzzer downstairs. It's been so long since I heard it. I walk to the intercom. The buzz comes again, then once more. Then I remember what I'm expected to say. A phrase that is ridiculously simple.

"Who is it?"

For a split second I stupidly imagine that it will be Dalia. "It was a terrible joke," she will say with a laugh. "Inspector Elliott helped me fool you."

Now a hollow voice comes from the intercom.

"It's K. Burke."

I buzz her inside. Moments later I open the door and let her into the loft.

"How did you know where to find me?" I ask.

"I called your cell twenty times. You never picked up. Then I called Dalia's place twenty times. You weren't there, *or* you weren't picking up. So I found this place listed as the home address in your HR file. If I didn't find you here, I was going to forget it. But I got lucky."

"No, K. Burke. *I got lucky.*"

I have no idea why I said something so sweet. But I think I mean it. Again, an idea that comes and goes in a split second: whoever is trying to destroy me—will he go after K. Burke next?

She gives me a smile. Then she says, "I'm about to say the thing that always annoys me when other people say it."

"And that is..."

"Is there anything I can do for you?"

I take a deep breath.

"You mean like brewing a pot of coffee or bringing me a bag of doughnuts or cleaning my bathroom or finding the son of a bitch who—"

"Okay, I got it," she says. "I understand. But actually, Nick Elliott and I did do something for you."

My forehead wrinkles, and I say, "What?"

"We tracked down Dalia's father. He's in Norway shooting a film."

"I was going to call him soon," I say. "But I was building up courage. Thank you." And just thinking about father and daughter begins to break my already severed heart.

"How did he accept the news?" As if I needed to ask.

"It was awful. He wailed. He screamed. He put his assistant on, and he eventually... well, he sort of composed himself and got back on the line."

My eyes begin filling with tears. My chin quivers. I rub my eyes. I am not trying to hide my emotions. I am merely trying to get through them.

"He sends you his love," K. Burke says. I nod.

"He is as fine a man as Dalia was a woman," I say.

"He asked me to tell you two things."

I can't imagine what Monsieur Boaz wanted to tell me.

"He said, 'Tell Luc that I will come to America when I finish my film, but he should bury Dalia as soon as possible. That is the Jewish way.'"

"I understand," I say. Then I ask, "And the other?"

"He said, 'Tell Luc thank you…for taking such good care of my girl.'"

This comment should make me weep, but instead I explode with anger. Not at Menashe Boaz, but at myself.

"That's not true!" I yell. "I did *not* take good care of her."

"Of course it's true," K. Burke says firmly. "You loved her totally. Everybody knows that."

"I…let…her…die."

"That's just stupid, Moncrief. And it smells a little of…" K. Burke abruptly stops talking.

"What? Finish your thought. It smells of what?" I say.

"It smells of…well…self-pity. Dalia was murdered. You could not have prevented it."

I walk to the floor-to-ceiling windows of the loft. I look down at Gansevoort Street. It's this year's chic hot-cool place to be— the expensive restaurants and expensive boutiques, the High Line, the cobblestone streets. It is packed with people. I am disgusted with them because I am disgusted with me. Because Dalia and I will never again be among those people.

I turn and face Detective Burke, and suddenly I am more peaceful. I am truly grateful that she is here. She has stopped by to offer the "personal touch" and I was hesitant at first. Afraid I would feel nervous or embarrassed. But K. Burke has done a good thing.

I walk back toward her and speak slowly, carefully.

"There is one thing we need to discuss very soon. You must realize that these two murders had nothing to do with prostitutes or Brazilian drug dealers or…well, all the things we have been guessing at."

"I realize that," she says. I continue speaking.

"The first murder, at a rich man's home, was to confuse us. The next murder, at a school where people learn to be police professionals—that was to torment us."

K. Burke nods in simple agreement.

"These murders have to do with *me*," I say.

"In that case," K. Burke says, "these murders have to do with *us*."

CHAPTER 31

"WHAT THE HELL IS the story with these two murders?"

This question keeps exploding off the walls of NYPD precincts. It is the commissioner's question. It is Nick Elliott's question. And—obsessively, interminably, awake or asleep—it is my question.

The question is asked a thousand times, and a thousand times the answer comes back the same.

"No idea. Just no goddamn idea."

Forensics brought in nothing. Surveillance cameras showed us nothing. Interviews at the scene turned up nothing.

So it is now time for me to do the only thing left to do: turn inward and rely entirely on my instincts. They have helped me in the past, and they have failed me, too. But instinct is all I have left.

I confront Nick Elliott. I tell him that the answer to the murders is obviously not in New York. The answer must be in Paris.

"Paris?" he shouts.

Then I say, "I need to go to Paris—look around, nose around, see if I can find something there."

Nick Elliott gives it a long pause and then says, "Maybe that's not a bad idea."

Then I tell him that I want to take K. Burke with me.

He pauses again, another long pause. Then he speaks. "Now, *that's* a bad idea."

"Inspector, this is no holiday I'm planning. This is work. K. Burke and I will be examining cases that—"

"Okay, okay, let me think about it," Elliott says. "Maybe it'll help. On the other hand, it might end up being a waste of time and money."

I think quickly and say, "Then it will be a waste of *my* time and *my* money. I'll supply the money for the trip. I only care about getting to the bottom of these murders."

"I guess so," says Elliott.

I say, "I'll take that as a yes."

A minute later I am telling K. Burke to go home and pack.

Her reaction? "I've never been to Paris."

My reaction? "Why am I not surprised?"

CHAPTER 32

K. BURKE AND I are sitting at a steel desk in a small room with bad internet service at Les Archives de la Préfecture de Police, the dreary building on the periphery of Paris where all the old police records are kept. Here you can examine every recorded police case since the end of the Great War. Here you can discover the names of the French collaborators during the Vichy regime. You can examine the records of the Parisian bakers who have been accused of using tainted yeast in their bread. Here are the records of the thousands of murders, assaults, knife attacks, shootings, and traffic violations that have occurred in the past hundred years in the City of Light.

It is also here that K. Burke and I hope to find some small (or, better yet, large) clue that could connect us to whoever is responsible for the brutal deaths of Maria Martinez and my beloved Dalia.

To find the person who wishes to hurt me so deeply.

"Here," says Detective Burke, pointing to my name on the screen of the archive's computer. "*L. Moncrief était responsable…*"

I translate: "L. Moncrief was responsible for the evidence linking the Algerian diplomat to the cartel posing as Dominican priests in the 15th arrondissement."

I press a computer key and say to Burke, "Listen: after years of being dragged to church by my mother, I know a real priest when I see one, and no *prêtre* I'd ever seen had such a well-groomed beard and mustache. Then I noticed that his shoes...eh, never mind. See what's next."

We study my other cases. Some of those I worked on are ridiculously small—a Citroën stolen because the owner left the keys in the ignition; a lost child who stopped for a free *jus d'orange* on his way home from school; a homeless man arrested for singing loudly in a public library.

Other cases are much more significant. Along with the phony Dominicans, there was the drug bust in Pigalle, the case I built my reputation on. But there was also a gruesome murder in Montmartre, on rue Caulaincourt, during which a pimp's hands and feet were amputated.

In this last case my instincts led me to a pet cemetery in Asnières-sur-Seine. Both the severed hands and feet were found at the grave of the pimp's childhood pet, a spaniel. Instinct.

But nothing in the police archive is resonating with me. I do not feel, either through logic or instinct, any link from these past cases and the awful deaths of my two beloved women.

"I think I need another café au lait, Moncrief," K. Burke says. Her eyelids are covering half her eyes. Jet lag has definitely attacked her.

"What you need is a taxi back to Le Meurice," I say. "It is now *quatorze heures....*"

K. Burke looks confused.

I translate. "Two o'clock in the afternoon."

"Gotcha," she says.

"Go back to the hotel. Take a nap, and I will come knocking on your door at *dix-sept heures*. Forgive me. I will come knocking at five o'clock."

I add, "Good-bye, K. Burke."

"Au revoir," she says. Her accent makes me cringe, then smile.

"You see?" I add. "You're here just seven hours, and already you're on your way to becoming a true *Parisienne*."

CHAPTER 33

WE MEET AT FIVE.

"I am not a happy man," I say to K. Burke after I give our destination to the cabdriver. Then I say, "Perhaps I will never be a completely happy man again, but I am *un peu content* when I am in Paris." Burke says nothing for a few seconds.

"Perhaps someday you will be happi*er.*" She speaks with an emphasis on the last syllable. Perhaps someday I will be.

Then I explain to her that because we will have to get back to our investigation tomorrow—"And, like many things, it might come to a frustrating end," I caution—this early evening will be the only chance for me to show her the glory of Paris.

Then I quickly add, "But not the Eiffel Tower or the Louvre or Notre Dame. You can see those on your own. I will show you the special places in Paris. Places that are visited by only the very wise and the very curious."

Detective Burke says, *"Merci, Monsieur Moncrief. "*

I smile at her, and then I say to the cabdriver, *"Nous sommes arrivés."* We are here.

Burke reads the sign on the building aloud. Her accent is amusingly American-sounding: "Museé...des...Arts...Forains?"

"It is the circus museum," I say. And soon we are standing in a huge warehouse that holds the forty carousels and games and bright neon signs that a rich man thought were worth preserving.

"I can't decide whether this is a dream or a nightmare," Burke says.

"I think that it is *both*."

We ride a carousel that whirls amazingly fast. "I feel like I'm five again!" shouts K. Burke. We play a game that involves plaster puppets and cloth-covered bulls. K. Burke wins the game. Then we are out and on our way again.

This time out I tell our cabdriver to take us to Paris Descartes University.

"*Vous êtes médecin?*" the cabdriver asks.

I tell him that my companion and I are doctors of crime, which seems both to surprise and upset him. A few minutes later we are ascending in the lift to view the Musée d'Anatomie Delmas-Orfila-Rouvière. The place is almost crazier than the circus museum. It's a medical museum with hundreds of shelves displaying skulls and skeletons and wax models of diseased human parts. It is at once astonishing and disgusting.

At one point Burke says, "We're the only people here."

"You need special permission to enter."

"Aren't we the lucky ones?" Burke says, with only slight sarcasm.

From there we take another cab ride—to the Pont des Arts,

a pedestrian bridge across the Seine. I show her the "love locks," the thousands of small padlocks attached to the rails of the bridge by lovers.

"They are going to relocate some of the locks," I tell Burke. "There are so many that they fear the bridge may collapse."

So much love, I think. And for a moment my heart hurts. But then I hail another cab. I point out the Pitié-Salpêtrière hospital, and we both laugh when I explain that it was once an asylum for "hysterical women."

"Don't get any ideas, Moncrief," Burke says.

Since our bodies are still on New York time, it is almost lunchtime for us, and I ask K. Burke if she is hungry.

"Tu as faim?" I ask.

"Très, très hungry. Famished, in fact."

Ten minutes later, we are in the rough-and-tumble Pigalle area. I tell Detective Burke that she can always dine at the famous Parisian restaurants—Taillevent, Guy Savoy, even the dining room in our hotel. But tonight, I am taking her to my favorite restaurant, Le Petit Canard.

"Isn't this the area where you made your famous drug bust?" Burke asks.

"C'est vrai," I tell her. "You have a good memory."

She is looking out the taxi window. The tourists have disappeared from the streets. The artists must be inside smoking weed. Only vagrants and prostitutes are hanging around.

"Ignore the neighborhood. Le Petit Canard is amazing. I used to come here a great deal when I lived in Paris. With friends, with my father, with..."

She says, "With Dalia, I'm sure." She pauses and says, "I am so sorry for you, Moncrief. So sorry."

Softly, I mutter, "Thank you."

Then I add, "And thank you for allowing me to take you to the crazy tourist sights. It lifted my spirits. It made me feel a little better, Katherine."

Burke appears slightly startled. We both realize that for the first time I have called Detective Burke by her proper first name.

I look closely at Burke's face, a lovely face, a face that goes well with such a lovely evening in such a beautiful city.

"Okay," I say loudly and with great heartiness. "Let me call for the wine list, and we shall begin. We will enjoy a glorious dinner tonight."

I fake an overly serious sad face, a frown. "Because you know that tomorrow... *retour au travail.* Do you know what those three French words mean?"

"I'm afraid so," she says. "'Back to work.'"

CHAPTER 34

MONCRIEF AND K. BURKE return to the hotel. If you were unaware of the details of their relationship, you would assume that they were just another rich and beautiful couple strolling through the ornate lobby of the Meurice.

Much to Moncrief's surprise and pleasure, K. Burke had brought along an outfit that was quite chic—a long white shirt over which hung a gray cashmere sweater. That sweater fell over a slim black skirt. It was finished with short black boots. Burke could *possibly* pass as a fashionable Parisian, and she could *certainly* pass as a fashionable American. Moncrief had told her how "snappy" she looked.

"You look snappy yourself, Moncrief," she had said to him. This was, of course, true: a black Christian Dior suit with a slight sheen to it; a white shirt with a deep burgundy-colored tie.

Moncrief walked K. Burke back to her room and said good night. He listened while Burke locked her door behind her. Then he walked to the end of the hallway, to his own room.

It was a dinner between friends, between colleagues. K. Burke had expected nothing more. In fact, K. Burke *wanted* nothing more. It had been a spectacular day—the odd museums, then the extraordinary dinner: foie-gras ravioli, Muscovy duckling with mango sherbet, those wonderful little chocolates that fancy French restaurants always bring you with your coffee (or so Moncrief told her).

The night had turned out to be soothing and fun and friendly. He referred to Dalia a few times, and it was with nostalgia, sadness. But there was no darkness when he reminisced about his late girlfriend.

Now, as Burke unscrews and removes her tiny diamond studs, she wonders: *Can you have such a wonderful time with a charming, handsome man and not think about romance?*

Of course you can, she tells herself. But then again, it's impossible to put a man and a woman together—the electrician who comes to fix the wiring, the traffic cop who stops you for speeding, the attorney who is updating your will—and not consider the possibilities of *What if... at another time... under different conditions...*

Burke removes her shirt and sweater. She sits on the bench at the white wood dressing table and removes her boots. As she massages her toes she shakes her head slowly; she is ashamed that she is even having such thoughts. Despite the pleasant dinner, she knows that Moncrief has not remotely begun to recover from Dalia's awful, sudden, horrible death. *And yet here I am, selfishly thinking of how great we look together, like one of those beautiful couples in a perfume ad.*

"Enough nonsense." She actually says these two words out loud.

Then she goes into the bathroom, removes her makeup, brushes her teeth, and takes the two antique combs out of her hair. She slips her T-shirt (GO RANGERS) over her head, then she removes her contact lenses and drops them into solution. There is only one more thing to do.

She goes to her pocketbook to do what she does instinctively every night before bed: check the safety on her service weapon. Then she remembers—she doesn't have a gun. The French police said that she and Moncrief were on official business for New York, *not* for Paris. No firearms permits would be issued.

She remembers what Moncrief said to her when she complained.

"Do you feel naked without your gun, K. Burke?"

"No," she had answered. "Just a little underdressed."

CHAPTER 35

THE SAME CRAMPED AND ugly little room. The same primitive air-conditioning. The same stale air. The same inadequate internet service. But most of all, the same rotten luck in finding "the fingerprint," the instinctive connection between one of my past investigations and the tragedies in New York.

Detective Burke and I keep working. We are once again seated in the police archives building, outside Paris. We have been studying the screen so intently that we decided to invest in a shared bottle of eyedrops.

The screen scrolls through old cases, some of which I had actually forgotten—a molestation case that involved a disgusting pediatrician who was also the father of five children; a case of a government official who, not surprisingly, was collecting significant bribes for issuing false health-inspection reports; a case of race fixing at the Longchamp racecourse.

"This looks bigger than fixing a horse race," she says. "The pages go on forever."

"Print them," I say. "I'll look at them more thoroughly later."

Forty pages come spitting out of the printer. Burke says, "It looks like this was a very complicated case."

"Not really," I say. "No case is ever *that* complicated. Either there's a crime or there isn't. The Longchamp case began with a horse trainer. Marcel Ballard was his name. Not a bad guy, I think, but Ballard was weary of fixing the races. So he fought physically—punching, kicking—with the owner and trainer who were running the fix. *And* Ballard had a knife. *And* Ballard killed the owner and cut the other trainer badly."

K. Burke continues scrolling through the cases on the screen. She says, "Keep going, Moncrief. I'm listening."

"I met with Ballard's wife. She had a newborn, three months old, their fourth child. So I did her a favor, but not without asking for something in return. I persuaded Ballard to confess to the crime and to help us identify the other trainers who were drugging the horses. He cooperated. So thanks to my intervention—and that of my superiors—he was allowed to plead to a lesser charge. Instead of *homicide volontaire,* he was only charged with—"

"Let me guess," says K. Burke. *"Homicide* in*volontaire."*

"You are both a legal and linguistic genius, K. Burke."

I grab some of the Longchamp papers and go through them quickly. "I'm glad I did what I did," I say. "Madame Ballard is a good woman."

"And the husband? Is he grateful?" K. Burke asks as she continues to study the screen intensely.

"He has written to me many times in gratitude. But one must keep in mind that he did kill a man."

Burke presses a computer key and begins reading about a drug gang working out of Saint-Denis.

"What does this mean, Moncrief? *Logement social.*"

"In New York they call it public housing. A group of heroin dealers had set up a virtual drug supermarket in the basement there. Once I realized that some of our Parisian detectives were involved in the scheme, it was fairly easy— but frightening—to bust."

"How'd you figure out that your own cops were involved?" she asks.

"I simply *felt* it," I say.

"Of course," she says with a bit of sarcasm. "I should have known."

We continue flipping through the cases on the computer. But like the race fixing and murder at Longchamp, like the drug bust in Saint-Denis, all my former cases seem to be a million miles away from New York. No instinct propelled me. No fingerprint arose.

We studied the cold cases also. The kidnapping of the Ugandan ambassador's daughter (unsolved). The rape of an elderly nun at midnight in the Bois de Boulogne (unsolved, but what in hell was an elderly nun doing in that huge park at midnight?). An American woman with whom I had a brief romantic fling, Callie Hansen, who had been abducted for three days by a notorious husband-and-wife team that we were never able to apprehend. Again, nothing clicked.

We come across a street murder near Moulin Rouge. According to the report on the computer screen, one of the witnesses was a woman named Monica Ansel. Aha! Blaise Ansel had been the owner of Taylor Antiquities, the store on East 71st Street. Could Monica Ansel be his wife? But Monica

Ansel, the woman who witnessed the crime at Moulin Rouge, was seventy-one years old.

"Damn!" I say, and I toss the papers from the Longchamp report to the floor. "I have wasted my time and yours, K. Burke. Plus I have wasted a good deal of money. And what do I have to show for it? *De la merde.*"

Even with her limited knowledge of French, K. Burke is able to translate.

"I agree," she says. "Shit."

CHAPTER 36

K. BURKE SITS OUTDOORS at a small bistro table on rue Vieille du Temple. She is alone. Moncrief had asked if he could be by himself for a while. "I must walk. I must think. Perhaps I must mourn. Do you mind?" Moncrief had said.

"I understand," she had said, and she did understand. "I don't need a chaperone."

She sips a glass of strong cider and eats a buckwheat crepe stuffed with ham and Gruyère. It is eight o'clock, a fairly early dinner by French standards. At one table sits a family of German tourists—very blond parents with two very beautiful teenage daughters. At another, an older couple (French, Burke suspects) eating and chewing and drinking slowly and carefully. Finally, there are two young Frenchwomen who appear to be...yes, K. Burke is right...very much in love with each other.

Burke's own heart is still breaking for Moncrief, but she must admit that she is enjoying being alone for a few hours.

Back in her hotel room, she takes a warm bath. A healthy dose of lavender bath oils; a natural sea sponge. Afterward, she dries herself off with the thick white bath sheets and douses herself with a nice dose of the accompanying lavender powder.

She slips on her sleep shirt, and she's about to slide under the sheets when her phone buzzes. A text message.

R U back in yr room? All is well?

She imagines Moncrief in some mysterious part of Paris, at a zinc bar with a big snifter of brandy. She is thankful for his thoughtfulness.

Yes.

But then, for just a moment she considers her own uneasiness. She simply cannot get used to not having a gun to check. So she does the next best thing: she checks that the door is double-locked. She adjusts the air-conditioning, making the temperature low enough for her to happily snuggle under the thick satin comforter. Within a few minutes she is asleep.

Two hours later, she is wide awake. It is barely past midnight, and Burke is afraid that jet lag is playing games with her sleep schedule. Now she may be up for hours. She takes a few deep breaths. The air makes her feel at least a little better. Maybe she will get back to sleep. Maybe she should use the bathroom. Yes, maybe. Or maybe that will prevent her from falling asleep again. On the other hand ...

There is a sound in the room. At first she thinks it's the air conditioner kicking back into gear. Perhaps it is the noise from the busy rue de Rivoli below. She sits up in bed. The noise. Again. Burke realizes now that the sound is coming from the door to her hotel room. Some sort of key? What the hell?

"Who's there?" she shouts.

No answer.

"Who's there?"

Goddamnit. Why doesn't she have a gun?

She should have insisted that Moncrief get them guns. He was right. She feels naked without it.

She rolls quickly—catching herself in the thick covers, afraid in the dark—toward the other side of the bed. She drops to the floor and slides beneath the bed just as a shaft of bright light from the hallway pierces the darkness. Someone else is in the room with her. She moves farther underneath the bed. *Jesus Christ,* she thinks. *This is an awful comedy, a French farce—the woman hiding beneath the bed.*

As soon as she hears the door close, the light from the hallway disappears.

"Don't move, Detective!" a muffled, foreign-sounding voice hisses.

Then a gunshot.

The bullet hits the floor about a foot away from her hand. There's a quick loud snapping sound. A spark on the blue carpet. She tries to move farther under the bed. There is no room. It is so unlike her to not know what to do, to not fight back, to not plot an escape. This feeling of fright is foreign to her.

Another bullet. This one spits its way fiercely through the mattress above her. It hits the floor also.

Another bullet. No spark. No connection.

A groan. A quick thud.

Then a voice.

"K. Burke! It is safe. All is well."

CHAPTER 37

HOTEL MANAGEMENT AND GUESTS in their pajamas almost immediately begin gathering in the hall.

K. Burke emerges from under the bed. We embrace each other the way friends do, friends who have successfully come through a horrible experience together.

"You saved..." she begins. She is shaking. She folds her arms in front of herself. She is working to compose herself.

"I know," I say. I pat her on the back. I am like an old soccer coach with an injured player.

Burke pulls away from me. She blinks—on purpose— a few times, and those simple eye gestures seem to clear her head and calm her nerves. She is immediately back to a completely professional state. She has become the efficient K. Burke I am used to. We both look down at the body. She moves to a nearby closet and wraps herself quickly in a Le Meurice terry-cloth bathrobe.

The dead man fell backward near the foot of the bed. He wears jeans, a white dress shirt, and Adidas sneakers. His bald head lies in a large and ever-growing pool of blood. It forms a kind of scarlet halo around his face.

The crowd in the hallway seems afraid to enter the room. A man wearing a blue blazer with LE MEURICE embroidered on the breast pocket appears. He pushes through the crowd. He is immediately followed by two men wearing identical blazers.

I briefly explain what happened, planning to give the police a more detailed story when they arrive.

K. Burke then kneels at the man's head. I watch her touch the man's neck. I can tell by the blood loss, by simply looking at him, that she is merely performing an official act. The guy is gone. Burke stands back up.

"Do you know him, Moncrief?" Burke asks.

"I have never seen him before in my life," I say. "Have you?"

"Of course not," she says. She pauses. Then she says, "He was going to kill me."

"You would have been...the third victim."

She nods. "How did you know that this was happening here, that someone was actually going to break in...threaten my life...try to kill me?"

"Instinct. When I texted you I asked if all was well. So I drank my whiskey.

"But fifteen minutes later, when I am walking back to the hotel, I found myself walking faster and faster, until I was actually running...I just had a feeling. I can't explain it."

"You never can," she says.

CHAPTER 38

THE NEXT MORNING.

Eleven o'clock. I meet K. Burke in the lobby of the hotel.

"So here we are," she says. "Everything is back to *ab*normal."

Even I realize that this is a bad play on words. But it does perfectly describe our situation.

"Look," I say. "A mere apology is unsuitable. I am totally responsible for the near tragedy of last night."

"There's nothing to apologize for. It goes with the territory," she says, but I can see from her red eyes that she did not sleep well. I try to say something helpful.

"I suspect what happened a few hours ago is that the enemy saw us together at some point here in Paris and assumed that we were a couple, which of course we are not."

I realize immediately that my words are insulting, as if it would be impossible to consider us a romantic item. So I speak again, this time more quickly.

"Of course, they might have been correct in the assumption. After all, a lovely-looking woman like you could—"

"Turn it off, Moncrief. I was *not* offended."

I smile. Then I hold K. Burke by the shoulders, look into her weary eyes, and speak.

"Listen. Out of something awful that almost happened last evening... something good has come. I believe I have an insight. I think I may now know the fingerprint of this case."

She asks me to share the theory with her.

"I cannot tell you yet. Not for secrecy reasons, but because I must first be sure, in order to keep my own mind clear. *On y va.*"

"Okay," she says. Then she translates: "Let's go."

We walk outside. I speak to one of the doormen.

"Ma voiture, s'il vous plaît," I say.

"Elle est là, Monsieur Moncrief."

"Your car is here?" Burke asks, and as she speaks my incredibly beautiful 1960 Porsche 356B pulls up and the valet gets out.

"C'est magnifique," Burke says.

The Porsche is painted a brilliantly shiny black. Inside is a custom mahogany instrument panel and a pair of plush black leather seats. I explain to Detective Burke that I had been keeping the car at my father's country house, near Avignon.

"But two days ago I had the car brought up to Paris. And so today we shall use it."

I turn right on the rue de Rivoli, and the Porsche heads out of the city.

After the usual mess of too many people and triple-parked cars and thousands of careless bicycle riders, we are outside Paris, on our way south.

K. Burke twists in her seat and faces me.

"Okay, Moncrief. I have a question that's been bugging me all night."

"I hope to have the answer," I say, trying not to sound anxious.

"The gun that you used last night. Where did you get it?"

I laugh, and with the wind in our hair and the sun in our eyes I fight the urge to throw my head back like an actor in a movie.

"Oh, the gun. Well, when Papa's driver dropped off the car two days ago, I looked in that little compartment, the one in front of your seat, and voilà! Driving gloves, chewing gum, driver's license, and my beautiful antique Nagant revolver. I thought it might come in handy someday."

In the countryside I pick up speed, a great deal of speed. K. Burke does not seem at all alarmed by fast driving. After a few minutes of silence I tell her that I am taking the country roads instead of the A5 *autoroute* so that she might enjoy the summer scenery.

She does not say a word. She is asleep, and she remains so until I make a somewhat sharp right turn at our destination.

K. Burke blinks, rubs her eyes, and speaks.

"Where are we, Moncrief?"

Ahead of us is a long, low, flat gray building. It is big and gloomy. Not like a haunted house or a lost castle. Just a huge grim pile of concrete. She reads the name of the building, carved into the stone.

PRISON CLAIRVAUX

She does a double take.

"What are we doing here, Moncrief?"

"We are here to meet the killer of Maria Martinez and Dalia Boaz."

CHAPTER 39

A FEW YEARS AGO, a detective with the Paris police described the prison at Clairvaux as "hell, but without any of the fun." I think the detective was being kind.

As K. Burke and I present identification to the entrance guards, I tell her, "Centuries ago this was a Cistercian abbey, a place of monks and prayer and chanting."

"Well," she says as she looks around the stained gray walls. "There isn't a trace of God left here."

Burke and I are scanned with an electronic wand, then we step through an X-ray machine and are finally escorted to a large vacant room—no chairs, no tables, no window. We stand waiting a few minutes. The door opens, and an official-looking man as tall as the six-foot doorway enters. He is thin and old. His left eye is made of glass. His name is Tomas Wren. We shake hands.

"Detective Moncrief, I was delighted to hear your message this morning that you would be paying us a visit."

"*Merci,*" I say. "Thank you for accommodating us on such short notice."

Wren looks at Detective Burke and speaks.

"And you, of course, must be Madame Moncrief."

"Non, monsieur, je suis Katherine Burke. Je suis la collègue de Monsieur Moncrief."

"Ah, mille pardons," Wren says. Then Wren turns to me. He is suddenly all business.

"I have told Ballard that you are coming to see him."

"His reaction?" I ask.

"His face lit up."

"I'm glad to hear that," I say.

"You never know with Ballard. He can be a dangerous customer," says Wren. "But he owes you a great deal."

With a touch of levity, I say, "And I owe him a great deal. Without his help I would never have made the arrests that made my career take off."

Wren shrugs, then says, "I have set aside one of the private meeting rooms for you and Mademoiselle Burke."

We follow him down another stained and gray hallway. The private room is small—perhaps merely a dormitory cell from the days of the Cistercian brothers—but it has four comfortable desk chairs around a small maple table. A bit more uninviting, however, are the *bouton d'urgence*—the emergency button—and two heavy metal clubs.

Wren says that he will be back in a moment. "With Ballard," he says.

As soon as Wren exits, Burke speaks.

"I remember this case from the other day, Moncrief. On the computer. Ballard is the horse trainer who killed some guy and wounded another at the Longchamp racecourse."

"Yes, indeed, Detective."

"But I don't totally get what's going on here now."

"You will," I say.

"If you say so," she answers.

I nod, and as I do I feel myself becoming…quiet…no, the proper word is…frightened. A kind of soft anxiety begins falling over me. No man can ever feel happy being in a prison, even for a visit. It is a citadel of punishment and futility. But this is something way beyond simple unhappiness. Burke senses that something is wrong.

"Are you okay, Moncrief?" she says.

"No, I am not. I am twice a widower of sorts. And now I feel I am in the house where those plans were made. No, Detective. I am not okay. But you know what? I don't ever expect to be okay. Excuse me if that sounds like self-pity."

"No need to apologize. I understand."

CHAPTER 40

A CREAKING SOUND, LIKE one you would hear in an old horror movie, comes from the door. It opens, and a burst of light surges into the bleak room.

Wren has returned, and with him is a young prison guard. The guard escorts the prisoner—Marcel Ballard.

Ballard is ugly. His fat face is scarred on both cheeks. Another scar is embedded on the right side of his neck. The three scars show the marks of crude surgical stitching. Prison fights, perhaps?

His head is completely bald. He is unreasonably heavy for a man who dines only on prison rations; he must be trading something of value for extra food.

The guard removes the handcuffs from Ballard.

Ballard comes rushing toward me. He is shouting.

The guard moves to pull Ballard away from me, but Ballard is too fast for him.

"*Moncrief, mon ami, mon pote!*" he yells. Then he embraces me in a tight bear hug. In accented English, the guard translates, "My friend! My best friend!"

Then Ballard kisses me on both cheeks.

CHAPTER 41

IT IS BALLARD WHO enlightens K. Burke.

"You wonder why we embrace, mademoiselle?"

"Not really," says K. Burke. "I know about you and the detective. I know that you received a lesser sentence because of *him,* and I know that he received some valuable information because of *you.*"

Ballard smiles. I look away from the two of them.

"Detective Moncrief, you have not told your colleague the entire story of our relationship?" Ballard asks, his eyes almost comically wide.

For a reason I can't explain, I am becoming angry. With a snappish tone I respond, "No. I didn't think it was necessary. I thought it was between the two of us."

"But many others know," Ballard responds. "May I tell her?"

"Do whatever you like," I say. The bleakness of the prison, the memory of the Longchamp arrests, and the indelible pain of Maria and Dalia's deaths all close in on me. I am sinking into a depression. There is no reason why I should be angry that Burke will be hearing the story of Ballard and me. Still, he hesitates.

I try to restore a lighter tone to the conversation. "No, really. If you want to tell her, go right ahead."

After a pause, Ballard tells her, "When I was arrested I was the father of an infant, and I was also the father of three other children, all of them under the age of five years."

He pauses, and with a smile says, "Yes, we are a very Catholic family. Four children in five years." Burke does not smile back.

Then he continues. "Life would have been desperate for my wife, Marlene, without me. The children would have starved. When I was sentenced to the two decades in the prison, I worried and prayed, and my prayers were answered.

"In my second month inside this hell, Marlene writes to me with news. She is receiving a monthly stipend, a generous stipend, from Monsieur Moncrief."

He pauses, then adds, "I was overwhelmed with gratitude for his extreme generosity."

Burke nods at Ballard. Then she turns to me and says, "Good man, Detective."

I do not care to slosh around in sentimentality. I gruffly announce, "Look, Ballard. I am here for a reason. An important reason. You may be able to pay me back for that 'extreme generosity.'"

CHAPTER 42

THE GOSSIP NETWORK IN a prison is long and strong.

Ballard confirms this. "I was overcome with sadness and anger when I heard about your police friend and your girlfriend, Detective. I could not write to you. I could not telephone. I did not know what to say. And, I am ashamed to admit, I was afraid. If the other prisoners found out that I was speaking to a member of the Paris police, I might be in danger."

"I understand," I say. "Besides, Marlene wrote me and expressed her outrage and sympathy."

"*Très bien,*" he says. "Marlene is a good woman."

I am silent. I want to speak, but I cannot. Suddenly everything is rushing back—the sight of Maria in the lavish Park Avenue apartment, the sight of Dalia on the gurney, the crazed run that I made through Hermès and the wine shop.

I think Burke senses that I have wandered off to a deeper, darker place. She keeps a steady gaze on me.

Ballard looks confused. He is waiting for me to say something. My tongue freezes as if it's too big for my mouth. My brain is too big for my head, and my heart is too broken to function.

Ballard reaches across the little table and places his rough hand on mine.

"The heart breaks, Detective."

I remain silent. Ballard speaks.

"What can I do, my friend?"

My head is filling with pain. Then I speak.

"Listen to me, Marcel. I believe that someone being held in this prison arranged for the executions of my partner, Maria, and my lover, Dalia. I think whoever it was also planned to kill my current partner, the person sitting here."

I cannot help but notice that Ballard does not react in any way to what I'm saying. He finally removes his hand from mine. He continues to listen silently. If he is anything, he is afraid, stunned.

"It is pure revenge, Ballard. There are men here in Clairvaux who detest me. They don't blame their crimes for their imprisonment. They blame *me*. They think that by killing the people I am close to...they are killing me...and you know something, Ballard? They are right."

Again silence. A long silence. The minute that feels like an hour.

Ballard interrupts the quiet. He is calm. "*C'est vrai, monsieur le lieutenant.* Someone who hates you is killing the women you love."

"Tell me, Marcel. Tell me if you truly have gratitude for what I've done to help your wife and children: do you have any idea who ordered these murders?"

Ballard looks at Burke. Then he looks at me. Then he

looks down at the table. When he looks back up again a few moments later his eyes are wet with tears. He speaks.

"Everyone inside this asylum is cruel. You have to learn to be cruel to survive here."

I am awestruck at Ballard's intensity. He continues.

"But there is only one man who has the power to buy such a horror in the outside world. And I think you know who that is. I think you know without my even saying his name."

And I know the person we should bring in.

CHAPTER 43

BURKE AND I WAIT for Adrien Ramus.

We wait in a smaller, bleaker room than the one in which we met with Ballard. This room is located within the high-security area, where the most treacherous prisoners are kept. It is not solitary confinement, but it is the next worst thing. Isolation, only relieved for food and fifteen minutes of recreation a day in the yard.

The room has no table, no chairs. It is bare except for the emergency button, three clubs, and three mace cartridges that hang on the wall.

The door opens with the same horror-film creak as the door in the previous interview room. Tomas Wren once again accompanies the prisoner, but Ramus apparently warrants *three* guards to keep him under control. What's more, I suspect that the handcuffs behind Ramus's back will not be removed.

Ramus is gaunt, thin as a man with a disease. His nose is too big for his face. His eyes are too small for his face. Yet all his characteristics come together to form a frightening but handsome man. He could be an aging fashion model.

Years ago, during his booking, his trials, and his sentencing, Ramus spat on the floor whenever he saw me. When this vulgarity earned him a club to the head from a policeman or a prison guard, Ramus didn't care. It was worth a little pain to demonstrate his hatred for the detective who had brought him down.

Ramus does not disappoint this time. Upon seeing me he immediately lobs a small puddle of spittle in my direction.

I sense madness—not only in Ramus but also in myself. I reach across and grab him by the chin. I push his head back as far as it will go without snapping it off. I know the guards probably hate Ramus as much as I do. I know they won't stop me. I could beat Ramus if I wished to.

"My partner! My lover!" I shout. "It was you!"

He just stares at me. He twists his neck forcefully, trying to relieve the pain of my assault. I let go of his chin, then shout again.

"You have sources on the outside who can do such things!"

Now Ramus smiles. Then he speaks. The voice is rough, the words staccato.

"You are a fool, Moncrief. I have sources, yes. But anyone inside this pit of hell can buy influence outside. Put the pieces together, Moncrief. Are you so stupid?"

He spits again. Then he just stares at me. I speak more softly now.

"You will burn in hell . . . and I cannot wait for that time! I cannot wait for God to burn you. And you will do more than die and burn. You will first *suffer.* And then die and burn. I will see to it."

He says, "When I heard that your two women friends were killed I was happy. I was joyful."

My heart is beating hard. My chest is heaving up and down. Ramus continues.

"Some men are very powerful . . . sometimes even *more* powerful in the shadows of a prison than they are on the streets of the city."

I feel my hand and both my arms tense up completely. In seconds I will be at him once again. This time I will force my hand around his neck. Then I will force my fingers around his Adam's apple. Then . . .

He speaks again.

"Believe whatever you want, Moncrief. It is of no meaning to me. As I say, you are a stupid, pathetic fool. When will you learn? Where I am concerned, you are powerless. The boss? He is Ramus."

The tension and strength suddenly drain from my body. My arms fall to my side. I am the victim of a perfect crime.

I bow my head. *I have solved the case, but the women closest to me are gone.*

I try to control my shaking limbs. I try to hold my feelings inside me.

"Get him out of here," I say to the guards.

Ramus says nothing more. They lead him out. It's over.

CHAPTER 44

THE NEXT AFTERNOON K. Burke and I fly back to New York City.

Closure. K. Burke is smart enough and now knows me well enough not to talk about "closure," a glib and wishful concept. Nothing closes. At least not completely.

Friends and colleagues and family will say (and some have said already), "You're lucky. At least you're young and rich and handsome. You'll get over this. You'll find a way to learn to move on."

I will nod affirmatively, but only to stop their chatter. Then my response will be simple: "No. Those qualities—youth, wealth, physical attributes—are randomly distributed. They protect you from very little of life's real agonies."

Menashe Boaz and I speak on the telephone. He is still in Norway with his film—"wrapping in three days." His voice, predictably, is somber. I am one of the few people who knows precisely how he feels. With my complete agreement, he decides that he will send two assistants to New York to oversee clearing out Dalia's apartment. Sad? It is beyond sad. Menashe and I cannot have this conversation without the occasional tear. It is a miracle that we can have the conversation at all.

"I don't want a thing from Dalia's apartment," I tell him. I never want to enter the place again.

Any book I've left there I will never finish reading. Any suit in her closet I will never wear again. The real keepsakes are all inside me. A handful of wonderful photographs are on my phone.

Full of jet lag, fatigue, tension, and sorrow, K. Burke and I speak with Inspector Elliott at the precinct. I describe in broad strokes our time in Paris. Burke describes the same thing, but in much greater detail. I say the words I've been aching to say: "The case is solved."

When our two hours with Elliott are over, I tell K. Burke, that her memory is "astonishing. I mean it."

She says, "Almost as good as yours. I mean it."

We return to the detective pool—piles of files, the endless recorded phone messages, the crime blotter. I see that Burke is not her usual ambitious self. She is shuffling papers, typing slowly on her computer.

"Something is troubling you, Detective?" I say.

She looks up at me and speaks. "I'm angry that Ramus has brought us down. I know that's stupid. I know the case is solved. But he *has* committed the perfect crime. He can kill and get away with it. It really pisses me off. I can only imagine how you must feel."

"Life goes on, K. Burke. Who knows? Maybe tomorrow will be a little bit better," I say.

Detective Burke smiles. Then she speaks.

"Exactly. Who knows?"

CHAPTER 45

La maison centrale de Clairvaux

ALL PRISONERS ARE EQUAL in the mess hall. At least that's the way it's supposed to be. Same horrid food, same rancid beverages. But in prison, those who have money also have influence. And those with money and influence live a little better.

Marcel Ballard supplies two kitchen workers with a weekly supply of filtered Gauloises cigarettes. So the workers show their gratitude by heaping larger mounds of instant mashed potatoes on Ballard's plate and by giving him a double serving of the awful industrial cheese that is supplied after the meal. On some lucky occasions, Ballard goes to take a slug of water from his tin cup and finds that a kitchen ally has replaced the water with beer or, better still, a good amount of Pernod.

Adrien Ramus has even more influence than Ballard. Ramus, you see, has even more bribery material at his disposal. Even Tomas Wren has snapped at the bait Ramus dangles. Because he gives Wren the occasional gift of a few grams of cocaine, Ramus has a relatively easy time of it in isolation—

a private cell, a radio. Ramus sells many things to many prisoners. He always has a supply of marijuana for those who want to get high and access to local attorneys for those who want to get out.

It is Tuesday's supper. The menu never changes. Sunday is a greasy chicken thigh with canned asparagus spears that smell like socks. Monday is spaghetti in a tasteless oil. And then Tuesday. Tuesday at Clairvaux is always—unalterably, predictably—white beans, gray meat in brown gravy, canned spinach, and a thin slice of cheap unidentifiable white cheese.

Guards patrol the aisles.

No conversation is allowed. But that rule is constantly broken, usually with a shout-out declaring, "This food is shit." Sometimes there's a warning from someone just on the edge of sanity, a "Stop staring at me or I'll slice off your balls" or "You are vomiting on me, *gros trou du cul.*" That charming phrase translates as "you big asshole."

This evening is relatively quiet until one man slashes another man's thigh, and as both victim and abuser are hauled away, most of the other prisoners cheer like small stupid boys watching a game. Two other men fight, then they are separated. Two more men fight, and the guards, for their own amusement, allow the fight to proceed for a few minutes until, finally, one man lies semiconscious on the floor.

Suppertime, an allotment of twenty minutes, has almost ended. Some men, like Marcel Ballard, have, for a few euros, bought their neighbor's beans or cheese. Ballard stuffs the food into his round mouth.

Other prisoners have not even touched their plates. Most likely they have chocolate bars and bread hidden in their cells;

most likely such luxuries have been supplied—for a price, of course—by Adrien Ramus.

Hundreds of years ago this mess hall was the refectory of Clairvaux Abbey. Here the hood-clad monks chanted their *"Benedic, Domine,"* the grace said before meals. The faded image of Saint Robert of Molesme, the founder of the Cistercian order, is barely visible above the doors to the kitchen. Often, when some angry prisoner decides to throw a pile of potatoes, the mess ends up on Saint Robert's faded face.

The men are ordered to pass their individual bowls to the end of each table. Most do so quietly. Others find that this chore gives them the opportunity to call a fellow diner a prick or, sometimes more gently, a bitch.

Lukewarm coffee is passed around in tin pitchers. Nothing is ever served hot. Too dangerous. Boiling soup or steaming coffee could be poured over an enemy inmate's head. Almost everyone pours large amounts of sugar into their cups. Almost everyone drinks the coffee, including one of the most prominent and influential prisoners, who sits silently at the end of a table.

That prisoner takes a gulp of coffee. He then places the cup on the wooden table. Suddenly the man's right hand flies to his neck, his left hand to his belly. He lets out a hoarse and stifled gasp. His head begins shaking, and a putrid green liquid surges from his mouth. The prisoners near him move away. Two guards move in on the victim. As trained, two other guards rush to protect the exit doors. This might easily be a scheme to start an uprising.

This, however, turns out not to be a trick. The stricken prisoner falls forward onto the wooden table. His head bounces twice on the wood. His poisoned coffee spills onto the floor. He is dead.

Prisoners are shouting. Guards are swinging their clubs.

Adrien Ramus remains seated. No smile. No anger. No expression. He is satisfied.

At this exact same time, the rest of the world continues turning.

In Paris, a group of French hotel workers are busy replacing the bullet-scarred carpeting where K. Burke was attacked.

In Norway, Menashe Boaz is calling "Cut" and then saying, "Fifteen-minute break." He must be alone.

In New York, Luc Moncrief, who has just come in from running four miles on the West Side bike path, sits in a big leather chair in his apartment. He is sweaty and tired and sad. But for some unknowable reason he finds that he is suddenly at peace.

CHAPTER 46

"I THOUGHT YOU WERE out today," K. Burke says to me, as crisp and confident as ever. Whatever jet-lag body-clock adjustment she had to make has been made.

"I was," I say. "But I had to see you. I must show you something on the computer."

"What's with you, Moncrief? You sound a little—I don't know...creepy. It's like your energy level is down a few notches."

"Yes, Detective. I am stunned. I am walking in a dream. Maybe half a dream and half a nightmare."

As always, about a dozen other New York City detectives are very interested in our conversation. Everyone is aware of the murders. Now many are aware of the attack on Burke in Paris.

"Interview room 4 is free. I checked. Let's go there," I say.

Perhaps for the benefit of our police colleagues, Burke shrugs her shoulders in that I-dunno-maybe-he's-a-little-crazy way. Then she follows me down the hall to the interview room.

I close the curtain to prevent anyone from spying on us

through the two-way mirror. I place my laptop on the table, open it, and tap a few buttons.

"I've read it maybe fifty times," I say. "Now it's your turn. Please read. Then I am going to delete it."

K. Burke looks vaguely frightened, but she is also curious. I can tell. Her eyes widen, then they relax. Then her forehead wrinkles. She begins to read.

Monsieur Moncrief:

I believe that the following information will be of interest to you.

Three hours ago, at 1800 hours Paris, an inmate in my charge died, the direct result of poison administered to his coffee.

He was a man of your acquaintance: Marcel Ballard.

Burke looks away from the screen. She looks directly at me. "Ballard?" she says. "But I thought . . . no. Not Ballard!" "Keep reading," I say.

Ballard's death was obviously planned and perpetrated by someone inside La maison centrale de Clairvaux.

I know that it was your belief that the murders of Maria Martinez and Dalia Boaz were ordered by another prisoner, Adrien Ramus.

I must inform you, however, that evidence taken here at this scene after today's murder proves otherwise.

An investigation of Ballard's cell revealed a laptop computer hidden within a broken tile beneath the toilet.

An examination of the laptop's contents showed frequent correspondence between Ballard and two Frenchmen who were in the United States on visitor visas. One of them, Thierry Mondeville, returned to France a few days ago. Mondeville has now been identified as the attacker in the incident involving Katherine Burke and yourself.

Further correspondence indicates Ballard's extreme anger at his imprisonment and the role you played in causing it. Ballard explicitly held you responsible for "destroying my life and destroying my family."

Upon its release by the police I will forward a file containing the complete contents of Ballard's computer as well as the findings and conclusions of the official investigation.

Je vous prie d'agréer, Monsieur, mes
respectueuses salutations,
Tomas Wren

Burke and I say nothing for a few moments.

Then she looks at me and speaks. "Do you believe this is true?"

I nod, and, for assurance, I say, "I am certain."

I walk to the other side of the room. I look out the perpetually dirty window. The tops of the brownstones look like figures drawn in charcoal when seen through the dirt on the glass.

"But, Moncrief, you mean...all these years you were helping Ballard, and all these years he was planning to destroy your life?" she says. "You must be amazed at this."

"To be honest, I am not amazed. *I knew.*"

Now Burke is the one who is amazed. She is speechless.

"Ramus is indeed a wretched excuse for a human being. But if he had ordered the executions he would have happily bragged to me about them. He would have told me directly that he was the talent behind the killings. But...he stopped just short of bragging.

"That is why I assaulted him. But I could not drive him to say what he would have been glad to say. He would not admit to being the force behind the killings.

"Then we add the fact that Ballard was so effusive in his thanks to me. Bah! I put him in prison for most of his life. Do you think he cares what happens to his family? Do you think he cares about their welfare? I instinctively knew he was throwing the *connerie*, the bullshit, at me."

I can tell she wants to smile, but this moment is too serious.

"But most important, *I could not have put Ramus in prison if Ballard had not given me information on him*. I knew that someday Ramus would punish Ballard. This was timing *parfait*. Ballard falsely pinned the crimes on Ramus *and* Ballard had previously betrayed him. So, *le poison dans le café*."

"So the case is solved," she says. But she speaks softly, cautiously.

"I guess so," I say. I know, however, that there is sorrow in my voice.

I walk back to the table where the opened laptop rests. Then I push the button marked DELETE.

CHAPTER 47

I LEAVE THE PRECINCT and head toward Fifth Avenue and 52nd Street. I am standing outside a fabulous shop, Versace. I pause and then walk through the great arched center door.

This was one of Dalia's favorite stores. I can remember almost every single item Dalia ever bought here.

The black skirt. If I looked hard I could see through the tightly woven material and catch a glimpse of Dalia's exquisite legs.

The shoes with thick cork platforms that made Dalia a half inch or so taller than I am. We always laughed at that.

The belts with golden buckles. The black leather shopping totes. The crazy shirts with variously colored geometric shapes that shout at you.

"Signor Moncrief. It has been a thousand years since we have seen you," says the store manager, Giuliana. "Welcome. You have been away, perhaps?" she adds.

"Yes. I've been away. Far away."

Giuliana tilts her head to one side. "I heard of the tragedy of Miss Boaz, of course. We were all so sad."

"Thank you," I say. "I read your condolence note. I read it more than once."

"We liked her so very much," says Giuliana. Then she says, "I will leave you alone. Call on me if I can help you."

"I will," I say. *"Grazie."*

She walks away, and I remain still, moving only my head. I take in the lights from the golden fixtures. The multitude of wallets laid out in their cases in neat overlapping rows.

It is late summer. So they are showing fall coats, fall dresses, fall scarves. Reds and browns and dark yellows. Black jeans and white jeans. And lots and lots of sunglasses. Even the mannequins are wearing sunglasses.

"Sunglasses are always in season," Dalia used to say.

I am about to move deeper into the store. I am calm. Not completely calm, but I am calm.

Then my phone rings. The caller is identified as "K. Burke." I answer.

"Good afternoon, K. Burke. Don't tell me. There's been a murder."

"How did you know?" she says.

"I just knew. Somehow I just knew."

THE CHRISTMAS MYSTERY

JAMES PATTERSON
AND RICHARD DiLALLO

PROLOGUE

ONE

CHAOS AND CONFUSION reign in New York City's most glamorous department store, Bloomingdale's.

A dozen beautiful women—perfect makeup, perfect clothing—are strutting around the first floor, armed. No one escapes these women. They are shooting customers...with spritzes of expensive perfume.

Enough fragrance fills the air to create a lethal cloud of nausea. The effect is somewhere between expensive flower shop and cheap brothel.

"Unbelievable! This place is packed," says K. Burke.

"Yes," I say. "You'd think it was almost Christmas."

"It *is* almost Chris—" Burke begins to say. She stops, then adds, "Don't be a wiseass, Moncrief. We've got a long day ahead of us."

K. Burke and I are police detective partners from Manhattan's Midtown East. Our chief inspector, Nick Elliott, has assigned us to undercover security at this famous and glamorous department store. I told the inspector that I preferred more challenging assignments, "like trapping terrorists and capturing murderers."

Elliott's response?

"Feel free to trap any terrorists or capture any murderers you come across. Meanwhile, keep your eyes open for purse-snatchers and shoplifters."

K. Burke, ever the cooperative pro, said, "I understand, sir."

I said nothing.

In any event, K. Burke and I at this moment are standing in a fog of Caron Poivre and Chanel No. 5 in Bloomingdale's perfume department.

"So, how are we going to split up, Moncrief?" asks Burke.

"You decide," I say. My enthusiasm is not overwhelming.

"Okay," Burke says. "I'll take the second floor...women's designer clothes. Why don't you take high-end gifts? China, crystal, silver."

"May I suggest," I say, "that you take women's designer clothing on the *fourth* floor, not the *second*. Second floor is Donna Karan and Calvin. Fourth floor is Dolce & Gabbana, Prada, Valentino. Much classier."

Burke shakes her head. "It's amazing, the stuff you know."

We test-check the red buttons on our cell phones, the communication keys that give us immediate contact with each other.

Burke says that she'll also notify regular store security and tell them that their special request NYPD patrol is there, as planned.

"I've got to get out of this perfume storm," she says. She's just about to move toward the central escalator when a well-dressed middle-aged woman approaches. The woman speaks directly to Burke.

"Where can I buy one of these?" the woman says.

"I got the last one," Burke says. The woman laughs and walks away.

I'm completely confused. "What was that lady asking about?" I say.

"She was asking about you," Burke says. "As if you didn't know."

Burke walks quickly toward the up escalator.

TWO

WITHIN THREE MINUTES I'm standing in the fine china and silver section of Bloomingdale's sixth floor. If there is a problem with the economy in New York City, someone failed to tell the frantic shoppers snapping up Wedgwood soup tureens and sterling silver dinner forks. It's only ten thirty in the morning, yet the line at gift-wrap is already eight customers deep.

My cell phone is connected to hundreds of store security cameras. These cameras are trained on entrance areas, exit doors, credit card registers—all areas where intruders can enter, exit, and operate quickly.

I keep my head still, but my eyes dart around the area. Like Christmas itself, all is calm, all is bright. I make my way through the crowd of wealthy-looking women in fur, prosperous-looking men with five-hundred-dollar cashmere scarves.

Then a loud buzz. Insistent. Urgent. I glance quickly at my phone. The red light. I listen to K. Burke's voice.

"Second floor. Right now," she says. She immediately clicks off.

Damn it. I told her to go to the fourth floor. Burke makes her own decisions.

Within a few seconds I'm at the Bloomingdale's internal staircase. I skip the stairs three at a time. I burst through the second floor door.

Chaos. Screaming. Customers crowding the aisles near the down escalators. Salespeople crouched behind counters.

"Location Monitor" on my cell notifies me that Burke is no longer on the original second floor location. Her new location is men's furnishings—ties, wallets, aftershave. Ground floor.

I reverse my course and rush toward the rear escalator near Third Avenue. I push a few men and women out of my path. Now I'm struggling to execute a classic crazy move— I'm running *down* an escalator that's running *up*.

I land on the floor. I see K. Burke moving quickly past display cases of sweaters and shirts. Burke sees me.

She shouts one word.

"Punks!"

It's a perfect description. In a split second I see two young women—teens probably, both in dark-gray hoodies. The pair open a door marked EMPLOYEES ONLY. They go through. The door closes behind them.

Burke and I almost collide at that door. We know from our surveillance planning that this is one of Bloomingdale's "snare" closets—purposely mismarked to snare shoplifters and muggers on the run. This time it works like a Christmas charm. We enter the small space and see two tough-looking teenage girls—nose piercings, eyebrow piercings, tats, the whole getup. One of them is holding an opened switchblade. I squeeze her wrist between my thumb and index finger. The knife falls to the ground. As K. Burke scoops up the knife, she speaks.

"These two assholes knocked over a woman old enough to be their grandmother and took off with her shopping bag," Burke says. "They also managed to slash her leg—the long way. EMU is taking care of her."

"It ain't us. You're messed up. Look. No shopping bags," one of the girls says. Her voice is arrogant, angry.

"Store security has the shopping bag. And they've got enough video on the two of you to make a feature film," Burke adds.

It's clear to the young thieves that they'll get no place good with Burke. One of them decides to play me.

"Give us a break, man. It probably isn't even us on the video. I know all about this shit. Come on."

I smile at the young lady.

"You know all about this shit? Let me tell you something." I pause for a moment, then continue quietly. "In some cases, with the holidays approaching, I might say: give the kids a warning and release them."

"That'd be way cool," says her friend.

K. Burke looks at me. I know that she's afraid my liberal soft spot is going to erupt.

"But this is not one of those cases," I say.

"Man, no. Why?" asks the girl.

"I believe my colleague summed it up a few minutes ago," I say.

"What the hell?" the girl says.

I answer. "Punks!"

THE CHRISTMAS MYSTERY

CHAPTER 1

Almost Thanksgiving

WHEN DALIA BOAZ died a few months ago, I believed that my own life had ended along with hers.

Friends suggested that, with time, the agony of the loss would diminish.

They were wrong. Day after day I ache for Dalia, the love of my life. Yet life rattles on. Unstoppable. Yes, there are moments when I am joyful. Other times are inevitably heartbreaking: Dalia's birthday, my birthday, the anniversary of a special romantic event. Holidays are a special problem, of course, because I am surrounded by celebration—Easter baskets overflowing, fireworks erupting, bright lights hanging from evergreen trees.

Thanksgiving Day is a unique problem. There is nothing remotely like it in France. When Dalia was alive, if I was not on duty, we stayed in bed and streamed a few movies, whipped up some omelets, topped them with beluga caviar, and were thankful that we did not have to eat sweet potatoes with melted marshmallows.

This Thanksgiving proved a challenge. A few detective

colleagues generously and sincerely invited me to join them. No, that wasn't for me. So I volunteered for holiday assignment. But Inspector Elliott informed me that Thanksgiving was well staffed with both detectives and officers (mostly divorced parents who traded seeing their children on Thanksgiving Day for seeing them on Christmas Day).

For a moment I wondered how my partner would be spending her holiday. Although my knowledge of K. Burke's private life was sparse, I knew that both her parents were deceased.

Casually I asked her, "Where are you going for Thanksgiving?"

"The gym," was her answer.

In an unlikely explosion of sentiment that surprised even myself I said, "Come to my place. I'll fix Thanksgiving dinner for both of us."

"Yeah, sure," was her sarcastic reaction. "And I'll bake a pumpkin pie."

"No. I'm serious."

"You are?" she said, trying to hide her surprise.

With only a hint of confusion she spoke slowly and quietly. "Oh, my God. This feels like a date."

"I assure you, it is not," I said.

Both Burke and I knew that I meant it.

Then I added, "But please do *not* bake a pumpkin pie."

CHAPTER 2

Thanksgiving

"THIS PLACE IS . . . well, it's sort of unbelievable," K. Burke says. She stands in the entrance gallery to my new apartment and spreads her arms in amazement.

"Merci," I say. "I had to find a new home after Dalia died. I could not stay in her place. I could not stay in mine. Too many . . ." I pause.

Detective Burke nods. Of course, she knows. Too many memories. I take her on a brief tour of the place. A loft on Madison Square, a single three-thousand-foot room with a view of the Flatiron Building to the south and the Empire State Building to the north. The huge room is sparse—purposely so. Steel furniture, glass side tables, black-and-white Cartier-Bresson photographs of Paris.

We eventually move to the table for Thanksgiving dinner. The small black lacquered table is set with my great-grandmother's vintage Limoges.

As we begin the main course of the dinner, K. Burke says, "The only thing more impressive than this apartment is this meal."

Another *Merci.*

"Moncrief, I've known you almost a year. I've spent hundreds of hours with you. I've been on a police case in Europe with you. I...I never knew you could cook like this. I just can't believe you can make a meal like this."

"Well, K. Burke. I *cannot* make a meal like this. But fortunately Steve Miller, the senior sous-chef at Gramercy Tavern, was happy to make such a meal."

And what a feast it is.

Burke and I begin with a truffled chestnut soup. Then, instead of a big bird plopped in the middle of the table, Miller has layered thin slices of turkey breast in a creamy sauce of Gruyère cheese and porcini mushrooms. Instead of the dreaded sweet potatoes, we are dining on crisp pommes frites and a delicious cool salad, a combination of shredded brussels sprouts and pomegranate seeds.

"This is what the food in heaven tastes like," K. Burke says.

"No, this is what the food in Gramercy Tavern tastes like."

I pour us each some wine.

"What shall we toast to?" she says.

I say, "Let us toast to a good friendship during a difficult year."

She hesitates just for a moment. Then K. Burke says, "Yes. To a good friendship."

We clink glasses. We drink.

She holds up her glass again.

"One more thing I want to toast to," Burke says.

"Yes?" I say, hoping it will not be sentimental, hoping it will not be about Dalia, hoping...

"Let's toast to you and me really trying to see eye to eye from now on."

"Excellent idea," I say. We clink glasses again. We continue to devour the wonderful food.

And then her cell phone rings. Burke quickly puts down her fork and slips the phone out of her pocket. She reads the name.

"It's Inspector Elliott."

"Don't answer it," I say.

"We've got to answer it, Moncrief."

"Don't answer it," I repeat. "*We* are having dinner."

"*You* are a lunatic," she says.

I roll my eyes and speak.

"So much for trying to see eye to eye."

CHAPTER 3

OF COURSE, K. BURKE triumphs. She takes Inspector Elliott's call.

Fifteen minutes later we're in the detective squad room of Midtown East watching Elliott eat a slice of pie. K. Burke later tells me that it is filled with something called mincemeat, made out of beef fat and brandy. *Incroyable!*

"This could have waited until tomorrow, but you both told me that you wanted to work today. So I assumed you'd be free," Elliott says.

Then he looks us both up and down closely, Burke in a simple, elegant gray skirt with a black shirt; me in a navy-blue Brioni bespoke suit.

"But you both are dressed like you've just come from the White House."

Neither Burke nor I speak. We are certainly not going to tell our boss where we were dining fifteen minutes earlier.

"In any event, I decided to come in and do some desk work. My wife packed me some pie. And I figured I could watch

Green Bay kick the Bears' ass on my iPad instead of watching it on TV with my brother-in-law."

Then he gets down to business.

"I thought this problem might go away, but it's real. Very real. Potentially dangerous. And it involves some New York City big shots."

Elliott swallows the last chunk of his pie. Then he continues speaking. He's energetic, anxious. Whatever it is, it's going to be a big deal.

"You two ever heard of the Namanworth Gallery up on 57th Street?"

"I think so," says Burke. "Just off Park Avenue."

"That's the one," says Elliott. "You know the place, Moncrief? It sounds like something you'd be down with."

"As a matter of fact, I *do* know that gallery. They handled the sale of a Kandinsky to a friend of mine a few months ago, and a few years back my father was talking to them about a Rothko. Nothing came of it."

"Well, your dad might have lucked out," says Elliott. "We've got some pretty heavy evidence that they've been dealing in the most impeccable forgeries in New York. A lot of collectors have been screwed over by them."

I speak.

"Namanworth hasn't owned that place for thirty years. A husband and wife are the owners. Sophia and Andre Krane. I think she claims to have been a countess or duchess or something."

"We don't know about her royal blood. But we do know that Barney Wexler, the guy who owns that cosmetics company, paid them thirty-five million dollars for a Klimt painting. And he thinks it was . . ."

I finish his sentence for him. "...not painted by Klimt."

Elliott says, "And Wexler's lined up two experts who can back him up."

"Although the case sounds really exciting..." Burke says, "there's a special division for art-and-antique counterfeit work."

"Yeah," says Elliott. "But with these big players, there may be more to it than simple forgery. Where there's smoke, there's usually fire. And where there's valuable artwork, there's possible fraud, possible money-laundering—ultimately, possible homicides. So they want us to stick our dirty noses in it. We can call on counterfeit if we want."

I speak. "I don't think we'll want to do that."

"That's what I thought you'd say, Moncrief." Then he taps a button on his computer. "There, I've just sent you all the info on the case. You'll see. It's not just Wexler. These are the money-men *and* the money-women who rock this town.

"By the way, there's a special pain in the ass about this case..."

"Isn't there always?" Burke says.

"This is particularly painful," says Elliott. "The Kranes aren't talking. They're comfy in their eight-hundred-acre Catskills estate."

"The hell with that," says Burke. "We'll get an order from justice."

"No, you won't, not when the attorney general of the state of New York says they don't have to cooperate."

"What the hell is that all about?" I say.

"Exactly," says Elliott. "What the hell is that all about?"

He lets out a long breath of air and swivels to face his PC.

As we walk away from Elliott's desk, K. Burke lays out her

plan to download all information on the Namanworth Gallery, all information on Barney Wexler, all information on Sophia and Andre Krane, and all classified insurance information on important international collectors.

"What's your plan, Moncrief?" she asks.

"First, I think we should return to my home and finish our dinner."

"And then?" she asks.

"And then I'll call my friends who collect art."

CHAPTER 4

K. BURKE LIKES to do things by the book. I like to do things by the gut. This is our professional relationship. This is also our ongoing problem.

"It looks like we'll be spending the day at this desk, Moncrief," she says. Do I detect a note of smug satisfaction in her voice?

But of course I do.

Black Friday, the day after Thanksgiving. Almost everyone will be open for what America calls door-busting sales, but the truly fashionable establishments—certainly the 57th Street galleries—will be locked up tight. No wealthy collector is going to be shopping for a Jasper Johns today.

"I have been at this desk for thirty minutes, and I've accomplished nothing," I say to Detective Burke.

"Try turning the computer *on*," Burke says.

I stand and inform her that I'll be doing a little "on-the-street wandering." Burke simply shakes her head and smiles. She knows by now that both of us will be better off if I'm out doing "my kind of police work."

Twenty minutes later I am entering a shop at the corner of Lexington Avenue and 63rd Street, J. Pocker, the finest art framer in New York City.

"I think you may have used us before," says the very gracious (and very pretty) Asian woman who greets me.

"Yes," I say. "A few years ago. You framed two photographs for me."

"Yes, you're the Frenchman. You brought in those Dorothea Lange portraits. Depressing, but very beautiful," she says.

"Isn't that sometimes the way?" I ask. I feel myself shifting into Automatic Flirt.

I look through the glass partition behind the huge measuring table at the rear of the shop. Two bearded young men are working with wood and glass and metal wire.

"So, how may I help you today, sir?" the woman says.

I pull out my personal cell phone. A photograph of a painting by Gary Kuehn comes up. It is essentially a pencil, ink, and oil drawing of a slice of the moon. The moon is a deep dark blue. It hangs against an equally dark gray-brown sky. It is beautiful, and it hung in the bedroom that Dalia and I once shared.

"I need to have this piece reframed. The frame is a cheap black thing. I had it done in Germany some time ago, when I bought the piece."

"It's a Kuehn," she says. "I like his work."

She walks to the measuring table and pulls out a sample of maple and one of thin shiny steel.

"I think either of these would be worth considering. I prefer simple subject matter to have a corresponding simple frame. I know that the French prefer contrast—a Klee inside an ornate Renaissance-type frame, but consider..."

I cut her off. "The Frenchman agrees with your suggestion."

"Please take the samples with you. You can return them after you've made your choice."

I thank her, and as I am about to leave she says, "I've seen a lot of Kuehn's work lately. He's older. But he's become very popular recently."

"As a fan of his, I must ask, how much of his work have you seen recently?"

"Certainly three or four canvases," she says. "Many of them— I think—are similar to the one you own. Curves. Circles. A sort of defiance of space."

Ah, the babble and bullshit of the art world.

"Yes," I repeat. "A defiance of space."

She smiles.

I tell her that I will be back. Yes. I will definitely be back.

CHAPTER 5

I WATCH THE SHOPPERS. Today's shopping could be classified as a sort of athletic event. People barely able to carry their exploding shopping bags. Huge flat-screen television sets lugged by happy men. Packs of happy people, angry people, exhausted people.

I have seen the videos of women punching one another to snatch the last green Shetland sweater at H&M. Entire families—mothers, fathers, wailing children—waiting outside Macy's since four in the morning so they can be the first to race down the aisles.

I take in all the madness as I walk the six blocks down and one avenue over from 63rd Street to 57th Street. I turn right. Yes, Namanworth Gallery will be shut tight, but I am so close that I must visit.

An ornate carved steel door covers the entrance. The one front window holds a single easel that holds a single large impressionist canvas. It is famous. A painting by Monet. The painting is framed with baroque gold-leaf wood. It is one painting in Monet's series of haystacks.

The subtle beauty of color and craft eludes me. I cannot help myself. I examine it purely as a possible forgery.

I pull up the series of paintings on my phone and quickly find the one I'm looking at. I know I am on a fool's errand. The tiny phone photo and the gorgeous real painting cannot be compared. Is a straw out of place? Is *that* smudge of cloud identical to *that* smudge of cloud?

Wait. What about the artist's signature?

I recently read that a woman had a Jackson Pollock painting hanging in her entrance hall for twenty years. No one—not the woman, not her guests—ever noticed that the artist's signature was spelled incorrectly: "Pollack" instead of "Pollock."

No such luck. A big bold signature: Claude Monet. Not Manet. Not Maret.

"Monet" is "Monet." How could I expect to be so lucky?

I decide to take a few photographs of the painting. I am not sure why I need photographs, but they might somehow someday come in handy. I move to the left, then right. I try to avoid the glare on the window.

Now I hear a voice from behind me. "You taking a picture for the folks back home?"

Mon Dieu! I have been mistaken for a tourist.

I turn and see a portly middle-aged man. He is wearing an inexpensive gray suit with an inexpensive gray tie. He wears a heavy raincoat and a brown fedora. He is smoking a cigarette.

"Beautiful painting," the man says.

"It certainly is," I say, as I slip my phone into my suit jacket.

"I'm one of the security people for Namanworth's," the man says. "You've been looking at that picture for quite a while."

There is no threat in his voice, no anger.

"I have a great interest in Monet," I say. "The Haystacks series in particular."

"Apparently a lot of people have an interest in this stuff," the man says. "I work out of that second floor front office. Just me and my binoculars."

He gestures in the direction of the elegant stationery store across the street. It is the same store where I have my business cards engraved.

"I just thought I'd come ask what's so intriguing about that painting. It seems to have caught a lot of attention today. Not just the usual shoppers and tourists," he says.

"Well, who else, then?" I ask as casually as I can.

"Well, there was a man and a woman, a young couple. They were driving a Bentley. Double-parked it. Then they began shooting their iPhones at the painting. Little later two guys in one of those Mercedes SUVs jumped out; these guys had big fancy cameras, real professional-looking. Then I saw you... and anyway, I needed a smoke."

"And do you have any idea what the others wanted?" I ask.

"Just art lovers, I guess. Anyway, they looked kinda rich. Sorta like you—now that I see you close up. I guess you're too fancy to be a tourist."

A twinge of relief. Then the security man flicks his cigarette onto 57th Street.

"Did you record the license numbers of the cars?" I ask.

"No. They weren't doing anything *that* unusual. Could be they were thinking of buying it. I'm just here to make sure nobody breaks the window... though it's as unbreakable as you can get."

"I'm sure it is," I say.

"Well, you have a good day," the man says. He walks to the curb, looks both ways. He turns back toward me and speaks.

"You're French, right?"

"I am, yes."

"I thought so."

I am so obviously French that I might as well have a statue of the Eiffel Tower on my head. But the man is pleased with his detective work. Then he crosses the street.

I take a final look at the Monet.

I am about to make my way to Madison Avenue when, without warning, I think about Dalia. I freeze in place. People walk around me, past me.

Suddenly I am overwhelmed by sadness. It is not depression. It is not physical. It is…well, it is a sort of disease of the heart. It always comes without warning. It is always dreadful, painful.

Fortunately, I know just what to do.

CHAPTER 6

SHOPPING IS THE ANSWER. For me it is almost always the answer. So I join the holiday madness. An uncontrolled shopping spree, for some unfathomable reason, always brings me peace.

My mind clicks madly away as to how I can best visit the many extraordinary stores on 57th Street.

Like a recovering alcoholic who studiously avoids bars, I almost always avoid this area. The merchandise is so tempting, so upscale, so expensive.

Where to start? That's so easy. The Namanworth Gallery is a block away from Robinson Antiques. Surprisingly, it's open. This shop is only for the wealthy cognoscenti of New York—eighteenth-century silver sugar shakers, Sheffield candelabras that hold twelve candles, a rare oil painting of a cocker spaniel or a hunting dog, another of a Thoroughbred at Ascot. A mahogany wig stand, one whose provenance says that it was one of twenty that once stood in the Houses of Parliament. The distinguished-looking old salesman says, "May I help you?" Five minutes later I have become the proud owner of four sterling silver Georgian marrow scoops. Seventy-three-hundred dollars.

The salesman wants to explain the insignia of King George III on the reverse side of the scoops. I tell him to please hurry. "I have to be someplace."

The place "I have to be" is also nearby—Niketown. One of the first things K. Burke said when we began working together was, "You are the only person I've ever met who can find sneakers that look as if they were made by a Renaissance artist."

Burke was right. The sneakers she had seen were black high-tops with a small brass clasp, Nike by Giuseppe Zanotti. Today the store manager escorts me to "The Vault," a small room in the back of the very busy store. When I leave the Vault I am wearing a pair of black Ferragamo Nikes—black with thin white soles, the distinctive Gancini buckle. As I exit Niketown I think, *I must be insane. Except to play an occasional game of squash, I never wear sneakers.* This thought, however, lasts only for a minute. By then I am back across 57th Street at Louis Vuitton where I'm examining an oversized overnight bag. It is made with simple soft brown leather. It does not have the ostentatious LV pattern on it. It is beautiful. It is perfect. Not at all like my life.

Now I am only a few yards from the Van Cleef & Arpels entrance at Bergdorf Goodman. I can do some real damage here.

The Van Cleef doorman is still holding the door open when my phone buzzes. The red light. Burke.

"Your day's just beginning, Moncrief," she says

"What's going on?"

"I see you're at 57th and Fifth."

"Right," I say.

"Get over to 61st and Park, number 535. Somebody decided to murder the elderly Mrs. Ramona Driver Dunlop. Or as they still call her on the gossip blogs, Baby D."

"Ramona Dunlop?" I say. "I didn't know she was still alive."

"She's not," Burke says.

"Good one, Detective. Very good."

CHAPTER 7

I **EXPECT THE** usual homicide pandemonium. But this is over-the-top madness. Twice the sirens, twice the flashing lights, twice the news reporters. I should not be surprised.

After all, this was Baby D. In 1944 she was Debutante of the Year. In 1946 she married Ray Dunlop, a Philadelphia millionaire who had inherited extremely valuable patents on ballpoint pens and mechanical pencils. In 1948 she divorced Dunlop and took up with a waiter from the Stork Club.

The lobby of 535 Park is cluttered with the usual detectives and forensic folks. An NYPD detective holds up four fingers. Then he nods toward the elevator. An elevator man takes me up to the fourth floor. The elevator doors open directly into the foyer of the Dunlop apartment. K. Burke is standing with four senior officers. She waves at me, and then approaches.

"You waved?" I say. "Did you think I wouldn't be able to find you in that ocean of blue?"

Burke ignores my comment, glances at my shopping bags, and says, "Little man, you've had a busy day."

"In a manner of speaking, yes," I say.

"Follow me," she says. Burke and I turn right and walk down a long narrow hallway.

These hall walls are cluttered with photos and paintings and framed documents: an invitation to President Kennedy's inauguration; a cover of LIFE magazine that verifies Baby D as "New York's Debutante of the Year." Then I see a large Lichtenstein cartoon panel. It hangs next to a much smaller Hockney diving board and swimming pool. I linger for a moment and take in the paintings.

Then we are in Mrs. Dunlop's bedroom. Also in the bedroom are Nick Elliott and assistant ME, Dr. Rosita Guittierez.

"Where's Nicole Reeves?" I ask. Elliott understands, of course, that I am referring to the fact that Guittierez is an *assistant,* while Reeves is the big boss.

"She must be out shopping," Elliott says.

"Like everyone else," Burke adds.

The late Mrs. Ramona Driver Dunlop is resting, very dead, in her king-sized bed with the powder-blue satin-covered headboard. Mrs. Dunlop is covered with protective plastic police cloth, from her shoulders down to and including her feet. What's left exposed is the dry bloody slash that begins at the jawbone below one ear and extends the entire width of the neck to the other ear. The face is thin and, as with many women of a certain age, has the high-puffed chipmunk-like cheeks that only a significant facelift can guarantee.

Burke asks Elliott for the details. Elliott hands the floor over to Rosita Guittierez.

"Looks like we're talking about six o'clock this morning when this happened. Sharp-bladed instrument, probably a knife. You can see the wound is U-shaped. So it got all the jugulars—internal, external, posterior. It got the carotids. She partially bled out. No sign of force. They got the old girl while she was still asleep."

Burke listens carefully. I pretend to listen, but I am more interested in looking around the room—light-blue walls matching the satin on the headboard, an ornate crystal chandelier more appropriate for a ballroom, mock Provincial side tables, and bureaus with random dabs of white and gray paint to give a distressed antique look. And one odd detail: Except for a full-length mirror behind the bathroom door, nothing is hanging on the walls. Absolutely nothing.

CHAPTER 8

WE LEARN WHAT little else is left to learn.

Mrs. Dunlop spent most of Thanksgiving Day at her son and daughter-in-law's house in Bedford. The only other person who was in the apartment after her return was a maid. The maid discovered the victim at the time she always woke Mrs. Dunlop.

Three medical staff police now pack up Mrs. Dunlop and wheel her out.

Elliott speaks.

"What do you guys think?"

"My guess is that it's a burglary gone bad," says Burke. "Holiday weekend. Lots of places empty. The intruder could have had inside information. What do you think, Moncrief?"

"Perhaps," I say. "Always perhaps. I see nothing to prove otherwise, but I also see nothing to support the theory. So for the time being, let's embrace Detective Burke's theory."

Elliott nods and says—as only an American detective can

say easily and without irony—"I'll see you guys back at the morgue."

He leaves, and K. Burke speaks. "Thanks for supporting my theory. I wasn't really expecting that."

I smile. "Don't get used to it, K. Burke. I am not so concerned with this murder as I am concerned with the circumstances *surrounding* this murder."

"And that means?" says Burke.

"The victim was almost ninety years old. May God bless her and welcome her into His paradise. Baby D has lived a life of enormous pleasure and wealth. *But*...fresh off our investigation of the Namanworth Gallery...I notice something interesting. Hanging outside her bedroom are paintings by Lichtenstein and Hockney. Only they are forgeries. The small dots in the 'talk bubbles' on the Lichtenstein are too neatly spaced to be authentic. And the swimming pool in the Hockney should be more rectangular."

Burke says exactly what I am expecting her to say.

"You can't be the first person to have noticed that."

"Perhaps. Perhaps not. But I don't think that too many art connoisseurs traverse that hallway. The possibility may also exist that Baby D knew that her pieces were forgeries and it made little difference to her. Like a print of the *Mona Lisa* in a small apartment in Clichy. It brings the owners joy. Perhaps the same was true with Madame Dunlop and her modern masterpieces."

"We need to tell Elliott about this," Burke says.

"I don't want him breathing down our necks. At least not yet. We will return tomorrow morning, let the others finish the interviews. We'll have more information and more space to examine the apartment closely, see what we can see, find what we can find."

"This is not going to end well, Moncrief. I don't like doing things this way."

"I know you don't," I say. "That's what makes it such an adventure."

CHAPTER 9

THERE ARE ONLY three things in this world that I truly hate: overcooked vegetables, flannel sheets, and whenever K. Burke is right about something.

This next day is one of those times.

We arrive at 535 Park Avenue at 8:00 a.m. There is still a "modified police presence"—one NYPD officer at the corner of Park and 61st Street, a second officer in the small mailroom, a plainclothesman in the lobby. It's the usual set-up for a post-homicide scene.

Burke and I bring with us two big evidence cases marked "NYPD." These will be used to carry the forged Lichtenstein and Hockney. When the elevator opens at the Dunlop apartment we exchange hellos with Ralph Ortiz, a smart up-and-coming rookie who's stuck guarding the crime scene.

"*Allons-y*," I say. "Let's go."

"I know what *allons* means, Moncrief," she says. "I've only told you a few thousand times. You do *not* have to translate for me. I know French. That's one of the reasons they teamed us up."

"*Ah, oui*," I say. Then I say, "That means 'yes.'"

Burke ignores me as we walk toward the hallway.

And then…son of a bitch! The paintings are missing.

Softly Burke says, "Goddamnit."

I turn quickly and rush down the hallway to Officer Ortiz.

"How long have you been on duty?"

"Since midnight," he says. Ortiz senses that something's not right. He immediately answers the question I would have asked.

"Nobody's been in or out. Nobody. Not a soul," he says. And then, because he's as sharp as any kid I know in the NYPD, he says, "And I never heard anyone. I never saw anyone. I checked on the master bedroom and the other rooms every hour. I know…"

"Okay, okay," I say. "I'm sure nothing got by you."

"Only something *did* get by him," Burke says. "A bunch of officers and detectives on surveillance and two paintings disappear."

"Listen, these things happen. These things…" But she cuts me off.

"Goddamnit," says Burke. "I should never have listened to you. We should have gotten the info to Elliott and *then* together the three of us could proceed. But you. You have your own ways. The goddamn *instinct*."

My anger about the paintings, along with Burke's rant, now makes me explode.

"Yes. And my ways are good ways, smart ways. History proves it. My ways usually work!"

Burke shakes her head and talks in a calm, normal voice.

"The operative word here is 'usually.' I'm going back to the precinct house."

"I'll join you shortly," I say. We are quiet.

I know this brief two-sentence conversation is as close as Burke and I will come to signing a peace treaty.

As soon as K. Burke leaves, Ortiz and I check the apartment, walking the rooms for any detail that might stand out. Nothing. Pantry. Maid's rooms. Butler's pantry. Service hall. *Nothing.* Silver closet. China closet. Powder rooms. *Nothing.* Dressing rooms. Kitchen (and impressive wine collection). Office. Dining room. *Nothing. Nothing. Nothing.*

I rush back to the hallway wall where the Lichtenstein and Hockney once hung. I study the two empty spaces of the wall—as if the paintings might magically have reappeared, as if I could magically "wish" them back to the wall.

Finally, I say to Ortiz, "I cannot stay in this apartment any longer. If I do, I will explode like a human bomb."

CHAPTER 10

IT IS BARELY ELEVEN in the morning when I leave Baby D's apartment. The day is cold and crisp, and to the happy person...Christmas is in the air. The sadness that I've come to know so well begins to descend. As the doctors say, "Rate your pain on a scale of one to ten, ten being the most painful." I would call it a six or seven.

I walk down Park Avenue and turn left on 59th Street. I am at a store I enjoy enormously, Argosy, the home of rare maps and prints, antiquarian books. Perhaps a $30,000 volume of hand-colored Audubon birds will lift my spirits. Perhaps a letter addressed to John Adams and signed by Benjamin Franklin will cheer me up. I touch the soft leather on the binding of a first-edition *Madame Bovary*. I study a fifteenth-century map of my native land—a survey of France so misshapen and inaccurate, it might as well be a picture of a dead fish. But I buy nothing.

The same happens to me in Pesca, a swimsuit shop, where Dalia once bought a pale-yellow bikini for five hundred dollars, where I could buy an old-fashioned pair of trunks with a bronze buckle in front for $550 and look just like *mon grand-père* on the beach in Deauville. I move on to other shops.

But nothing is for me. Not the art deco silver ashtrays, not the leather iPad cases that cost more than the iPads that they hold.

No. Not for me. But also not for me are the street corner Santa Clauses, the exquisite twinkling white lights in the windows of the town houses, the impromptu Christmas tree lots on Third Avenue.

In the season of buying I have, for once, bought nothing.

CHAPTER 11

I REALLY DO intend to return to Midtown East and meet with K. Burke. Really. But then other instincts take over. I decide to return to 535 Park Avenue. I must make a dent in this case. I must redeem myself.

I walk back toward Baby D's building. This morning I interviewed the super, a handsome middle-aged guy named Ed Petrillo. Like most Park Avenue supers Petrillo wears a suit, has an office, and thinks he's running a business like General Motors or Microsoft. He says he was at his weekend house (the super has a weekend house!) for Thanksgiving.

I also spoke with the first-shift doorman, Jing-Ho. He was not aware of anything unusual. He suggested that I talk to George, the doorman who came on after him. I let other detectives speak to George, but now I need to stick my own fingers into this pie.

I arrive at the building and exchange a few words with the police guard at the corner of Park and 61st. "Nothing suspicious, nothing extraordinary." He's seen a bunch of limos outside the Regency Hotel across the street. He's seen a celebrity—either Taylor Swift *or* Carrie Underwood. He's not sure. (Hell, even I would know the difference.)

George the Doorman has the full name of George Brooks. The dark-blue uniform with gold braid fits him well. He wears black leather gloves.

"In winter we wear leather gloves. Other times of the year it's strictly white gloves. White gloves are what separates the 'good' buildings from the 'cheesy' buildings."

He is a polite guy, maybe thirty-five.

"Listen, Detective, not to be uncooperative or anything, but two other detectives have already asked me a bunch of questions—all I can do is tell you what I told them. I really don't know much. I mean, Mrs. Dunlop didn't have many guests. Just the usual deliveries through the service entrance—groceries, flowers, Amazon, liquor."

"Just tell me anything unusual about the day she died," I say. "Even if you think it's not important, just tell me."

"Nothing. Really nothing. She had come back Thursday night from the country. Her regular driver dropped her off." He pauses for a moment. "I didn't like the driver, but who the hell cares about what I think."

"I care quite a bit about what you think. Why didn't you like him?"

"He wasn't here long, but he thought he was better than the building staff. Because he drove a rich lady around in a car. A big black Caddy, an Escalade. Who gives a shit? Here's a good example: drivers are not supposed to wait in the lobby. That's the rule. They either stay in the car or go downstairs to the locker room. The driver was always standing outside smoking or sitting on the bench right here by the intercom phone. So I tell Mr. Petrillo about it..."

"The super," I say.

"The super, yeah. So Mr. P. tells him he can't do it anymore, and Simon says that that's bullshit. He says he's going to tell Mrs. Dunlop. Mr. Petrillo says go right ahead. Well, I guess Mrs. Dunlop agrees with the rules of the building. So the next thing you know—*bam!*—Mrs. Dunlop is getting a new driver."

I've read all this previously, in the interviews taken down by the other detectives, but I do notice a small trace of triumph in George Brooks's face when he arrives at the climax of his story.

I also know that the driver, whose full name is the very impressive moniker "Preston Parker Simon," did *not* say he was fired. According to his manager, he'd quit. K. Burke had checked Simon out with Domestic Bliss, an employment agency that places maids, laundresses, chauffeurs, and the occasional butler. Simon hadn't answered her calls, but a manager at Domestic Bliss, Miss Devida Pickering, told Burke that Simon was honest and dependable. But, she said, Mrs. Dunlop only used him part-time, and Simon wanted to be a full-time chauffeur. So that was that. But as that is never *really* that, we would need to track him down. He was the last person to see Baby D alive. I thank George. He offers me his hand to shake. I, of course, shake it.

I tell him thank you.

He says, "It's been great talking with you, absolutely great."

CHAPTER 12

A MINUTE LATER, I am in the basement of the building. My interviewee is fifty-four years old and is wearing khaki pants with a matching shirt. The shirt has the words "535 Park" emblazoned in red thread on the pocket.

The man's name is Angel Corrido, and Angel stands in the doorway of the service elevator. As we talk he removes clear plastic bags of very classy recycling. Along with the newspapers and Q-tips boxes are empty bottles of excellent Bordeaux and Johnnie Walker Black Label, empty take-out containers from Café Boulud.

I've already been briefed on his initial interviews on the scene, so my first question is the old standby: "Could you tell me anything I might not know about Mrs. Dunlop?"

He shrugs, then speaks. "No, nothing. Mrs. Dunlop never sees Angel Corrido."

"Never?"

"Eh, maybe sometimes." He removes a bundled stack of magazines.

"When I see her…Mrs. Dunlop…she is nice. She says, 'Hello, Angel. How are the wife and the children?'"

Angel laughs and says, "I have stopped telling her that I don't have a wife and I don't have children. She don't remember. She is nice, but a man who runs the back elevator blends in with the other men who run back elevators and shovel snow and take out garbage."

Angel does not sound angry at this. He actually seems to think it's amusing.

"Were you working here on Thanksgiving?" I ask.

"No, I come to work early the next morning. No back elevator on Thanksgiving."

He takes the last bag of recycling from the elevator. Then he throws a glance at the stairs leading down from the lobby above.

"But Angel *can* tell you something you do not know. But it is not about Mrs. Dunlop. It is about someone else."

"Yeah?"

He says nothing.

"So what is it?"

Still silence.

Then I do what no NYPD detective is ever supposed to do. I take a fifty-dollar bill from my pocket and hand it to him.

"So?"

"So maybe you should know something about that big-shot *el cabrón* who holds the door open for people, George Brooks," says Angel.

"Go on," I say.

"You know the way you just tipped me?"

"Yeah."

"That is the way the *chofer* for Mrs. Dunlop used to tip George every week. One hundred dollars when he delivers Mrs. Dunlop the big packages from the art gallery."

"The Namanworth Gallery?" I ask.

Angel speaks.

"Yes, maybe that is the name. I am not always good when I try to remember names. You know, when you are not born in this country—it is sometimes hard."

"Yes," I say. "It is sometimes *very* hard."

I thank him. I run up the stairs.

I text K. Burke: Need more info on driver P Simon. Let's find him.

CHAPTER 13

BURKE TELEPHONES DOMESTIC BLISS again. They have no current address for Preston Parker Simon, but she finds out that he is now driving for the CEO of a large and very successful comedy video website.

Making up for their failure to maintain addresses for their employees, Domestic Bliss does have the capability to track their drivers while they're driving clients. In a few minutes Burke finds out that the Escalade, presumably with Preston Parker Simon in the driver's seat, is parked outside the Four Seasons Hotel.

All roads in this case seem to lead to 57th Street. The Four Seasons is neatly bookended with Brioni, the men's fashion hot spot, on one side and Zilli, the French luxury brand, on the other side.

Burke and I meet up outside the hotel. A parade of limos, SUVs, and two Bentleys are waiting there. Their engines are running, poised to whisk away some business tycoon or rap star or foreign princess.

Burke punches some buttons on her phone, and soon we're asking Simon to step out of the Escalade.

He turns out to be a good-looking blond guy, certainly no older than thirty. He's charming, cooperative, and he has a fancy British accent that fits perfectly with his fancy British name.

Burke tells him that we're investigating the murder of Mrs. Ramona Dunlop. As soon as we do, a look of horror crosses his face.

"I heard. I saw it on the telly yesterday. Quite horrid. You know, I worked briefly for Mrs. Dunlop."

"Up until yesterday, you were her chauffeur," Burke says.

"Lovely woman. Remarkably spry for her age," Simon says.

He pulls out a tortoiseshell cigarette case from his jacket and offers us a cigarette.

"Have a fag?" he asks. Then he adds, "I love saying that to Americans. Always good for a laugh."

Burke and I decline the cigarette. We also decline to laugh.

"How long did you work for Mrs. Dunlop?" Burke asks.

"Not more than a month. She had a home in East Hampton. So a few times I took her out there. But she only really needed me for an occasional trip to the Colony Club for lunch, sometimes the opera, once or twice to her son's house in Bedford. It was not working out financially for me. I sought other clients."

"You drove her up to her son's house Thanksgiving Day, correct?" I ask.

"Quite correct."

"Though you had already given your notice?"

"Yes. She had hired a new driver, but we agreed I'd work through the holiday."

"How long were you and Mrs. Dunlop up there?" I ask.

"About four hours. We left for the city around six o'clock. I think I had her back on her doorstep by seven fifteen, maybe seven thirty."

Burke says, "Did you help her into the building with her things?"

"Things?" Simon asks, confused.

"Yeah," says Burke. "Things. Luggage. Packages. Leftover stuffing."

"Oh, no, no, no. There was a doorman. Very posh place. Lovely mansion," says Simon.

"535 Park Avenue is an apartment building, a co-op," says Burke.

I speak. "In England an apartment building sometimes is called 'a mansion.'"

"Live and learn, I guess," says Burke.

When did he officially resign from his job with Mrs. Dunlop? Yesterday.

Has he had reason to return to 535 Park since her death? No.

Who's he working for now?

"Danny Abosch, a dot-com prince," he says. "Lovely young chap."

As if on cue, a guy who looks like a college student who's late for class exits the hotel.

"Mr. Abosch is approaching," says Simon. "I really have to dash."

K. Burke responds to a crackle from her radio. I tell Simon that we may want to talk to him again. He says, "Surely," but his attention is on his boss, the young man in a blue Shetland sweater and a red ski parka walking toward us.

As Preston Parker Simon moves to open the car door he hands me a "calling card"—name, number, email. Engraved. Beige paper. Garamond type.

A chauffeur with his own calling card.

And they say I'm fancy.

CHAPTER 14

K. BURKE AND I begin walking from the Four Seasons Hotel down Fifth Avenue. We're headed back to police headquarters on East 51st Street.

A few minutes pass in silence. Then I speak.

"Preston Parker Simon is not an Englishman," I say.

"He sure does a good imitation of one," K. Burke says.

"Precisely," I answer. "His accent is purely *theatrical*. It is not authentic. In England someone from Yorkshire sounds distinctly different from someone from Cornwall. *Monsieur le chauffeur* has an all-purpose stage accent, the kind Gwyneth Paltrow uses in the cinema."

"You're good, Moncrief," Burke says. "Very good."

"*Merci,*" I say.

"But you aren't telling me anything I don't already know."

"You could detect it also?" I ask.

"No. Simon might as well have been Prince Charles as far as I could tell."

We stop to look at the Christmas display in the windows of Bergdorf Goodman. It is sparkly and sexy and crazy. Neptune and half-dressed female statues and the Baby Jesus. Toward the back of all this opulence is a crystal Eiffel Tower—homage to the horror of the hideous Paris terrorist attacks. I turn away.

"So, go on," I say to Burke. She speaks.

"While we were finishing up with Simon I received a 'birth and background' file from downtown. They found out that Preston Parker Simon's real name is Rudy Brunetti. He's from Morristown, New Jersey. He was born and raised there, and then…"

"And then he became an actor," I venture.

"Don't try to speed ahead of me, Moncrief."

"Forgive my enthusiasm," I say.

"*Then* Simon went to Lincoln Technical Institute. That's in Edison, New Jersey. *Then* he became a karate instructor. *Then* he became an actor."

"And after that he became a chauffeur," I say.

"What did I tell you about speeding ahead of me? No."

She takes out her iPad and consults it for the rest of Simon's bio.

"Then he signed up with Domestic Bliss. He got a job as a personal assistant to one of Ralph Lauren's designers. Then for a year he was a butler at the French consulate.…"

"And he fooled the French?" I exclaim as if I were shocked. "*Mon Dieu!*"

"*Then* he became a driver. First to Mrs. Dunlop. Now to this Abosch kid at the comedy website. By the way, neither the police nor Domestic Bliss has an address for him, just a post office box in Grand Central."

Burke and I are about to turn onto 51st Street. We pause to

admire the huge wreath on the front of St. Patrick's Cathedral. It is lighted with thousands of lights.

Then I lose interest in the wreath. My mind still lingers on the window of Bergdorf Goodman—the crystal *Tour Eiffel* a few blocks away, the wrought-iron *Tour Eiffel* a few thousand miles away.

I should be used to Burke's amazing sensitivity, but this time I am truly astonished.

"You're thinking of the Paris attacks, aren't you, Moncrief?" she says.

"You are a very wise woman, K. Burke."

"My heart breaks for you and your countrymen."

I nod. Then I say, "I know. I know it does. But enough gloom for now. Tell me. What do you think the next steps should be with Rudy Brunetti?"

"Let's go pick him up and find out what the story is, yes?"

I speak slowly, thoughtfully.

"No. I have another idea. Let us wait a few hours. My plan may turn out to be more helpful."

CHAPTER 15

NINE O'CLOCK THAT EVENING.

Burke and I sit in a car on Tenth Avenue and 20th Street in the shadow of Manhattan's newest beloved tourist attraction, the High Line.

I had wanted to drive my 1962 light-blue Corvette for this job. K. Burke's reaction to that idea?

"Forget it, Moncrief. You might as well have a brass band marching in front of that Corvette. They designed that car to attract attention," she said. Grudgingly, I told her she was correct.

So we sit in an unmarked NYPD patrol car. A Honda? A Chevy? Who cares? We are watching Preston Parker Simon, who is sitting in his black Escalade outside a brand-new thirty-five-story building. The three of us are waiting for the same thing—the young internet video tycoon. Once Simon picks up the "rich kid" we will tail them. Domestic Bliss can only track him when he's on the clock; our objective is to discover the location of the place that Simon calls home.

Fifteen minutes later we see Simon get out of his SUV. He

holds the door open for Danny Abosch. They exchange what appear to be some pleasant words. The kid steps inside the car. They take off.

Simon's car turns right onto 20th Street. Another right onto Ninth Avenue. Whether the tycoon is going to dinner or just going home he is, of course, going to Alphabet City. Apparently every person in New York below the age of thirty goes to the Alphabet City.

The car eventually stops on Saint Marks and Avenue A. Abosch is home. Or possibly at a friend's home. Or possibly at a girlfriend's home. Or... it doesn't matter. Whatever might come next is what matters.

Shortly I'm tailing Simon's car on the East River Drive, heading north. A fairly heavy snow begins. I stay "glued by two." I learned that this is the expression for tailing a car while allowing one other car in front of you for camouflage.

Simon exits the Drive and starts moving west all the way across Manhattan, then north on the Henry Hudson Parkway, across the Henry Hudson Bridge into the Bronx.

My tour guide, Detective Katherine Burke, explains the Bronx to me in two easy sentences.

"Riverdale is the fancy-ass part of the Bronx. Everything else is meh."

Traffic lightens, then slows. The snow dusts the road. "Glued by two" has to end. Now I keep some space behind Simon. He pulls off the main road, crosses even farther east. The street sign says "Independence Avenue." Then Simon pulls into a long circular driveway of a very elegant apartment building.

Two men come out of the building. One is clearly a

doorman—the hat, the coat, the gloves. The other is smaller, in a black wool pea coat, a dark woolen ski cap pulled down over his head.

Simon hands the doorman a very large, flat, wrapped package.

"You don't have to be a detective to figure out that Simon just gave the doorman a painting," says Burke. "I wonder if…"

But I interrupt her. I speak loudly.

"Son of a bitch!" I say.

"What's the matter?"

"The other man," I say.

We watch as Simon hands the other man a similar-looking wrapped package.

"Do you know him?" she asks.

"I sure as hell do."

"Who is he?" asks Burke.

"It's the little guy on the back elevator. It's Angel Corrido."

CHAPTER 16

ANGEL AND THE DOORMAN carry the paintings into the building. The doorman returns immediately. Angel remains inside.

We watch Simon and the doorman closely. They seem to be having a very intense conversation. The pantomime goes like this: The doorman moves close to Simon. The doorman looks like he is screaming. Then it appears that Simon is having none of it. Simon, using both hands, pushes the doorman. Although the doorman is larger than Simon, and the shove doesn't seem particularly violent, the doorman staggers backward and falls to the sidewalk.

As the doorman staggers to his feet, Simon puts his hand in his coat pocket. I am expecting a knife or a gun to be pulled out. Instead he hands the doorman something I don't recognize.

"Looks like Simon may have just slipped the doorman some cash," I say.

"I'm not sure, Moncrief. He handed him something. It looked like a tiny package."

"Some rolled-up bills," I say.

"No," says Burke. "My guess is he gave him a good noseful of coke." Then she adds, "And by the way, don't you think we should call him by his real name? He is *not* 'Preston Parker Simon.' He is Rudy Brunetti. Let's stop calling him Simon."

I think that this is a... what?... the kind of correction that Burke enjoys. Ah, well, it is easier for me to agree. So I nod. Then I say, "Brunetti it is."

Now we watch Simon... er, Brunetti... go back inside the building. The building doorman gets into the car and drives it into an attached building marked GARAGE.

He's back on the door in less than five. I immediately drive up to the building entrance.

"Who are you here to see, sir?" says the doorman, a very thin man, two days' growth, a dark stain on the lapel of his heavy brown coat.

He's only spoken a few words, but I can tell that he has an accent. My guess is Danish.

I lean across Burke and say, "We're here to see you."

"Me?" he says. And he looks genuinely confused. He blinks his eyes quickly. He wipes his lips with his gloved right hand.

"Yes, we'd like to talk to you about the gentlemen who you just assisted with the paintings...." I begin.

"What paintings?" he says.

I realize that this guy has a bad attitude *and* a drug problem. I am sure that Burke is onto this also. The symptoms are simple and obvious—quivering hands, milky pink eyes, perspiration on his upper lip. Dirty, matted wisps of blond hair stick out from beneath his hat.

K. Burke gets out of the car and stands next to the doorman. She flashes her ID.

I get out of the car and stand next to Burke. I touch the inner suit pocket where I carry the Glock I'm not supposed to carry.

"NYPD, sir," she says. "We'd like to see some ID immediately."

"What for? For helping a tenant with packages?"

"No. Possible possession of drugs. ID, please," I say.

I don't know a bit of Danish, but I think this guy just taught me the Danish word for "Shit."

CHAPTER 17

THE DOORMAN-DRUGGIE'S NAME IS Peter Lund.
He was in the Royal Danish Navy. He jumped ship seven years
ago. I guess I can buy that story.

Early on in the interview he says, "Yes, I like the heroin
too much." A minute later, with very little prodding from us,
he adds, "And yes, it is possible that Mr. Brunetti and Mr. C.
bring the works of art in and out of the apartment."

He rubs his lips.

Major rule of an interview: If a suspect starts talking, let
him keep talking. Don't interrupt.

"Mr. Brunetti tips me generous, and he sometimes gives me
my H, and it is none of my business to ask the tenant what
are his parcels in and out. Not my job."

I believe him. Burke nods. A signal to me that she also
believes him. Okay, now we know that Brunetti is storing
artwork here. But we need more.

Then I have an idea, an idea that might get us information.

"It would be a great help if you would take us to see Mr.
Brunetti's car," I say.

"But he would be angry," says Lund.

"Then you will be arrested for drug possession," says Burke. "How's that for a trade-off?"

"Come on," I say. "Show us where Brunetti's car is parked."

Lund answers quickly. "Which one?"

Three minutes later we are standing in the underground garage of 2737 Independence Avenue, Riverdale, Bronx, New York.

Peter Lund points to three identical black Escalades parked side-by-side-by-side. We look in the windows. Just the usual: black leather seats, high-tech dashboards. Burke takes a quick picture of the cars, the interiors, the plates. With one client, what does Brunetti need a fleet of SUVs for? This, and the involvement of Angel Corrido, suggests that the operation is bigger than we thought.

Burke tells Lund that we'll probably be back to talk some more. She suggests he try to stay as clean as he can *and* try to keep his mouth shut.

On the ride back to Manhattan, Burke says to me, "I'll do the write-up when we get back. We can't keep screwing around, avoiding Nick Elliott. We've got to build a file for him."

"Do you have reason to believe he's become impatient?" I ask.

"Yeah, I do. Let me read you a message." Then she reads from her cell phone: "What the hell are you two doing? Barney Wexler is up my ass. And the commissioner is standing right next to Wexler." Then Burke looks up at me and adds, "Maybe if you read your messages…"

"We will have something for him tomorrow. Next day at the latest," I say.

"No, Moncrief. We've got to get something to Elliott now."

"You are much too worried about the upper echelon, K. Burke."

"No. I'm worried that we are getting in way over our heads. Put a choke hold on your arrogance, Moncrief. We don't know for sure what we've got. Art forgeries? Drugs? It's time we got the rest of the team caught up."

"Give me one more day without any interference."

"No. Listen. It's not me. It's the case. We've got the facts— the stolen art, Rudy, Angel, a dead society dame, drugs. But we don't know where it's leading or how the hell to put it all together."

"I know how to put it together. Please, K. Burke. One more day to follow my arrogance. Please. Don't make me beg."

"You're not *begging* me, Moncrief. You're *bullshitting* me. But fine, I'll give you one more shot, one more day to piss in the ocean. Then we call in the cavalry."

CHAPTER 18

ETIENNE DUCHAMPS IS a billionaire and a very important art collector. He is also my friend. I have known Etienne since we were both four years old and attended *la petite école*.

Etienne has arranged a private viewing of the Monet at the Namanworth Gallery. Only the best of customers receive this kind of treatment.

I tell K. Burke that she and I will be introduced to the gallery owners as Mr. and Mrs. Luc Moncrief, *les amis intimes de Monsieur Duchamps*. Burke is angry with such a charade. She is even angrier by what I say next.

"So, it would be good for you to dress in the style of a wife of a man who can afford to purchase a Monet," I say.

"In that case I'll wear clean chinos," she says, then curls her lips with annoyance.

Amazingly, when she shows up at my apartment the next morning she looks...well...*chic*. In fact, *très chic*. Slim black slacks, black silk blouse, beige cashmere cardigan sweater.

Her black hair is shiny, piled up fashionably carelessly. A brown silk scarf and a short sheared beaver jacket pull the look together.

"What have you done with Katherine Burke?" I say as I open the door.

"Don't expect me to ever look like this again, Moncrief. Everything but my underwear is borrowed from my friend Christine, who happens to be a buyer at Neiman Marcus."

"You look like a woman who has a château that is chock-full of Monets. But I would add one or two little touches, if Madame Moncrief does not mind."

"What exactly are those 'touches'?"

"You'll see in a moment." Then I walk into my bedroom and quickly return.

"Here, put these on," I say.

I hand her a bracelet with two rows of twenty small square-cut diamonds on each row. The clasp that keeps it together fastens onto a large citrine stone. I also hand her a thin gold chain from which hangs an antique ruby and diamond pendant.

"This type of jewelry is what my mother used to call 'daytime jewelry,'" I say, forcing a smile.

"I don't feel comfortable wearing these things," she says, as I help her with the necklace clasp.

"You look exactly like the wife of a wealthy art collector," I say. Then I look away from her.

"Moncrief," she says. "I can't. Didn't this jewelry belong to . . . ?"

"Yes, of course. But they have been sitting like sad orphans in Dalia's jewelry safe," I say.

Is my voice cracking? Can Burke hear my heart beating? What the hell am I doing?

"Think about this. It's not right," Burke says.

I glance at her. She does look lovely. Then I speak loudly.

"Enough with the jibber-jabber. Let's go," I say. "We have a Monet to examine."

CHAPTER 19

THE OWNERS, SOPHIA and Andre Krane, are waiting for us at the shop door.

"I drove in from the country this morning. I so wanted to greet you myself," Sophia Krane says. She is a phony, but the kind that Dalia used to call "a *real* phony."

Sophia looks to be about seventy-five years old. Elegant, well preserved, slow-moving, fake-golden hair pulled back tight. She says she's a countess. Even if she is lying, she carries herself like royalty.

Her husband, Andre, must be at least ten years older. Andre is not nearly so well preserved. Overweight, balding, he wears a herringbone sports jacket with leather elbow patches. Later K. Burke will say, "The coveted New England college professor look."

The Monet has been moved from the window to a large easel. It is a wonder of the impressionist's art. When we stand close to the canvas we see a blur of overlapping colors, a clown's scarf, a paint-by-numbers set. A few steps back the viewer is transported to a breathtakingly beautiful field in Giverny.

Just as Sophia Krane appears to be a real countess, so, too, does this painting appear to be a real Monet. But what do I know? Burke and I are not there as art experts; we are there as sniffing-around detectives.

Andre Krane speaks: "And how does Madame Moncrief like the piece?"

To my astonishment Burke speaks with a graceful and very believable French inflection. I am amazed at her acting. I've seen her "play" tough. I've seen her "play" sentimental, but I've never seen her transform herself into a woman of high society.

"As expected, it is magnificent," Burke says, a charming and slight smile enhancing her performance.

"I will tell you," says Sophia, "that we have had an offer of forty. The offer is from an American, seventy-five percent is in cash, the remainder in stock holdings . . . dot-com stock, of course."

"Of course," Burke says.

I nod and stifle the urge to stroke my chin in contemplation.

"Not to change the subject too much," I say, "but are you by chance representing any of the Moderns?"

"Not many," says Andre.

"A minor Utrillo," says Sophia. "A few other things."

Andre speaks conspiratorially, lowering his voice. "Follow us. We'll take you someplace very special—the Back Room. It's where we keep the work that we don't show just anybody."

CHAPTER 20

THE "BACK ROOM" turns out to be nothing more than a kind of storage space. On the near wall are two unframed canvases. Both have the graffiti touch of a Basquiat. Sophia Krane flicks her hand dismissively toward the unframed pieces.

"You won't want these," she says. "They're second-rate examples. I knew Basquiat well."

As if to prove her friendship, she now refers to him by his first name. "Jean-Michel has much better work. We just don't have any of it at the moment."

Then she walks to three framed canvases on the floor. They lean against the opposite wall, behind one another.

"Now these..." she says. Andre flips on an overhead fluorescent bulb. Sophia continues in her casual tone.

"This is a good Hopper. It comes from a private collection in Philadelphia. I think there was something going on between Hopper and the woman who originally owned it."

She slides the painting to the side. She reveals a three-dimensional painting of a toy fire truck.

"Feldman. He's hot again," says Sophia.

"Whoever thought he'd be back on top?" says her husband. Sophia shoots Andre a mean glance, then says, "I did, darling."

The third painting is a series of bowls on a shelf—simple, geometric, flat.

Sophia speaks.

"Ed Baynard is back, too. At least he's back for the wealthy couples in Sanibel and Palm Beach. The rich people in Florida can't decorate a media room without one of these pretty little Baynards hanging near their recliner chairs."

Sophia's art lesson has ended, and, although I find the Baynard paintings quite appealing, I am smart enough to remain silent.

Suddenly my fake–French wife speaks.

"I really would like to look at them further...but at a later time," Burke says. "Luc and I are meeting our mutual friend, Etienne, for drinks...."

"Etienne is in town? I didn't know that," says Andre.

Burke is, I think, becoming a bit too impressed by her own charade. We need to get out. Burke speaks.

"Just for the day. An unexpected business meeting. So we will be in touch about the Monet and perhaps the Feldman. But, you know, I do have a question."

"Of course," says Sophia.

Burke continues.

"Isn't it unusual to have such valuable pieces stacked one on top of another, leaning against the wall, on a dirty floor?"

"That's how the artists often keep them in their studios," says Andre.

"But this is not a studio," Burke says, her charming smile in place.

Detective Burke and Mrs. Krane exchange tense smiles. But I know Burke well enough to realize that she is heading somewhere in this conversation.

"I was so hoping," she says, "that you would sift through those three paintings and reveal a fourth canvas. I was foolishly hoping for a piece by Frida Kahlo. One of the self-portraits."

"Yes, everyone loves the self-portraits," says Andre. "The perfect scarves, the interesting headdress..."

"You know..." says Sophia.

"I know what you're thinking," says Andre. (I prepare myself for an avalanche of bullshit.)

Sophia speaks directly to K. Burke. Here it comes.

"You know, there is a collector, a very discreet individual, who has acquired three Kahlos over the years. The collector is away for the Christmas holidays. Saint Martin, I think. The French side, of course. I can get in touch, though. Would you be interested?"

"It would be a dream come true for Madame Moncrief," I say.

Burke touches my shoulder. She smiles at me. She speaks.

"What a sweet Christmas gift that could be...." Her voice trails off. And we say our good-byes.

As soon as we step onto 57th Street I say, "A magnificent performance, K. Burke."

"I'd like to thank the Academy...." she says. "And we might get a fake Frida Kahlo piece out of this."

But I am already plotting our next steps.

"I hope you are not too exhausted for tonight's job, when we follow Simon again," I say.

"No, we're not flying solo anymore. It's time to brief Elliott on our suspicions."

"Tonight will be our last time, K. Burke," I say.

"No way," says Burke. "No freakin' way." She is angry.

I smile my most charming smile and say, "Tonight if we get Simon we will be able to arrest him."

Burke speaks slowly, firmly.

"If you go on surveillance again, Moncrief, you're doing it without me."

I speak, barely able to spit out the words. I am angry also.

"If that's the way you want it, then stay back tonight. Stay and punch the numbers, search the file. I will do real police work. Go on back to Elliott now. Tell him whatever you like. As for me, I'm going into the Sherry-Netherland for a martini."

CHAPTER 21

I SIT WITH a frosty gin martini—straight up—at the bar of the Sherry-Netherland. The happy quiver of the first sip calms me, at least for a moment. Then my phone buzzes. A message from K. Burke. She texts: Read this. Then call me or come to precinct.

I read the following, from the *New York Post*'s website:

Bye-Bye, Baby D

Mrs. Ramona Driver Dunlop, the society matron known popularly as "Baby D," was bid farewell today at a lavish memorial service at St. Thomas Episcopal Church on Fifth Avenue and 53rd Street. White lilies and Bach cantatas filled the air as friends and family remembered the glamorous life of the social queen. Understandably, none of the speakers mentioned Baby D's earthly farewell—a particularly gruesome murder.

"There are more detectives and cops here than there are friends," said nightlife gossip blogger Teddy Galperin.

"Let's hope one of them can finally make some headway in the case."

His comment was a reference to the NYPD's inability to make any progress in solving the murder of Mrs. Dunlop Friday. NYPD has thus far offered no clues as to the story behind the grisly death of the elderly woman.

In her youth Mrs. Dunlop was named New York Debutante of the Year. In recent years, the wealthy widow had turned her considerable energy and fortune to helping charities involved with the scourge of drug abuse. A lover and collector of fine art, Mrs. Dunlop also served on the boards of many museums, including the Frick and the Metropolitan Museum of Art. She is survived by her son and daughter-in-law.

I do not call K. Burke. I know what she will tell me: *No more screwing around, Moncrief! We must get help!*

I text K. Burke: Hold Elliott off until tomorrow. Don't be angry.

Burke texts me back: Not angry. Just worried.

CHAPTER 22

I'M WAITING EXACTLY where I waited the previous night. But this time, I'm waiting in the car that Dalia had christened "The Baby Blue from '62." And K. Burke isn't here to tell me that driving a flashy Corvette is a foolish idea.

Simon/Brunetti sits in his Escalade. The "rich kid" comes out of the building and slides into the backseat. When they take off, I take off after them.

Okay. A slight variation this time around: Simon deposits Abosch at Dirt Candy, a hip vegetarian restaurant on Allen Street.

This time Simon heads back to the Henry Hudson, only we take the George Washington Bridge into New Jersey. Simon speeds...85...90....I speed, too. It seems like Simon knows all the speed traps. He slows down three times, always unexpectedly. Then back up to 85...90....The Baby Blue from '62 and I are loving it. *Detective Burke, you don't know what you're missing.*

An hour and a half later, we're in Monticello, New York.

A few minutes later we're maneuvering around dark roads in the Catskills.

I turn off my headlights and drop back to a safe distance. The guardrails and ditches on the country roads become my guide. If I lose track of Simon's car, I'll be adrift.

Occasionally I see a house decorated with Christmas lights. A few Nativity scenes on front lawns. Neon wreaths. But mostly murky darkness.

Ten...fifteen...twenty minutes. Amazingly at a certain point I see Simon's car flash a right-turn signal. Is it a driver's reflex? Or, as Americans say: Is this guy just messing with me?

CHAPTER 23

A TOUCH OF winter moonlight provides just enough illumination to watch the Escalade pull into a very long dirt driveway. At the end of the driveway is a large Tudor-style mansion. I park on the road.

Two in the morning, but most of the windows are bright with lights. Simon leaves his car. He carries two packages. I'm assuming that they're the same paintings from last evening in Riverdale. But why drop them in storage instead of coming straight here? Maybe for discretion.

He rings the doorbell and looks around him. Yup, he's nervous. In a few moments Andre Krane opens the door. Simon disappears inside.

Now I exit my car. I stretch. I step into the woods a few feet. I survey the area. Woods and woods and then more woods. Giant trees—bare oaks, bare elms, hundreds of pines and evergreens. Tiny-sized to majestic-tremendous. The ground is covered with snow, tree limbs peeking out. Not far from the house is an ice-gray lake. More evergreens surround the lake, a lake so big that I can't even tell where it ends.

I return to the car and open the glove compartment. I unwrap a perfectly ripe piece of Camembert. I push a piece of sliced baguette into the soft cheese and enjoy my meal. A crisp Belgian ale, a perfect heirloom apple. A good snack along with this simple fact: I love solo detective work so much that even these bizarre and boring stakeouts are enjoyable to me. I'm a hunter after the game. There is a prize at the end for my perfect patience.

I crack the car window open an inch. The cold air rushes in.

Then I turn on the engine and warm the car. This on-and-off engine procedure occurs four times in the next hour. My eyes remain fixed on the house. I watch the lights go out. The mansion is draped in darkness. But I will not sleep.

At three o'clock I exit the car again. I bend and touch my toes a few times. I tie my silk scarf snug around my neck and chin. The snow begins again. The night is relentlessly cold.

I decide to move closer to the Krane house. *Histoire de voir.* I'll see what I can see.

CHAPTER 24

THROUGH THE LEAD-FRAMED windows of the dining room, when my eyes adjust to the dark, I see a giant oak table with chairs that look like Tudor thrones. If I expected to see a Matisse or an O'Keeffe hanging on the wall, I am disappointed. Four British fox-hunting prints. Nothing else.

I walk to the rear of the house and look into the huge kitchen. Two old stoves. Two deep sinks. A refrigerator from the 1950s. A marble-topped pastry table. A butler's pantry.

The ground is frozen hard, yet beneath the snow are deep hidden holes. I look toward the lake. The dock is covered with layers of tarp.

I move cautiously through the ice and snow. I now stand at the windows to the living room. Nothing on the wall except some African carvings and bronze antique sabers.

I decide to head back to my car. Too cold. Too icy. Also I must be there if Simon suddenly leaves.

I hear the door to the house open, and voices. There he is. I begin to run—then I trip. A hole? A branch? A discarded fake Picasso? I am not hurt. I get up quickly. But my fall has apparently tipped someone off to my presence.

Suddenly the unmistakable sound of a bullet cracks the air. It shatters a piece of the stucco wall near where I stand and lands significantly away from where I'm standing. But a bullet can never land far enough away.

Then another bullet.

Another shot. Because the woods appear thicker near the lake I try to run there as fast as possible. To hide. To escape. I take out my gun, but I'm not acting in a Western. Real life offers no chance for me to spin on my heels and actually shoot my pursuer.

My knees are bent. I run close to the ground. If I fall I have less chance of getting hurt.

Then a scream in the darkness.

"I *will* get you, Moncrief."

The dumbest detective in America could identify the British-sounding voice. It is, of course, Preston Parker Simon/ Rudy Brunetti.

I keep running as fast as possible toward the lake. What once looked like a short distance seems like a marathon challenge.

Another bullet. Then immediately another.

My shoes and ankles and calves are soaked with melted snow and ice.

Another bullet.

As I get closer to the lake, a voice comes at me: "You'd better be able to swim that lake, asshole." He's stalling. Probably reloading.

Simon is closer. But now he sounds simpler, cruder, American. I get it. He's slipped into being his real self. He's not

Preston Parker Simon. He's Rudy Brunetti. Now I am at the water's edge. In the dim moonlight I can see Simon. He is getting closer.

He fires three more bullets in succession. The bullets land close enough to where I stand that I can see sections of the icy surface shatter.

He fires two more shots.

He suddenly shouts, "Who the hell...? Angel, is that you?"

No response.

"Angel? Angel?"

Still no response.

Another yell from Simon: "Krane. Is it you? Are you there?"

I can see Simon clearly now. I watch him raise his gun. He fires in my direction. He fires again. He misses. He aims carefully. I fall to the snowy icy ground. He lowers his aim just a bit. He sees me.

He raises his arm slightly. He reevaluates the situation.

I am like a scared child. I close my eyes tightly.

Then...one more bullet shot. It comes nowhere near me.

I wait for the next bullet. And I wait. I only hear the sounds of nature. Winter birds cackling in the sky. Strong winds whipping through the pine trees.

Then a voice calls out.

"You okay, Moncrief?"

I know that voice. It is K. Burke.

CHAPTER 25

THE CHEESY TUDOR-STYLE living room—like something out of Disneyland—fills up quickly with lots of local law enforcement.

The New York State police arrive: seven burly men and two substantial-looking women. The local Monticello police arrive: two detectives, two coroners, four police officers. This may be the entire town police department. The local press arrives, as eager and noisy as anything in Manhattan or Paris. The coroners do a quick on-site examination of Rudy Brunetti. Then they begin to transfer the body to an ambulance.

I stand at an open window and watch them speedily move the body to the ambulance. The coroner sees me and explains what I already know: "We need to minimize dermal contamination."

Why do American officials enjoy using big words? Couldn't he just have said "skin decay"?

Detective Burke and I are at different corners of the room. We see each other, and I immediately join my colleague, the person who just saved my life.

"So, K. Burke," I say. "You *did* accompany me after all." I squeeze her shoulders, as close to a loving gesture as we have ever shared.

"You probably predicted that I'd be following you," she says. I tell her the truth.

"Not this time, I must say. This time I thought our disagreement was too great for it to mend quickly."

There is a pause. Then she looks at me with intense eyes. Softly she says, "I could never let you down, Moncrief."

My head turns to the ground. My throat aches with anxiety. I know that I should be lying dead on the icy ground. I shake. My neck hurts. I speak.

"*Merci, merci beaucoup.* You have saved my life. I am beyond grateful."

Burke smiles. Her eyes sparkle.

"As you should be."

I smile. This will not grow any further into a sentimental moment. That is simply not the way Burke and I behave.

And anyway, we must not allow the local police to take over. No. Now we must take control, as all the little puzzle pieces of the investigation begin to fall into place.

The results turn out to be fairly much as we expected. The elegant Sophia and Andre Krane are the masterminds in this grand fraud scheme. They maintain a large basement studio at this home. It looks like a classroom at a university's fine arts painting course. Easels with half-finished canvases dot the room—a large Picasso here, a tiny Rubens there, a Schnabel that looks like every other Schnabel, a Warhol "Liz Taylor" that looks like a thousand others.

Handcuffs are locked onto the Kranes. Sophia Krane is

calm, stoic, almost bored, as she stands with three police officers guarding her.

"Rudy was a fool. I told him all he had to do was steal some goddamn paintings, from her bedroom. He didn't have to kill the old lady," she says.

"But he did," K. Burke says.

Now the Kranes are led out of their gloomy house to join Angel, who is already in a police car.

Burke and I question and Andre quickly admits that they sold the Hockney and Lichtenstein forgeries to Baby D. Only too eager to sell out their pal Rudy, he described how they had planted him—already an accomplice in art forgery sales— as her driver, when other clients of the gallery had started to raise alarm about the legitimacy of their pieces.

Rudy was supposed to gain access and steal the paintings back, but she'd sniffed him out and fired him before he had the opportunity. Desperate, after their last drive Rudy had killed her—but was too cowardly to take the paintings then, sniffed Sophia.

So they'd enlisted Angel Corrido to "retrieve" them from the apartment after her death. Their fear at that point, of course, had become that Mrs. Dunlop's estate would identify the pieces as forgeries. "You might as well look in Baby D's second maid's room," Sophia tells us. "She has a box spring with a secret compartment. Right now you'll probably find a Giotto wood panel and a group of architectural drawings from Horace Walpole's country home that Angel couldn't manage to get out. And...oh, yes...ten animation cels from Disney's *Snow White and the Seven Dwarfs.*"

"No one can say we don't offer a variety," says Andre.

The local chief of police, the Monticello district attorney, and the sergeant of the county police approach us like a pumped-up sports team. I know what they want: a quarrel. Will these three criminals be tried in Sullivan County where they were arrested? Or will they be tried in Manhattan where their crimes were committed? I'm way too weary to deal with this.

"K. Burke, you have given me the greatest gift that one person can possibly give another. Thanks to you, I am still alive."

"All in a day's work," she says, with only a trace of irony in her voice.

"Now I must ask for one more favor, a small favor," I say.

She simply rolls her eyes.

"What is it, Moncrief? Do you want me to give you a kidney?"

"Actually, worse than that. Would you please deal with these three local police people? I have an errand to run."

"An errand? It's five thirty in the morning. We're at a crime scene in the middle of the woods a hundred miles from home base . . . and you've got an errand to run?"

"*Merci,* K. Burke. *Merci, merci,* and for good luck, one more *merci.*"

CHAPTER 26

IT IS DARK as midnight when I walk outside. The late-November morning is misty and cold. It is snowing lightly, just enough to make the air wet and icy. It is a perfect environment for sadness. The frozen lake, the dark night, the icy air...it should be ideal for depression. Yet I am strangely buoyant. I am calmer than I have been in months. I know it is the result of a successful end to the art forgery case. The usual sense of smugness that runs through me is stronger than ever. I look forward to discussing the details with Elliott. I know that some of my New York colleagues will have a touch of envy that this French interloper cracked the case. But most of all I am deeply warmed by Katherine Burke's extraordinary role in saving my life. Beyond friendship, and even, in a certain way, beyond romantic love.

I look down toward the lake. I stand still. I imagine the scene of a few hours ago, a scene of terror as a man with a gun pursued me through the dark. Now the entire area is one of peace and beauty.

A wooden shed sits not far from the main house. I have

seen sheds like this outside some of the very old châteaux of France; they are remnants from hundreds of years earlier— outdoor bathrooms, basically toilets for the servants.

I look through the one small glass window in the shed's wooden door. The tiny household's gardening equipment— old-fashioned hand mowers, clippers, axes, shovels. I open the door and see a rusty bow saw hanging on a hook. I take it down and walk toward the lake.

In this forest of dead winter branches and hundreds of evergreens, I find a pine tree that is precisely the same height as myself—six feet, no taller, no shorter. It is not a tree from a storybook—not a scrawny lonely tree, yet not a great thick beauty. A tree. Simple. Lovely. A good representation of the work of God...if you are happy enough with life to still believe in God.

The trunk is soft. I cut through easily. As I do, I notice how completely ruined my shoes and trousers are—stained with water and ice and snow and the feces of deer and dogs.

I give the severed trunk an easy shove, and the tree falls forward. Just as I slip the bow saw over my shoulder and lift the bottom end of the trunk to drag the tree back toward the house, I hear a man's voice calling.

He shouts my name. He calls, "Detective Moncrief. Over here."

I wave at him, and he continues toward me. I recognize him as one of the Monticello police officers on the crime scene. He is no boy. He may be as old as thirty. As he comes closer I see that he is tall and blond and handsome, no doubt a local girl's dream.

But as is always the way with me, I am hesitant, suspicious.

Perhaps the Kranes and Rudy Brunetti had a cabal of helpers up here. It would not be incredible—a few facilitators in the police force, in city hall, in the highway department.

I drop the tree and slip the bow saw from my shoulder to my hand. I grip the saw handle tightly.

The police officer stands next to me.

"I can give you a hand with that," he says. "I saw you from way up there."

"Ah, you caught me in the act of thievery," I say.

"I think you can help yourself to anything you want around here. You and Detective Burke are heroes. This is pretty amazing, the way you solved this case."

He nods his head nervously. He looks a bit goofy.

"Persistence," I say. "All it takes is persistence . . . and a great deal of patience."

"Yeah, I'm sure," he says. Then he speaks quickly.

"I was talking to your partner," he says. "Um . . . I asked her . . . well, I hope you won't be mad, but I asked her if you and her were anything more than partners."

I know exactly what the young man means, but I pretend otherwise.

"More than partners?" I ask.

"You know . . . God, I can't believe I'm doing this . . . like . . ." He cannot get it out.

"What did Detective Burke say?" I ask.

"She said 'absolutely not,' but then she told me to ask you."

"She is teasing you, *monsieur*. Detective Burke and I are partners professionally, but we are just friends."

"Just friends," he repeats. "So I could see her, go on a date with her?"

"You could go to the moon with her," I say.

"I'll help you with the tree," he says. Then he adds, "You take the lighter end."

"I'm fine with this end," I say. So we carry the tree. I see K. Burke is standing, waiting for us near the toolshed.

"*That's* where you were, Moncrief. Cutting down a tree?" she says with a smile. "I can't believe it."

The police officer, K. Burke, and I are standing, admiring the tree.

"Christmas is a few weeks away, K. Burke. Here is my gift to you. For Christmas and for saving my crazy little life. We can tie the tree to the roof of the car and bring it back to the city. This strapping young man can help us."

She looks at me. I speak.

"Merry Christmas, Detective," I say.

"Merry Christmas, Detective," she says.

Then K. Burke begins to cry. I also feel my eyes fill with tears. The young police officer speaks.

"Just friends," he says. "Sure. Just friends."

CHAPTER 27

CHRISTMAS IS COMING. And as my favorite American expression goes:

I couldn't care less.

In the past I would have been in deep consultation with Miranda, my traditional Cartier shopping assistant. Miranda had a 1.000 batting average in helping me select the perfect Christmas gift for Dalia. Not too flashy, but not too boring. Something with sparkle, but something that did not call attention to itself... like Dalia herself.

It is December 20, and whatever gift-giving I am doing these few days is taken care of with a checkbook. I write gift checks for the daily maid, the twice-a-week laundress, the wine merchant at Astor who advises me when a particular Bordeaux is at its peak, Xavier who cuts my hair at Roman K, and... and that is it.

I consider giving something special to Detective Burke. But what do you give a person who has saved your life? An expensive car, an expensive trip, an expensive bracelet? They each sound ridiculous, and I think perhaps that any of them would insult Katherine Burke.

The days since the arrests of the art forgery gang have been dull. Elliott suggested that we take some time off. I tried to do so, but a man can only play so much squash and attend so many exhibitions at MoMA and the Morgan.

K. Burke takes a few days to do some Christmas shopping with her nieces and nephews in New Jersey. I decline to accompany them to the Short Hills mall.

When we return to work we catch up on the paperwork for the forgery case. We make an easy arrest of a drug dealer outside Julia Richman High School on East 67th Street. Elliott asks us to spend two days renewing our former Bloomingdale's assignment. We are reluctant and grumpy and unpleasant about the assignment, but the department store is a block away from Le Veau d'Or, where we have lunch this afternoon. The impeccably old-fashioned French restaurant on 60th Street still knows how to make perfect veal kidneys in a mustard sauce. And this afternoon Le Veau d'Or becomes the first (and most likely, last) restaurant where K. Burke has *tripes à la mode de Caen*. When I tell her that tripe is the stomach lining of a cow, she simply shrugs and says, "All I know is that it tastes good. Thanks for the reco." I think she is lying. But such a lie means that she must finish eating the dish.

Bloomingdale's closes at 10:00 p.m. Fifteen minutes later I am sitting in my apartment, sifting through Christmas cards wishing me *Joyeux Noël et Bonne Année*.

I stand and pour myself a small glass of Pepto-Bismol. Have I grown too old for veal kidneys?

The phone rings. The Caller ID shows the familiar 161 area

code for Paris, but the remainder of the phone number means nothing to me.

As I reach for the phone I remember that it is about five in the morning in Paris.

"Luc," she says. "It is Babette."

Babette Moreau is my father's personal secretary. She has been his secretary for forty years, maybe longer.

My instincts tell me why she is calling.

"Votre père est mort."

Your father has died.

My first instinct is to feign sadness. I do not want Mademoiselle Babette to have proof of what she already knows: my father and I had a distant, sometimes angry relationship. He was a man of great financial achievement and great emotional distance. Early on—when it became clear that he and I had nothing in common except that we were related—he, a young widower, dispatched me to the care of nannies and tutors and tennis instructors and private schools. He thought that my interest in police work was ridiculous, and, while he was extremely generous with his money, he was extremely sparing with his love and companionship. This system worked. He did not care much about me. And I surely did not care very much about him.

A different son might burst into tears. A different son might express over-the-top shock at the news. But I am not that son. And I am a detective, not an actor.

"A heart attack," Babette says. "No pain. He was at his desk, of course."

"Of course," I say.

"The arrangements?" I ask.

"Notre Dame," she says. "That is what he would have wanted."

"Yes," I reply. "That is certainly what he would have wanted."

A pause, and then she asks what she is afraid to ask.

"Will you attend?" she says.

I do not pause.

"Of course," I say. It is an honest response. No, I am not moved by his death. But for a son not to attend his father's funeral is an extraordinary offense.

I tell her that I will leave tomorrow for Paris. She tells me that she will schedule the funeral after my arrival. I tell her to call me if there is anything else I need to know. The conversation ends.

What do I do next? I telephone K. Burke.

"That's awful, Moncrief," she says. Then a pause. Then... "Listen. I know you and your father didn't have the best relationship. But *he was your father*. Nothing changes that. Do you want me to come by and be with you?"

"No," I say. "No. But there is something you can do to help me through this."

"Of course. What is it?"

"Tomorrow afternoon...come to Paris with me."

CHAPTER 28

"I AM EMBARRASSED to be enjoying this flight so much," says K. Burke.

The premier cabin is spacious and elegant. Aside from an exotic-looking sheik who is traveling with a valet, Burke and I are the only other passengers in the first-class compartment of this Air France flight to Paris. The luxury is, even for a spoiled brat like me who has flown first class his entire life, extraordinary. It is slightly intoxicating to be above the Atlantic Ocean with so much *stuff* at one's disposal: flatbed seats for perfect sleeping, each bed with a small dressing room attached; perfectly chilled bottles of Dom Pérignon; access to first-run movies.

"And you are embarrassed...why?" I ask.

"Because we are going to Paris for a funeral. Not a wedding, not a birthday party, not even a business meeting. A funeral."

"Just pretend that it is one of the pleasanter events you just mentioned," I say. "Or call it business. I'm certain business will be discussed. I have already received two emails from my late father's personal assistant Babette and *three* emails from his protégé, Julien Carpentier."

"Julien Carpentier," Burke repeats. "That's a new name for me."

"Julien is his 'business assistant.' Julien is the new and improved version of the son I was supposed to be. If I had turned out to be the person my father wished me to be— ambitious, serious, businesslike—I would have been Julien. Instead I became what my father called *un policier fou,* a foolish policeman."

"And Julien is an asshole, I suppose?" K. Burke asks as she piles a generous spoonful of beluga caviar onto a warm blini.

"Surprisingly not. I do not know him well, but the few times I've seen or spoken with Julien, he has been quite...I don't know the word precisely...pleasant...authentic...yes, that is it, authentic. I think he is happy with his luck to have such an important position. Plus he diverts my father's attention from me. Julien and Babette are both probably truly saddened by my father's death. While you and I are sitting in luxury, sipping the bubble-water, soon to go to sleep on Pratesi bed linens, Julien is tending to the comings and goings of the company."

The flight attendant stops at our seats. She is carrying the 500mg tin of beluga with her. Pointing at the tin with her mother-of-pearl caviar spoon, she asks if we would like some more.

Burke hesitates.

"Go ahead," I say. "Have some more. Caviar builds strength. You will need all you can get for our important meetings."

I smile, but the flight attendant takes my remarks seriously.

"Ah, you are in France on business?" she says.

"In a manner of speaking," I say.

"I hope you will meet with great success," she says.

When the pretty young woman leaves us, Detective Burke speaks.

"By the way, Moncrief. I did do something that *you* forgot to do," she says.

"Whatever we failed to pack will be available at my father's house," I say.

"Don't be so smug. It's nothing as simple as dental floss or underwear. You forgot to tell Inspector Elliott that we are disappearing for three days."

"We are not *disappearing*, K. Burke. We are on holiday," I say.

"Well, maybe you can be cavalier about this. But not me. I need this job. Anyway, I called Elliott earlier and told him that he was right, we both needed a real break, that the work from the forgery case finally caught up with us. So we were taking a few days off."

"And he said what?"

"He said 'You two guys deserve it. Have fun.'"

I begin to laugh. Burke looks confused. My laughter grows louder.

"What's so funny, Moncrief?"

"Don't you see? Our boss thinks that we're off on a romantic journey."

I keep on laughing. Detective Burke does not.

CHAPTER 29

EIGHT O'CLOCK IN the morning at Charles de Gaulle airport.

Burke and I are fast-tracked through customs. We are suffering from "Dom Pérignon Syndrome," an alcohol-fueled sleep followed by a walloping morning headache.

In the reception lounge K. Burke says to me, "There he is. There's Julien Carpentier." She points to a handsome man in his late twenties, perhaps his early thirties. Six feet tall or so. Light-brown hair. A well-cut, dark-blue overcoat, a dark-blue silk scarf.

"How did you know that man is Julien?" I ask. "You've never seen him before."

"Correct. But I know it's Julien Carpentier because he looks exactly like you."

It has been at least a year since I have seen Julien, but for some reason this time, in the bright unflattering light of the airport, I see the truth of K. Burke's observation. He is not a mirror image of me, not a twin, but we both have a sharp nose, straight long hair, green eyes.

Julien is accompanied by a beautiful woman who is formally dressed in a chauffeur's uniform—black suit, brass buttons, large cap. I cannot help but think that this is the beginning of a pornographic film.

Julien moves toward me quickly and embraces me like a brother, which perhaps he thinks he is. I return the hug with a lot less vigor.

"*Mon ami, Luc.* Welcome. Welcome." He turns to Katherine Burke and makes a small quick bow from the waist. "And this, of course, is Mademoiselle Burke, a fine companion to have at this sorrowful time."

Julien takes Burke's hand, bows once again, and—well, he doesn't quite *kiss* her hand—he gently *brushes* Burke's hand beneath his lips.

"I only wish that we might have met under happier circumstances," Julien says. K. Burke says that she agrees.

"Huguette and I will go gather your luggage," Julien says. "We will meet you at the doorway marked D-E." As they leave for the luggage carousel Burke mumbles, "No. Don't . . . it's all right. I . . ." In the noise of the terminal they do not hear her.

"Let them go," I say. "We will have to listen to Julien chatter all the ride into Paris. Let's take a short break from him right now."

"But, Moncrief. There's only one little suitcase, mine. You said you didn't need to bring anything, that you had a lot of clothing at your father's. Julien and that hot-looking driver are going to be looking for your stuff. And then they'll . . ."

"Listen. I have only been with Julien about sixty seconds, and he is already annoying me with yak-yak-yak."

"You're wrong. I think he's genuinely glad to see you. *And* I think he's far more broken up about your father's death than you are."

"The woman who served us dinner on the plane was more broken up about my father's death than I am," I say.

I take a deep breath. I squeeze a few eyedrops into my eyes and say to K. Burke, "Very well. Let's go to the luggage area and find them. We'll tell them that we were so jet-lagged that we forgot we only had one small piece of luggage."

"You're impossible, Moncrief."

"Let's go find them, but..."

"But what?" Burke says.

"But let us walk very, very slowly."

CHAPTER 30

AS PREDICTED, JULIEN talks incessantly on the ride into Paris.

"Your father was a tough boss, but a fair boss."

"The factory workers in Lille and Beijing are all anxious about their future."

"*Monsieur le docteur* said the heart attack came fast. He did not suffer."

"I wanted the funeral at Sacré-Cœur. Babette wanted Notre Dame. She, of course, got her way. It is only right. She knew him best."

"The American ambassador, the ambassadors from Brazil and Poland, even the Russian ambassador, the one your father detested, will be there."

"We are prepared with security for the paparazzi. They will come for the television and cinema personalities."

"The presidents of *all* your father's offices are attending, of course."

"I am so grateful that the heart attack came quickly. Not

that it was not expected after the two bypass surgeries and the ongoing atrial fibrillation."

"There will be a children's choir at the mass as well as the regular Notre Dame chorus."

K. Burke listens intently. I think she may actually be intrigued by the details of this grand affair. Julien and Babette have planned my father's funeral as if it were a royal wedding— red floral arrangements, Paris Archbishop André Vingt-Trois to officiate, Fauchon to cater the luncheon after the burial.

I tune out of Julien's lecture early on. His words come as a sort of sweet background music in my odd world of jet-lagged half sleep.

Then I hear a woman's voice.

"Luc," she says. "Luc," she repeats. It sounds very much like Burke's voice, but...well, she never uses my Christian name—"Luc." I am always "Moncrief" to her. She is always "K. Burke" to me.

"Luc," again. Yes, it is Burke speaking. I open my eyes. I turn my head toward her. I understand. With Julien and the driver here she will be using my first name. I smile and say, "Yes. What is it . . . Katherine?"

"Monsieur Carpentier asked you a question."

"I'm sorry. I must have dozed off," I say.

"Understandable. The jet lag. The long flight. The sadness," says Julien. "I merely wanted to know if you cared to stop and refresh yourselves at your father's house before we go to the *pompes funèbres* to view your father's body."

I have already told Burke that we would be staying at my father's huge house on rue de Montaigne, rather than my own apartment in the Marais. Burke knows the reason: I cannot go back to my own place, the apartment where I spent so many joyful days and nights with Dalia.

"Yes, I *do* want to go to the house," I say. "A bath, a change of clothes, an icy bottle of Perrier. Is that all right with you, *Katherine?*"

K. Burke realizes that I am having entirely too much fun saying her name.

"That's just perfect for me, *Luc.*"

"So, Julien," I say. "That's the plan. Perhaps we can allot a few hours for that, but then... well, I think we can hold off on the viewing of the body..."

I pause and suppress the urge to add, *"My father will not be going anywhere."*

"I see," says Julien. "I just thought that you would..."

I speak now matter-of-factly, not arrogantly, not unpleasantly.

"Would this perhaps be a better expenditure of time instead to meet with Valex attorneys, get a bit of a head start on the legal work?" I ask.

"You're in charge, Luc," says Julien, but his voice does not ring with sincerity.

"Thank you," I say. "What I'd like you to do is assemble my father's legal staff. Invite Babette, of course. We can meet in my father's private library on the third floor. I am sure there are many matters they have to discuss with me. Ask anyone else who should be there to please be there. Only necessary people—division presidents, department heads. This may also be a convenient time to reveal the main points of the will."

Julien is furiously tapping these instructions into his iPad. I have one final thought.

"The important personages who are not here for the funeral—North America, A-Pac, Africa—Skype them in."

I am finished talking, but then K. Burke speaks up.

"What about other family members, Luc?" she asks.

There is a pause. Then Julien speaks.

"Luc is the only living family member."

"As I may have mentioned, *Katherine,* my father had two daughters and a son out of wedlock. I never met them. The girls are younger than I. The boy is a bit older. But arrangements have been made. Correct, Julien?"

"Correct. The lawyers settled trust funds upon them years ago," he says. He nods, but there is no complicit smile attached to the statement. "They have been dealt with quite a while ago."

Meanwhile Julien continues to tap away at his iPad. The car is now closing in on Central Paris. Julien looks up and speaks again.

"I have texted the IT staff. They are on their way to the house now. They will set up Skype and two video cameras, a backup generator...the whole thing."

"What about sleeping arrangements?" I ask. I look to see if there is a change of expression on Julien's face. Nothing.

"All the bedrooms are made up. You may, of course, do what you wish," says Julien.

"What I wish is for Mademoiselle Burke to have my old bedroom. It is quite large. It has a pleasant sitting room, and it looks out over the Avenue."

I look at Burke and add, "You will like it."

"I'm sure," she says.

"As for me, I will sleep in the *salon d'été.*" The summer

room. It is spacious and well ventilated and close to my father's library. It was where I always slept during the summer months when I was a child. It is no longer summer. And I am no longer a child. But I can forget both those facts.

"Very well, Luc. As you wish. I will have a Call button installed, so you can summon a maid if you need one," Julien says as he flicks his iPad back on.

"Thank you," I say. "But that won't be necessary. I doubt if I'll have any need to summon a maid."

Julien smiles and speaks.

"As you wish, my friend."

CHAPTER 31

BABETTE ENTERS THE LIBRARY. She is dressed entirely in black, the whole mourning costume—stockings, gloves, even *une petit chapeau avec un voile*. Drama and fashion are her two passions, so my father's funeral is a glorious opportunity to indulge those interests.

"*Luc. Mon petit Luc,*" she says loudly. She embraces me. She flips the short black veil from her forehead. Then she kisses me on both my cheeks. She is not an exaggerated comic character. She is, however, one of those French women trained to behave a certain way—formal, slightly over-the-top, unashamed.

She keeps talking.

"*Mon triste petit bébé.*"

"I will agree to be your *bébé*, Babette, but not your 'sad little baby.'"

She ignores what I say and moves on to a subject that will interest her.

"And this, of course, must be the very important police partner, Mademoiselle Katherine Burke of New York City."

"I'm delighted to meet you, Mademoiselle Babette," says K. Burke.

Detective Burke extends her hand to shake, but Babette has a different idea. She goes in for the double-cheek kiss.

The attorneys are arranging stacks of papers on the long marble table in the center of the room. Two of the housemaids, along with my father's butler, Carl, are arranging chairs facing that table. Three rows of authentic Louis XV chairs. We will be like an audience at a chamber music recital.

The attorneys introduce themselves to me. They extend their sympathies on "the loss of this magnificent man, your father." "He was one of the greats, the last of his kind."

One of the attorneys, Patrice LaFleur, the oldest person in the room, the only attorney I actually know, asks me if I would like to join him and his colleagues at the library table. I decline.

The doors to the book-lined room remain open. Well-dressed men and women enter and take seats.

"They are employees of Valex, important employees," Julien says.

Some of them smile at me. Some give a tiny bow.

"I'm a New York City cop, Julien. I'm not accustomed to such respect."

Julien Carpentier takes me by the shoulders. He looks directly into my eyes. He moves his head uncomfortably closer to mine. He speaks.

"This is a gigantic company. Sixteen offices. Twelve factories. Valex manufactures everything from antacids to cancer drugs. Thousands of people are dependent on Valex for their employment, hundreds of thousands are dependent on Valex for their health. You are their boss's son. *Allow* them to respect you."

I am a little nervous. I am a little confused.

"But this is not my company," I say. "It's my father's enterprise."

"But it is your responsibility," Julien says. I want very much to trust his sincerity, to trust Babette. But I have spent so much time in my life listening to the lies of heroin dealers and murderers that I cannot wholly embrace the sincerity of my father's two most trusted employees.

I nod at Julien. He smiles. Then I sit. Front row center. The best seat in the house.

Julien is to my left. K. Burke is to my right.

"What are you thinking, Moncrief?" whispers Burke.

"You know me too well, K. Burke. You can perceive that my instincts are telling me something."

The room is settling down. All is quiet. Burke leans in toward me. She whispers.

"Can you ask the lawyers to hold off for a few minutes, so you and I can talk?"

"No. What you and I have to say can wait."

CHAPTER 32

THE LEAD TRUSTS, wills, and estates attorney is Claude Dupain, a short-nosed, large-eared methodical little man who has devoted his entire life to my father's personal legal matters.

"Good afternoon to the family, friends, and business colleagues of my late, great friend, Luc Paul Moncrief. Monsieur Moncrief's funeral memorial, as you know, will take place tomorrow. Today, however, at the request of his family, we are deposing of Luc's... forgive me... Monsieur Moncrief's will... forgive me once again... I am, of course, referring to Luc Moncrief père, Moncrief the elder. He is the Moncrief I shall be speaking of here.

"In the upcoming months, Monsieur Moncrief's bureau of attorneys will begin the complex filing of all business documents, debt documents, mortgages, and other Valex-related items. As you all know, Monsieur Moncrief paid strict attention to detail. While his death was terribly unexpected, he recently had become... shall we say... somewhat preoccupied with preparations for death. He brought his will and estate planning up to date in the last few weeks. And that recent planning is reflected in what I announce at this gathering.

"I must add that while it will take many months, even years, to honor all legal procedures in company matters, Monsieur Moncrief's wishes in other matters, personal matters and bequests, are quite simple and very clear."

I realize easily what Dupain's legal babble means: Valex is a monstrosity of a company, so it will take a great deal of time to sort out its future. However, my father's personal directions about his estate will be, like my father himself, easy to understand.

Dupain opens a leather portfolio and removes a few pieces of paper. I bow my head. I look down at the floor. The attorney speaks. And, as promised, the information is simple.

Babette will receive a yearly income of 150,000 euros with annual appropriate cost-of-living increases. She will also receive rent-free housing in her current house at Avenue George V. After her death, her heirs will receive the same annual amount for one hundred years.

Julien Carpentier is to continue at his annual salary of 850,000 euros annually. And, subject to the approval of the board of directors, Julien will be named Chairman and CEO of Valex and its subsidiaries.

The American phrase comes to mind again: I could not care less.

There now follows a long list—at least forty names—of disbursements to office personnel and household staff members in Paris, as well as at my father's London house, his château in Normandy, his house in Portofino, and—a stunning surprise to me—his apartment at 850 Fifth Avenue in New York.

The amounts of the disbursements are generous, excessive by traditional standards. Housemaids will be able to stop scrubbing and dusting. Butlers will retire to Cannes. Gardeners will become country squires. Frankly, I am delighted for all of them.

After the listing of the bequeathals to the staff members, Dupain dabs at his forehead with a handkerchief. An assistant presents him with a large glass of ice water. He drinks the water in one long gulp. Then he says, "There is but one item left. I shall read it directly from Monsieur Moncrief's testament."

Dupain removes a single paper from yet another leather envelope. He reads:

"To my son, Luc Paul Moncrief, I leave all my homes and household goods, all attachments to those homes and household goods, all real estate, all attachments to that real estate. I further leave to him all monies and investments that I may own or control.

"*With the following stipulation:* After assigning this distribution to my son Luc Paul Moncrief, any monies remaining *in excess of three billion euros* will be divided equally among the Luc and Georgette Moncrief Foundation, the Louvre Museum, the Red Cross of France, and the Museum of Jewish Heritage in the United States."

There is a long pause, a very long pause. It is the kind of pause that comes when you hear that someone has just inherited three billion euros.

My head remains bowed. I continue to stare at the floor. The silence is punctuated by an occasional sob, a smattering of whispering. Finally, Dupain the attorney speaks again.

"I believe that it is now appropriate for the remainder of

this meeting to be conducted, not by me, but by Luc Moncrief the younger."

I hold up my head. But I do not rise from my seat.

"Monsieur Dupain. I think that there is nothing more for me to add to the proceedings. However, I would like to ask a question of you," I say. "And I ask it here in the presence of all assembled, because it has troubled me since I was first informed of my father's death."

"But of course, monsieur."

"Are there police reports *or* medical reports *or* coroner reports *or* any kind of reports available concerning the death of my father?"

Dupain appears startled by the question, but he does not hesitate to answer.

"As you must know, Luc...er...Monsieur Moncrief, your father was a man in his late seventies. He had suffered from heart disease. He was discovered dead at his desk. Of course, there is an official death certificate signed by Doctor Martin Abel of the French Police Department."

"And that is all?" I ask.

"That is all that seemed necessary."

It is then...finally...that I feel my eyes fill with tears.

CHAPTER 33

WHEN I WAS YOUNGER, much younger—ten years old, fifteen years old—I visited magnificent homes of my school friends: huge châteaux in western France, thirty-room hunting lodges in Scotland, outlandishly large London town homes smack in the middle of Belgravia.

Many of these houses had rooms dedicated solely to pastimes like billiards and swimming and cigar-smoking and wine-tasting. Many had entire floors that housed ten to twenty servants. Some of the houses had stables with rooms put aside for tanning saddles and polishing stirrups.

But I had never seen in any other home the sort of room that we had in our house on rue du Montaigne.

Our house had a "silver room."

This room was about the size of a normal family dining room. It had perhaps fifty open shelves. These shelves were loaded with sterling silver serving pieces—everything from finger bowls to soup tureens, asparagus servers to butter pats, charger plates the size of platters, water goblets as ornate as altar chalices. Open bins were neatly filled with stacks of dinnerware assorted into categories like "Cristofle" and "Buccellati" and "Tiffany." Subcategories were sets of silver dinnerware wrapped with red velvet ribbon, each bin marked with a note signifying when the pieces had been used:

1788, one year before the Revolution
1872, one year after the ending of the Franco-Prussian War
1943, a dinner for General Eisenhower and his secretary, Kay Summersby
Babette, Birthday
Luc, Partie de Baptême

In the middle of the room is a simple pine table. It can easily seat eight butlers to polish and buff silver. It can also seat eight people for a party.

This early evening it seats only K. Burke and myself.

We sit facing each other. We sip a St. Emilion. The wine's château and vineyard names mean little to me and nothing to K. Burke.

Our moods are...well, I can only speak for me. I am slightly touched now with sadness, and yet I am happy that the process of the will has ended. Tomorrow is the funeral to get through, but then—after perhaps a day or two of shopping and museum-hopping—we will return to our favorite pastime—NYPD detective work.

We ignore the fruit and cheeses and charcuterie that the kitchen has assembled for us. We drink our wine.

Finally, Burke speaks.

"I see the newspaper headline now," Burke says. "Luc Moncrief, the Gloomiest Billionaire on Earth. Sob. Sob. Sob."

"K. Burke, surely you, of all people, are smart enough to know that a great big pot full of money does not make a person happy. Too many people in my position have jumped from skyscrapers, overdosed on drugs, murdered their lovers, died alone…money is a fine thing, especially if you do not have it, but it guarantees nothing other than money."

"Skip the lecture, Moncrief. Of course I know all that. And I also know that your heart was broken into pieces when Dalia died. There's no amount in the world—no money, no work of art, no beautiful woman—who can repair that."

A pause, and then I say, "It is because of that wisdom that you and I are such fine friends."

"So, what's the problem, Moncrief? Is it just that your father has been good to you in death and that you wish that he had…"

"No. No. It is not the usual, not the obvious."

I decide to be blunt. I speak.

"I believe that my father was murdered."

Burke does not flinch. She barely reacts. Her eyes do not pop open. Her jaw does not drop. If anything she is a woman acting as if she's heard a very interesting piece of casual gossip.

"Hence, your one and only question to the attorney. The question about the doctor's report," she says.

"Of course. I knew you would deduce that."

"What makes you believe that…other than your impeccable instinct?" she asks.

"Sarcasm does not flatter you, K. Burke." I pause. Then I say, "Yes, it is my instinct, of course. But there are two small issues. *One,* my father was a man of great importance and great wealth. You know that the newspapers and political blogs referred to him as *le vrai président,* the real president. Surely the police and detectives would require an autopsy or some sort of medical investigation to assure that there was no foul play. That would be done for a cabinet minister or an ambassador's wife. But it was not done for one of the most important men in France? *Ridicule!*"

K. Burke takes a long gulp of her wine. She nods, but she says nothing. I have something else to add.

"Now, another thing, something perhaps a bit subtler, but not to be overlooked: Julien Carpentier mentioned innumerable times that my father died of a heart attack, that my father had heart disease, that my father passed painlessly because of the speed of his heart attack. How many times was it necessary to tell us that? Likewise, from Babette's very first phone call to me in the States, she too kept insisting that it was a heart attack, a heart attack, a heart attack. Dupain the attorney mentioned it....Why so much attention to this? Yes, surely he may very well have died from a heart attack, but is it necessary to mention it so many times?"

I pour us more wine. Then Detective Burke lifts her purse from the floor. It is her big black leather satchel of a purse. She unzips the bag and puts her hand inside. She retrieves a business-sized envelope. It is cream-colored. It looks like fine heavyweight paper.

Burke hands the envelope to me. On the reverse side,

just below my father's engraved initials, the envelope is held closed by a bit of red sealing wax.

"I found this envelope where I am staying, in your bedroom. It was leaning against the bronze inkstand on your desk. The envelope was meant to be discovered," she says.

I flip the envelope over. There, in my father's precise handwriting, are these words: *à mon fils*. To my son.

I grab a dinner knife from one of the bins. Then I slit the envelope open. I read the letter aloud.

My Dear Luc,

This letter assumes that you are now in Paris for my funeral, that you are in our house, in your former bedroom.

Here is what I wish you to know.

In April I received word from Julien Carpentier that our most important new product—Prezinol, a breakthrough treatment for childhood diabetes—was facing serious problems. Prezinol was to be my last great achievement. Valex had worked on it for decades.

Then this awful news arrived. Thirty percent of three hundred juvenile test volunteers in Warsaw suffered a dreadful reaction to the drug—kidney failure or stage one cancer of the liver.

Julien immediately (and without consulting me) dispatched a team of doctors to Poland. By the time Julien involved me in the matter, the doctors reported back that the kidney and liver damage were irreversible. They advised that we stop all testing immediately, and that we cancel our plans for a similar test in São Paulo.

I disagreed with this strategy. I could not allow Prezinol to fail. I posited that we might receive different results in São Paulo. I also knew from experience that it would take the Polish bureau of health a few months to take action against Valex.

I instructed Julien to proceed with everything as planned. He refused. In fact, he accused me of being—and I quote— "a senile old devil." He said that my entire life was driven by greed and ego.

The fact is this: Julien was correct. I realized the truth of his observation. It is one that you yourself had sometimes made.

That evening I instructed Julien to stop all testing in Warsaw, to cancel plans for the testing in São Paulo, and to arrange significant compensation for the Polish children who suffered such unspeakable damage.

I then considered what else I might do to compensate for my history of abhorrent behavior. Sadly I realized that there was no suitable punishment.

I realized I was just another old man with arthritis and heart disease. My financial success was everything and nothing.

I decided to address my situation as follows.

First, to name Julien as my successor at Valex. Julien has the skills and moral fiber to act in a way that will allow Valex to create pharmaceuticals that will advance worldwide health.

Second, to leave to you the vast portion of my wealth. Out of guilt certainly for my years of paternal neglect, but also because you will use my fortune not merely to live well, but to live wisely.

Finally, to have delivered to me a shipment of fifty capsules of Prezinol.

My dear Luc, more than anything, I wish you the love I kept locked in my heart.

Votre père

CHAPTER 34

THE SONGWRITER WAS wrong when he wrote the lyrics that said he even loved "Paris in the winter, when it drizzles." I tell this to K. Burke as she and I walk the Boulevard Haussmann toward the enormous shopping cathedral known as Galeries Lafayette, after my father's funeral.

"The drizzle, it even gets through the finest wool coat," I complain.

"You should wear a good puffy ski jacket like mine," says Burke.

"I would rather wear a circus clown costume than a ski jacket."

"Say what you want, but I'm warm and dry, and you're cold and wet."

The morning had been a blur, but it was a mercifully short, respectful service with no gathering after. Except that I called Julien and Babette to meet with us. We ate homemade breakfast brioche and discussed my father's suicide.

Julien and Babette readily admitted that they knew the *full* story, and, yes, they had been complicit in hiding the method from me. They swore that they were going to tell me the truth and to put that truth "in context." That my father was suffering from advanced heart disease, that the children's diabetes drug had caused grave damage to many in the test group, that my father had, in fact, ended his own life by taking more than four dozen Prezinol capsules.

"We merely wanted to get through the funeral, Luc. With so many business matters and the will, it seemed like the right thing," Julien said. "I am sorry if we miscalculated."

I was inclined to believe him. I still am. You see, the simple truth is: What difference does it make? We move on. My father is gone. Babette is a sad old lady. Julien is set for a lifetime of overwhelming work. We move on. At least we try.

As for me, I am and will always be without my beloved Dalia. To have a death that meaningful in your life is to always have the tiniest cloud over even the greatest joy. My police work may fascinate me. Good friends like Burke will support me. France may win the World Cup. I may sip a magnificent Romanée-Conti. I may even fall in love again. Even that I cannot rule out. But: no matter. Dalia will not be here with me.

K. Burke and I continue our walk. Now we are within a block of the Galeries Lafayette. Christmas lights hang from the chestnut trees. Candles sit shining in the shop windows.

"You know, Moncrief. You're a real Frenchman," she says.

"Did you ever doubt it?" I ask.

"No. Here's why: you do what many Frenchmen do. I noticed. You don't walk. You *stroll*. Long strides, a little hip swing, head back. You're like a little cartoon of a French guy."

"There's a compliment hidden somewhere in those words, K. Burke. I just haven't found it yet."

So we stroll. We approach the Haussmann entrance to the store. Burke asks that we pause for a moment. We do, and she says, "So, you were right. Your instincts were true. Your father was murdered."

"But, of course not, K. Burke. Not murder. My father committed suicide."

"I guess, but…" she says. "He was a murderer who… murdered himself."

I tell Burke how I feel. That sometimes I believe his suicide was an old-fashioned noble gesture; that he had committed sins that could never be forgiven. So, *poof.* He punished himself.

"But then," I tell her, "I think he was an old-fashioned coward. The mere thought of *earthly* punishment—jail, humiliation—told him to escape. He up and left us. He left Babette, a woman who loved him. He left Julien, a young man who idolized him. And he left me, his son, the boy he barely knew, the man he *never* knew."

We walk inside the gilded department store. It looks like a Christmas tree turned upside down. Sparkle and glitter and thirty-feet-high gift boxes suspended from the vaulted ceiling. Burke looks upward, her neck stretching backward, as if she were standing in the Sistine Chapel. Her mouth literally opens in awe. The Christmas shoppers crowd the floor.

Then she says, "Let's start shopping before you start wanting to move on. I want to buy a few things to take back."

"I can assure you, K. Burke, there is almost nothing worth purchasing here."

"Well, thanks for the advice, Moncrief. But I think I'm about to prove that statement wrong."

I limit her, however, to one hour. In that short time she purchases a green Mark Cross Villa Tote bag, a pair of real silk stockings (the sort that also requires her to buy simple but quite intriguing garters), two tiny bronze replicas of the Arc de Triomphe (*"Vous touriste!"* I tell her), and four silk scarves (blue for her cousin Sandi, red for her cousin Elyce, yellow for her cousin Maddy, white for her cousin Marilyn). The scarves are my treat. I insist.

I also came out of the store with a purchase of my own. A five-pound tenderloin of venison.

"I shall give this venison to my father's cook, Reynaud, and you shall feast in a way you never have before."

"I'll say that it was interesting being in a butcher store inside a department store. But really . . . venison? Deer meat?"

"What is so odd about that?" I ask.

"I can tell you in one word: Bambi."

CHAPTER 35

I MUST ADMIT the truth: I am enjoying my day with K. Burke.

She is constantly refreshing, authentic. She has a complete honesty to her behavior. On the job she is not always charming, but here she always is. Burke is like a provincial schoolgirl on her first trip to Paris—wide-eyed and enthusiastic, but never irritating or vulgar. Burke has the purity that I have experienced in one other woman.

"We are going someplace really special now," I say.

"Galeries Lafayette was special enough for me," she says.

"Cease the humility, K. Burke. Where we are going next is...is almost..."

"*Incroyable?*"

"*Oui.* Almost unbelievable."

"It is only a short walk. It is on the Place Vendôme. But the drizzle is still drizzling. I'll try to get us a taxi."

"No, we'll walk," she says.

"But the rain. It is cold. It is icy."

"We'll walk."

So we walk, and I try to remember not to "stroll." K. Burke can't get enough of the Parisian excitement. Her head seems as if it's attached to a well-oiled fulcrum that allows her to snap her eyes from side to side in only a second.

We pass the furriers and jewelers and even the occasional hat store on our walk. Then, in front of a chocolate shop, of all places, I make a grave error.

"If there's anything you want, just say so, and we can get it," I say.

She stops walking. The smile leaves her face, and her head remains motionless.

"I don't want you to buy me anything . . . anything. I shouldn't have let you buy those expensive scarves for my cousins. I don't want *things*. Frankly, if you want to give me something, do it by giving *yourself* a gift . . . the gift of joy, some peace. What would truly make me happy is for you to be happy."

She brushes her cheeks with her hand, and I cannot be sure whether she is brushing away tears or merely brushing away the icy drizzle.

"You are a true friend, K. Burke," I say.

"I try to be," she says, her voice choking just a bit. "But it's hard to be a friend to a lucky man who has had some very bad luck."

"You are doing just fine," I say.

We continue our walk.

We are about to turn onto the Place Vendôme when she says, "By the way, Moncrief, you can stroll if you want to."

"I am walking slow because I am contemplating a problem," I say.

Burke looks nervous, serious.

"What's the matter?" she says.

"I have a problem that only you can solve."

"And that is?"

"That is this: we are going to a place where I had planned on purchasing you a combination Christmas–New Years–Friendship–Thank You gift. And now you say…" (I do a comic imitation of an angry woman) *"I don't want you to buy me anything!"*

"That's the problem?" she says.

"For me, that is a problem. Can you solve it?"

"Okay, *mon ami*. You may buy me one more thing. Just one. And then that's it."

CHAPTER 36

THE FLAG THAT is pinned over the doorway is not too big, not too small. It is surely not an elegant sign, although the small building itself is a beautifully designed nineteenth-century town house. The sign is wet from the rain, so it is wrinkled in many spots. Dark-purple letters—only three letters—are printed against a white background.

JAR

Quite logically K. Burke says, "Is it a store that sells jars? Or do the letters stand for something?"

"The letters stand for something," I say. "It is a man's name. Joel Arthur Rosenthal. He is the finest jeweler in the world, and, not surprisingly, he is here in Paris."

"Moncrief, when I said one more gift, I did not say jewelry. This is out of the question. I'm not going to allow..."

I put an index finger gently on her lips.

"I am going to ring the bell. I have an appointment. Let's try to keep our voices down."

Within seconds we are greeted by a very handsome young man in gray slacks and a blue blazer. We exchange greetings in French, and then I introduce him to Detective Burke.

"*Mademoiselle Katherine Burke, je voudrais vous presenter Richard Ranftle,* the assistant to Monsieur Rosenthal."

"*Je suis enchanté, Mademoiselle.* I am also very much admiring of your coat. The North Face ski jacket has become everyone's favorite."

"*Merci,* Richard," Burke says. Then she smiles at me.

"Monsieur Rosenthal regrets that he is not here to assist the both of you, but your phone call came only this morning, Monsieur Moncrief, and Monsieur Rosenthal had already left for his home in Morocco. He likes to escape Paris during the Christmas season."

A maid enters. She is dressed in full maid regalia—starched white cap, black dress, starched white apron with ruffle.

She asks if we would like tea or coffee or wine.

We decline.

"Perhaps some champagne," says Richard.

We decline again.

We follow Richard a few steps into what looks like the parlor of a small elegant apartment on the rue du Faubourg Saint-Honoré. A two-seat sofa in gray. A few mid-century wooden chairs with darker gray seats. A very bright crystal chandelier in the center of the ceiling. The only thing that distinguishes the room from a private residence are the four glass jewelry showcases.

Katherine Burke runs her hands along the glass enclosures. I watch her closely. We both seem to be nearly overwhelmed by the beauty of the jewels. Not merely the size of the diamonds but the unusual designs of the bracelets and earrings and necklaces and rings.

"I know very little about jewelry, and it has been a few years since I have visited here, but these stones all seem to be enormous," I say.

"Joel...er, Monsieur Rosenthal, likes to work on a large canvas. You see, even when he uses small stones, as in a pavé setting, he sets them so close to one another that they look like a wall of diamonds."

He points, as an example, to a ring with something called an "apricot" diamond at its center. The tiny diamonds around it look like a starry night.

Richard Ranftle shows us something called a "thread ring." If there were a piece of sewing thread composed of tiny diamonds, then flung into the air, then eventually landing in a messy heap, it would be this enormous ring. For good luck, Rosenthal seems to have decided that a very large amethyst should sit on top of this pile of extraordinary thread.

"Mademoiselle seems most interested in the rings, eh?" says Richard.

I note with amusement that Richard has perfected an amazing style. He is helpful without being condescending. He is courteous without being obnoxious. We are three people having fun. Million-dollar fun, but fun nonetheless.

Burke is slightly stoned, I think, on the jewelry on display.

"Look at that," she says, and she points to an enormous round green stone.

Richard immediately goes to work.

"It is a twelve-carat emerald. Monsieur Rosenthal was inspired to set the stone upside down. Then he surrounded it with a platinum and garnet rope. It is beyond nontraditional. He says it looks like 'a turtle from paradise.'"

Richard removes the ring from the glass case. He places it on a dark-purple velvet tray.

"Let me slip it onto your middle finger," says Richard. Then he pauses and says, "Unless you would care to do so, Monsieur Moncrief."

"No, no. Go right ahead," I say.

"My God," says Burke. "This is about the same size as my Toyota Camry."

"If you like, then, you can drive it out of the showroom," says Richard. We all smile.

She looks at the ring. She holds up her hand.

"I wish you'd told me we were coming here, Moncrief. I would have given myself a manicure."

The ring looks spectacular, huge and spectacular, beautiful and spectacular. I tell Burke to take it. She says, "Oh, no." I insist. She insists no. I say that it's a Christmas gift. She says this is ridiculous. I tell her that she promised I would be allowed to give her "just one gift." Then as an extra argument I say something that is probably not even true: "Look, Detective, how expensive can it be? It's only an emerald, not even a diamond."

For about three minutes the room remains completely silent. I do not know what is going through her head, of course. But when she finally speaks, she says, "Okay."

I smile. She smiles. Richard smiles. Richard hands me a

small blue paper on which is written: "540,000 EU." I slip the paper into the wet pocket of my coat, and I continue to smile.

And that is how Detective Katherine Burke came to own the ring that came to be called "The Emerald Turtle."

CHAPTER 37

CHRISTMAS DAY IN PARIS is for family. Grand-père carving the goose. Grand-mère snoring from too much Rémy Martin. It is a day for children and chocolate.

I will not violate the spirit of the feast. Indeed, Reynaud, my late father's exceptional chef, will roast the tenderloin of venison. I have invited Babette and Julien and Julien's girlfriend, Anne. (Who knew Julien had a girlfriend? Who knew Julien had a life apart from Valex?)

So that will be Christmas Day. For Christmas Eve, however, I have made a special plan. Burke and I will have a night of fine dining.

"It will be a night perfect for wearing 'The Emerald Turtle,'" I say.

"I'm so nervous wearing it," says Burke. "If I lose it ... if ..."

"If you lose it, there are plenty more emeralds in the world," I say. "And if I sound like a spoiled rich kid, so be it. I am. At least for Christmas."

"I'm still nervous."

But, of course, she wears it.

The evening begins with—what else?—chilled Dom Pérignon in the warm and cozy backseat of the limo.

"Our first stop will be Les Ambassadeurs inside the Hôtel de Crillon," I tell K. Burke.

"Our *first* stop?" says Burke.

"*Oui*. The first course of seven courses," I say. "A different course at a different restaurant. I can imagine no finer way to welcome Christmas. This took much planning on my part."

We arrive at the Place de la Concorde. Five minutes later we are tasting artichoke soup with black truffle shavings. Exceptional.

Fifteen minutes later we are back in the car and headed for *le poisson,* the fish course. At L'Arpège my friend, Alain Passard, has prepared his three-hour turbot with green apples.

Just when we think nothing can surpass the turbot we move on to Lasserre. Here the magical dish is a delicate pigeon with a warm fig and hazelnut compote.

The maître d' at George V's Le Cinq describes a dish that both Burke and I think is ridiculous—a seaweed consommé with bits of turnip, parsnip, and golden beets floating on top. It is, of course, magnificent.

When we return to the car Burke announces, "I don't know how to say this properly. But I am full without really being full."

"You are *satisfied,*" I say. "Small portions of exquisite food. The French never fill themselves. They eat. They think. They enjoy."

"Sure. That's it exactly," says K. Burke. Then, with a giggle in her voice, she says, "A bit more champagne, please."

The first four restaurants we have visited are classic Parisian restaurants. They have been filling famous bellies for many years—royalty and food writers and a few pretentious snobs. But always the food has remained magnificent.

"Now we are going to have something completely modern," I tell my dining companion. "We are going to one of the famous new places that I call 'mish-mash-mosh' restaurants. You don't know whether you are eating Indian or French or Hungarian or Cambodian food. The classical chefs turn in their graves, but it is the future, and we must try one of them."

So Burke and I, a little tipsy from champagne and wine, sit at Le Chateaubriand, a fancy French name for a restaurant that looks like a 1950s American diner. The duck breast we are served is covered with fennel seeds and bits of… "What is this?" I ask the captain. He replies, "Tiny pieces of orange candy." This fabulous concoction sits next to a purée of strawberries that tastes a little bit of maple syrup, a little bit of tangerine.

K. Burke describes it perfectly: "It tastes like something wonderful, like something you'd get at a carnival in heaven."

"You have the vocabulary of a restaurant critic, K. Burke," I say.

We leave the heavenly carnival, and a short time later we are at Le Jules Verne, the foolishly named restaurant on top of the beloved *tour Eiffel*.

The alcohol is making me too happy, too giddy, and surely too talkative. "This is a restaurant that has maintained its integrity, even though it is in the very tourist heart of Paris," I say.

"I'm not ashamed to be a tourist," says Burke.

"Nor am I," I say. Then we sit down and look out at

the marvel of Paris at night while we eat an impeccable piece of filet mignon—big beefy flavor in every meltingly tender bite.

"And now. On to dessert," I say.

"I should say 'I couldn't.' But the truth is...I could," Burke says.

"We will finish at my favorite place in all of Paris," I say. Soon our car is making its way through the narrow streets of the Marais.

All the chic little shops are closed. A small kosher restaurant is shutting down for the evening. "The best hummus in Europe," I say.

A few students are singing Christmas songs. They swig from open bottles of wine. Lights twinkle from many windows.

The car stops at a tiny corner shop on rue Vieille du Temple, very near the rue de Rivoli.

Burke reads the sign on the shop aloud, "Amorino." Then she says, "Whatever it is, it looks closed."

"*Un moment*," I say, and I hit a few numbers on my phone. "*Nous sommes ici.*" We are here. A young woman appears at the shop door. She is smiling. She gestures to us. We go inside.

"It's an ice cream parlor," Burke says.

"Yes and no. It is a gelato shop. When I lived in Paris— before moving to New York—no evening was complete unless we had a two-scoop chocolate and amaretto cone at Amorino. What flavors do you like? The pistachio is magnificent."

She looks away from me. When she faces me again she is blinking her eyes.

"Would you think I'm rude if I skip the gelato?" she says.

"But you would love it," I say.

"It's been a great evening. I appreciate it. I really do," she says. "But I've had enough."

Then it hits my thoughtless French brain. Suddenly, as if a big rock fell on my stupid little head.

"Oh, K. Burke. I am sorry. I am awful and stupid. I am sorry."

"You have nothing to be sorry about," she says. "It was a wonderful night. It is a beautiful ring. This is the nicest Christmas I've ever had."

Then I find the courage to say what I should say.

"Forgive me, Katherine. I gave you a night of glamour without the romance that should accompany it. Forgive me."

She smiles at me.

"There's nothing to forgive, Moncrief. You're terrific. You're the best friend I've ever had."

EPILOGUE

IF I REALLY wanted to stretch the truth, I could say that my partner K. Burke and I are spending New Year's Eve at the Plaza Hotel. But as I say, that would be stretching the truth. A lot.

The fact is, the two of us are spending New Year's Eve in the underground loading alley under the kitchens of the Plaza Hotel.

It seems that our boss, Inspector Nick Elliott, wanted to bring us back to reality after our time in Paris. So Burke and I are on a drug stakeout in the repugnant, disgusting garbage zone beneath the fancy hotel. We are waiting for a potential "chalk drop." That's cop-talk for a major delivery of methamphetamine, a fairly wicked drug for some of the New Year's Eve revelers.

The smell of garbage, the whip of the winter wind, and the knowledge that most of New York is dancing the night away does nothing to relieve our boredom. And as with most stakeouts, the boredom is excruciating.

"So this is how it goes, right, Moncrief?" Burke says. "A

week ago we were on top of the Eiffel Tower. Tonight we're in a hole under the Plaza."

I laugh and say, "That's life. Even for a rich kid." I pause for a moment as I watch a rat scurry past us. Then I say, "You know, K. Burke, the truth is, I am enjoying this surveillance routine almost as much as—but not *quite* as much as—our Christmas Eve in Paris. Simply put, I love doing detective work. Can you believe that?"

She does not hesitate. She says, "Yes, Moncrief. I can believe that."

Before I can even smile there is a great eruption of firecrackers and noisemakers and the noise of people shouting with joy.

"Listen closely, Moncrief. You can hear the music," Burke says.

She is right. From somewhere inside the hotel the orchestra is playing "Auld Lang Syne."

I lean in and kiss her on her cheek.

"Happy New Year, K. Burke," I say.

She leans in and kisses me on *my* cheek.

She speaks.

"Happy New Year, my friend."

FRENCH TWIST

JAMES PATTERSON
AND RICHARD DiLALLO

CHAPTER 1

"I HAVE ABSOLUTELY NO appetite! Absolutely none! So don't waste your money, Moncrief!"

This is Katherine Burke speaking. K. Burke is my NYPD detective partner and she is furious with me. This is not an unusual state of affairs between us.

"We're supposed to be on the job, and instead we're sitting in this ridiculously fancy restaurant having a thousand-dollar lunch," she says.

"But you have never tasted anything so magnificent as the oyster and pearls appetizer served here at Per Se," I say.

I raise a small spoonful of the appetizer and move it toward her.

"White sturgeon caviar, icy just-shucked oysters, a dollop of sweet tapioca and…"

"Get that food away from me," she says. "I am way too angry to eat."

"But I am not," I say, and I pop the spoonful into my mouth and put an exaggerated expression of ecstasy on my face.

Don't get the wrong impression. K. Burke and I are great

friends *and* a great detective team. Our methods, however, are very different. Burke is a tough native New Yorker. She plays by the book—strict procedure, always sticking to the rules. I, on the other hand, believe in going with my instinct—feelings, intuition. By the way, I am a native Frenchman, Luc Moncrief.

These different approaches lead to occasional disagreements. They also enable solutions to very tough cases.

I eat my appetizer in absolute silence. Then I say, "If you're not going to eat yours…"

She pulls the plate back toward herself and takes a bite. If a woman is able to chew angrily, then K. Burke chews angrily. In a few seconds, however, her mood transforms into peacefulness.

"This time you are pushing things too far. It's almost three o'clock. We should not be sitting here still having lunch."

"K. Burke, please, if you will. Our assignment is completed. And I must remind you that it was an assignment that amounted to absolutely nothing. A complete waste of time. In any event, we did what we were told to do. Now we should enjoy ourselves."

I signal the waiter to pour us each some more Bâtard-Montrachet.

I am, by the way, telling K. Burke the absolute truth about the assignment. And she knows it. Here is how it all went down…

Per the instructions of our boss, Nick Elliott, we arrived at Pier 94 on 54th Street and the Hudson River at 5 a.m. Let me repeat the time. Five a.m.! When I was a young man in Paris, 5 a.m. was when the evening ended.

In any event, Inspector Elliott said that he had unimpeachable, impeccable, irreproachable information that the stolen parts of rare 1950s-era American automobiles—Nash Ramblers, Packards, Studebakers—were being shipped to collectors worldwide, ingeniously smuggled into supply boxes for cruise ships at the 54th Street shipping pier.

We arrived (at 5 a.m.!) with detectives from Arts and Antiquities, four officers from the New York Motor Vehicles Bureau, and three NYPD officers with .38 Special handguns.

Beginning at 6 a.m. the officers, using crowbars and electric chainsaws, began uncrating large wooden boxes that were about to be loaded on board. Or, as K. Burke informed me, "laded on board." Apparently her second cousin was a longshoreman. K. Burke is full of revelations.

To no one's complete surprise, the crates marked "Steinway & Sons" contained pianos. The crates marked "Seagram's" contained whiskey. The crates marked "Frozen Ostrich Meat" contained...you guessed it.

By eleven o'clock we had uncovered properly tax-receipted crates of video games, mattresses, antacids, bolts of silk, *but* no automotive parts.

At noon I texted Nick Elliott and told him that we discovered nothing.

He texted back an infuriating, Are you sure?

I refused to answer the insulting question. So Detective Burke texted back, Yes, Moncrief is sure.

While Burke was texting Elliott, I was texting Per Se, making a lunch reservation. And that is where we now sit.

"You always make me sound like a hard-ass workaholic, Moncrief," Burke says.

"Hard-ass?" I say. "I think not. A little difficult. A little stubborn. But not a hard-ass. You are a woman, and because you are a woman..."

"Don't you dare say anything vulgar or sexist, Moncrief. I swear I'll report you to NYPD Internal Affairs."

"But I never say anything vulgar or sexist," I say.

Burke squints for a moment, puts down her salad fork, then says, "You know something? Come to think of it, you never do. I apologize."

"*Ce n'est rien.* It's nothing."

Burke lets a small smile sneak on to her face. We're aligned again. And that's truly important. Her friendship means the world to me. I've had a very bad year, to say the least. My beloved girlfriend, Dalia, died, and I was left with an impossibly broken heart. Shortly after Dalia's death my *not* very beloved father died. This left me with an obscenely large inheritance, but a great sum of money did nothing to repair my heart. Only my friend and partner K. Burke kept me sane through all of it.

Two waiters now swoop in and lift our empty appetizer plates from the table. Almost immediately two different waiters swoop in with our main course of butter-poached sable with a mission fig jam. The sable is accompanied by toasted hazelnuts and...

K. Burke's cell phone rings.

"I asked you to turn off that foolish machine," I say.

"Yes, you did, and I told you that I would not."

She looks at her phone. Then she looks at me.

"We are wanted at 754 Fifth Avenue," she says.

"Bergdorf Goodman, the store for rich women," I say.

"You got it."

"Well, we cannot leave before we are served our main course."

"Yes, we can. There's a dead woman in a dressing room at Bergdorf Goodman. Inspector Elliott will meet us there in fifteen minutes."

I toss my napkin onto the table.

"I know we cannot decline the job, K. Burke. But I am disappointed," I say.

She stands at her chair and speaks.

"Why not ask the waiter for *le petit sac pour emporter les restes*?"

"This is a French expression that *you* know and that I do not," I say.

She smiles broadly.

"Translation: a doggy bag."

CHAPTER 2

THE VERY EFFICIENT K. Burke calls for a squad car as I sign my Per Se house account receipt. The police car speeds us along Central Park South. In five minutes we are at Bergdorf Goodman.

We exit the squad car, and we both immediately realize that something very weird is going on. Burke and I are *not* greeted with the usual crime scene madness. There's *nothing* to indicate that a homicide has occurred inside this famous store. *No* flashing lights, *no* zigzag of yellow DO NOT CROSS POLICE LINE tape, *no* police officers holding back a curious crowd.

"What the hell is going on here?" Burke asks. "It looks so...so...not like a crime scene."

For a second I think we may have the wrong location. As if she could read my mind, Burke says, "I know this is the right place. But...let's go in and see."

Inside, the same thing. A busy day for the wealthy. Everything is calm and beautiful. Elegant women and an occasional man examine five-thousand-dollar handbags, perfumes in crystal bottles, costume jewelry as expensive as the real thing.

Our boss, Nick Elliott, is waiting right inside the entrance for us.

Elliott looks serious and concerned. His greeting is typical: "You two are finally here." Then he gets right to the point.

"Before I take you upstairs I've got to tell you something. This scene plays out like a typical natural death. A twenty-five-year-old woman, name of Tessa Fulbright, suddenly drops dead in a dressing room. Maybe a heart attack or a drug OD or a brain aneurysm. But it's not. It's a shitload bigger than that."

Elliott says that he'll give us the most important details upstairs in a few minutes.

"They gave me details in the car on the way over, but nobody thought to mention what floor it's on. Lemme check," Elliott says. He begins to punch into his cell phone. Before he gets the correct floor number, I speak.

"It's the sixth floor," I say.

Almost in perfect unison Elliott and Burke say, "How'd you know that?"

"Floor six has the youthful designer clothing."

They know what I am not going to say: I am remembering the days before Dalia died.

Two minutes later, with a store detective and a floor manager accompanying us, Burke, Elliott, and I are standing in a very large, very lovely dressing room. It is furnished with two armchairs and a small sofa, both of them upholstered in pale purple, the signature color of the store.

One other thing: there is a stunning, beautiful, red-haired young woman lying on the floor. She is wearing a Chloé summer gown with the price tag still attached.

Burke and I kneel and examine the body closely. Other than the dead woman's beauty, there is nothing unusual about her.

"I assume you noticed the tattoo behind the right ear," says Burke.

"The tiny star? We got it," says Elliott. Then he looks down at the deceased, shakes his head, and speaks to the small police staff around him.

"You can take Ms. Fulbright downtown. Don't dare release the body. She belongs to us until I say so."

The medical examiner nods. Then Elliott looks at me and Burke.

"Here's the deal," he says. "In the last two weeks there have been two other deaths *exactly like this one*. The first one was in Saks Fifth Avenue, ten blocks away."

Elliott explains that a twenty-three-year-old woman, Mara Monahan, died suddenly—literally dropped dead—while she was paying for shoes. Elliott and his teenage daughter were having lunch around the corner at Burger Heaven when the call came in. So after lunch, when Elliott's daughter took off, he went over to Saks to take a quick look-see.

"So this Mara Monahan turns out to be the wife of Clifton Monahan, the congressman from the Upper East Side. Maybe you've seen her picture online or something. This Mara Monahan is a beautiful, I mean *beautiful,* blonde."

"I heard about this," K. Burke says. "The *Post* and *Daily News* were having a field day with their covers. She was beautiful."

I interject. "I was at her table at the gala dinner for the Holy Apostles Soup Kitchen. She was a knockout."

"Could we refocus on the *pertinent parts* of the case, gentlemen?" Burke says.

"Anyway. I figure I'd better make nice to her husband, the congressman. I'll be under a crushing amount of pressure and scrutiny to close this case. So I go see him. He's broken up. Really broken up, I mean. Two days later there's a funeral. I go. Lots of big shots. Cuomo's there, Cardinal Dolan does the service. Over and out. Sad stuff."

But there's one more chapter in Nick Elliott's story. He tells us that the following Monday, almost a week after the Monahan woman dies, a few days before today's date, a second-string Broadway actress dropped dead in one of the only restaurants in New York as expensive as Per Se. It's called Eleven Madison Park, and yes, the woman was young and beautiful and . . .

"Brunette this time," I say.

"No," Elliott says. "This one is blond, also."

One quick glance at Burke, and I can tell that she's pleased that my hunch was wrong.

Elliott explains that this woman is the understudy to the female lead in the latest Broadway smash hit. But, perhaps as a measure in case her acting career doesn't work out, the woman, Jenna Lee Austin, recently married a multimillionaire hedge funder. Elliott also points out that the medical examiner's reports in both deaths show *no* sign of trauma, *no* injuries, or, almost as important, no sign of any foreign substance in the victims' systems, nothing that could indicate a cause of death. And looking at victim number three here, she seems like she's going to match the pattern.

So, NYPD has three young, beautiful, rich women, all of them apparently dead from natural causes, all of them dead in the middle of an ordinary day in three of the fanciest places in Manhattan.

"What do you need us to do?" K. Burke asks.

"Frankly, everything. Hit the computers. Pull all the info on all the women, their husbands, their friends. The first one seemed like a tragedy, the second more suspicious, and now with three—there's obviously some sort of connection. And we don't have one goddamn idea what it is. So I want you two to take over from Banks and Lin, who are working the first two. See them and get caught up."

I nod. Burke gives her typically enthusiastic "Got it, sir."

Elliott says, "I'll see you at the precinct tomorrow."

"A small problem, Inspector," I say. Then Burke jumps in.

"We have one of our rare long weekends. But we can cancel all that and come in to work."

I interrupt her quickly, almost rudely.

"No, we cannot," I say. "Detective Burke seems to have forgotten. We *do* have some plans for the weekend."

K. Burke looks slightly startled, but she is smart enough to know that she'd better trust me on this one.

"Okay," Elliott says. "Bang the hell out of the computers tonight. See what you can find. By Sunday you'll have the ME's report. I'll assume you two will be in on Sunday?"

"But of course," I say.

He nods to the store detective. They both begin to walk toward the elevator. Then Elliott stops for just a moment. His face has the barest trace of a smile. Then he speaks, "Have a good time." God only knows what he is assuming about Burke and me.

Nick Elliott makes his way through the sea of Carolina

Herrera dresses and Stella McCartney jackets. Katherine Burke looks at me. Her eyes narrow slightly.

"Okay, Moncrief. What the hell is going on?"

"What's going on is this: I shall pick you up at your apartment tomorrow morning at six. And please, K. Burke, be sure to bring some nice clothes. Yes, this case looks very interesting. But, my friend, so is this little trip that I've planned."

CHAPTER 3

VERY LITTLE TRAFFIC IN Manhattan. Very little traffic on the Hutchinson River Parkway. Very little traffic on Purchase Street. Everything is going our way. So, in thirty-five minutes K. Burke and I are walking through the Westchester County Airport in White Plains, New York.

Burke is, after all, a detective, accustomed to ridiculously early hours. So she is wide-awake and bright-eyed, and also a trifle confused. We walk through a small gate marked PRIVATE AIRCRAFT. I am about to show my driver's license to the security guard as ID, but the young man waves his hand casually and says, "No need, Mr. Moncrief. Welcome aboard."

Five minutes later we are in the sky.

"First question," she says. "What's with this fancy jet? Don't tell me you rented a private plane."

"No. I did not rent it," I say. "I bought it. It is called a Gulfstream G650, and it contains enough fuel to fly for about seven thousand miles. That's my complete knowledge of the vehicle."

She shakes her head slowly and says, "They should give

one of these planes to every NYPD detective. It would make days off so much more fun."

Then she says, "Question number two. Tell me where we're going, Moncrief, or I'm walking off this plane."

"No need to prepare your parachute, K. Burke. We are going to a city named Louisville, in the state of Kentucky."

As I say the word "Kentucky," the attractive young woman who greeted us as we boarded crouches beside us, rests her hand on mine, and asks if we would like some champagne or coffee. (I hear K. Burke mutter, "Oh, brother.") Both Burke and I decline the offer of champagne and settle for a perfectly pulled cappuccino. As if the coffee was a magical elixir that filled her with special knowledge, K. Burke suddenly shouts.

"The Derby!" she says loudly. "Tomorrow is the Kentucky Derby!"

"Congratulations. You are a detective *parfaite*," I say.

"Since when did you become a horse-racing fan? And please don't tell me you bought a horse and managed to get him into the Kentucky Derby."

"No, although I did think about it. But the dearest friends of my late parents have a horse running tomorrow at Churchill Downs. They have been racing horses ever since I can remember. Madame and Monsieur Savatier, Marguerite and Nicolas. The name of their extraordinary horse is *Garçon*, although his full name is *Vilain Garçon*, which means 'naughty boy.'"

"So, they named the horse after you," she laughs.

"An easy joke, K. Burke. Too easy."

"Irresistible," she says.

"In any event, the Savatiers have been in Louisville for two months while Garçon was training. For Nicolas and

Marguerite the Kentucky Derby has been their dream. They have rented a house, and we will be staying with them. They will meet us when we land."

Burke and I each have another cappuccino, and less than an hour later we arrive at Louisville International Airport.

We exit the plane. At the bottom of the steps waits an elegant old woman wearing an elegant gray suit and a large white hat. Next to her stands an equally elegant-looking man of a similar age. He, too, wears a suit of gray. He also wears an old-fashioned straw boater. They both carry gold-handled canes.

"*Bienvenue, Luc. Bonjour, mon ami bien-aimé.*" Welcome, my beloved friend.

We embrace.

"*Madame et Monsieur Savatier,* I wish to present my best friend, Mademoiselle Katherine Burke," I say. "Miss Burke, Marguerite and Nicolas Savatier."

The three of them exchange gentle handshakes. K. Burke says that she has heard wonderful things about them as well as "your great horse, Vilain Garçon."

"*Merci,*" says Madame Savatier. "And I must say this. Since Luc just called you *his* best friend, that makes you also *our* best friend."

Monsieur Savatier speaks. I immediately recall what a stern and funny old Frenchman he can be.

"Please, everyone," he says. "This is all very touching. But we must hurry. In less than a half hour they will be having the final workout of the horses. And no friendship is worth being late for that."

CHAPTER 4

THE FIRST SATURDAY IN May. That's the date of the Kentucky Derby. May promises sunny weather. But today, May does not make good on that promise. The sky is overcast. The temperatures are in the mid-forties. The only sunshine is the excitement in the noisy, boozy, very colorful crowd. Katherine Burke, the Savatiers, and I are standing outside the super-elite Infield Club. This is where the horse owners and their friends gather. Here most women are dressed as if they are attending a British royal wedding: huge floral print dresses, most of them in bright primary colors; necklaces and brooches and earrings with sparkling diamonds, emeralds, and rubies. The women's hats are each a crazy story unto themselves—huge affairs that must be pinned and clipped to remain afloat, in colors that perfectly match or clash with the colors of their dresses.

The men are in morning suits or are dressed in classic-cut blazers—each a different rainbow color. Bright club ties, striped ties, bow ties. The whole area has the feeling of happy anxiety and big money. And of course no one is without a smartphone, constantly raised to capture the moment. This has to be the most thoroughly photographed Kentucky Derby in history.

I give K. Burke two hundred dollars.

"Bet one hundred on Garçon for me, one hundred on Garçon for yourself," I tell her.

"I'm not going to take your money," she says.

"But this time you must. To watch the race with a bet riding on it makes it a million times more exciting. But I must prepare you for the worst."

She looks surprised.

"Garçon has little chance of winning. The oddsmakers have his chances at forty to one."

"I don't care," she says, in the true spirit of the Derby. "He's our horse." And she is off to the betting window. She's become a real racing fan.

K. Burke clutches our tickets tightly. She is dressed more casually than most of the women in the infield, but she looks enchanting. Marguerite Savatier has given Burke a piece of Garçon's silks—a red, white, and yellow swatch of cloth. Burke has tied it around her waist as a belt. She looks terrific in a simple white billowing cotton dress. And if anyone present thinks Burke is out of her social element, all they need do is glance at the huge emerald necklace, the gift that I gave her this past Christmas in Paris.

Then it is time for the race.

Grooms snap lead shanks onto their horses and escort them out of their stalls. Then comes the traditional parade. The horses are conducted past the clubhouse turn, then under the twin spires of Churchill Downs. Finally, the horses are brought into the paddock to be saddled.

Nicolas and Marguerite Savatier speak to Garçon's jockey and trainers. They save their most important words for . . . who else? Garçon. Both Savatiers stroke the horse's nose. Marguerite touches his cheek. Then they move away.

Now comes the moment that most people, myself among them, find the most touching. It begins with a simple, sad piece of music. A college band begins playing a very old Stephen Foster song. Everyone at the Derby sings along, right down to the heartbreaking final verse:

Weep no more my lady.
Oh! Weep no more today.
We will sing one song
For my old Kentucky home.
For the old Kentucky home, far away.

And the race begins.

For me there is no sporting event that does not excite me when I am watching in person. Boxing. Basketball. Tennis. Hockey. But nothing compares to horse-racing. And nothing in horse-racing compares to the Kentucky Derby.

It is even more incredible to be watching the race with owners of one of the racehorses. It is almost as exciting watching K. Burke transform from a no-nonsense NYPD detective into a crazed racing fan. She clenches her fingers into fists. She screams the word "Garçon" over and over, literally without stopping for breath.

And the race itself?

If I could have "fixed" the race, I am ashamed to say, I would have taken all of my father's inheritance and done so. Nothing would please me more than to see my frail elderly friends, Marguerite and Nicolas, break down in tears as Vilain Garçon crossed first at the finish line. Nothing would please me more than to see my best friend in her white cotton dress jump for joy, her emerald necklace flapping up and down. Yes, it would have been worth my fortune to see that happen.

As it turns out, I did not have to spend a penny.

The voice on the loudspeaker, above the cheering, came out shouting, with a perfect Southern accent, "And the winner, by half a length, is VILL-EN GAR-ÇON!"

CHAPTER 5

THE BEST THING ABOUT being the governor of Kentucky must be hosting the Winner's Party for the Kentucky Derby.

We watch the giant wreath of roses being placed upon Garçon. Then we head to the Kentucky Derby Museum for the Winner's Party. K. Burke and I are sort of maid of honor and best man at a royal wedding. We get to enter with the bride and groom, Marguerite and Nicolas. Shouts. Cheers. Music.

"I bet that most of the people here think that we're the son and daughter of the Savatiers," K. Burke says.

"Or the son and daughter-*in-law*," I say. Burke acts as if she did not hear what I just said.

Armand Joscoe, the tough little French jockey who is hugely responsible for Garçon's victory, is carried around the room on a chair, like a bride at a Jewish wedding.

"He's adorable," says K. Burke.

"When I was a lad everyone called him *Petit Nez*, Little Nose. He has been with the Savatiers forever. This win is a wonderful day for him."

"No more *Petit Nez* for him," says Burke. I now look at the commotion around the Savatiers.

The charming old couple is, as always, composed and courteous as they field the questions from society magazines, racing magazines, newspaper and TV reporters from all over the world, and gossip blogs. Marguerite's gentle voice is barely audible among the thousands of clicks from the cameras and cell phones. It is their show. Burke and I stand many feet away from the stars.

"Have you tasted the mint julep?" I ask K. Burke.

"I'm an Irish girl. I prefer my whiskey straight up," she says. "I just don't understand the combination of mint and bourbon."

As if on cue a waiter passes by with a tray of chilled mint juleps. I take two from the waiter and hand one to K. Burke.

"As a good guest and adventurer you must try the local drink," I say.

Reluctantly she says, "Okay." We both hold our drinks in the air.

"To Garçon and his owners," I say.

"To you, Moncrief, with a big thank you for this trip," Burke says.

"My pleasure, partner," I say. We clink. We sip. She speaks.

"Hmmm. I think I may have been wrong about bourbon and mint leaves. I could easily get used to this concoction," she says.

I frown and say, "Not me. A white Bordeaux will always be my drink."

"Over there," Burke says, pointing to a nearby waiter with a tray of good-looking hors d'oeuvres. Then she adds, "What do you think those things are?"

"Hush puppies with country ham," I say.

"I didn't know you were such an expert on Kentucky food," Burke says. "You're just full of surprises, Moncrief."

We are poised to grab a few bites from the hors d'oeuvres tray when the orchestra suddenly lets go with a musical fanfare. A commotion seems to be taking place in the area where the Savatiers are being interviewed and photographed. Always on the job, Burke shoots me a look and heads toward our friends.

As we push our way through the crowd, a spotlight hits the older couple. A gigantic arrangement of red roses is being carried in. It's even larger than the garland of roses that was draped on Garçon. The floral arrangement is so large that it takes four men to carry it. They place it in front of the Savatiers. Marguerite and Nicolas's heads disappear behind the huge red rose arrangement.

One of the unidentified four men holds a mic. It clicks on with a screeching noise.

"Five hundred American Beauty roses for one wonderful French woman," he says. His accent is tough, New York–ish.

Both Savatiers seem confused. The two Derby officials with the Savatiers also seem confused. The four men walk away quickly.

"Was that some official part of the winner's ceremony?" Burke asks.

I shrug my shoulders. "So much of what you Americans do is a little bit crazy. Let's go find the waiter with the hors d'oeuvres."

In the next hour Burke and I set some kind of record for "Most Hors d'Oeuvres and Canapés Consumed at Churchill

Downs." We set a similar record for "Most Mint Juleps Consumed at Churchill Downs."

We are drunk enough to have trouble forming words when we kiss the Savatiers farewell. Our thanks are heartfelt and garbled. Fortunately, the Savatiers' chauffeur drives us to the airport. Moments later we are aloft. On our way back to New York. On our way back to the murders of the three beautiful young women.

I try to do some mental theorizing about the case. But I am tired, and my brain is muddled, and K. Burke's head is resting on my shoulder.

CHAPTER 6

KATHERINE MARY BURKE UNLOCKS the three dead bolts that will allow her to enter her apartment. After the door is finally opened, she surveys the one-room apartment on East 90th Street where she has lived for the past five years.

All those keys and locks to keep this little place safe. *Is this cramped little studio even worth protecting?* she thinks. The dark-green sofa, dotted with stains. It's the sofa that her cousin Maddy was going to throw out. The two needlepoint pillows that a friend made. The first one says, THERE'S NO PLACE LIKE HOME. The second one says, YOU CALL THIS PLACE HOME?

When she first rented the apartment it seemed spacious and bright. That was before she set up the fake-pine IKEA coffee table with the wobbly fourth leg. That's before she made the decision to keep the Murphy bed permanently opened and unmade. That's before the club chair from the Salvation Army became the *de facto* storage unit for her pile of shirts, jeans, slacks, and tights, plus an occasional shoe, boot, or sneaker.

Yet Burke came to love the place. It was simple. It was sweet. Most of all, it was hers. Okay, her best friend Moncrief may live in a loft big enough to host a basketball game, but life has a way of evening out sorrow and joy. She would never trade her simple life for Luc's wealthy world, a world scarred by death and tragedy. Sometimes she wonders how he gets through the day without crying.

And what the hell, right now Burke is feeling rich, too. The $4,000 she won on Garçon is the biggest single amount she has had since...since...well, since ever. She could pay her Time Warner Cable bill, she could buy a really cool first communion gift for her niece Emma Rose, she could bank some of it so that when Christmas came she could buy Moncrief something a bit fancier than a fake Cross pen and pencil set (which he does, however, keep on his desk and actually use).

Burke drops her luggage on the floor. Then she plugs in her laptop and her smartphone for recharging.

She unpins her hair and removes her bright silk belt. The juleps are catching up with her.

One last look at her email. It has been a few hours since she checked it. There might be important info on the three murder cases that she and Moncrief are jumping on top of tomorrow.

Nothing urgent. Some new files about the victims' cell phones, no important DNA material from any of the crime scenes, a few useless pieces from the gossip sites TMZ and Dlisted about the alleged affair between Tessa Fulbright's husband and a twenty-year-old Yankees farm-team player. Hmm. He's in the closet? Interesting but probably irrelevant.

Finally, there is an email from Mike Delaney. Mike is part-owner and weekend bartender at a place called, what else?

Delaney's. Mike isn't the sharpest guy Burke has ever met, but...Mike is sort of like her apartment. Mike is simple. He's sweet. And she knows she could have him for the asking.

She falls backward on the bed. Her head hurts. Her feet hurt. But she is full of happy memories of the Derby, the roses, the party, the juleps...and a friend like Moncrief.

Friend. The word "friend" seems to stick uneasily in her mind. What do you call a male friend who's rich and hand-some and funny, and when you accidentally-on-purpose fall asleep on his shoulder you feel warm and comfortable?

I guess you just call it...a Moncrief, she thinks.

Then she falls asleep.

CHAPTER 7

"ALL RIGHT, I HAVE it entirely figured out," I say as K. Burke, wearing I've-got-a-hangover sunglasses, walks into the precinct.

"Can it wait five minutes until I put a little coffee in my engine?"

"K. Burke, it is ten o'clock Sunday morning. We agreed to meet at nine a.m.? I assume you were not at church," I say.

"Moncrief, already you're making me crazy, so I'm going to give you my mother's two favorite words of warning," Burke says. "Two simple words."

"Please, nothing obscene," I say.

"Obscene? My mother? No way. Here are the two words." Then she shouts: *"Don't start!"*

I am stunned for a moment, but just for a moment.

"But why would I not *start?"* I ask. Then I launch into my analysis.

"There was no cause of death determined in the post-mortem on the first two victims, but you have no doubt read the autopsy report from the medical examiner concerning Ms. Tessa Fulbright, the dead woman in Bergdorf?"

"No, I have not, but I'm sure you'll tell me what I need to know," says Burke.

"With pleasure. As we noted, there was no physical abuse, no bruising, no fractures. Beyond that there were no unusual substances in her blood…"

"Unusual? You mean like poison?" Burke says.

"Correct. Unless, like me, you consider a small amount of instant oatmeal and trace amounts of pomegranate juice to be poison."

"That's it?" Burke asks. I can tell by the wrinkled forehead and the speed with which she gulps her coffee that she's listening hard.

"Yes, that's it for the examination, but that's not the end of the information I have found. I called Tessa Fulbright's pharmacy this morning and received some interesting information."

"How'd you know what drugstore to call? From her husband?"

"No. But I figured it out easily. We knew she bought her wardrobe at Bergdorf's. So I correctly assumed that she bought her medicines at C.O. Bigelow, the most glamorous pharmacy in Manhattan. Tessa Fulbright did not seem like the kind of woman who would wait on line at Duane Reade."

"So what did you find out?"

"Not much. Not really much at all. She was due for a refill on Nembutal, which as you know is…"

It's K. Burke's turn to show off a bit.

"It's a pretty popular antidepressant, a pentobarbital pill-pop. You'd have to swallow an awful lot to kill yourself.

Marilyn Monroe left town on it. Anyway, if it wasn't showing up in Fulbright's autopsy, I'd rule it out."

"*Moi aussi.* Me too, but, I am sad to report that the only other thing the postmortem examination showed in her blood was a high amount of sugar and a certain amount of a medication named..."

Here I pause and refer to my iPad for the name. "Dulcolax. It is a stool softener."

"I know what Dulcolax is," she says.

"Ah, so the hardened stool is a problem that you suffer from, K. Burke?"

"I'm not going to say it again, Moncrief. *Don't start!*"

CHAPTER 8

I AM, OF COURSE, laughing at my little joke. And I believe that she, too, is suppressing a smile.

"Okay," I say, almost ready to rub my hands together with enthusiasm, "Now for the big insight. Turn on your computer. I have something more to show you. Something important."

Burke quickly boots up the desktop and enters a code. She turns away from the beeping computer sounds as if they are making her head hurt.

"Okay, the computer's ready. I'm ready. What's up?" she says.

"Here's what's up!" I say, and in my enthusiasm begin very quickly calling up some pages on the screen.

"*Alors!*" I shout. "Look at this."

She studies the screen for a few moments and then eyes me suspiciously.

"It's photographs of the three dead women," Burke says. She gives a short shrug. "So what? We have photos of . . . lemme see if I remember right . . . this is the redhead from Bergdorf, Tessa Fulbright. This one is the blonde who died in the restaurant. The 21 Club."

I interrupt. "No, *not* 21 Club, *but* there is a number in the restaurant name—Eleven Madison Park."

"Her name is Jenna Lee Austin. She's the actress. The understudy. Married to the hedge funder."

"*C'est magnifique.* Now. The final *Jeopardy!* answer is...?"

Katherine Burke does not hesitate. She taps the screen photo of the third victim.

"Mara Monahan. Shoe department, Saks Fifth Avenue."

"You go home with a million dollars!" I yell.

"Great," she says. "I'll just add it to the four thousand bucks from yesterday."

"And now I will show you something else," I say.

I quickly tap a few keys on Burke's computer. "See?"

Under the photo of each dead woman appears a photo of a different man. Beneath Tessa's photo is a strapping young blond lifeguard type. Under Mara's is one of those nerdy-handsome guys, the black eyeglass frames, the slightly startled smile. Under Jenna's photo is the "older gentleman," who looks amazingly like the former French Minister of Agriculture (but is not).

"Who are these guys? Their husbands?" K. Burke asks.

"A good guess," I say. *"Mais non."*

"Do I get a second chance?" she asks.

And then she knows.

"They're the boyfriends, aren't they?"

"Precisely," I say.

"How'd you figure it out, Moncrief? Instinct?"

"No, no, K. Burke. Not at all."

"Then how'd you find them?"

"On Facebook, of course."

CHAPTER 9

WHEN KATHERINE BURKE AND I go to work we really go to work.

On the sixth floor of Saks Fifth Avenue, where a simple pair of Louboutin heels can cost more than the monthly rent on a Sutton Place one-bedroom, we ignore the exquisite merchandise (and I ignore the smooth, sexy curves of the customers' legs).

"If you could just take us through the movements that Mrs. Monahan made as you remember them," Burke says to Cory Lawrence, the department manager. Young Cory looks as if he'd be right at home on a prep school tennis team or a Southampton polo club.

"Well, as I understand it from the store representative helping her..."

Burke interrupts, "That store representative is the same thing as a *salesman?*"

"That's right," Cory Lawrence says. He is not unpleasant, but his voice does have a touch of *you're obviously unfamiliar with the ways of fancy stores.*

"Okay, if you could walk us through it," I say.

Cory Lawrence speaks softly. He says that he would like to do this as quietly and unobtrusively as possible, so as not to annoy the "clients." "Clients" is apparently the new word for "customers."

"Okay, Mrs. Monahan tried on some shoes, made her choices, and then she slipped back into her Tory Burch sandals. I escorted her to the sales counter. Because she's a frequent, valued customer she has access to our exclusive app, available only to customers who spend a hundred thousand a year with us, where she can just pay with a tap of her phone. And that was it."

"Did she say anything? Did you have any sense that she wasn't feeling well?" Burke asks.

"No, not at all. She said something when the phones tapped, like 'Oh, this is like a little kiss.' Then I noticed that she stopped smiling. I was about to ask whether she wanted the shoes sent to her home, and...*bam*...she just sort of collapsed to the ground."

"What did you do then?" Burke asks.

"What did I do? I thought she had fainted. I touched her face gently. Her eyes were adrift. And then a young man—in a black Ferragamo suit, I couldn't help but notice—rushed over and began calling her name. Then there was store security, and we called 911. But then the EMT said...that she was...she was dead."

"Anything else?" I ask.

"Well, the police came with the ambulance, and then some important police boss arrived. His name was Elliott something, I think. And then they took Mrs. Monahan away."

"What about the young man in the black suit?" Burke asks.

"I guess that he left with them. I assumed he was Mrs. Monahan's assistant or her driver," says Cory Lawrence.

"Did you really *assume* that?" I ask with a tiny smirk.

"I always assume that," says Cory Lawrence.

"You are a wise young man, Mr. Lawrence. In a decade or so you will be running this store."

"Thank you, sir."

"But for the time being…Don't look now, but I would discreetly direct your eyes to the woman seated approximately ten yards to your left. She is wearing white slacks and a black silk shirt. You will notice that she has slipped on a brand new pair of Isabel Marant ankle boots, replacing them in the box with her scuffed and worn-out Blahnik pumps. *Merci et au revoir, Monsieur Lawrence.*"

CHAPTER 10

AN HOUR LATER DETECTIVE Burke and I walk into the art deco splendor of Eleven Madison Park.

"My God," says Burke. "I feel like I'm in an old black-and-white musical."

Suddenly, Marcella, the tall, thin, copper-haired beauty from the front desk, walks quickly toward me with her arms extended. Her smile is huge.

"Oh, here we go," says Burke.

She and I embrace.

"Luc, you're back. It's been at least a month," she says, shaking her hair. "Let me check on your table," she adds. "Have a flute of champagne while you're waiting. It's on the house, of course."

"*Merci,*" I say.

As the lovely Marcella walks away, Burke says, "*Merci,* my foot! What's going on, Moncrief? She's checking a table? We're on the job."

"But if the job takes place in one of New York's finest restaurants, it would actually be foolish not to partake of lunch."

"No. It would actually be foolish if we *were* to partake of lunch. About as unprofessional as you can get."

"Oh, K. Burke. You know I can always be much more unprofessional than this."

Needless to say, Burke does not laugh. She also refuses to join me in a glass of champagne. So we stand and wait in angry silence.

A few minutes later we are seated at a corner table.

"I'm not going to eat," says Burke.

"Didn't we have this identical conversation just last week?" I ask. As soon as I finish asking that question, a handsome fifty-ish man with close-cropped gray hair approaches the table.

"Mr. Moncrief, a pleasure, as always."

"This is my colleague, Detective Burke," I say. "This is the restaurant's manager, Paul deBarros."

As K. Burke gives a quick cold nod, deBarros pulls out a chair from the table and sits down.

Burke looks surprised, until I explain that deBarros witnessed the death of Jenna Lee Austin.

"Mrs. Austin was here at least once a week for lunch, and often for dinner," says the manager.

Burke and I follow the training rule: when the witness starts talking, do not interrupt. Let him get going. Sit back and listen.

"Sometimes Mrs. Austin dined with her husband. Sometimes she was with her mother. But the unfortunate day she died, she was dining alone. She told the front desk—Marcella was on that day—that perhaps she would be joined for coffee. She was not sure."

DeBarros takes a deep breath and shrugs his shoulders.

"Honestly, there's not much more to say. I welcomed her. I asked after her health. I asked after Mr. Austin. She was, as always, very bubbly and happy. I asked if she'd like something to drink before she ordered. She said she'd like a glass of San Pellegrino. A minute later, when I delivered it, she looked up at me. Then her head crashed onto the table."

"Who else saw this happen?" Burke asks.

"I'm not sure anyone else saw Mrs. Austin pass out. But when her head hit the table I shouted for help. So, of course, other diners looked, but it was early in the luncheon service, only a bit before noon. So there were not that many people here."

DeBarros describes how Jenna Austin was unresponsive to anything, although he admits that he did not follow the 911 operator's explicit instructions not to move her.

"I did not want to cause a disturbance for the other diners. So we carried Mrs. Austin to the passageway between the kitchen and the dining room. I'm certain she did not want people to see her in that condition."

"In *that* condition?" I ask. "Did you think she was drunk?"

"Oh, but of course not," he says. "I did not think she would want to be seen unconscious."

"Anything else, Detective?" I ask Burke. "The police? The ambulance?"

"Yes, all that. They gave her oxygen, I think, but the EMT said she was dead. I think they took her to Beth Israel hospital."

"Actually, it was NYU," Burke says.

"Thank you, Paul," I say. Burke thanks him also.

The captain rises from his seat. He gently pushes the chair back into place.

"Now, to travel from something tragic to something peaceful...if indeed you have no further questions..."

I have no further questions. The pattern is emerging, and that pattern is simple: no clue from any eyewitnesses. We will have to make sense of the boyfriend angle.

I ask K. Burke if she wants to ask anything. She shakes her head.

"In that case, Miss Burke, Mr. Moncrief, I have ordered a simple but interesting luncheon. To start with, a refreshing lobster ceviche with watermelon and lime ice. Then, if you agree, a Muscovy duck breast with lavender honey."

"Sounds wonderful," I say.

"Just coffee for me," says Burke.

"Bring Detective Burke the lobster ceviche. She may change her mind."

As soon as deBarros leaves, Burke hisses at me, "No. I told you I'm not doing this. I'm not eating. This is outrageous."

A few minutes later, after I've selected a Hugel Riesling as our wine, the lobster ceviche appears.

It is my pleasure to inform you that K. Burke ate every bit of it.

CHAPTER 11

ABOUT FIVE SECONDS AFTER Dalia died, I was certain of only one thing—that life was truly not worth living.

Yet everything else around me remained the same. People clogged the subways at rush hour. The *Mona Lisa* still smiled at the Louvre. Washington still crossed the Delaware at the Met. I was rich enough and skinny enough to wear the idiotic Milan fashion show suits, but I could bring myself to wear only Levi's and black T-shirts. People made love. People made war. I did neither.

Although I did not eat much, I made dinner reservations. I scheduled sessions with my personal trainer. And when my impeccably restored '65 Mustang needed work, I drove it to the mechanic in Yonkers who loved the car like a man loves his child.

I did go back to work, and that—along with my friendship with K. Burke—kept me from leaping from the rooftops.

I did make one big change, however. I never returned to the apartment I had shared with Dalia. I could not go back.

I lived briefly at the St. Regis Hotel. It was pleasant, and midtown Manhattan was certainly convenient. Hotel services made life easy—clean, crisp sheets every day, 4 a.m. room service deliveries of Caesar salads and Opus One wine. But after K. Burke persisted in jokingly calling me a "rich vagabond," I did as she suggested. I purchased a new apart-ment. A temple of simple luxury—cement flooring, spacious uncluttered walls, an occasional piece of iron or copper or steel furniture.

I return here this evening. After a day of investigation at Saks and Eleven Madison Park, I should be invigorated. Case work is my joy in life. Instead, the inevitable gloom of loneliness passes over me. I knew if I returned to our old apartment, I would never stop expecting to hear Dalia's voice from another room, to see her coat and scarf and pocketbook on the hall-way chair, to hear her sound system blasting Selena Gomez. I wish. I wish I could hear her playing that obnoxious music again. I wish I could yell, "Turn off that crap!" I wish.

I do what I always do when I first arrive home from work, whether it is early in the evening or five in the morning. I take a shower—piercingly hot, Kiehl's coriander body wash, rinse with icy cold water. I step into sweat shorts and walk into the kitchen.

Lunch at Eleven Madison Park with K. Burke was delicious (and yes, I admit that we shared the orange chocolate bonbon for dessert), but it was a long time ago, so now I crack three eggs into a bowl. I whisk with a fork. Then I move to the eight-burner Wolf oven. (No, I did not forget the salt; Dalia was trying to make me cut down.) I melt a big knob of (unsalted) butter until it bubbles from the heat. I am about to pour the mixture into a pan when an echo-like disembodied voice fills the air. I know it well. The phone message machine is programmed to speak to me twenty minutes after I turn off the entrance door security alarm.

"You have two new messages," announces the small silver box on the kitchen island. Two? I seldom share my landline phone number, so there are usually *no* messages. Tonight there are *two*.

The first message promises to be a long, boring, and complicated piece of information from one of my late father's accountants. Something to do with German bonds and electronic stock certificates. I know that the accountant will call back. I move to the silver box and click Next.

The second message is a potentially important one.

"Mon cher enfant." My dear boy…with those three words I recognize the voice of Nicolas Savatier. He continues in French: "We have just arrived in Baltimore…preparing for the Preakness Stakes. . . . It would be most helpful if you could get in touch with us soon, very soon. We are heading to the Four Seasons on the harbor, where we are staying, but we always have our cell phones at hand. Please, if you would call soon."

In the background I hear Marguerite Savatier speaking loudly, *"Immédiatement."*

Then, from Nicolas, another *"immédiatement"* followed by a soft and courteous *"Merci."*

I return the call *immédiatement*.

CHAPTER 12

"MON CHER LUC, WE did not want to alarm you," says Nicolas, ever the perfect French gentleman.

"Give me the phone, Nicolas," I hear Marguerite say, in French. Then I hear her voice clearly on the phone.

"Luc. It is you?"

"Mais oui," I say. "What is the problem?"

We both switch to French.

"We are not quite certain that it is an actual problem. And, of course, we do not want to alarm you . . ."

"Or trouble you," comes the voice of Nicolas, now relegated to the background.

"Please," I almost shout. "You are *not* alarming me. You are *not* troubling me. What is the matter? Speak, please, speak."

Marguerite continues.

"Perhaps it is not worth getting excited about," she says.

I am thinking that if they were with me in person I would wring their aristocratic necks, or at least toss a glass of Veuve Clicquot in their faces. Finally, Marguerite speaks. Her voice is trembling:

"I have received two dozen red roses," Marguerite says. "A deliveryman was waiting with them when we landed in Baltimore."

I, of course, instinctively know that there is more to this phone call, that not everything has been revealed. Even a slightly dotty elderly couple would not become frightened by a box of flowers. However, I proceed as if all will turn out normally.

"How delightful. Who sent the roses?" I ask.

"We do not know," Marguerite says. "It is anonymous. And *c'est ça le problème*."

Suddenly, Nicolas's voice is on the phone.

"You see, the greater problem is that, yes, it is unsigned, *but* there *is* a note with the roses. Let me read it to you."

Nicolas's frail voice becomes strong: "'Win the Preakness. Or you will suffer the consequences.'"

I keep my own voice calm, but this is surely not the sort of note anyone wishes to receive.

"Did you try contacting the florist?" I ask. (Yes, I know, a foolish and obvious question.)

"*Encore une fois, mon cher Luc.* We may be old but we are not stupid," says Nicolas. "There was no name on the card or on the box. We signed for them without thinking, figuring it was just more congratulatory flowers. It wasn't until we were in the cab that we even thought to look at the card. It is so mysterious."

I am thinking that it is not just mysterious, but it is so creepy, really creepy. Is it a threat? A joke? A mistake?

To put the Savatiers at ease I say something that I don't fully believe. "This is nothing to be alarmed about."

Then I quickly add, "Listen. The Preakness is next Saturday. I've got work to do up here. But if you need me, I'll drop everything and join you. Okay?"

"Okay," says Nicolas.

In the background, just before I hang up, I hear Marguerite's voice in a loud stage whisper: "Tell him to come down now."

Click.

The butter for the eggs is now burnt to a foul brown grease, and the smoke detector is screaming at me. So my dinner becomes a bowl of Special K and two large glasses of Bouchard Montrachet.

I don't sleep. Not a wink. My bedtime companion is the relentless stream of grim BBC detective shows and one more glass of the soft chardonnay. Between the ending of *Wallander* and the start of *Vera* comes dawn.

CHAPTER 13

Mara Monahan
2 East 79th Street

TODAY BURKE AND I visit the Manhattan apartments of the three beautiful murder victims. Burke has made some interesting connections in the three cases: Each one of the murdered women was, of course, beautiful and wealthy. But there's something more. Each of them had an only child below the age of three. All these rich women, of course, also had household help—maids, drivers, housemen, house-keepers, cooks, nannies. It's the nannies who interest Burke and me. In reading the reports, Burke noticed that all three of the nannies were placed by the same employment agency in London. Funny. In detective work you have to be very careful of coincidences, and then again, you can't be *too* careful.

An attractive, excessively energetic young woman with a de-mure hairstyle opens the door of the Monahan apartment.

The young woman wants to appear properly somber, but she cannot hide the sometimes chronic American characteristic of perkiness.

"I'm Congressman Monahan's District Assistant, Chloe Garrison," she says. "Please come in." We walk into a big foyer with traditional Upper East Side black-and-white tiled marble floors.

"The congressman wanted to be here himself to speak with you," she says, then quickly adds, "But he was on the first flight down to DC today. There's an environmental waste bill in debate...and...well, he thought it would be most helpful if he got back to work." We agree again.

"NYPD has already spoken to Mr. Monahan," Burke says. "He's been very cooperative...especially given the painfulness of the situation."

Chloe nods. "Congressman Monahan is taking Henry, their little boy, out to Montauk this weekend. Like you said, the whole death thing is pretty...tough."

"No doubt about it," Burke says.

The assistant grants our request to speak to Henry's nanny, Mrs. Meade-Grafton. "If it's all right, you'll meet in Congressman Monahan's home office."

The home office has a spectacular view of Central Park, and Mrs. Meade-Grafton does not remotely look like what I thought a British nanny named "Mrs. Meade-Grafton" would. She is wearing stretch jeans that cling quite snuggly to her ample hips and thighs. She sits on a black leather sofa, and her legs are tucked beneath her. Her white T-shirt has these words printed on the front:

I LISTEN TO BANDS THAT DON'T EXIST YET.

We introduce ourselves. Mrs. Meade-Grafton does not stand to greet us, but she does extend her very fleshy hand. The congressional aide leaves the room.

"Is young Henry around?" Burke asks.

"Oh, the little one is watchin' telly. Cook's keepin' an eye on 'im," the nanny says. English is definitely *my* second language, but you don't have to be 'enry 'iggins to know that it is a fairly lower-class accent.

I ask how she and the late Mrs. Monahan got along.

"Like two peas," she says. "An' why not? We didn't see very much of one 'nother. I was with little 'enry when she wasn't. And when she was seein' to the little lad then myself mostly wasn't there. But Mrs. M was a decent enough sort. Quite a loss, o' course. Not sure the 'usband 'as took it all in yet. An' to be honest, little 'enry might be thinkin' his mum's still just out shoppin'."

She laughs. A lot.

CHAPTER 14

Jenna Lee Austin
156 Perry Street

JULIA HIGHRIDGE PREFERS TO be called *Miss* Highridge, *and* she prefers to be called a governess, not a nanny. Wardrobe? A dark plaid tweed suit, sensible shoes, hair in a bun. Miss Highridge is probably forty years old, but with her grooming and wardrobe she could pass for fifty. She is as formal as Mrs. Meade-Grafton was informal.

We sit in the first floor Victorian parlor of an impeccably decorated Greenwich Village town house. We are only a block from the West Side Highway, the Hudson River just on the other side of that.

"So, you look after Ethan?" Burke asks.

"That would be *Master* Ethan. And yes, Master Ethan is my charge."

Then she gestures to a small table. On the table is a silver tray covered with a silver teapot, teacups, a large plate of cookies, and various pastries.

"I thought you might need some tea. I've also had the cook bring in some puddings and cakes. You may not be familiar with all of them, these especially..."

"I am happy to tell you that I am completely familiar with these. They are *canelés,* and I have not seen them ever before here in New York," I say. *"Je les adore."* I adore them. "They are my favorite."

I am not merely being a polite guest. I am telling the truth about the crunchy little dome-like butter pastries that are in every patisserie in Paris. I've not found any that taste as good as they do there.

"Ah," Miss Highridge says. "An authentic Frenchman. Perhaps you would like to conduct the interview in French. I'm fluent."

"No," I say. "I think English is the more appropriate language for an NYPD investigation. Plus, my colleague might not..."

Burke interrupts. She is not at all amused. "Have a canelé, Detective Moncrief. And let's get on with it."

Miss Highridge goes on to tell us that she was enormously fond of Mrs. Lenz—"That would be *Mrs.* Austin to you."

Burke, losing none of her edge, says, "We know her husband is Bernard Lenz. He's been interviewed twice already."

We ask for her opinion of Jenna Lee Austin.

Her answer: "She was an actress. That should tell you everything." Then she proceeds to pop a third canelé into her mouth.

"That really does *not* tell us very much, Miss Highridge," I say.

"Then let me explain. She knew how to *act* like a mother. Just as she knew how to *act* like a good wife. But...please, have another cake..."

Both Burke and I decline.

"In any event, I suppose she wanted to be a good mother.

But her career came first. She cared so very much about her career. The lessons, and the private trainer and the yoga instructor and the homeopathic doctor and the nutritionist and...oh, so many people to help her. But Mr. Lenz didn't seem to mind."

Miss Highridge pauses, pops another pastry, then speaks: "Her husband had *his* life. She had *hers*. And Master Ethan had *me*."

We talk some more. Miss Highridge says that Jenna Lee seemed to have a lot of friends.

"How about her marriage?"

"The marriage was what most marriages are. A series of small compromises."

When we are ready to leave, she agrees to get in touch if she thinks of anything helpful. But, she tells us, "That seems unlikely."

Then she says, "Let me have these extra canelés wrapped for you. You can take them with you."

"*Non merci, mademoiselle.* You enjoy them."

"Oh, dear. It's the last thing I need," she says. She pats her significantly round belly, and we escape without the little cakes.

CHAPTER 15

Tessa Fulbright
River House, 435 East 52nd Street

MAZIE McCRAY LOVED TESSA Fulbright. My instincts tell me that immediately.

"First I raised her mother, Mrs. Pierce. Then I raised Tessa... I mean, of course, Mrs. Fulbright. And now my last job will be raising Andrew. But I never expected not having his mother by my side while doing it."

Mazie dabs at her eyes with a crumbled tissue. Mazie is Black and round and perfectly charming. Mazie, Burke, and I are sitting on low, children-sized benches in Andrew's bright-yellow nursery. Andrew toddles around, chubby arms extended. He falls. He giggles. He laughs. He gets up and walks some more.

Suddenly Mazie stands up and walks quickly to Andrew. Mazie lifts the child. He rests in Mazie's arms, and Mazie uses her free hands to cover the boy's ears.

"Tessa, Andrew's mother, was fine, absolutely fine, a wonderful child, a wonderful woman. Then she married Mr. Fulbright. Then she started in with 'I'm not pretty enough.

I'm not young enough.'" Mazie shakes her head thoughtfully, and then fixes her eyes on Burke and me.

"You two saw her," she says. "You must've seen photos. She was beautiful. The most beautiful woman. Even more important, she was a *good* woman. I knew her. I raised her. I knew her better than anyone."

A long pause. Then K. Burke speaks softly.

"What do you think happened?"

Mazie places Andrew back on the floor. The little boy returns to his giddy, happy walking. Mazie takes a deep breath, shakes her head, and speaks.

"I wish I knew. Dear Lord, I just wish I knew."

CHAPTER 16

I SLEEP WELL. BUT don't assume that sleep comes to me easily. No, not at all. My sleep is a chemical and musical trick. It requires 10mg of Ambien, followed a half hour later by 5mg of Xanax, and then I queue up the Luc Moncrief Artist of the Week on the sound system. This can be anything from Chopin to the Rolling Stones. This week, I'm sleeping with the little-known Vienna Teng. Her music is just slow enough to lullaby me a bit, just fast enough to let me know I'm still breathing.

Sleep arrives suddenly. And just as suddenly I am awake. The telephone is ringing. It is morning. The big bedroom is filled with soft morning light.

I grab the receiver.

"Yes, what is it?"

"Luc? It is so early," comes the old woman's voice. I recognize it immediately.

"Marguerite, what's wrong?" I say.

My neck hurts. My lips are dry. An Ambien-induced sleep brings sleep, but it rarely brings peace.

"Many things. I'll put Nicolas on."

"The news is bad," he says.

I can only imagine. And I want to know everything right this moment. I do not want the Servatiers to begin dithering.

"*Stop! Do not tell me anything except what the goddamn problem is*," I say. I have purposely chosen the curse word to demonstrate my seriousness.

"It is a murder!" the old man shouts back at me.

"A murder. A murder of whom? Tell me. Keep talking."

I don't understand what he's saying at first...then I deduce a horse has been killed.

"Which horse?" I ask. Nicolas says something I don't understand in half-French, half-English.

"Say it again, sir. Say the horse's name again." I hear something like "Charlene Bay."

"Charlene Bay?" I ask, just one impatient step away from a shout.

"No. Not Charlene," he says.

"A bay? The horse is a bay?"

"Luc. You are not listening properly," Nicolas says.

I restrain myself from becoming angry at the anxious old man.

"Speak slower...slower and louder," I say.

He says the name again. Slower and louder.

This time I get it. "Charlie-Boy? The horse's name is Charlie-Boy?" I ask.

"*Ah, oui. Son nom est Shar-lee-Boy*. Charlie-Boy."

He continues.

"The security people say they heard a noise. They go into the stable, and there he lay. His throat was sliced, they think, with the electrical saw, the machine a man uses to cut down a tree. It made me sick. Marguerite wept."

My response is "Holy shit!"

Nicolas has yet more information.

"Charlie-Boy was the Pimlico exercise horse. The warm-ups. As you know, the warm-ups are so important."

I remember. Only a few days ago Nicolas described the important job of the warm-up horse to K. Burke and me. But the lesson here, in the most graphic terms possible, was: Do as I say, or Garçon is next.

As I am recalling that excellent lesson, Nicolas passes the phone to his wife.

"What should we do?" says Marguerite.

I am, of course, thinking of the note the Savatiers received. *Win the Preakness. Or you will suffer the consequences.*

There is just one thing to do. I tell them what they want to hear.

"I have to come down there immediately," I say.

She conveys this news to Nicolas. I can hear him talking loudly in the background.

"No, Luc. We do not want to be a bother. We only..."

"*Au revoir, mes amis.* I'll see you both soon."

"But Luc..." I hear Marguerite, and I am forced to be an American.

"Gotta go, guys." Click.

CHAPTER 17

WE WALK TOWARD STABLE A-2 at Pimlico Race Course.

It is almost noon on Wednesday. The sky is clear. The temperature is seventy-six degrees.

"I wish we could bottle this weather and save it for next Saturday's race," says Detective Kwame Clarke of the Baltimore Police Department.

I am walking with Detective Clarke, Marguerite and Nicolas Savatier, two Pimlico officials, and Nina Helstein. Miss Helstein is an investigating officer from TOBA, the Thoroughbred Owners and Breeders Association. They have kept the scene intact for us.

We walk, almost like people in a funeral procession, into the stable.

We stare down at the lifeless body of Charlie-Boy.

My father raised horses at his home in Avignon, but they never particularly interested me (especially since Avignon was only a two-hour drive to the beaches of Nice, with their beautiful waters and topless women).

Perhaps because I have spent so little time with horses,

whenever I see these animals I am always surprised that they are so big.

This dead horse, Charlie-Boy, looks…well…gigantic. A huge dead pile of tremendous muscles, a heap of giant thighs and legs and torso. Yards of white linen bandages are tied tightly around Charlie-Boy's massive neck. The bandages are splotched with red blood. Bloody hay is scattered around the horse's neck and head. The straw is also caked with blood.

Marguerite looks down at the floor. Nicolas looks up toward the wooden rafters. After what feels like an appropriate amount of time, Detective Clarke speaks quietly to me.

"There's a trainers' lounge in Stable A-4. I'll wait for you there. Say, in about ten minutes."

I nod yes, and then I walk with the Savatiers to another stable, the stable where Garçon is being kept. Both Marguerite and Nicolas break into sobs when they see their horse. Armand Joscoe, Garçon's jockey, smiles gently. Joscoe and a tall young man are methodically stroking Garçon's neck and back.

"Ah, Monsieur Moncrief," says Armand. *"Une véritable tragédie."*

The young man with Joscoe addresses me: *"Bonjour, Monsieur Moncrief."*

I have no idea who this teenager is. Then Armand Joscoe tells me in French that "Perhaps you remember Léon, my little boy. He is all grown up."

"He certainly is," I say. I am amazed Léon has become a veritable six-footer. He is quite handsome, freshly showered, and I can't help but notice that he is impeccably dressed. I also can't help but notice how expensive his clothing is. He looks more like one of the well-heeled spectators than his hardworking father.

The Joscoe men and I all smile at the different heights of father and son, but our smiles do not come from the heart. It is impossible. The stable is too filled with sadness and fear.

Here, the second step on the way to the Triple Crown, a wonderful horse with wonderful owners, an occasion that should be so festive. Now it is all so terribly grim.

A few minutes later I walk into a room attached to Stable A-4. The room is small, with two worn leather sofas, a stack of dirty, smelly jodhpurs in one corner, a soda machine in another corner.

Detective Clarke smiles when I enter.

"You were probably expecting something a bit fancier for Pimlico," he says.

"I never expect anything," I say. "That way I'm never disappointed."

"That's a perfect New York philosophy," says Clarke.

"It is also a French philosophy, I think."

Clarke is a small man, Black, and completely bald. He also wears a suit (I can't help myself from comment here) whose cut and quality seem quite elegant for what I know a detective's pay level to be, especially in Kentucky. In any event, he is smart, and he is extremely likable.

"Your friends have filled me in," he says. "And Miss Helstein is talking to yet more of the track officials."

"The Savatiers are terribly frightened," I say.

"With good cause," he says.

He hands me a neatly folded letter-sized piece of paper. I

open it and see that it is a copy of the threatening note that was sent to the Savatiers.

Win the Preakness. Or you will suffer the consequences.

"What do you think?" I ask.

"I think that it is very much what it appears to be—a scary, gruesome, inscrutable threat. I really wish you or the Savatiers had contacted me earlier…"

"They only told me about it yesterday."

"Doesn't matter. Anyway, I sent the original note to the lab. Frankly, I don't think they'll come up with anything. Prints and stuff like that only happen on TV. All we can do is keep watching Pimlico, up and down, east to west."

"Any other suggestions?" I say.

"Well, I would strongly suggest they try to persuade their horse to win the race on Saturday."

"I wish I had thought of that," I say.

Kwame Clarke laughs. We both give very weak smiles. Then Clarke says, "My instincts tell me that the horse-murder and the threatening note are *not* connected. I've got absolutely no proof. But I just feel that if there was a connection we'd see it. The whole thing is just a little too baroque, bizarre. You know what I mean?"

Another detective with *instinct*. I knew I liked this guy.

"My instinct's the same as yours," I say. Then I add, "Two cops with the same unsubstantiated idea. We must be wrong, huh?"

We're in no mood to laugh. I speak.

"Look, my friends are scared. And I don't blame them."

"I don't, either. We've put three plainclothes people—two men, one woman—around the stables. We've got three other detectives checking everyone and everything coming in— florists, caterers, workers, set-up people, tent people."

"How about you assign some protection for my friends?"

"Detective, I don't know about the NYPD, but here in Baltimore there's always a shortage in manpower. I can't loosen one or two people for a civilian guard."

"Let me ask this. Do you have anyone who's looking for some freelance work on their days off?"

"Plenty of those, but like I just said, there's no budget for it."

"Do me a favor, if you don't mind. Get three people to follow the Savatiers. I'll feel a whole lot better. And I'll come up with the cash. I'm going to be back down here next Friday night for the race on Saturday. I'll give you cash to pay your guys."

Clarke does a goofy over-the-top double-take.

"Way to go, New York!" he shouts.

Kwame Clarke throws his right hand up into the air. *Shit.* I must try to execute a high-five, always a disaster for me. We complete the gesture clumsily (on my end, at least), and almost immediately my cell phone rings.

Of course, I know who it is, and I know what the greeting will be. I click on the phone.

"Where the hell are you, Moncrief?"

I answer the question.

"And good day to you also. I'm afraid, K. Burke, that our work has followed us to the races."

CHAPTER 18

AFTER MY PLANE TAKES off from Baltimore's Thurgood Marshall Airport we receive information that travel from our reserved airport, White Plains, into Manhattan is a mess. I don't know how my pilot does it, but he manages to get last-minute clearance at LaGuardia.

I walk through the private aircraft gate and immediately hear a shout.

"Moncrief! Over here!"

It can only be K. Burke.

"I've got a patrol car and driver outside. We've got to get our butts over to Central Park West. We can catch up on the way," she says. I follow her quick step toward the exit.

Instead of asking why "our butts" are so urgently required on Central Park West, I ask, "How did you know I'd be here, at *this* airport?"

"I have top-secret access to a special communication device. It's called a telephone. I used it to track you down."

I stop myself from saying that I thought perhaps she had the powers of a gypsy woman. Instead I simply say, "Ingenious, K. Burke. You should become a detective."

"And right now you should become familiar with what's going on at 145 Central Park West. It seems..."

The police siren blares as our car enters the expressway.

"One-forty-five?" I say. "That's the San Remo. 74th Street. *Très élégant*; I have a good friend who lives there..."

"Why am I not surprised?" Burke says. "Who?"

"Juan Carlos Vilca, the Peruvian polo player, and his wife, Gabriela," I say. "She's a professional model. She is exquisite."

"Do you know anyone who isn't exquisite?" A quick pause, then she says, "Wait. Don't answer that. I just thought of someone who isn't. And you're sitting next to her."

"That is *your* opinion, K. Burke," I say. That conversation goes no further. She moves on.

"Meanwhile, there are a few facts you should know about a dead neighbor of your Peruvian friends."

Burke tells me that at two o'clock this afternoon a personal assistant to a rich young woman by the name of Elspeth Tweddle found her dead in her bedroom.

"Tweddle?" I ask. "That is a real name? It sounds like the name of a talking duck in a child's storybook."

"Elspeth Tweddle is a very real name, and Elspeth Tweddle is a very dead woman. And, there's a bit of background information. She's twenty-five years old. And take a look. As you would say, truly exquisite."

K. Burke clicks a photo of Elspeth Tweddle on her iPad. The woman may be twenty-five, but she could pass for eighteen.

This woman *is* exquisite, truly beautiful. A big pouty look on her face, with light-green eyes, and chestnut hair with the fashionable blond streaks.

Burke tells me that they are called champagne streaks.

"When the streaks have more gold in them than blond," she explains, "the color is called champagne."

"I love to learn, K. Burke. And that is good, because you love to teach."

Burke ignores me. Then she tells me more about the woman with the champagne streaks.

The woman's personal assistant came in at two. He usually arrived at ten, but the woman had a dentist appointment and he had arranged to not arrive until after lunch.

"The assistant found her sprawled on the floor, and since Tweddle was rich and beautiful, 911 actually remembered to call us. She was dead when the ME got there."

At this moment our squad car pulls up to the first of the two San Remo apartment towers. The doorman opens the car door.

"Good morning, Mr. Moncrief. Is Mr. Vilca expecting you?" he asks.

"No, Ernie. I am here today on official business."

K. Burke takes charge. "I'm Detective Burke, and apparently you already know Detective Moncrief. We will be joining a few other members of the NYPD on the . . ."

Ernie finishes her sentence. "The twelfth floor. There are quite a few people up there already. Take a left at the end of this hall, and that'll be your elevator."

As we wait for the elevator I ask Burke, "So, what are you thinking? Do we know if this case fits the same pattern as the other three?"

"The only thing that fits is that the victim or the 'dead woman,' if you prefer, is very pretty, very young, and very rich. There the similarities end. Miss Tweddle is *not* married. Miss Tweddle does *not* have children. And so Miss Tweddle does *not* have an overweight nanny."

"Hmmm. Yet it *feels…it feels…*" I begin to say. Burke holds her hand up like a traffic cop. She speaks.

"I'm with you. It sure as hell smells like the other three deaths."

"Mademoiselle Tweddle lives alone?"

Burke looks down at her notes.

"Well, there's a live-in cook, a live-in maid, and another maid who doesn't live there. Miss Tweddle's personal assistant comes in five days a week. But there are a few other things I've got to tell you…"

Then the elevator arrives. The elevator man pulls wide the bronze gates, and two young boys wearing blue blazers and gray flannel slacks get off the elevator.

Burke and I ride up to the twelfth floor in silence. She's not about to tell me anything in front of the elevator man.

We finally arrive on twelve. Two police officers nod and gesture toward the open apartment door. But Burke pauses before we enter.

"Let me finish the background," she says. "Elspeth Tweddle lives here, but this is her mother's apartment. The victim grew up in this apartment. Elspeth never moved out."

"The mother is deceased?"

"No, she's very much alive. Elspeth's mother, Rose Jensen Tweddle, is currently the American ambassador to Italy."

CHAPTER 19

THE POLICE SCENE HAS not been touched. Pristine. Just the way we like it when we show up.

The victim is lying on her back on the bedroom floor. She wears only a sports bra and cut-off gray sweatpants.

Jonny Liang, the assistant medical examiner, approaches us immediately. Jonny handled Tessa Fulbright's case.

"A quick on-site blood test is telling us no drug abuse, but we won't know for sure until we get the full autopsy going," Jonny says.

Jonny's a smart guy. Before Burke or I can say a word, he anticipates our next question.

"I know. From a circumstantial point of view, it looks just like your other three 'rich gal' cases. Yet so far the forensics don't support that conclusion. Wait until tonight or tomorrow morning. I'll get you the information fast."

"Assuming there *is* information," Burke says. I share her skepticism, but something is bugging me. Before I can even think about what that nagging feeling might be, a handsome young blond man—no more than thirty years old—approaches us.

"Good morning, detectives. I'm Ian Hart. I'm Miss Tweddle's personal assistant."

"I'm happy to tell you what I told the police officers," Hart says. My instinct is that this guy is a sleazebag—too handsome for his own good. I notice his four-hundred-dollar jeans, and consider that he spends each day with the ambassador's beautiful daughter.

I immediately glance at the bed and consider if more than one person has been in it. No. Just one side of the king-size bed looks slept in.

But I rethink that instinct as he speaks. This guy comes across as smart and strong. He's also somber, like a guy who is authentically sad that he's lost a friend.

For the most part I learn nothing that I haven't already heard from K. Burke. He does, however, point to a small desk near the window. On that desk is a coffee mug with the initials "ET" on it.

"She had a lot of ET stuff," Hart says. "Her initials, you know."

Burke nods. She obviously figured that out. Elspeth Tweddle.

I also nod. I would never tell this to Burke, but I did not figure that out.

Burke tells one of the officers to "bag" the coffee mug contents and get it to the lab.

"What exactly were your responsibilities with Miss Tweddle?" I ask.

"The usual PA stuff—lunch reservations, dinner reservations, dealing with what little correspondence she had.

But a lot of the things she did…well, we did together. We played squash. We went to parties together. We'd run in the park. We went riding in the park a lot. And she was working on this documentary. She had all these home videos of her and her family's summers on Fishers Island."

Clearly Ian Hart interprets our silence and our occasional nods as indication that we thought his boss's life—not to mention his own job—was pretty frivolous.

He says, "Listen. I know it kind of sounds like I was being paid to be Elspeth's friend. And in a way I was. But I really liked the days I spent with her. She was smart and she was pretty and she was fun."

He looks away from us. He blinks his eyes quickly. He looks back at us, composed. He smiles.

"She was my friend," he says.

Later, as we wait for the elevator, Burke says, "You know one of the toughest things in detective work?"

She does not wait for my answer. Instead she gives her own answer.

"It's whether grieving people are telling the truth. In those moments, I never quite know for sure when someone is bullshitting me—or even being honest with them-selves."

"I am not so good at it myself," I say. We are silent for a few seconds.

Then Burke says, "So, they went riding a lot. You've got quite a few horses in your life these days, Moncrief."

As we walk from the elevator to the door I say to Burke, "*Alors.* You have reminded me. You know that white dress in which you looked so magnificent at the Kentucky Derby?"

"What about that dress?" She asks the question suspiciously.

"Have it washed and ironed. Next Friday night we are leaving for Baltimore. The next day is..."

She knows. She yells, "The Preakness!"

CHAPTER 20

THE SAVATIERS' HORSE, GARÇON, came to Louisville as an anonymous foreigner. He comes to Baltimore as a worldwide celebrity, the favorite.

Garçon now has a really good shot at capturing the Triple Crown, the honor that goes to the rare horse who wins the Kentucky Derby, the Preakness Stakes, and the Belmont Stakes. This possibility is beyond thrilling—only twelve times, in more than one hundred years of thoroughbred racing, has a horse won the Triple Crown.

Only a few days ago I was here to view the remains of a horse, a mysterious and disgusting slaughter. But we carry on. We have tried our best to tuck the event in the back of our brains. Even the ominous threats and flowers sent to the Savatiers cannot eradicate our nervous hopes. The Savatiers are worried, but they are certainly not defeated. The hired bodyguards and Detective Kwame Clarke have been staying very close to them.

Now, if only the weather would cooperate.

It is a miserable day. Cold rain everywhere. Umbrellas are

everywhere. Serious raincoat weather. Pimlico Race Course is becoming Pimlico River.

K. Burke and I wait in the stable with the Savatiers. Wet hay sticks to our water-soaked shoes. Rain pelts the stable roof.

But Garçon's jockey, Armand Joscoe, keeps smiling and tells Burke and me not to worry. Then he gives us some information to keep us calm.

"*Le cheval aime la boue,*" the little guy says.

"*Très bien, Armand. Très bien.*" Then I turn to Burke and translate.

"The horse likes mud!" I say.

"*Merci,*" Burke says. "And may I remind you for the hundredth time that I speak French." She speaks sweetly, but there is a touch of irritation in her voice.

"Where is your son, Armand?" I ask. He tells me that Léon is occupied elsewhere. But of course, he will be watching.

Burke speaks.

"Have you noticed, Moncrief, that you, me, Marguerite, and Nicolas are all wearing the same clothes we wore at the Derby?"

I look.

"*Mon Dieu,*" I say. "Unbelievable." But it is not really unbelievable.

The four of us seem to be honoring a superstition: Everything must be as it was in Louisville. Marguerite is in her bright floral suit. Nicolas in his perfectly cut gray slacks and blue blazer. Katherine Burke in her white linen dress with the Savatiers' racing silk colors belted around her waist.

I move in close to K. Burke and whisper, "Do you think

Madame Savatier is wearing the same undergarments as she did in Louisville?"

K. Burke looks away from me, as if I am a naughty-minded schoolboy and she is the little girl I chose to shock.

Then a tremendous blare of trumpets. The moment is upon us.

CHAPTER 21

THIRTY SECONDS LATER AN announcement comes from the loudspeakers: "Horses and jockeys will now proceed to the track!"

We walk a few yards with Armand Joscoe and Garçon. After a few minutes the horse and rider turn. They walk toward the water-drenched track, and the rest of us find our places in the owners' circle.

The parade is magnificent, a combination of beauty and strength. Marguerite is seated to my right. She holds my hand. Katherine Burke sits to my left. She holds a pair of high-powered binoculars. Me? I occasionally glance at the equine parade, but mostly I keep a keen eye on the many people seated near us. Who might be watching us? Who might want to harm the Savatiers?

I would like to report that the sun broke out before the race began. It did not. The rain keeps on raining, but it seems a little more cooperative. It seems to fall in a softer, more peaceful rhythm. We wait for the race to start.

I say, "You will recall, K. Burke, that during the plane ride down here you insisted that I was *not* to place a bet for you on Garçon?"

"Of course I do. It was just a sudden superstition on my part. I didn't think he'd win this time if we placed a bet."

"Well, I disobeyed and did so anyway," I say. "But I bet only a hundred dollars."

She's pissed. She turns away from me and mutters, "Damn it. Do you ever listen?"

I say nothing. So she speaks again.

"When I specifically asked you not to? It's bad karma, Moncrief. You're pushing your luck...my luck...our luck."

"But, K. Burke, we are trying to do everything in the same way as we did in Kentucky, *n'est-ce pas?*" I say.

"*N'est-ce pas,* my foot. I think it feels selfish to bet, to feel so smug about winning. If Garçon loses, I'm blaming it on you."

"We shall see. And please, not to worry. This time cannot be exactly like last time. At the Derby Garçon was a long shot. Today he is the favorite. Today his odds are a measly two-to-one. Even if he wins you will only...."

But my attention is suddenly elsewhere. A few yards away from K. Burke I see Detective Kwame Clarke taking a seat. Clarke watches us. Our eyes meet. He tips his umbrella handle in my direction. We both nod to each other.

Marguerite speaks to me.

"I am scared, Luc. Very scared," she says.

"There is no reason..."

"Yes. Yes. I know that you have the private guards watching us. And I know Detective Clarke is nearby. But I am nonetheless frightened."

"You have no need to be," I say. "All is secure."

But I am wise enough to know that, like me, Marguerite is thinking about that dark and threatening note.

Win the Preakness. Or you will suffer the consequences.

"What if Garçon does not win?" she says.

I don't have time to answer. We hear the sound of a bell. Marguerite grabs my hand.

The race begins.

CHAPTER 22

ARMAND JOSCOE, THE JOCKEY *extraordinaire,* turns out to be a psychic *extraordinaire.*

Joscoe's assurance that Garçon "likes mud" turns out to be absolutely true! It becomes clear in the first few moments of the race that Garçon doesn't merely *like* mud. Garçon *loves* mud! Physically, spiritually, indisputably. With mud painting his hooves and legs, Garçon does not merely gallop, he flies.

Yes, we remain nervous. We are still anxious. But it is so much better to be nervous and anxious with a winning horse.

But not only does he win, he wins *decisively.* We all go nuts, and for the second time in two weeks, we are celebrating like crazy people.

The Savatiers are ecstatic, but it is also clear to me that both of them are anxious. Marguerite's hands tremble. Her head keeps turning back and forth. Officials (including Kwame Clarke) arrive quickly to lead the couple to the presentation circle.

"My friends must come with us," Marguerite says to Detective Clarke.

"No, no," I say. "You will be well cared for, and Detective Burke and I will be standing nearby."

Burke leans into me.

"Moncrief, she's shaking. She's a nervous mess. What difference does it make? Let's go with them."

Burke's logic is impeccable, of course.

"Very well," I say. Marguerite Savatier turns to Burke: "*You, Mademoiselle Burke,* are a very fine influence on our Luc." Hmmm. I could swear there was a flash of romantic mischief in Marguerite's eyes.

So we join the owners. Then, a few moments later, the four of us join the triumphant horse and the smiling jockey. Garçon is covered in a huge blanket of yellow flowers.

"Those are Viking poms. They're meant to look like Black-Eyed Susans, the official state flower of Maryland," Burke says to me.

"Is there anything you do not know, K. Burke?" I ask.

"Well, I don't know how much money we won on that race," she says with a twinkle in her eye. Then we both turn our attention to the trophy presentation, as well as the presentation of a large bouquet of Black-Eyed Susans to Madame Savatier. The old woman smiles for the cameras. Applause. Smiles. The thousands of *click-click-click* from cameras.

I feel a buzz from my cell phone. I try looking at the screen as discreetly as possible. A message from Inspector Elliott.

Where the hell r u 2?

I text back. See u soon.

He texts back. WTF?

I slip the phone back into my pocket.

The speeches from corporate sponsors and the governor of Maryland are mercifully short. Then we stand at attention—for the third time—and listen to yet another rendition of "Maryland, My Maryland."

CHAPTER 23

THE MOMENT BURKE AND I break from our group and head to the after-party she says, "That message you got was from Elliott, wasn't it?"

"Indeed it was. He asked about our whereabouts. I told him that we would be in touch soon. Not to worry," I say.

"We should get back up to New York now," she says.

"In due time, K. Burke. For the moment, a celebration."

The party in the Pimlico Club room is lavish, even more so than the post-race party in Louisville. Instead of mint juleps, Pimlico serves a cocktail called the Black-Eyed Susan.

"I think they put every fruit juice in the world in this drink," says K. Burke.

I ask a nearby waiter what goes into this concoction. He practically quotes Burke: "Any fruit juice you can name—orange, pineapple, lime. Then a lot of vodka and a little bourbon."

Burke and I each put down a few drinks. Indeed, will Burke and I ever find a race-party cocktail that we do *not* like?

It should be a festive day. Garçon has won. The party is noisy and happy and fun. Instead of Louisville's tiny hush puppy hors d'oeuvres, we are served miniature crab cakes. The crowd is elegant. The music is loud. The DJ plays Randy Newman and Bruce Springsteen and Lyle Lovett and even Counting Crows. And every song is—amazingly—a song about Baltimore.

I pull out my phone and pull up my favorite horse-racing blog. I have to yell to be heard over the music and celebration, but I read this part to K. Burke:

"As a Frenchman loves champagne, so does Preakness favorite Vilain Garçon love mud. Yes, Vilain Garçon easily grabbed hold of step two in his bid for the Triple Crown. This extraordinary steed, owned by a charming elderly French couple, Marguerite and Nicolas (no "h," *s'il vous plait*), and ridden by the until-now unknown jockey Armand Joscoe, won the Preakness decisively this afternoon. Not by a nose, but by a full length. The rain-drenched crowd is reacting with wild shouts. As for this reporter, I will suggest to the Savatiers that, when the Belmont Stakes comes along, that they pray for rain. If their prayers are answered, then the Triple Crown is certain."

Burke pretends to listen, but she's chewing on the orange peel from her cocktail. As always, however, she is on the job.

"Shall we check in with your buddy Kwame and the Baltimore PD?" she asks.

"Certainly. If you ever finish your orange peel," I say. She makes a face and puts the peel back in the glass. Then we both walk to the entrance archway where Kwame Clarke and two men in gray suits are standing, bodyguards for the Savatiers. The cut of their boxy suits immediately tells me that these are two officers.

Introductions all around.

"Aha, now I finally meet the extraordinary K. Burke," says Kwame Clarke.

Burke nods her head in my direction and says to Clarke, "You didn't hear that word 'extraordinary' about me from Moncrief, I'm sure."

Smiles all around.

K. Burke and Kwame Clarke shake hands. Perhaps an unusually long handshake, I think.

It occurs to me that Burke and Clarke have noticed...how to put this?...how good-looking the other is.

Why does this annoy me?

Clarke introduces me to the officers—Vinnie Masucci and Olan Washington. They explain that they are eyeballing everybody who comes in.

"If the name's not on the invite list, they're not at the party," says Masucci.

We discuss the rain, of course. The weather and the triumphant Garçon are the subjects of the day. Then Clarke says that he and his "guys" are going to check out the kitchen once more.

"We can hang here," K. Burke volunteers.

And we do. We even have a serious discussion concerning the merits of crab cakes versus hush puppies. Then K. Burke, who must have been reading *Horse Racing for Dummies*, lectures me on the wonders of American Pharoah, the most recent horse to win the Triple Crown.

K. Burke ends her lecture abruptly and says, "I'm worried, Moncrief."

I shrug and say, "We have done all we can. They have

put ten plainclothesmen at the stables after the training horse was killed. They put thirty officers in the crowd today, two of them directly behind the Savatiers and us. They randomly tested all the food. They did backgrounds on the caterers, waiters, band…"

"Moncrief!" K. Burke says. "Over there."

She points to two young men walking toward us, wearing jeans and yellow rain slickers, carrying either side of a huge arrangement of roses. Holy shit! The floral display is identical to the arrangement Marguerite Savatier received at the Kentucky Derby.

"Where'd these roses come from?" asks K. Burke.

"I don't know. Some kid, a teenager, dropped 'em off. Matt and I were just working out there, parking cars, trying to stay dry. Then this kid shows up in this shitty old van. He gives us each twenty bucks and tells us to bring it inside to the party. He says they're for some old lady."

He then pulls a small gift card from his pocket and hands the envelope to Burke, who then passes it to me.

The roses are, of course, for Marguerite.

"You know where the old lady is?" says the guy who's helped carry in the floral arrangement.

"Yeah, we do," I say. "We'll make sure she gets them."

CHAPTER 24

BACK IN NEW YORK, at the Midtown East precinct, K. Burke and I receive an exceptionally warm welcome from our boss, Inspector Nick Elliott.

"Where the hell on Christ's green earth have you two lovebirds been?"

K. Burke now makes a huge mistake. She talks.

"Excuse me, Inspector Elliott. I just want to make it clear that Luc Moncrief and I are not—in any way, shape, or form—involved in a romantic or..."

Elliott interrupts.

"Thank you, Detective Burke. Your private life is your business."

K. Burke won't let go of it. Bad idea. She tries once more.

"This is the truth. Moncrief and I have never..."

Now Elliott interrupts loudly. No one is going to interrupt him again. He's moved back to the work discussion.

"As I was saying. Take a look at this. It's a surveillance video of a drug dealer in Central Park."

This time I speak.

"Inspector, forgive my rudeness, but finding a drug dealer in Central Park is as common as finding a blade of grass in Central Park."

"I don't disagree, Moncrief, but just take a look." Then he adds, "And do it quietly." By now both K. Burke and I have annoyed him.

Elliott motions to us with his finger from his desk chair. Burke and I move behind him and lean into the computer screen.

The black-and-white picture portrays—in muddy shades of light and dark gray—what looks like clouds. Eventually, as the scene comes into focus, everything is more easily identifiable as an unkempt area of trees and weeds and stone boulders.

"It looks like Sherwood Forest," Burke says. "Is it the Ramble?"

The Ramble is a wooded area of Central Park totally un-manicured and un-landscaped.

"Yup. During the day you see bird-watchers with their binoculars and notepads," says Elliott. Then, "At night it turns into a kind of playground for gay guys."

"I have been to this area. To the Ramble," I say.

Elliott looks up at me, slightly startled. Burke turns her head and looks at me. Also slightly startled.

"No. I am not a bird-watcher. But when I began working for you, Inspector, you may recall, my first assignment was searching for criminals who stole bicycles. For three weeks myself and Maria Martinez spent two days at the Bethesda Fountain, two days in the Sheep Meadow, and two days in the Ramble, all in pursuit of bicycle thieves."

"And as I remember, you and your partner didn't catch one goddamn bike thief," says Elliott.

"Ah, but I learned a great deal about the geography. Right now, in this video I can tell you the scene is located precisely between Harkness House on the East Side and the Museum of Natural History on the West Side."

"Great. Keep watching," says Elliott.

The camera suddenly makes a sharp downward turn. We zoom in for a medium close-up to record who is standing on the stone pathway that rambles through the Ramble.

Burke and I study the screen. It now shows a fairly sharp image—for a police surveillance video: a teenage boy. Tall, thin, with a great deal of blond hair. Perhaps he is seventeen.

"New York City rich kid," K. Burke says. "A common species."

She is correct. He wears a blue blazer with an indecipherable gold insignia on the front pocket. A white button-down shirt of the Brooks Brothers variety. Striped blue-and-yellow silk tie in a thin sloppy knot. Gray pants.

"In fact," she continues thoughtfully, "didn't we see one of those recently?"

I am distracted. "His rucksack is bursting," I say.

"Speak English, Moncrief," says Elliott. "What the hell is a *rucksack?*"

Burke cuts in again. "At Miss Tweddle's. Didn't we see..."

She trails off as two similarly dressed teenage boys approach. The blond boy reaches into his...backpack...and hands each of them a plastic bag.

"No exchange of money," says Burke. "Maybe the next customer."

"I think his clientele pay in advance or put it on the tab," says Elliott.

"The latter—the tab—that is the way the rich do it," I say.

No sooner has Burke predicted a 'next customer' than a pretty—and very curvy—brunette woman, maybe thirty years old, in athletic clothes approaches. Again, the blond boy reaches into his satchel and hands over a small plastic bag. And again no money is seen.

"This is why I called you to look at this," says Elliott. "Do you recognize that woman?"

"Oh, my God," says Burke. "The Monahans' nanny."

"Mrs. Meade-Grafton!" I remember her unsettling laughter.

"One of the officers who was at the Monahan apartment happened to be on this as well. Lucky stroke for us. Especially while you two are gallivanting around," Elliott says, with insinuation.

Burke's face is very red, but she lets it pass. "What I was going to say is that we saw two boys wearing blazers and gray pants exiting the elevator when we entered Miss Tweddle's building."

"Very good, Burke!" I exclaim. "I had forgotten. Your sartorial eye is getting better every day."

I do not think I deserve her glare.

We watch more transactions. Most of the buyers are young. Most of them are white. The entire video will continue for twelve minutes before the blond boy leaves the frame.

"We had no trouble identifying the teen pusher. He's been booked before, petty thievery once. Ready for this? He and his girlfriend bolted a bill at Daniel. The most expensive restaurant in the city. Plainclothes caught them two blocks away on Fifth Avenue."

"Beware the couple who attend the restroom at the same time," I say.

Elliott smiles slightly and recites the rest of the rap sheet: Weed outside a dance club on 28th Street. Assault of another student at a school basketball game.

"And no arrests that stuck?" Burke says.

"No. The kid's name is Reed Minton Reynolds. His father, Bill Reynolds, is that big deal weight-loss specialist, and, if you want, he'll give you a side order of plastic surgery. I've met him twice—actually a nice guy. Full disclosure, he's also responsible for 50 percent of the funding for the Police Athletic League."

"And 50 percent of the facelifts and breast augmentations in Manhattan," K. Burke says.

I can't resist. I turn and say, "You sound like you know something about these procedures, K. Burke."

Elliott shoots me an angry look.

"Don't start." A pause. Enough time for K. Burke to give a *somebody got in trouble* kind of smile. Elliott continues.

"Anyway, this Reed Reynolds kid is about to graduate Dalton, and he's signed, sealed, and soon-to-be-delivered to Yale. I'd like you two to track him for a day or two or three. Stay close to him. I want you to see where he goes, if he works anywhere else in the park. Do a 'smother job' on him. I'm not that interested in him, but...I think if we get a good fix on him, we can find out who's supplying him with his stash."

K. Burke gives one of her energetic responses: "Gotcha, Inspector."

As we reach Elliott's office door to leave I cannot resist

saying: "Oh, and by the way, Inspector. While we're in Central Park, I'll keep my eyes open for any stolen bicycles."

"Get the hell out of here, Moncrief."

"Gotcha, Inspector."

The last word I hear from Elliott's mouth is simple.

"Asshole!"

CHAPTER 25

Monday
3:15 p.m.

WE SPENT ALL YESTERDAY afternoon trying to track down this kid, but only saw him as he arrived at home at the end of the day, and never came back out. But we never saw him leave this morning, either, unless he left before dawn, so now K. Burke and I are waiting on the north side of East 89th Street. We watch students straggling out of the Dalton School. Some light cigarettes. Others hold hands. Reed Reynolds doesn't show.

"Let's get over to Central Park. Maybe he cut out of school early," I say.

"Or maybe he never went to school today," says Burke. "I remember my own last few days of high school. Once we got accepted to college or had a job lined up, we didn't care anymore."

We enter the park just south of the Metropolitan Museum. We walk over a wide grassy area where shirtless men and near-shirtless women are sunning themselves. We then make our way down a small dirt pathway that leads us into a large dark wooded area. The Ramble.

The skunky-sweet smell of weed is in the air. Burke and I quickly locate the general area where Reed Reynolds was recorded distributing drugs. A few people are around— tourists, dog-walkers—but there are others in more secluded corners, kissing and smoking. But it's the same as the wait at his house this morning and at his school this afternoon—no Reed Reynolds.

I suggest we walk farther into the woods. It pays off. Thank you, instinct. A slightly swampy overgrown area, a few people, a few pairs of people. And there he is, holding court on a bench, like a little kid running a lemonade stand. We watch, taking care to remain hidden in the trees.

There he is, smoking cigarettes, an occasional finger snap to the beat of the music coming through his phone. He pauses only when a buyer comes along. Reynolds hands out his little zip-lock bags, his plastic orange bottles of bennies or red balls or good old reliable speedballs. He's got a steady flow of customers. He seems to know exactly what they came for. No money changes hands. In about twenty minutes he's supplied about a dozen people.

Who are these folks? Your basic mixed bag of New Yorkers: the old, the young, the Black, the white. Some are dressed for sleeping on the street. Some are dressed for sleeping at the Carlyle. They're as varied as the crowd at a Knicks game. People like Mara Monahan and Tessa Fulbright, two of those young women who died, would fit seamlessly into this group.

"You're starting to get agitated, Moncrief," says K. Burke.

"It is true, K. Burke. I have a great agitation to put handcuffs on this little preppy shithead," I say.

"Our job right now is to watch him and follow him. Nothing more. Nothing less."

"*Oui, maman,*" I say.

Suddenly, K. Burke elbows me.

"Take a look at that guy with Reynolds now," she says.

I look to see a middle-aged man in annoyingly good shape. Sinewy muscles and forearms. He is wearing a ridiculous costume: tight black lycra shorts, a colorful yellow bicycling shirt, and a yellow helmet.

"I think that man has escaped from the circus," I say.

"No. He's that guy who gives massages. Remember that gift certificate you gave me for massages? That's him."

"Ah, *oui.* The Armenian masseur. Louis."

"*Non.* The Hungarian masseur. Laszlo."

"Whatever his name," I say, "he's spending my money on skag."

We study the other customers. Two of them are teenagers—very distressing. Two of the female purchasers are what are known as "yummy mummies," in a way that is also distressing.

We watch the ebb and flow of buyers.

"Aha, K. Burke," I suddenly say. "Now it is my turn to push my elbow into your side. You will please look at that woman who is approaching young Master Reynolds."

I point to an attractive Manhattan-type: Her perfectly cut chestnut-colored hair falls over a snug white T-shirt. She wears a pair of baggy black linen shorts. The woman is not beautiful, but she is impeccably put together. This woman is evidence of an observation my late beloved Dalia sometimes made: "She's done the best she can with what God gave her."

"Okay, Moncrief. Who is she?" asks K. Burke.

"You do not know her? You met her just a few days ago. She..."

"Holy shit!" says Burke, perhaps a little too loudly. "It's that frumpy English nanny...what's-her-name... the one who worked for what's-her-name."

"Well put, K. Burke. What's-her-name is correctly named Julia Highridge, who appears to have been transformed from a dowdy Miss Marple into a chic Manhattan mademoiselle."

"It's amazing how much better she looks," says Burke.

"A touch of makeup. And a six-hundred-dollar Frederic Fekkai haircut," I say.

Reed Reynolds hands Julia Highridge a plastic bag, and she walks in the direction of Central Park West. She seems to be the day's final customer.

Reed Reynolds stands alone. He makes a few quick notes on a small pad. Then he takes a silver flask from his bag and takes a long swig. He recaps the flask and slips it into his backpack. Reed Reynolds heads east to Fifth Avenue. He half walks. He half runs. He has youth on his side. We take off after him. Skipping, hopping, jogging, racing, or leaping over a stone wall, K. Burke and I keep up with him.

Now we're out of the park. He crosses Fifth Avenue. We stay on the Park side and watch him. Reynolds stops at 930 Fifth Avenue, a large gray-stone building. He nods to the doorman. The doorman touches the rim of his cap. Then Reed Reynolds enters the building.

He's home.

"Damn."

Now it is *my* turn to calm *her* down.

"K. Burke. Please. You will settle your nerves. We will follow him. Tomorrow. And the next day. We will learn from him. Then once we know how he does it and where he gets his inventory... *Voilà!*

"This young man believes he's going to Yale. But first... well, he may have to do an internship on Rikers Island."

CHAPTER 26

Tuesday
3:00 p.m.

EARLY THE NEXT MORNING, K. Burke and I visit the office of Megan Scott, the dean of students at the Dalton School. We have shown her our ID and begin our questions, politely of course.

"We need to know if Reed Reynolds was in class today," we say.

"Why do you *need* to know?" asks Megan Scott.

"That's an expression, Miss Scott," says K. Burke. "And this is an NYPD investigation."

Burke and I know that many of the students at this school are the children of the rich and powerful. That means little to me, and it means absolutely nothing to my partner.

"We give information out on our students only when it's necessary," says Megan Scott.

"*Mademoiselle,*" I say. "We have asked you for one piece of information. Was the boy in school today? That is not an inflammatory or provocative question."

Burke gives me a look that seems to say, "We're not going to let this bureaucrat obstruct our investigation."

"Very well," says Scott. "Reed was *in* class today, but he was not in this building. He's finishing up a special project at the Metropolitan Museum of Art. Okay. There's your answer. Now if I may ask a question, what's the problem?"

"Not a problem, really. We just want to talk to him," Burke says.

"This Reed Reynolds, he is a good student, a good young man?" I ask, trying hard to use as much French charm as I can muster.

"Yes, 'this Reed Reynolds' is a very good student. He's on his way to Yale. He's a wonderful young man. If you could see this project he's doing with the curator of Dutch Renaissance portraiture at the Met..."

K. Burke has heard all she cares to hear. She puts an end to it.

"Thanks, Miss Scott. Thanks for letting us take up your precious time," she says.

Later that day, we're back in the Ramble, witnessing a similar-looking stream of buyers.

Reed Reynolds is still, of course, totally prepped out—white button-down, striped tie, loafers. He looks like he should be on the front of a prep school recruitment brochure.

We watch the distribution of the plastic bags of...heroin? Weed? Speed? Buttons? The possibilities are endless.

Then I turn to Burke and say, "Okay. I'm going to try something."

"What?" she asks.

"I think I'll make a purchase," I say.

"It won't work, Moncrief. These are regulars. Don't be stupid."

I know that she's right, but there's nothing to lose. And if

I make a buy we can hook him into cuffs without chasing all over the city. As I walk toward him, I can practically *hear* K. Burke rolling her eyes.

"I was wondering if you could help me out?" I say.

"Probably not," he says. His voice is flat, dead, weak.

"Maybe just some loose weed," I say.

"No."

"I have two hundred dollars."

"No, man. Go away."

"Five hundred for two ounces?"

This time he doesn't even bother to say "no." He simply walks away.

I return to K. Burke.

"Please notice, Moncrief. I am not saying a word."

But Reed Reynolds doesn't go far, once he sees I'm gone. We watch from our hiding place as, like yesterday, he makes some brief notes and then takes a swig from his silver flask. This time, he does not head toward the Upper East Side but heads south through the park. We tail him past the lake, past Bethesda Fountain, on through the Sheep Meadow, then we are out of the park.

At 59th Street, just opposite the Plaza Hotel, Reed Reynolds hails a cab. We do the same. We follow them down Seventh Avenue, to the downtown corner where it changes to Varick Street. We're in SoHo now.

Reed Reynolds gets out of his cab at 300 Spring Street, a cement and steel monstrosity, a modernistic pile of crap in the midst of the great old SoHo ironclad buildings.

Burke is on her iPad.

Seconds later she says, "It's his father's office and clinic.

William Reynolds, MD. Let's go up. We can take a service elevator, maybe, or..."

"No," I say. "I know something better to do. And *you* will do it tomorrow."

"Me?" she asks. Burke looks confused. And suspicious.

"You will visit the eminent plastic surgeon, Dr. William Reynolds, *and* you will see if he will sell you some drugs."

"I'm not so..."

"Come, come, K. Burke. I can tell...You also think it is a good idea."

"Well...maybe...yes," she says. (Oh, how she hates to agree with me.)

"And for now I have another good idea."

"And that is?" she asks, also suspiciously.

"We are a mere three blocks from Dominique Ansel Bakery. Let's go and have some good coffee *and* one of Ansel's famous cronuts. *Allons-y!* Let's go!"

"I know how to speak French!" she explodes.

"Please, no angry attitude, K. Burke. Let's hurry! The bakery may soon be out of cronuts."

CHAPTER 27

I HAVE JUST SHARED with K. Burke my precise plan for tomorrow morning. The blueprint is not without some danger. And Burke will be the major player, practically the only player.

"Have you cleared any of this with Inspector Elliott?" K. Burke asks. I think she is nervous. And I don't blame her.

"Share it with Elliott? Of course not," I say. "I have cleared it with you, and I have already cleared it with myself. I think that will be sufficient approval."

"Sweet Jesus, Moncrief," she says.

We walk a few steps to the children's playground next door to Dominique Ansel Bakery. We begin eating our extraordinary cronuts.

As I watch the children in the wading pool and beneath the gentle sprinkler, I am transported—but just for a few moments—to that small unknown children's area in the Jardin du Luxembourg, a mostly hidden area of slides and swings and climbing ropes, an area where a grumpy old man performs absolutely terrible puppet shows, a childhood memory that...

"Moncrief, the plan. You were about to give me the details," Burke says.

My memory of the Jardin du Luxembourg explodes into the New York air, and I tell Burke the plan.

She will make an appointment to visit Dr. William Reynolds, father of drug dealer Reed Reynolds. Only an hour earlier we followed the son to his father's medical office. Only yesterday we watched an employee of one of the beautiful dead women purchase drugs from Reed Reynolds. Beyond that, we know that Dr. Reynolds is the go-to weight-loss specialist for the wealthy women of Manhattan.

"Listen, K. Burke. You are perfect for this job. You are attractive. You are slender. You are articulate. You are the perfect 'insecure rich woman.' We will buy you some decent clothing..."

Burke sneers a very tiny sneer. "Watch it, Moncrief."

"What did I say?"

"Just go on."

"No. It is simple. You go in. You say you are interested in...oh, I don't know...a little Botox here...a little lifting of the butt...maybe you discuss the nose, although I must say that your nose is a sweet little button, a gift from your Irish ancestors."

"Okay, Moncrief, let's stop right there," she says. "I'm actually with you on this idea. I hate to admit it, but it's good. As an idea. But I'm going to change something. Instead of surgery, I'll try asking Dr. Reynolds for drugs—weight-loss, relaxants, stimulants, that sort of thing."

"It is your setup and your scene. It is all up to you," I say.

I have been googling around on diet and weight-loss sites. I have learned about, I tell Burke, a desire on some women's parts to supplement their amphetamines and appetite suppressants with laxatives. I hand Burke my iPad. She reads a highlighted piece from Dr. William Reynolds's website, BeautifulYouInstantly.com.

Some patients believe that the additional use of diuretics and laxatives aids in reaching their weight-loss goal. This is a matter in which I try to dissuade them. Strong emetic medication, while fostering the sense of weight-loss, is a worthless medical methodology.

"But you're contradicting yourself. Reynolds is saying here that he does *not* approve of laxatives..." says Burke.

"*C'est vrai.* That is true, but my instinct tells me this: I am beginning to suspect that our four victims were using very strong purgatives. Such medications either contributed to their death or actually caused their death. Reynolds is invoking the 'reverse psychology' approach. Tell someone they don't need something, and, of course..."

Burke finishes my sentence: "And, of course, they will want it even more."

"Here's what I think. You remember the ME's reports, yes? No drugs, they said...except for an antidepressant or two, and a seemingly innocent laxative. So what do I think? That our victims died of laxative overdosing."

"Oh, my God," says Burke.

I continue. "I also believe, consciously or not, that he

was supplying his son's business with items that have street value. But to our victims, he supplied massive doses of laxatives—over-the-counter, prescription, even holistic herbs and teas. In any event when you go to see Reynolds, ask him to sell you one or two of the high-powered laxatives. Okay?"

I can see that Burke's enthusiasm is growing stronger.

"I'll do it, Moncrief, but I'm nervous."

"Not to have the worry. I will be there. I'll have a SWAT team on standby. Emergency medical will be standing by," I say.

"Medical?"

"Precautions, K. Burke. Laxatives can be…unpredictable." She doesn't laugh at my joke. "Don't worry. It is a harmless setup."

"Well if it's so easy, why don't you do it, Moncrief?"

I cannot resist. I say, "I would not be credible. What possible imperfection could Dr. Reynolds find in me?"

"Maybe he could change you from a smug asshole into a normal person," she says. Neither of us speaks for a moment.

"I will call." I dial the number from the website. A receptionist with a warm, calm voice answers. I exaggerate my French accent.

"Yes, I'd like to make an appointment for my client. She has not seen Dr. Reynolds before, but he is highly recommended. I am afraid my client needs to be seen right away—as in tomorrow. Her name is Marion Cotillard. Can you fit her in?"

I watch Burke's eyes widen. "Oh, you can? Thank you. She will see you tomorrow at five."

I hang up and she sputters, "Marion Cotillard?! She's a famous actress! I don't look anything like her."

"Does not matter," I say. "Now you're in. We never said you were *that* Marion Cotillard."

"What about when they ask for my identification?"

"You will have this."

I hand her a rolled-up wad of cash.

"Take this. Buy everything with cash."

"Why? The NYPD never allows personal money to..." she begins.

I ignore her. "It is thirty one-hundred-dollar bills. Three thousand dollars. Take it, and use it."

K. Burke nods. She takes the cash. We finish our cronuts and coffee.

Now the only thing left to do is to persuade K. Burke to walk with me to Alexander Wang and buy an outfit that's just a little bit more chic than her khaki pants and yellow Old Navy polo shirt.

"The weather is cooler," I say. "Let's walk around SoHo for a little bit."

"Sure," she says. "And while we're walking, let's stop at Alexander Wang and buy me some very cool clothes."

I laugh. Then I say, "You are something else, Katherine. I know that this plan will go very well."

"Holy shit," she says. "You must think this is important."

"And you say that because?"

"Because you actually called me Katherine."

CHAPTER 28

BURKE BLUSHED BUT WAS secretly proud when Nick Elliott first introduced her to Moncrief: "She learned it, she earned it. She's one of the best detectives around. *And* she's got guts to go with her brains." She knew it was true. She didn't often have the chance to do undercover operations, and was looking forward to this. Even so, Burke couldn't help feeling nervous about this operation.

She walks into Dr. William Reynolds's office the next day at 4 p.m., and her mind's eye virtually clicks a photograph of the waiting room—furnished with objects she only recognizes due to Moncrief's shopping addiction.

Creamy white walls. Two authentic—Le Corbusier, she thinks?—black leather couches facing each other. A glass-topped coffee table sitting between the couches. An authentic and huge photograph hanging on the wall that Burke recognizes thanks to an art crime case. It's Jeff Koons's *Made in Heaven*—a near-naked man and woman in a passionate embrace.

The couches, the Koons. Click. Brain picture.

Burke is the only patient in the waiting room. A receptionist sits behind a glass Parsons table. The only item on her table is a very small MacBook Air. Next to the table is a small gray cabinet.

The receptionist is gorgeous. Long blond hair. Perfect features on a perfectly shaped face. Burke remembers what her mother used to say about a beautiful woman or a handsome man: "God took extra care when He put that one together." The receptionist wears a simple sleeveless gray shift, matching the gray cabinet. Nice touch.

Burke approaches, and as she gets closer she notices a slightly theatrical shininess to the woman's face. Could she really be using pancake makeup? Greasepaint? The woman's figure is not merely thin, it is thinner than thin. Her clavicles are sharp and prominent.

The receptionist is possibly twenty-five years old, or thirty-five, or forty-five...Burke really cannot tell. The receptionist exists in plastic surgery time.

"Ms. Cotillard, welcome," she says. A warm voice, a quiet voice. Burke senses disappointment, but there is no comment. A moment later she is filling out forms on a tablet—the information is fictional, but she trusts she would be done before this was discovered. After a short wait, the receptionist leads Burke into a changing room. Burke slips into an unusually elegant examination gown—pale yellow, soft thick cotton, matching slippers.

A knock on the changing room door.

A man's voice. "Miss Cotillard. It's Bill Reynolds. May I come in?"

Burke opens the door. William Reynolds is a bigger-sized

cosmetically enhanced version of his son the drug dealer. No classic white doctor coat and stethoscope here. His blond hair is perfectly cut, his black suit fits perfectly, and his shirt is bespoke, like Moncrief's, allowing his slim frame to show some muscle.

He shakes Burke's hand. Reynolds does not indulge in ordinary clichés of greeting, no "Nice to meet you," no "Good to see you."

Instead he tenderly moves both his hands to Burke's shoulders and speaks gently: "Let me help you, Marion. Will you please let me help you?"

It should sound creepy, she thinks, but instead it sounds soothing. Burke wants to hear something dangerous or, at the very least, phony. Instead his voice makes her feel restful, trusting, and…oh, shit, she thinks…ever so slightly aroused.

CHAPTER 29

"MY OFFICE IS THIS way. Please, come with me, so we can talk before the exam."

Why am I wearing a gown? Through another door. Reynolds's office is sparse: another glass desk, a small gray cabinet. Some solemn-looking medical books on the shelves. An examining table with three measuring tapes and a small camera. Nothing else. It barely reads like a doctor's office. Reynolds gestures to the chair opposite his desk.

"What is your trouble? What is your dream? How can I help?" he asks.

She knows she must slip into the role she has come here to play. Reynolds's voice soothes her. But, damn it, she will, of course, be tougher. She's smarter. Clear the decks. Light the lights.

"I am just starting to hate the way I look. I mean, I know I'm sort of pretty. I also know the world's falling apart, and I'm worrying about the millimeter droop in my neck and my ears. But, well, I guess I should start by doing something about my weight..."

Burke knows that she is perfectly proportioned. She knows that if she ever truly complained to her cousins Maddy and Marilyn they'd laugh and criticize her for such self-involvement. God forbid she ever said something to Moncrief. He would force-feed her a hot fudge sundae.

"There's always room for improvement," Reynolds says. "That's the wonder of life."

That's the wonder of life? Burke thinks. *Jesus.*

Reynolds reaches into his filing cabinet and takes out two pamphlets. He hands one to her.

"Read along with me, Marion. Let's start on page three."

The page is titled "Help on Your Journey."

He begins reading:

"The judicious use of diet pills may lend you exactly the support you and your willpower need in order to learn and maintain sensible eating habits. Small doses of Dexedrine in limited quantities will give you the resilience you never knew you had."

Burke nods. Dexedrine, huh? On the street, in the clubs, in the best and worst neighborhoods, they're called Black Beauties.

"By the way," he says. "I know, of course, that my assistant, Nora, asked for the name of your pharmacy. That will be used strictly for emergencies. I will, for the sake of precision, put together a weekly packet of medication for you. It's a much wiser system, a safer system."

"But how do you know what . . . " Burke begins.

"I know, Marion. The Reynolds system is always the same, always foolproof. When you see a truly beautiful woman on Fifth Avenue, chances are great that she once sat where you're sitting now." He continues reading, in what is becoming the most bizarre doctor's visit she's ever had:

"Random and unpredictable sleeplessness is sometimes the result of even the most well-planned and supervised weight-loss plans, like the one you'll be embarking on. To compensate for the possible problem of insomnia, you will also be prescribed limited doses of Flunitrazepam, the medication that has been proven helpful to many European women."

Again Burke nods. She is sure that she remembers Moncrief saying that Flunitrazepam is called *le petit ami parfait*, "the perfect boyfriend," by wealthy Parisian women.

The reading from the gospel according to Reynolds continues. He tells Burke that her pill packet will also contain two forms of mescaline, as well as what Reynolds calls "a late afternoon relaxant."

Burke knows that on the streets of New York, these tablets are called roofies.

Reynolds stands at his desk.

"So that's it," he says. "I'll see you a week from today, anytime that's convenient and available."

"That's it?" she says, and she realizes that she may have sounded too surprised. Quickly she adds, "What I mean is: aren't you going to weigh me or take blood or urine or look in my eyes?"

"No need to right now. If we need those things at a later date, then we'll do them. But for now, it's better to just relax."

He hands her a small bag. It is made of a gray velvet-like material. The bag has a gold thread closure; it looks like it would contain a piece of silver given as a wedding gift, or a piece of jewelry given to a loved one.

Then Reynolds hands her a five-by-seven manila envelope. The envelope has nothing but the letter *A* written on it.

"These are helpful also. They're a mild laxative. Sometimes my clients find the act of bowel emission to be a helpful signal of how they're doing."

Burke has studied Moncrief's notes. She knows exactly what this medication is: Amatiza, a prescription laxative.

Reynolds keeps talking. "They're fairly large pills. So be sure to take plenty of water with them. Of course, you'll be staying away from all fruit juice. Too much sugar. Sugar and carbs. The dual enemy."

As he speaks she cannot resist squeezing the metal tab on the manila envelope. She pulls out one of the light-blue pills. By any estimation it is huge.

"Can I cut these in half?" Burke asks.

"You may get them down any way you choose," he says. "Put them on the tip of your husband's..." he begins to say. Then he laughs. Burke tries hard not to show that she's both surprised and repulsed by his joke.

"In any event, the medication chart for when you should take these pills is in the little bag," he says. "If you have any questions, Nora or I are always available."

Reynolds removes his suit jacket. He hangs it carefully on the back of his desk chair. He walks around the desk to where Burke is seated.

She thinks: *Why am I wearing an examination gown if he's not going to examine me?*

Now Dr. Reynolds stands in front of her, close to her.

"Do you have any questions?" he asks.

"No, I guess not," Burke asks.

But she realizes that this is now or never. She's got to get him to *sell* her some drugs. She pretends as if some new thought has just crossed her mind.

"Oh, yes. There is something. I'm glad you brought up the laxative thing," she says.

"Yes?"

"A friend of mine told me she occasionally uses something called...oh, I'm not sure...it's like...clementine... clemerol...some sort of laxative that really relaxes you inside... she says."

Burke is setting herself up to request an illegal drug, one banned by the FDA. It should be powerful. It's formulated for horses.

"You're probably thinking of Clenbuterol," Reynolds says. "And it *is* highly effective. But I'm not sure it 'relaxes you inside.'"

"I could swear that's what she said."

"It could help. Some women like it."

"I'd give it a try. I'm pretty serious about losing weight."

"I'll add it to the prescription package. But I must warn you..."

Oh, Burke thinks, this is when he warns me of serious side effects.

No. Reynolds says, "...that there will be an extra charge. I'll give you seven pills, until next week's visit. Like I say, they're pricey. One hundred dollars each."

"That's fine," says Burke.

"Very well. Now go get dressed, and on your way out stop

and see Nora. I'll tell her to add Clenbuterol to your 'goody bag.' It's been a pleasure meeting you."

"Same here," Burke says.

With a big smile on his face, Dr. William Reynolds speaks again. "Next week we can discuss what we might do about those droopy breasts of yours."

CHAPTER 30

KATHERINE BURKE DRESSES QUICKLY. The baggy black linen Alexander Wang pants tie easily at the waist. The simple white cotton T-shirt slips quickly over her shoulders. She grabs her pocketbook and she does a fast check of its contents: iPad, personal iPhone, work cell phone, roll of thirty hundred-dollar bills, and finally, the "Austrian Baby," which is what Moncrief calls the Glock 19 handgun that Burke and Moncrief carry.

Burke walks down the short hallway to the waiting room. She is certain that the lighting is dimmer than when she first entered. Yes, her quick police detective mind registers that the two Sonneman table lamps have been turned off. The track lighting has been turned down. The spotlight on the Koons photo is no longer on.

It's not scary, she thinks. *It's just gloomy.*

The very skinny, very pretty receptionist/assistant— Reynolds called her Nora—is not at the glass desk.

Then suddenly a noise, a human sound, not quite a cough, not quite a sniffle. Burke turns in the direction of one of the black couches. The back of the couch is facing her. Then Burke watches the receptionist beginning to sit up. Nora yawns the tiniest of yawns.

"Oh, Miss Cotillard, I'm sorry. I was just catching a nap while I was waiting for you. You're Dr. Reynolds's last patient. Forgive me," she says as she stands.

"What's to forgive? I wish I could grab a nap right now myself," says Burke.

Nora goes to her desk and begins tapping away at her iPad. "Let's just see what the total payment is. The consultation is one thousand..."

One thousand!

Burke tries not to show her astonishment when she hears the amount.

"The weight-loss medical package is another thousand," says Nora. "And I see here that Dr. Reynolds has dispensed additional medication, Clenbuterol. That's seven..."

Now Burke hears a noise coming from behind her. Nora must be hearing that noise also. Both women look toward the black couch where Nora had been napping. The cough comes again, louder. It is an intense cough, a man's cough, a sick man's cough, Burke thinks.

Suddenly a young man stands up. Burke can only assume that he also has been lying on that couch. The young man squints in the direction of both women. He seems confused, disoriented. He is blond, young, thin. The young man is Reed Reynolds.

"That's Dr. Reynolds's son. I think they're meeting for dinner," says Nora, who delivers the information calmly, matter-of-factly. Burke nods, as if this actually explained something.

"Your dad will be out momentarily, Reed," says Nora. Now she looks back to her iPad and says, "That will be a total of twenty-seven hundred dollars, Miss Cotillard."

Katherine Burke begins counting out hundred-dollar bills.

"Excellent," says Nora. "Cash."

Burke speaks. "Oh, and I'll need a receipt."

"I'll just email it to you," says Nora.

"Oh, I'd prefer a hard copy."

"If I email it you can just print it at home."

"Yes, but I really would prefer to leave with a piece of paper. I'm a dinosaur when it comes to receipts."

Suddenly a loud harsh voice comes from Reed Reynolds.

"Are you deaf *and* stupid, lady? She said she's going to email it to you."

"Reed, please..." says the receptionist.

The young man comes from around the black couch and approaches the glass desk.

"I know this bitch," says Reed Reynolds. "She doesn't *know* that I know her, but I do."

"I don't remember ever meeting you," says Burke, who is now really on edge. This kid is stoned or at least buzzed.

"You were with that asshole who tried to buy shit from me in the park. Like I didn't know you were feds or cops or some other kind of asshole."

Burke is not quite certain what she should say. But facing Reynolds, her arms and hands are shaking. Her stomach is churning. This operation is about to go up in flames. She turns away from Reed Reynolds to face Nora.

"Just ignore him," Nora says.

But Burke cannot. Reed Reynolds is walking toward her.

His long legs bend dramatically at the knees. His walk is almost cartoonish.

The combination of sneer-and-smile on Reynolds's mouth, the dramatic deep red outline of his dead eyes...there's nothing cartoonish about that.

She snaps open her pocketbook. She reaches in, but immediately realizes that her cell phone is in the compartment where her Glock should be.

Reynolds's voice comes at her, loud but slurred: "Move to the goddamn door, lady."

Burke freezes.

Reynolds's voice again: "Get her! Are you fucking deaf? Get her."

It takes Burke a millisecond to realize that Reynolds is shouting at Nora.

If the cell phone is sitting where the Glock should be, then the Glock should be where the...

Burke reaches into her pocketbook. Yes. I am a lucky sonofabitch, she thinks. Burke spins to face Nora.

Nora is holding a gun.

Burke's arm is still in her bag. Her hand is on the gun. But Nora is a second ahead of her. Nora aims her pistol in Burke's general direction.

Nora fires—and misses. The bullet hits the couch.

This is astonishing...to everyone except a cop. *"The 'general direction' IS NEVER GOOD ENOUGH!"* She can hear her firearms instructor's voice.

"Even if you're only three feet from your target it's still READY, AIM, and SHOOT. If you forget the AIM part, then chances are you're dead."

Katherine Burke does what Nora didn't do.

First she *aims*. And then she shoots.

Blood sprays from Nora's neck. She falls on top of the desk. Nora's blood is smearing like children's finger paint on the glass desk.

Then suddenly a hideous, retching, gagging sound comes from Reed. Sick and savage and loud, like a cannibal war cry.

Now Burke is alive in a kind of crazy way. She spins around and sees the boy fold at the waist. His head is almost at the floor, but he is still standing. He begins spewing a fountain of vomit, which splashes to the floor. Some of it hits his black pants as she uses her phone to call for Moncrief.

CHAPTER 31

I DIAL 911 AS I enter the reception room, along with Dr. William Reynolds. I see a dead woman facedown and bleeding out over a glass desk. I barely recognize Reed Reynolds, who is so unconscious that he appears to be dead, his head resting in his own pool of vomit. I ignore William Reynolds, staring at his dead receptionist and son. They will be dealt with when more officers arrive, which should be any minute.

When I look to the other corner, I see K. Burke standing, looking out the window. Her shoulders are shaking. She is sobbing, really sobbing, big bursts of tears mixed with squeaks and grunts and coughs.

I walk to her and from behind I put my arms on her shoulders and gently turn her around. She puts her head on my chest.

"It is all right, K. Burke. You behaved admirably. You have much to be proud of," I say softly.

I hold her, rubbing her back with my hands. Silence. Seconds. Minutes. Then Burke speaks.

"Moncrief, I just killed someone."

I imagine page after page after page of police forms and reports. Thousands of finger taps on so many cell phones and laptops. Photographers and photographs and the whooshing sounds of expensive cameras. More detectives. Medical examiners. More police officers. Inspector Elliott. A deputy mayor. The newscasters. The newswriters. The news photographers. The people in the neighborhood. The conversations.

"They say they killed Dr. Reynolds."

"No. Not Reynolds. They killed his girlfriend."

"No. They killed the nurse."

"The nurse *is* the girlfriend."

I can see in my head what is coming, a spectacle for a summer's night in New York City.

I tell Burke that I will take her home to her apartment, and, to my mild surprise, she does not object. She does, however, remain completely silent as the patrol car takes us from SoHo to her apartment in the East 90s.

At her apartment door we step over the messy pile of shoes, boots, and magazines.

"What sort of alcoholic beverages do you have here?" I ask.

"There's a bottle of Dewar's in the cabinet over the fridge, and there's some Gallo Hearty Burgundy next to it," she says. She cannot see the disgust on my face when she mentions the wine. But this, of course, is hardly a time for humor, even between such great friends. Also, these are the first words she has spoken since we left the mad carnival in Dr. William Reynolds's office. Reynolds has been taken to the precinct. Burke has been brought to her home. All has ended the way it should. Yet the air is heavy with misery.

Burke pauses only a few feet into the apartment. She stands perfectly still. Her hands hang at her side.

"K. Burke, what can I do to help you?" I ask. "We have had no nourishment since luncheon. I will order something. A little soup, some bread, some pastry."

"Nothing," she says. Her voice is soft.

"Do you need to refresh yourself? Do you want me to draw you a bath?"

Burke turns her head toward me. She speaks, "'Draw me a bath.' You said 'Draw me a bath.' That's so old-fashioned. So foreign. So...Moncrief-like."

"Well, what is your answer? A bath? A shower? A Dewar's on the rocks?"

It looks as if a small smile is creeping onto her face. I am delighted. The breaking of the ice, as they say. But I'm very wrong. The smile continues without a stop. It curves up and over her cheeks. Her eyes squint hard. Her entire face becomes contorted into sadness. Tears. Loud. Shaking shoulders. Hands to face. Then through her tears comes her ragged voice.

"I think she would have shot me, Moncrief. Do you think so? Moncrief, tell me that you think if I had waited she would have killed me."

I grab her by the arms. And I speak sternly.

"You do *not* have to ask me or torture yourself. You did what your job called for you to do."

She leans onto my shoulder. She sobs, but the sobs do not last long.

"I want to take a shower," she says.

"That is wise," I say. "Perhaps it will help to wash the day away."

"Perhaps," she says. Then, "Thank you for helping. You don't have to stay. I'll be fine."

"No," I say. "I will wait until you are ready for sleeping. I will have a Dewar's waiting for you when you come out of your shower."

Before she enters her tiny bathroom K. Burke turns to me. Her smile is small, but it is real. She speaks. "Draw me a bath? I don't think anyone has ever said that to me." She closes the bathroom door.

The room I'm left in is cluttered with small piles of clothing, an opened but unmade Murphy bed, stacks of magazines, a desk computer whose screen frame is littered with decals and Post-it notes.

I am suddenly thinking: *Who is this woman and what has she become to me? A friend? Of course. A sister? Somewhat. A daughter? Absurd. A woman who might be my lover? No answer to that one. More "no" than "yes." But maybe not.*

I walk to the bathroom door. I hear the shower. Somehow the mere sound of the shower water raining down helps soothe me also.

I do not believe that time heals everything, but in this case, this time . . . I so very much hope and pray that it will. This is not just anybody in my life. This is Katherine.

CHAPTER 32

I STAY THE NIGHT.

K. Burke and I drink our glasses of Scotch. She lies down on the "always-down" Murphy bed. I retreat to the green Barcalounger, which, I discover, is both incredibly ugly *and* incredibly comfortable.

When Detective Burke finishes her drink she holds out her glass. I move to the tiny kitchen area to pour more Scotch. I'm gone maybe thirty seconds, but K. Burke is sound asleep when I get back.

I remove my shoes, my socks, my shirt.

I do not remember falling asleep. But I certainly do remember being awakened by the buzzing of my cell phone. I am not exactly surprised by the caller.

"Luc, as always we call at the most inconvenient time. It is me, Nicolas." I glance quickly at the Felix the Cat clock on Burke's wall and see that it is ten minutes after three in the morning.

"Wait just one moment," I whisper. I take the phone into the bathroom and close the door so not to wake K. Burke. I still keep my voice low.

"Yes, yes. What is the problem?" I ask.

"It is the same. Only different. We are here in New York City, as you know, of course, for the upcoming Belmont. We are at the St. Regis, and...all of this is *très mal*...this..." he begins. I want to scream "Get to the point!" Then mercifully, the inevitable occurs: I hear Marguerite say, *"Donne-moi le télé-phone, Nicolas."* And Nicolas gives Marguerite the telephone. She begins talking.

"Luc, do you know what the time of day is?" she says.

Oh, shit. Is she going to be polite and long-winded also?

But I stay cool. Instead of saying, "Of course I know what the goddamn time is," I say, "Yes. Tell me the problem."

"There was a phone call from the lobby desk. Just a few minutes ago. The man at the desk said that there was a delivery for us. He said that the deliveryman insisted it be brought up to the room immediately. We are, you know, traveling without a maid or a secretary. So Nicolas answered the door buzzer and...*Voilà!*" She pauses.

This time I do not edit or censor my reaction.

"What was it, goddamnit?"

"An extraordinary wreath of roses. Hundreds of them. Hundreds and hundreds. Just like the roses we previously received."

"A card? A message?"

"Yes. I shall read it to you," she says. " 'Lose at Belmont. Or suffer the consequences.' "

I am silent. I am thinking. Then I say: "But of course. In the past they have delivered the roses at the victory party. This time they are certain that there will be no victory party."

Silence. Then Marguerite's voice again on the phone.

"Luc, are you still there?"

"Yes," I say. But I'm not completely *there*. My brain is traveling—filtering and sorting and clicking away. But it clicks slowly. I am weary from lack of sleep. My skin is wet with sweat. My eyes burn. My instincts fail to bring cohesion to my brain.

Marguerite's voice is just short of frantic. "What should we do, Luc?"

"Go back to bed. Try to sleep. I shall stop by your suite at nine a.m."

"Is there nothing else for us to do until then?" she asks.

"Yes. There is one thing."

"Of course," says Marguerite.

"Order coffee and croissants for a nine o'clock room service, and tell them to make certain that the coffee is very strong and the croissants are very flaky."

CHAPTER 33

I DO NOT FALL back to sleep. K. Burke, however, sleeps soundly. Indeed, she is still sleeping when I leave her apartment at 7 a.m.

Back at my own place, a shower, a shave, fifteen minutes in the sauna, another shower, and then a phone call to Jimmy Kocot, the man who is known as "Bookie to the Stars." He is so named because he does not accept bets below a thousand dollars. Further, he does not necessarily accept your bet if he does not personally care for the person placing the bet. How do I know all this? Via the recommendation of Inspector Elliott.

Yes, I know. Amazing. My police boss recommended my bookie. Here's how: Approximately one year ago I told Nick Elliott that I had a good friend who was competing in a—don't think me too foppish—cribbage tournament in Lyon. Because there was a one-day electronics strike in France I could not get through online or by phone to place a "win" on my friend.

Inspector Elliott said that he sometimes used a bookie

("Betting isn't really betting unless you can bet odds," he said, by way of explanation of his own breaking of the law). And so I spoke with Jimmy Kocot. I bet five thousand euros on my friend Pierre Settel. And so I lost five thousand euros.

"So, you got another frog buddy in a cribbage match, Mr. Moncrief?" Jimmy asks this morning when I call.

"No. I'm interested in the Belmont Stakes," I say.

"So's everyone else," he says.

"A great deal of wagering?" I ask.

"A very great deal," he says.

"What sort of odds are you giving on Garçon?"

"I'm not. The smart money is on Millie's Baby Boy and Rufus. They're both three-to-one to win. My clients are not keen on Garçon. I couldn't tell you why."

"No idea?" I ask.

"No. I've got no clue. But the other two nags are coming in, like I say, three-to-one for winning."

"And nothing new to cause this change?" I ask.

There is a pause. When Jimmy speaks again his voice is quieter, intimate, almost a whisper.

"Two guys told me the horse has a sesamoid fracture. That's the bones down around..."

I finish his sentence, "...the ankles."

"Ridiculous," I say. "I'm going with Garçon. I know the owners, and they've told me nothing," I say.

"Whatever you want. I make my money either way. If you'd rather listen to those two old French people instead of me, it's your loss." He says it as a joke, but there is a note of malice in the joke.

"In any event, what are the odds on Garçon?"

"I've got him at seven-to-one."

"I'll take it," I say.

"You say you don't know any inside stuff, but I'm sure you know stuff that I don't know," says Jimmy Kocot, Bookie to the Stars. "Anyway, how much you betting?"

"Fifty thousand."

"You want to tell me that one more time?"

"I think you heard me."

"You doing a group bet, huh?"

"No. It's all mine."

"Fifty is a mighty big bet, even for me. How are you covering it? You know I can only do cash."

"You'll have it in less than a minute. I'll wire it to you right now."

Jimmy and I say our good-byes. I punch in the codes and numbers that deliver fifty thousand to a site called starsbook472ko.com.

CHAPTER 34

AN HOUR LATER, PERFECT luxury is on perfect display in the Savatiers' suite at the St. Regis on East 55th Street.

The elderly couple is, of course, dressed elegantly, Marguerite in a simple white suit with navy-blue piping, as if she had stepped out of a Chanel showroom in 1955. Nicolas in a dark-gray suit with a vest, a wide red silk tie with a diamond pin.

A waiter and waitress are pouring coffee into the exquisite St. Regis china cups—cups and plates that ironically are designed with a delicate border of roses.

Nicolas quickly reminds me that there are real and dangerous roses to deal with. "The floral arrangement is in the bedroom," says Nicolas.

I step into the adjoining bedroom—the beds are already made, the carpet already vacuumed. I check this arrangement of roses against the photographs from the Derby and the Preakness on my phone. Indeed, all three arrangements are identical.

When I return to the living room Marguerite thrusts the

accompanying note toward me. A quick glance verifies that the request is to "Lose the Belmont." All I can do is read it and nod.

"Your croissants are getting cold, Luc," says Nicolas. There is a teasing smile on his face.

"My husband is not nearly so nervous as I am," says Marguerite, as we all sit down at the breakfast table.

"I am nervous, of course," explains Nicolas. "But what can happen to us? What are these 'consequences' we will suffer should we actually win—not lose—the Belmont tomorrow? Will they shoot us? So what? We will have won the Triple Crown. We have lived long and happy lives. People have died in far worse circumstances."

Marguerite sighs.

"No one loves her horses as much as I do, but I am not sure that I am willing to die for a horse race."

"Let me ask," I say. "Have you been in touch with the trainers and Belmont management about Garçon's health?"

"Of course, we speak to the head trainer every few hours. And our jockey Armand calls constantly..." begins Nicolas.

"He calls almost too often," Marguerite adds with a tiny laugh.

Nicolas: "And he is nervous but very optimistic about Saturday's race."

I am not surprised by this information. These trainers and Armand Joscoe have been with the Savatiers and their horses for many years. I nod, and then I take a big gulp of my coffee. I break off a crisp end piece from my croissant.

"Please, Luc. Tell us. What should we do?"

"First, we should finish our *petit déjeuner*. Then we should proceed as if all circumstances are normal. We will drive out to Long Island and watch Garçon go through his paces. Then we can decide what to do."

"Just one more question," says Nicolas.

"And that is?"

"Where is the delightful Mademoiselle Burke?"

"*Merci*," I say. "How could I forget about her?" I click the contact list on my cell phone and call K. Burke.

"Where are you, Moncrief?" comes the very grumpy, very sleepy voice of K. Burke.

"I am at breakfast with the Savatiers, downtown. You must brush your teeth and comb your hair. Put on your clothing and put on a smiling, happy face. The Savatiers and I will come fetch you in less than fifteen minutes."

"No way that I can…"

"We are on our way out to Belmont," I say.

"I don't know, Moncrief. I don't think I can."

"Please, K. Burke. Life goes on. Today is a day for working."

CHAPTER 35

Belmont.
The day before the race.

THE MERCEDES SUV THAT carries Marguerite and Nicolas Savatier, K. Burke, and myself is allowed through three different gates. At the last gate hangs an enormous red-lettered sign:

WARNING: TRACK OFFICIALS, OWNERS, AND
EMPLOYEES ONLY BEYOND THIS POINT.

As we pass through, Marguerite says, "Now *that* is a sign to warm the heart of a frightened old lady."

I nod, but I am more taken with the exceptional beauty of Belmont racetrack—the hundreds of yards of lush ivy blanketing the walls, the freshly painted blue and white grandstand. Men and women in police uniform, men and women in official Belmont Park uniforms nod at us as we pass. The skies are cloudless and clear.

As we walk toward the stables I say, "The weather is a perfect seventy-seven degrees."

K. Burke catches sight of Nicolas's puzzled look and

translates. "Seventy-seven degrees Fahrenheit is equal to about twenty-five degrees Celsius."

"*Merci,*" says Nicolas. "I am afraid our beloved young friend Luc has become transformed very much into the red-blooded American."

At the stable the Savatiers move as quickly as they are able toward Garçon. They stroke the horse's back. Nicolas looks into the horse's eyes.

There is a great deal of embracing and cheek-kissing between the Savatiers and the jockey, Armand Joscoe; between the Savatiers and *le docteur* Follderani, the vet that they've imported from France. Then begins the hugging and kissing between the owners and the trainers and the groomers. Finally, I receive a warm embrace from the jockey's tall son, Léon Joscoe. He looks very satisfied.

"Good to see you again, Léon," I say.

"And I'm tremendously happy to see you again, Monsieur Moncrief. It's been quite a ride for my father and me."

Now we have a great crowd of Frenchmen, all babbling excitedly at once. Actually a lovely occasion. Voices overlapping. Nervous laughter. Marguerite raises her voice; very unusual. Nicolas's eyes tear up; even more unusual.

K. Burke looks at me and says, "Okay. You win, Moncrief. I *do* speak French. But these folks are going way too fast for me. I don't understand very much."

"I assure you, it doesn't even make much sense to me."

Burke and I walk a few yards away from the small crowd of Frenchmen.

"So, we are alone for a moment. I am anxious to know: how are you feeling, K. Burke?" I ask.

"*Not* terrible," she says.

"*Not* terrible. Ah, compared to last night that is wonderful."

"And by the way," she says softly, "Thank you for helping me."

My voice now turns serious, a shift from banter between good friends.

"You shall feel even better in a very short while. I have deduced who it is that is threatening the Savatiers with the grotesque notes."

"You know who is...?" she begins. But I keep talking.

"*Ah, oui.* This must be the same person who murdered the training horse. The same person who has stolen all the joy and luster from winning the races. But that person is now done for."

"Who is it, Moncrief? How did you..."

"In a moment," I say. We move back near the French group.

I interrupt, but my voice has a genuine smile in it.

"Please, I must ask a favor of all of you: if you speak only French, please speak slowly. Better yet, if you can speak reasonable English, please try to do so. It would be helpful to all the Americans."

With a laugh Nicolas says, "Because English is the official language not only of our new American friend, Katherine Burke...but now it has also become the official language of our *old* American friend, Luc Moncrief."

Most of the crowd laughs.

Armand Joscoe, usually a quiet, shy man, says, "It is for me not much English. So I speak not much. But Léon speaks so good English. He will have to translate for me."

Almost everyone looks in the direction of Léon, who is fiercely tapping keys on his cell phone.

A sparse round of applause. Spirits are high. Nicolas shouts out, "Léon! *Ah! Quel bon garçon!* Such a good boy!"

Léon looks surprised at the sound of his name echoing through the stable. He looks up at the gathering. A moment of confusion on his face. I walk toward him slowly, without threat.

Léon speaks. His voice is thick with the nasal sounds of French pronunciation.

"*Mon papa,* he is very not correct. Very bad I am with the English," says Léon with the forced trace of a smile.

"I'm surprised to hear you say that. You spoke such fine English when I first came in. To quote, 'I'm tremendously happy' and 'It's been quite a ride.' Now that's impressive, excellent...impeccable English, each word used properly, spoken properly."

At first it seems as if he's going to remain silent. But he's a smart lad. Smart enough to trust his own brain. He speaks.

"You know how, *monsieur,* in the classes of English they teach first the American conversational English. The idiom expressions. *Oui.* It is a challenge they teach me good."

I interrupt.

"Did they teach you to say 'I'd like to bet ten grand on Rufus' or 'I'd like to place twenty thousand on Millie's Baby Boy'? How did you learn that?"

He is now a frightened little boy.

I snatch the phone from his hand. I find the last message sent and I read out loud the recipient: "starsbook472ko.com."

Then, holding the phone above my head, I say to the crowd, "It appears that Léon and I use the same bookie. Only this time Léon is betting *against* the horse his father rides."

I hand the cell phone to K. Burke. She looks at the screen and shakes her head.

"Jesus Christ!" she says. "Who would have thought?"

I move in, close to Léon. Then I speak. Directly to Léon.

"First, you thought you'd spread a rumor to get longer odds on Garçon. But you realized you stood to earn more from sabotaging and betting against the expected winners. How could you do this? To your father? To the Savatiers? How could you hurt and betray the best people in your life?"

K. Burke gets it, too. Her mind works fast.

"You needed the money, Léon, didn't you?" I say.

Burke begins explaining—in French—to Armand Joscoe and Madame and Monsieur Savatier what has happened.

Léon is the person who sent the threats and the arrangements of roses to Marguerite. Who murdered the training horse. That Léon threatened the Savatiers and told them to order his father to lose.

"Léon would make a fortune if Garçon lost this race," I add. "Though he wanted Garçon to win the Preakness—and knew he could, due to his father, since Garçon runs very well in mud—so that the bets would be sky-high for this final race in the Triple Crown."

The Savatiers' faces are saturated with shock, horror, and confusion. How could such a thing be? How could someone so close to them execute a scheme so hideous? They simply don't understand such an evil world.

Armand's face also looks sad, then horrified, and then... his face quickly turns to a red and wild rage.

"*Comment as-tu pu?*" he screams it over and over. How could you? How could you?

"J'ai le diable pour fils!" he screams. I have the devil for a son!
K. Burke and I move to either side of Léon.

Armand also moves closer to his son. He faces Léon. Tears are rolling down Armand's cheeks. I am expecting the symbolic slap across the face.

But there is no slap. Instead Armand moves swiftly. He throws his fist up high. That fist travels to his son's jaw with enormous force and a great cracking sound. Léon falls to the floor of the stable. He moans.

Armand looks down at his son and spits, then he screams and runs from the stable.

CHAPTER 36

Belmont.

Race day.

AT TEN IN THE morning, Marguerite and Nicolas Savatier, K. Burke, and I watch a young Cuban jockey taking Garçon on a gallop around a training track. Also watching the "audition" of the replacement jockey are assorted trainers, sports writers, Belmont officials, and even four competing jockeys. Garçon appears relaxed and ready.

"*Que pensez-vous, mes amis?*" I say to the owners. What do you think of it, my friends?

"He will have to do," says Nicolas.

Marguerite says what we are all thinking. "It is a tragedy. To come this far. To be this close. The Triple Crown within sight . . ."

The most senior of the Belmont officials says, "You can still withdraw the horse, Mrs. Savatier. It's happened before."

"No. I could not do that to Garçon. My wonderful horse has waited all his life for this," says Marguerite.

Everyone present has a point of view. One of the trainers thinks the Cuban jockey is "almost as good as Armand." Another thinks the Cuban jockey is *trop rapide avec la cravache.*

"Okay, Moncrief. I can't translate that one," K. Burke says.

"The jockey is 'too quick with the riding crop,'" I answer.

The talk grows faster, more passionate. I hear Marguerite say, "Garçon will race even if I have to ride him myself."

Then I watch Nicolas look toward the vibrant blue sky and say, *"Aidez-moi, s'il vous plaît, mon cher Dieu."* Please help me, dear God.

Then a man's voice comes from behind us. Startling all of us. It is sudden and strong.

"Who is riding my horse?" he shouts.

The voice belongs to Armand Joscoe.

"Armand..." says Marguerite. "We have not seen you since yesterday. We had no idea where you were."

Armand tells us that since yesterday morning he has been dealing with the Belmont New York police, as well as an assistant New York State attorney general, two representatives of the New York State Racing Commission, two attorneys who represent Belmont Park, and a son who has committed a serious and unforgivable crime.

Quickly Marguerite interrupts.

"No," she says. "Nothing is so serious that it cannot be forgiven."

"So true. So true," says Nicolas. "You are here with us now. We shall all be friends once again. You will see."

The Cuban jockey has alighted from Garçon. Armand Joscoe rushes toward "his" horse. Then he shouts for the trainers.

"Get the drying cloths immediately. He's wet. Walk him slowly. Cool him down. Feed him half of his usual food. Get him inside. Hurry!"

The only way to describe the faces of Marguerite and Nicolas is "joyful."

I turn to my partner.

"So, what do you think, K. Burke?"

"Well, with all the Savatiers' talk about forgiveness and everyone being friends again, I can only think one thing: those two would never make it in New York City."

I laugh and say, "K. Burke, *vous êtes un biscuit dur.*"

She smiles, but not with her eyes. "Not as tough a cookie as I seem."

CHAPTER 37

Belmont.
The race.

K. BURKE, NICOLAS AND Marguerite Savatier, Luc Moncrief. Together again at a horse race, for the third time.

In the owners' circle. The weather is perfect, even cool for summer. We are all tense, tired, a little shaky from raw nerves and too many glasses of pre-race champagne.

"You know, K. Burke, two years ago, when American Pharoah won this race, it had been almost forty years since any horse had captured the Triple Crown. The wise guys, the smart money, 'the horse guys,' they all say it will be another forty years before it happens again. They have weighed the odds. They know the facts. I worry for Garçon's chances."

Burke makes a skeptical face.

"That's what 'the horse guys' say. I guess I'm getting more and more like you, Moncrief. I say, 'Don't always go with the facts. Sometimes you have to go with your heart.'"

Nicolas has been listening to our conversation.

"My heart says that I am enormously grateful that Armand has returned to the job of jockey. You know, I don't really care if Garçon wins the race."

"Don't be insane, Nicolas. I certainly care," says Marguerite. "Indeed, feel however you like. I care enough for the both of us."

The four of us could easily banter and bicker until night falls, but the trumpet blows. The horses assemble within the starting gate. Of course, our attention is focused on Garçon. He seems under control, calm. I glance at Millie's Baby Boy. He's equally calm. Rufus, the only other real contender, is skittish.

The gun.

The race.

The cheers.

I am no expert at calling races, but from the start we all can see that it's going to be close. Garçon and Millie's Baby Boy take the lead together. They are, as the inevitable saying goes, neck-and-neck. So close that the two riders could carry on a conversation.

As always, Burke is amazingly excited. She shouts. "Hey, Millie, get off Garçon's ass!"

The two horses seem almost to run as a team. But then...as they close in on the finish, I am ecstatic to see that Millie's Baby Boy is falling behind. Not behind a great deal at first. Just a bit. Then a length. Then perhaps three lengths.

But now...as they approach the finish...what should be a glorious win for Garçon turns into a problem.

From fifth in the pack, Rufus has become Garçon's new partner.

And now...and now...

My eyes cannot see even a slight difference as they cross the finish line.

Different people erupt with different shouts. Rufus! Garçon! Rufus! Garçon! An announcement. The crowd quiets.

The photo sign will be posted and the results will be announced.

The waiting, of course, feels like a few hundred lifetimes.

The crowd turns even quieter.

Video screens play the finish over and over.

Finally, a voice echoes out of the loudspeakers:

"The winner, by a head, is Garçon."

EPILOGUE

K. BURKE AND I are together in Paris.

Why Paris? Because the Savatiers have decided to forgo the final important race in America, the Breeders' Cup. Instead, Garçon has been brought home to Paris to compete in the most important of French races, Le Prix de l'Arc de Triomphe.

Why together?

Frankly, because I find it impossible now to be in Paris without her. After our previous visits, visits that were touched with both tragedy and tenderness, Katherine Burke has given me new eyes to see Paris, from the glamorous shops on the Champs-Élysées to that perfect little bistro in Montmartre.

Burke and I are walking slowly through the Bois de Boulogne, the great forest-like park on the outskirts of Paris. It is also in the Bois where Parisians keep their own famous racetrack, Longchamp.

"Leave it to the French to build a racetrack smack dab in the middle of a beautiful park," says K. Burke.

"The park is for *fun*. The track is for *games*. Fun and games," I say.

"Whatever you say. Anyway, I'm always happy to be here," she says.

"And you will be even happier if tomorrow Garçon wins."

"Yes, I will. Especially that it's my own one hundred euros that I bet on him."

We walk without speaking for a few minutes.

It is October in Paris. Usually a rainy time of the year. But today the air is cool and the sky is bright. The trees are dripping with color—autumn reds and yellows.

"I hope the weather will be this great tomorrow," I say.

We are now walking so close to each other that our shoulders occasionally touch, our hands occasionally brush against each other's.

"And if the weather isn't so great, at least we're in Paris," she says.

"You have grown to like this city, eh, K. Burke?"

"I've grown to *love* this city," she says.

"Maybe we should both move here, live here," I say.

"If you'd said that a year ago I would simply say that you're crazy," she says. "But now I almost feel the same way."

I stop. I talk.

"That means we have become crazy together."

She says, "So now we're *both* crazy. I guess that's good."

I take her hand. We continue our walk.

ABOUT THE AUTHORS

James Patterson is the world's bestselling author. His enduring fictional characters and series include Alex Cross, the Women's Murder Club, Michael Bennett, Maximum Ride, Middle School, and Ali Cross, along with such acclaimed works of narrative nonfiction as *Walk in My Combat Boots,* *E.R. Nurses,* and his autobiography, *James Patterson by James Patterson.* Bill Clinton (*The President Is Missing*) and Dolly Parton (*Run, Rose, Run*) are among his notable literary collaborators. For his prodigious imagination and championship of literacy in America, Patterson was awarded the 2019 National Humanities Medal. The National Book Foundation presented him with the Literarian Award for Outstanding Service to the American Literary Community, and he is also the recipient of an Edgar Award and nine Emmy Awards. He lives in Florida with his family.

Richard DiLallo is a former advertising executive. He lives in Manhattan with his wife.

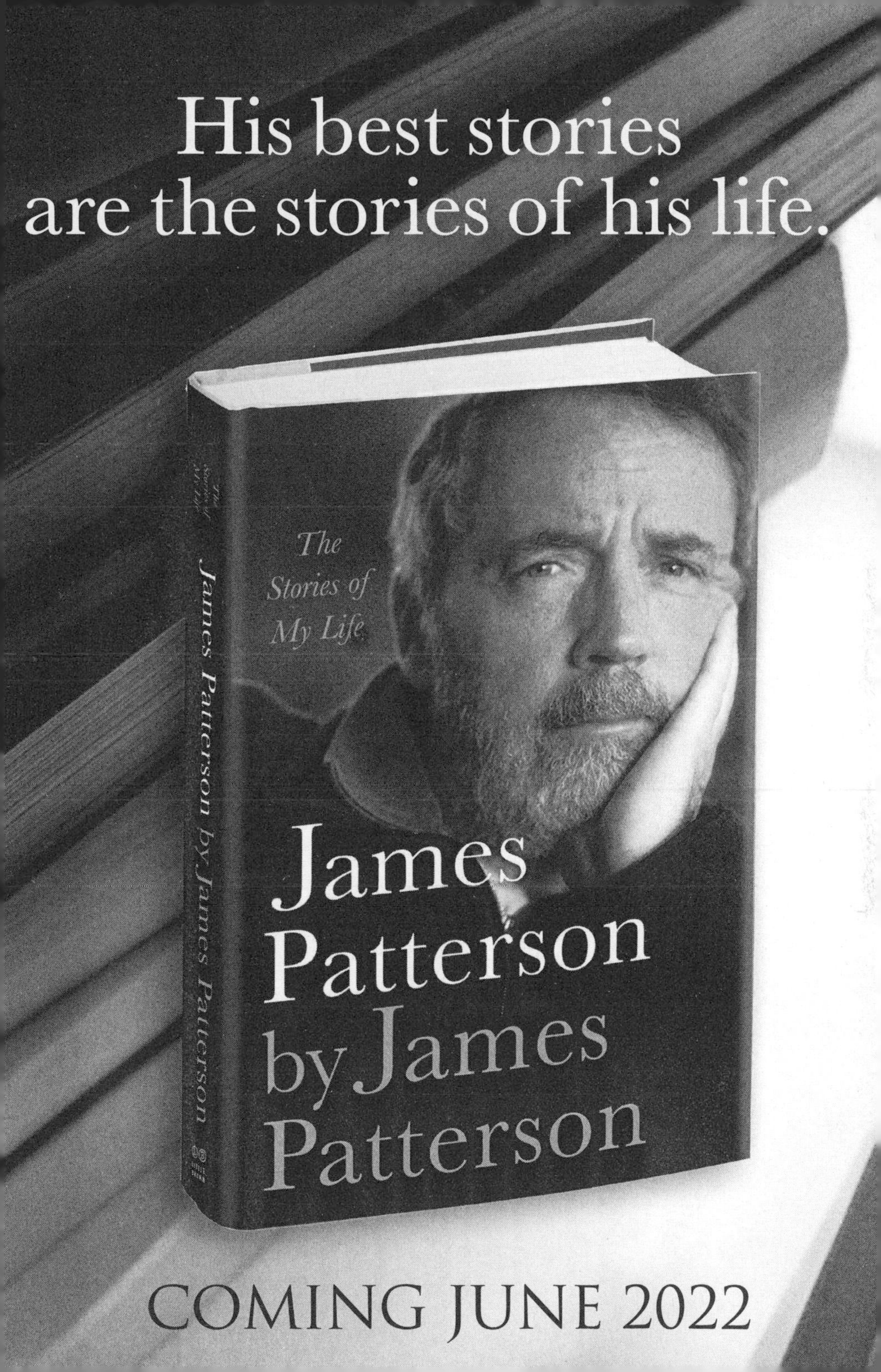

His best stories
are the stories of his life.
The
Stories of
My Life
James
Patterson
by James
Patterson
James Patterson by James Patterson
COMING JUNE 2022

JAMES
PATTERSON
RECOMMENDS

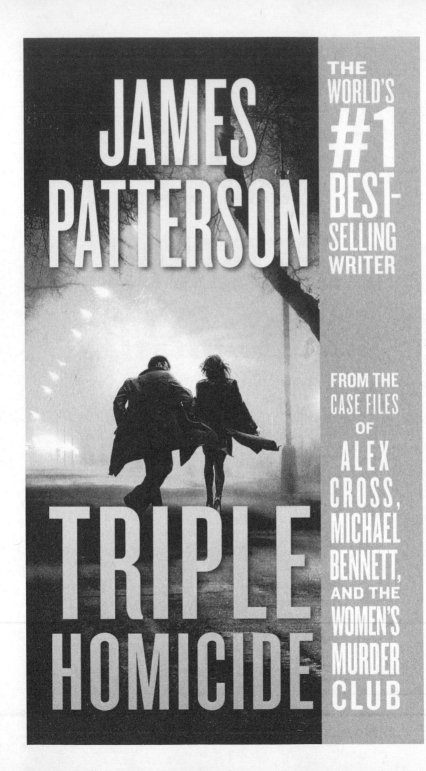

TRIPLE HOMICIDE

I couldn't resist the opportunity to bring my greatest detectives together in three shocking thrillers. Alex Cross receives an anonymous call threatening to set off deadly bombs in Washington, DC, and has to discover whether it's a cruel hoax, or the real deal. But will he find the truth too late? And then, in possibly my most twisted Women's Murder Club mystery yet, Detective Lindsey Boxer investigates a dead lover and a wounded millionaire who was left for dead. Finally, I make things personal for Michael Bennett as someone attacks the Thanksgiving Day Parade directly in front of him and his family. Can he solve the mystery of the "holiday terror"?

JAMES PATTERSON

THE FAMILY LAWYER

THE FAMILY LAWYER

The Family Lawyer combines three of my most pulse-pounding novels all in one book. There's Matthew Hovanes, who's living a parent's worst nightmare when his daughter is accused of bullying another girl into suicide. I test all of his attorney experience as he tries to clear his daughter's name and reveal the truth. Then there's Cheryl Mabern, who is one of my most brilliant detectives working for the NYPD. But does that brilliance help her when there's a calculating killer committing random murders? And finally, Dani Lawrence struggles with deciding whether to aid in an investigation that could put away her sister for the murder of her cheating husband. Or she can obstruct it by any means necessary.

THE HOUSE NEXT DOOR

There's something absolutely bone chilling about a danger that's right in front of you, and that concept fascinates me. Everyone always thinks there's safety in numbers, but it isn't always true, and those closest to you can sometimes be the most terrifying. In *The House Next Door*, Laura Sherman's neighbor seems like he's too good to be true; maybe he is. And then in *The Killer's Wife*, Detective McGrath is searching for six girls who have gone missing but finds himself dangerously close to his suspect's wife. Way too close. And finally, I venture out there in *We Are Not Alone*. Robert Barnett has found a message that will change the world: that there are others out there. And they're watching us.

For a complete list of books by

JAMES PATTERSON

VISIT
JamesPatterson.com

 Follow James Patterson on Facebook
@JamesPatterson

Follow James Patterson on Twitter
@JP_Books

 Follow James Patterson on Instagram
@jamespattersonbooks